"Charming. . . . An engaging whodunit."

—*Publishers Weekly*

"[A] delightful, and often funny, mystery series about a town that lives and dies by the love of books."

—Kings River Life Magazine

CLAUSE OF DEATH

Lorna Barrett

BERKLEY PRIME CRIME
New York

BERKLEY PRIME CRIME
Published by Berkley
An imprint of Penguin Random House LLC
penguinrandomhouse.com

Copyright © 2022 by Penguin Random House LLC
Excerpt from *A Questionable Character* by Lorna Barrett copyright © 2022 by
Penguin Random House LLC
Penguin Random House supports copyright. Copyright fuels creativity, encourages
diverse voices, promotes free speech, and creates a vibrant culture. Thank you for buying
an authorized edition of this book and for complying with copyright laws by not
reproducing, scanning, or distributing any part of it in any form without permission.
You are supporting writers and allowing Penguin Random House to continue to
publish books for every reader.

BERKLEY and the BERKLEY & B colophon are registered trademarks and
BERKLEY PRIME CRIME is a trademark of Penguin Random House LLC.

ISBN: 9780593333518

Berkley Prime Crime hardcover edition / June 2022
Berkley Prime Crime mass-market edition / June 2023

Printed in the United States of America

Book design by Laura K. Corless

For Ian Hart
Who wanted to see his name in print

CAST OF CHARACTERS

Tricia Miles, owner of Haven't Got a Clue vintage mystery bookstore

Angelica Miles, Tricia's older sister, owner of the Cookery, the Booked for Lunch café, Booked for Beauty day spa, and half owner of the Sheer Comfort Inn. Her alter ego is Nigela Ricita, the mysterious developer who has been pumping money and jobs into the village of Stoneham.

Pixie Poe, Tricia's assistant manager at Haven't Got a Clue

Mr. Everett, Tricia's employee at Haven't Got a Clue

Antonio Barbero, the public face of Nigela Ricita Associates; Angelica's son

Ginny Wilson-Barbero, Tricia's former assistant; wife of Antonio Barbero

Grace Harris-Everett, Mr. Everett's wife

Ian McDonald, former security chief of the *Celtic Lady* cruise ship

Edward Dowding, homeless man looking for work

Becca Dickson-Chandler, former tennis star, ex-wife of Marshall Cambridge

Dan Reed, owner of the Bookshelf Diner

Nadine, unhappy woman Tricia meets in the village square

Larry Harvick, owner of the Bee's Knees specialty shop

Rick Lavoy, owner of a craft beer brewery

Eli Meier, owner of the Inner Light bookstore

Clause of Death

ONE

Tricia Miles glanced over the notes she'd jotted down the previous evening in anticipation of that morning's Stoneham Chamber of Commerce meeting. How things had changed for the Chamber in just six months.

The previous October, the organization had been on the brink of insolvency, housed in a drafty warehouse unsuitable as a place for its members to meet, and was hemorrhaging warm, dues-paying bodies by the day. And then came the election with an outcome no one had anticipated. The two candidates hadn't received enough votes to win, but two write-in noncontenders were tied. And that's how Tricia and her sister, Angelica, were now co-presidents of the Chamber.

It was true that membership hadn't bounced back quite as fast as the sisters had hoped, but thanks to the generosity of their colleagues, they had obtained office space, a free meeting place, and office supplies. They could manage for the rest of the year, when it was hoped dues would once again float the Chamber's financial boat.

Tricia and Angelica had worked together during Angelica's tenure as the organization's leader, and Tricia volunteered while her vintage mystery bookstore, Haven't Got a Clue, was closed due to a fire. At that time, and under Angelica's leadership, the Chamber had thrived. Tricia was to be her heiress apparent but lost the contest by a mere three votes when Russ Smith had thrown his hat into the ring. When the elected leader had died of a heart attack, it was deemed Russ was the victor. He spent the next ten months on a quest to destroy the organization and would have succeeded if he hadn't been arrested for murder with a charge of embezzlement of the Chamber's assets thrown in for good measure. When he eventually came to trial, he was destined to spend many years, if not the rest of his life, as a guest of the New Hampshire penal system.

The Brookview Inn, owned by Nigela Ricita (known to only a few as Angelica herself), had graciously allowed the Chamber to meet there for the rest of the year with no fee. Chamber members did have to cough up ten bucks each to cover the cost of their continental breakfasts, but those who had bothered to check would have found that the cost to guests was actually 20 percent more. Perhaps not a bargain, but the meetings so far had been pretty well attended. Clearly, the members saw the benefit of the Miles sisters' leadership.

Angelica gave Tricia a nudge. "Hadn't you better start the meeting? The members will be eager to get back to their shops to start the workday."

"You're right."

Tricia got up from her seat and walked to the front of the restaurant, tested the microphone, and gave one last glance at her notes before speaking. "Welcome, everyone," she began, and waited for the voices to die down and the members present to give her their full attention.

"Before we start, let me remind you there are still plenty of the Brookview's marvelous pastries left, hot coffee, and juices, so feel free to enjoy them." She paused. "First on today's agenda are the summer flowers for Main Street. Once again, Nigela Ricita Associates has graciously agreed to provide them, as well as plants for the urns in front of the Main Street merchants' stores."

A polite ripple of applause met that statement.

"Next, we have a guest who's looking to open a new business here in Stoneham." Tricia nodded toward the table closest to the podium. "Mr. Rick Lavoy."

A man of about forty, dressed in a dark gray sports jacket, light gray shirt, and Dockers, stood. "Thanks for the welcome," he said to a polite smattering of applause.

"Why don't you tell us about your ideas for your new enterprise," Tricia said.

Lavoy turned to face the room. "My partners and I own a craft brewery in Nashua and we're looking for a property here in Stoneham to open a tasting room."

"To build or rent?" came a male voice from the back of the room.

"To rent, at first. If we're successful, we might like to build here in the village or close to the highway."

"Tell us more," Tricia encouraged him.

"We'd be open during regular hours all summer long and cut our hours during the off-season, probably only open on weekends."

Eli Meier, a not-so-longtime member of the Chamber, stood, waving a hand for recognition. He owned the Inner Light bookstore, two doors down from Tricia's shop. When she first arrived in Stoneham, his store stocked books on religion and spirituality, but of late, it had begun to carry more varied subjects on a variety of conspiracy theories, from lizard-like aliens about to take over the world to dark politics and beyond. Eli had seemed to transform as well, from being a mild-mannered gentleman to a paranoid individual who'd read too many of his own stocked items.

Tricia heaved a sigh and nodded in his direction.

Eli turned to Rick. "You *do* know Stoneham is known as *Booktown*, not beer-guzzling town." A nervous spate of murmuring rumbled through the room.

"Stoneham is a tourist destination," Tricia said. "Books drive the interest, but a diversity of businesses will bring in more than just book lovers. The more we have to offer, the greater our tourism reach. It's a win-win situation."

"For cretins," Eli scoffed. "Do we want a lot of low-class beer swillers in our midst?"

Rick cleared his throat loudly. "Excuse me, but our clientele are connoisseurs and we've done the market research to confirm it. They're also high-order readers, that's why we decided to establish a tasting room here in Stoneham. It was a no-brainer because your demographic audience is ours as well."

"I find that hard to believe," Eli jeered. "Stoneham was meant to resemble that fabled town in Wales, Hay-on-Wye. A *real* book town. *That's* what we should be striving to attain."

Well, yeah, except *that* village was steeped in history with Tudor buildings and old-world charm. The village of Stoneham was old by American standards, but not nearly as old as towns in Europe. Most of the buildings in Stoneham had been built in the early days of the twentieth century, and were, in most cases, merely dated. Most, but not all, were in good repair. That said, Hay-on-Wye's current claim to fame had only come about during the 1960s. Stoneham's rebirth was less than a decade old, but its moniker of Booktown had made it a reading destination in a lot shorter time.

Tricia directed her attention to Lavoy. "Are you working with NR Realty to locate a suitable property?" she asked.

"Ms. Johnson is showing me a possibility in an hour or so."

"We wish you good luck," Tricia said, and then encouraged Rick to join the chapter.

Rick threw a sour glance in Eli's direction but nodded anyway.

"Next up—" Tricia began.

"I'd like to make a motion!" came a voice from the back of the room. Again, Eli stood, waving a hand for recognition.

"And that is?" Tricia asked, and sighed yet again. Eli had been making a pest of himself for months.

"That the Chamber stop encouraging non-book-related businesses from opening up on Main Street. Us bookstore owners are being squeezed out."

Tricia shot her sister an annoyed glance. This wasn't the first time Eli had harangued them on the subject.

Dan Reed stood. "I second that motion." Dan owned the Bookshelf Diner and had a long-standing grudge against Angelica for daring to open her retro café, Booked for Lunch, which served one meal a day, just doors down from his full-service diner that was open from six o'clock in the morning until nine at night. It seemed to Tricia that he, too, lived to cause trouble at the Chamber meetings just to irritate the co-presidents.

"I third it," came a voice from the left side of the room. Though she'd been one of the original booksellers recruited to Booktown nearly eight years before, Betty Barnes from Barney's Book Barn, Stoneham's children's bookstore, was new to the Chamber. Did Betty even understand parliamentary procedures, where there was no thirding of a motion?

Tricia took a breath, determined to keep her cool. Ignoring Dan and Betty, Tricia addressed her comments toward Eli.

"Eli, you know the Chamber has no power to stop businesses from renting space on Main Street. In fact, it helps the entire village when all the storefronts are occupied. As of now, there are three empty establishments on the east side of Main Street, including the one next to your own shop, and only one on the other."

"Well, then, it should be up to you—as head of the Chamber—to recruit new *used* bookstores to the village. That's what Bob Kelly did!"

A rumble of agreement went around the room, but not everyone was in Eli's court.

Larry Harvick stood. "Are you saying I'm not welcome in Stoneham?" he challenged Eli. Harvick was a former county sheriff's deputy and had opened the Bee's Knees, a gift shop that featured products from his hives. They also carried other bee-related items, including books. They were new volumes, whereas most of the booksellers stocked mostly used books with some new stock. Eli also carried some newly published books, so what was he squawking about?

"Our village is known as *Booktown*, not *bee town*," Eli challenged.

"Yes, but we've always had other businesses," Tricia pointed out. "Like Leona Ferguson's shop that sells new and vintage dishware."

Leona leapt to her feet. "I was one of the first businesses to take a chance on Bob Kelly's little experiment here in Stoneham," she said indignantly. "He certainly welcomed me with open arms."

"That's only because you rented one of *his* empty buildings," Eli replied with a sneer in his voice.

"Well, I now *own* the building," Leona countered, "and I'm staying put." She turned on Dan Reed. "And why would you second the motion? You don't even sell books."

"Maybe not, but I have the word 'book' in my business name and my restaurant is decorated with old books that customers are free to buy if they wish. They're all priced for sale."

"And covered in years' worth of diner grease," Leona muttered loud enough for some to hear and giggle over.

"Now, now," Tricia chided. "As you know, the old warehouse where the Chamber was briefly located has been razed. There's room for several more storefronts—including bookstores."

"Yeah, and who bought the lots?" Eli demanded. "And what businesses are going to go in them?"

Again, Tricia sighed. "A limited liability company bought the property only hours after it went on the market. We don't know who owns it or what their plans are for the land."

"So, it's not Nigela Ricita Associates?" Mary Fairchild asked from the table closest to the podium. "Everybody figured that since she already owned half the village, it was *her* who was going to develop it."

She would have liked to, Tricia thought, but didn't share that information with Mary.

"Well, the least you can do is recruit more bookstores—just like Bob Kelly did!" Eli practically shouted at Tricia.

Oh, yeah, saintly Bob Kelly who'd started the Chamber and recruited the businesses for his own enrichment. He'd bought up most of Main Street for a song and advertised for booksellers, who'd relocated and paid him rent. At that moment, Bob was languishing in state prison with a very long sentence for murder. Tricia had to bite her tongue not to bring up that last little piece of history.

Angelica raised her hand and Tricia acknowledged her. "Eli, perhaps you'd like to form a committee to investigate the recruitment of more bookstores," she said sweetly. "Dan, maybe you'd like to be the first member to join Eli on such a recruitment effort."

Dan glowered at her.

"I second that motion!" Mary called.

"It wasn't presented as a motion," Eli growled at her. "And I don't have time to spend on a stupid committee."

"You didn't think it was stupid when you suggested it," Harvick commented sourly.

"Why don't we table this discussion for another time," Tricia said, hoping to regain control of the meeting.

"I second that motion!" Terry McDonald of All Heroes Comics called. He gave Tricia a smile and what could be described only as a cheeky thumbs-up.

"That wasn't a motion, either!" Eli complained.

"I move that we end the meeting," Leona called out.

"I second that," Mary agreed.

Tricia had no gavel—and should have rectified that problem long before then—and called, "So moved." She let out a breath. She'd barely touched on her list of things to bring up before the assemblage. She gave her sister a sour look, but Angelica merely shrugged. She'd have to face the group and preside over the next meeting. Good luck to her!

"Well, that went splendidly," Angelica said, and threw a look over her left shoulder to see the members get up from their seats, some heading for the pastry table to fill their pockets and purses with paper-napkin-covered mini Danish, croissants, and doughnuts. Well, better that than for them to be thrown away.

"So, honestly—how do you think the meeting went?" Tricia asked.

"Not nearly as contentious as I thought, which means we'd better have a lot of good news to share next time."

"And how do we accomplish that?"

"Miracles *do* happen," Angelica said, and rose from her seat. "It's time to thank the wait and kitchen staff. As always, they've gone above and beyond the call of duty to provide us with a lovely breakfast."

But as the sisters made their way toward the kitchen's swinging door, Eli stepped out in front of them, stopping them in their tracks. "You didn't have to cut me off," he complained to Tricia.

She stood her ground. "If you recall, it was Leona Ferguson and Mary Fairchild who moved to end the meeting."

"Probably from a signal from you."

Tricia wasn't going to argue with the man. "If you'll excuse us."

"Excuse? Never. And mark my words, we *will* be discussing the lack of new booksellers at the next meeting."

Tricia smiled sweetly. "I'll be sure to add it to the agenda."

Eli muttered an oath and pivoted, nearly running into the inn's manager, Hank Curtis.

"Whoa!" Hank called. "Everything okay here?"

Eli growled something unintelligible and shoved Hank aside, striding toward the exit. They watched him leave. "Was there a problem?" Hank asked.

Tricia shook her head. "Mr. Meier was a little upset by the abrupt end to the meeting."

"We were on our way to thank the staff for the lovely breakfast they provided," Angelica said, and batted her eyelashes. She seemed to think she had a chance at a relationship with Hank, but so far he'd resisted all her attempts at engagement.

"Were you able to sit in on much of the meeting?" Tricia asked.

Hank shook his head. "Too busy."

"But isn't it in the inn's best interest to know what's going on within the Chamber in case it could pertain to the inn?" Angelica asked.

"I get most of what I need from the Chamber bulletin."

Tricia beamed. *She* was in charge of the monthly newsletter. "I'm glad you find it useful."

Hank looked at his watch. "We've got a lunch meeting that begins in about ninety minutes. I'd better make sure we'll be ready. I'll convey your thanks to the staff." He gave them a curt nod. "I'm sure I'll see you soon, ladies," he said, and left them.

Angelica watched him go and heaved a great sigh.

"You have too much on your plate right now to enter into a relationship," Tricia reminded her sister.

"Who says I need a relationship? But I wouldn't mind a little romp in the hay once in a while."

Tricia glared at Angelica.

She gave her head a shake. "You're right. Besides all my business ventures, I've got a new grandbaby arriving soon, too."

Someone cleared his throat, and Tricia turned to face Rick Lavoy.

"Mr. Lavoy—?"

"Call me Rick."

"Rick. You must have a terrible impression of our organization. I'm so sorry you weren't greeted with more enthusiasm. My co-president and I"—Tricia waved a hand in Angelica's general direction—"think your tasting room would be an enormous asset to the village."

"There's always a couple of crabs in every group. I can assure you that everyone at my table was welcoming and seemed quite interested in my establishing a tasting room here in the village. I've already spoken with the manager at the Dog-Eared Page, who expressed an interest in selling several of our draft beers. I still think Stoneham would be a good fit. And to keep in the Booktown spirit, we plan to stock a variety of books on the subject. They may be more focused on current titles, but then the village is known as Booktown, not necessarily *used* Booktown."

"That's true." Tricia's specialty at Haven't Got a Clue was vintage mysteries, but they were getting harder and harder to find. Her stock and trade were still used books, but she sold many new books by current authors and hosted author signings as well.

"Perhaps we could do lunch sometime to discuss the matter further," Rick suggested. "I know my wife would love to pick your brains. She does most of the marketing for us. It was she who suggested we investigate locating the tasting room here."

"We'd love to meet her," Angelica said. She handed Rick a business card. "Feel free to give us a call so we can arrange it."

Rick pocketed the card. "I'll do that. Nice meeting you ladies, and hope to see you again soon."

They watched him go and Angelica sighed.

"Sorry, he's married," Tricia teased.

Angelica sighed. "All the good ones are."

The sisters headed for the inn's back entrance. "Maybe we should give Eli's suggestion some real thought. How does one recruit booksellers to Stoneham, anyhow?" Angelica asked. It hadn't been a problem under her Chamber leadership.

"The same way Bob Kelly did. Place ads in magazines. That's how I found out about the place. I called him, we chatted, and then I came to visit."

"But as I recall, at the time the place was pretty much dead," Angelica said as they started down the steps to the parking lot.

"It was. But Bob had a glib tongue and darned if he wasn't right. Look at where Booktown is now."

"We're bustling all right," Angelica said, taking out her key fob and unlocking her car doors. "But I refuse to give Bob all the credit." Especially since it was Angelica who'd invested the most capital to bring prosperity back to the village. They got in the car.

"I still want to know who bought the warehouse site and what they plan to do with it."

Tricia fastened her seat belt. Angelica did likewise. "I thought Antonio"—Angelica's son—"was looking into it?"

Angelica backed the car out of the parking space. "He keeps coming up against brick walls. It looks like a shell company is guarding the true ownership."

Tricia gave a stifled laugh. "That term always sounds sinister to me. Like someone is trying to hide something."

"Was that remark directed at me?" Angelica asked, sounding miffed.

"Well, your shell company *is* Nigela Ricita Associates. You *are* hiding your identity behind the name."

"I had a very good reason for doing that."

"Which you never told me," Tricia said.

Angelica's gaze was fixed on the road. "If you must know, it was so Daddy wouldn't find out about it. He'd just want a little loan—or *five*."

Yes, their grifter of a father had borrowed money (and never repaid it) from people who were now his ex-friends. Their mother controlled the finances and kept their father on a short leash. If she hadn't, he'd probably be in jail for the next ten to twenty years.

"But I think you're right," Angelica said as they approached the municipal parking lot on Main Street. "I can't help but think that whoever bought that lot did it deliberately to keep me from purchasing it."

Tricia laughed. "Now you're starting to sound like Eli with his conspiracy theories."

"Sometimes," Angelica said, her voice deadly, "conspiracy theories are based on fact."

Angelica parked her car in the village's municipal lot and the sisters got out, starting off for the sidewalk that lined Main Street.

"I've got to go to the bank," Tricia said.

Angelica looked appalled. "Do you mean to say you had yesterday's receipts in your purse this whole time?"

"Of course."

"But what if you'd been mugged? What if someone got into your purse while you were getting a coffee refill at the inn?"

"It's not high tourist season so it's not a huge sum, as we haven't exactly been inundated with customers."

Angelica shook her head disapprovingly. "You be careful," she warned. "Heaven only knows who you might run into."

"You worry too much. I'll be fine. I'll see you tonight. It's my turn to host happy hour."

"What are we having for dinner?"

"It's a surprise." Yes, it was, because Tricia had to hit the grocery store in Milford to get *something*, or else they'd be dining on stale crackers and canned pâté cat food.

"See you later."

Angelica gave a wave and Tricia headed for the sidewalk and the village's only stoplight. She crossed the road and covered the two-block distance in five minutes. As she hit the first step of three in front of the bank's granite edifice, a tall good-looking man, probably in his midforties, a little beefy, with a close-cropped ginger beard, came barreling out and nearly knocked her over.

"I'm terribly sorry," he said, his voice carrying the hint of an Irish lilt. Tricia's memory flashed and her breath caught in her throat.

"Ian? Ian McDonald?"

"Tricia Miles? Is it really you?" he asked, and laughed.

The two had met two years before aboard the *Celtic Lady* cruise ship. Tricia had found the door to a cabin open. When she'd reported it, Ian had arrived. He'd been the ship's security officer who ended up investigating the death of one of the authors on the cruise.

"What are you doing here in Stoneham?" Tricia asked.

"I'm staying with my cousin, Terry."

"Terry McDonald from All Heroes Comics is your cousin?" Tricia asked, aghast.

"That's right. We both spit in a tube for one of those

ancestry DNA searches, found we were second cousins, and here I am."

"That's amazing," Tricia said, a little overwhelmed by the revelation.

"I knew you lived in New England, but I had no idea it was Stoneham. It truly is a small world," Ian said, his grin wide.

"In fact, I own the mystery bookstore right next to Terry's shop. It's called Haven't Got a Clue."

"Its facade is charming. I'm a huge Sherlock Holmes fan. You've done a great job replicating the front of his home. I planned on stopping in either later today or tomorrow."

"You're welcome anytime."

Ian glanced at his watch. "Much as I'd love to catch up with you right now, I'm afraid I've got an important errand to run. I promise to come visit you in the next day or so. Perhaps we could go to dinner?"

"That would be nice," Tricia said, a warm glow coursing through her.

Ian flashed a winning smile and clasped her hand. "I'll be in touch." He gave it a tighter squeeze and then let go, giving her another smile and a brief wave before he headed north up Main Street.

Tricia watched him for a few moments before she heaved a heavy sigh and continued into the bank.

After making her deposit, Tricia turned south to go back to her store. Was it unusual that second cousins crossed vast expanses of ocean just to meet? Back on the ship, Ian had told her that he spent most of his limited vacation time with his sister and her family in Ireland. As Tricia walked, she idly wondered how long Ian would be staying in the village. Because of the nature of his job, it couldn't be for more than a few days. She had to admit, she'd been intrigued with the dashing ship's officer. And though he'd made it clear there was no fraternizing with the cruise passengers, now that they were both off the ship . . .

Stop it, she commanded. Thanks to her unhappy past, she was done with men—with the whole concept of romance. She'd heard the locals whisper. She *was* unlucky in love and everyone in the village knew it. Some had even taken to calling her the Black Widow, since it seemed every man she was involved with met some terrible, if not fatal, end.

To be the Black Widow *and* the village jinx was too much to take. Still, tight-lipped, she strode toward her store with her head held high.

Tricia thought back to what Ian had said: he had an important errand to run. Here in Stoneham? He'd just left the bank. What else could be called important? A visit to the post office or the liquor store in nearby Milford? And he'd headed north on foot. Tricia couldn't imagine what business would attract him. The day spa? No. He was going in the wrong direction for that. Besides, his hair had looked perfectly coiffed and his beard neatly trimmed. Did he need a chocolate fix from the Sweet as Can Be candy store?

Tricia shook her head. She'd just have to wait until Ian visited her store or they could speak more candidly at the dinner he'd proposed. She frowned. It had been a lonely six months since she'd had a date or even an intimate conversation with a man. She wasn't sure she was ready for another relationship—and wasn't she jumping the gun to even be thinking about Ian McDonald in that way? He'd most likely be here and gone within days.

The spring in her step had vanished and Tricia slogged along the sidewalk until she reached Haven't Got a Clue. With a heavy heart, she yanked open the plate glass door. It looked like it could be a long day.

TWO

 Tricia's assistant manager, Pixie Poe, was with a customer when Tricia returned to Haven't Got a Clue half an hour after the store's official opening. Or rather, someone was trying to sell Tricia's assistant a carton of paperbacks. Tricia meandered to the shelves near the glass display case that doubled as the checkout, eavesdropping on their conversation.

"You *need* these books," the young man was saying. He was skinny, with sallow skin, shoulder-length, greasy hair, and it looked like he hadn't bathed in a while. Tricia wasn't close enough to give him the sniff test—and was just as happy about it.

"They aren't all mysteries," Pixie said with authority, "and the ones that are aren't in good shape. We can't sell books where the pages are falling out," she said, holding up a copy of a former bestseller that was in tatters.

"Look, just give me twenty bucks and—"

"I'm sorry, but no," Pixie said firmly.

The young man grabbed the box, uttered a string of expletives, and huffed his way out of the store, letting the door slam with a bang. They watched him pass by the big glass display window, where he threw Pixie a one-finger salute and muttered another naughty word.

"Well, he wasn't a happy camper," Tricia muttered.

Pixie shrugged, unconcerned. "I got a text from June telling me to look out for him. Apparently, he's been all over the village trying to sell those dirty, damaged books."

"Maybe we should feel sorry for him," Tricia suggested.

"I feel sorry that he doesn't have any manners," Pixie agreed, but she did seem just a little rattled. "He's not our problem. How did the Chamber meeting go?"

Tricia shook her head and stowed her purse behind the counter. "Don't ask."

"That bad, huh?"

"Eli Meier—" she began, but Pixie held up a hand to stop her.

"Say no more."

Tricia grinned. But then she looked around the store. "Where's Mr. Everett?" Tricia asked after her other employee, an elderly gentleman who truly was a gentle man.

"He called to say he'd be a little late. Doctor's appointment."

"Oh, he didn't mention it the other day."

"He thought he might have strained a muscle or something. Grace was taking him."

"Oh, dear. Well, let's cross our fingers and hope it's nothing more serious."

"I'm sure it won't be."

Maybe. But Tricia knew if Mr. Everett's leg was hanging by a thread, he'd just tell them it was a scratch and not to worry.

Tricia hung her jacket up on a peg at the back of the store and looked up as the bell over the door rang cheerfully and in came Mr. Everett with his arm in a sling. Tricia and Pixie noticed it at once and both women practically ran to intercept the old man.

"What happened?" Tricia asked, her concern skyrocketing, which was an over-the-top reaction, but sympathy for her friend outweighed logic.

"Come sit down," Pixie encouraged, waving a hand

toward the reader's nook. "Would you like some coffee? Cookies? An ice bag?"

Mr. Everett shook his head, but he did allow himself to be guided toward the comfortable upholstered chairs where he settled himself.

Almost immediately, Miss Marple jumped onto the old man's lap and immediately began to purr. He gazed at the cat and petted her with his left hand.

"So?" Tricia prompted, taking an adjacent seat, with Pixie taking another.

"It seems I've broken my wrist," Mr. Everett said sadly.

"How?" Pixie asked.

"I was getting ready to feed the cats last night and Penny was a bit exuberant. She kept winding around my legs and I wasn't as observant as I should have been," he answered sheepishly.

"Did she trip you?" Pixie asked.

"More like I stumbled over her. I went down and, of course, threw out a hand to break my fall—breaking my wrist at the same time. I'm told it could have been worse. I could have broken both of them."

"Thank goodness for that," Tricia said.

"Yes, however, both cats will be happy for more of my company while I sit at home for six to eight weeks of enforced boredom while I mend."

"Why would you have to do that?" Pixie asked.

"I can hardly restock books or run the register like this," he said sadly, and proffered the cast around his wrist.

"Mr. Everett," Tricia said with just a little consternation, "that is hardly why I pay you to work at Haven't Got a Clue."

He blinked in surprise. "I beg your pardon?"

"I hired you—and Pixie—for your encyclopedic knowledge of the mystery genre. Not only do you know about the classics, but your expertise encompasses contemporary authors and their series as well, not to mention the excellent customer service you give all our patrons."

"And the store would just feel terribly lonely without you," Pixie added sincerely.

"That's true," Tricia agreed. "Now, that said, we certainly want you to feel well before you come back."

"That's just it—I feel perfectly fine. Just confined by this blasted cast."

Both Tricia and Pixie started. Those were fierce words from such a mild-mannered man.

"Then it's all settled."

"I can pick you up and take you home every day until you can drive once again," Pixie offered.

"That's very kind of you, but I can ride along with Grace, although would it be too much trouble for me to ride along on days Grace has other plans?"

"Between the two of us, I'm sure we can work something out," Tricia said, and patted his good arm reassuringly.

"Thank you, Ms. Miles. And you, too, Pixie."

Miss Marple gave a small cry as though protesting. "And you, too," Mr. Everett said, and patted Miss Marple's head. Again, her purring revved up and the three of them laughed.

It felt good to laugh. After the morning Tricia had had, she'd needed it. Now if she could just get through the rest of the day without another major hitch, she'd be all set. But as it was not even eleven o'clock, the bulk of the day was ahead of her. She'd just have to cross her fingers and hope.

Pixie and Mr. Everett went out for an early lunch, with Pixie promising to cut his food if necessary, leaving Tricia to woman the helm at Haven't Got a Clue. She busied herself with her laptop, looking over the latest publisher online catalogs to pick the books she'd stock for the summer season, and lamenting that it would be a couple more months before there'd be tag sales for Pixie to attend to look for vintage books. Still, she did check out estate sales and thrift shops around the area on a regular basis and was able to find some stock.

A ping from Tricia's phone interrupted her work. A text message from Angelica.

No lunch today. Work intrudes. See you tonight at your place. Yer sisti.

That was okay. It would give Tricia time to hit the grocery store and grab a variety of items to make several dinners.

Once Pixie and Mr. Everett had returned, and Tricia had run her errands, the rest of the day flew by. As it was Tricia's turn to host happy hour and dinner, she excused herself an hour before closing, leaving the care of her shop in Pixie's capable hands while she got the meal prep out of the way.

Lately, she'd taken to choosing recipes from the copy of her grandmother's favorite cookbook that Angelica had gifted her with. While the majority of the vintage book's recipes were quite good, some of them were just plain bizarre—which made them rather fun to make.

She'd perused the appetizers section and considered chicken liver bonbons, containing bacon and chopped ripe olives set in brown paper candy wrappers or pecans with anchovy paste adhering them together like tiny nutty sandwiches but rejected both ideas, deciding they wouldn't pair well with gin. Instead, she decided to whip up some hot cheese puffs. They, at least, sounded like normal food. Aside from the puffs, she decided the entrée would be cottage pie. She idly wondered if Ian was a fan. Perhaps Terry had already taken him to Stoneham's resident pub to test their version of this meal from across the pond. Maybe Tricia should have just bought a couple of orders to go . . . but what fun was that?

After assembling the entrée, she put it in the fridge and mixed the ingredients for the cheese puffs. She'd just popped them into the oven when her phone pinged once more. She glanced at it.

Grace picked up Mr. E a few minutes ago. Locking up for the night, Pixie texted. Should I send Miss Marple up or let Angelica do that?

Send her up, Tricia replied, and opened the door to her apartment.

Seconds later, the door to the stairwell opened. "Here she comes," Pixie called. "See you tomorrow."

"Good night," Tricia called.

Miss Marple scampered up the stairs. She seemed to know what nights Angelica was expected because she headed straight for the kitchen and her treat bowl.

"Can you at least wait until Angelica gets here?"

Miss Marple looked at her empty bowl with disdain and then decided to lick her front paws as though to prepare for *her* appetizer.

Tricia shook her head and took out the gin and vermouth. She'd just settled the vintage-etched martini pitcher into her fridge to chill when she heard her sister yoo-hoo in the stairwell. Her footfalls further announced her presence before she opened the apartment door that Tricia had closed only moments before.

"Hey there," Tricia called.

"Hey yourself." Angelica closed the door and headed for the kitchen. Taking off her jacket, she settled it on the back of a stool at the kitchen island and took a seat. "What smells so good?"

"Hot cheese puffs."

Angelica grinned. "Grandma Miles used to make them for us when we were kids. They were *so* good." But then her expression soured. "Mother thought they were too common to serve at her preposterously over-the-top cocktail parties."

Tricia rolled her eyes. She remembered far too many Friday or Saturday evenings when she and Angelica had been banished to the second floor of the family home while a host of strangers invaded to soak up copious amounts of alcohol and enjoy the exotic catered nibbles on offer.

Tricia shook herself. She didn't like to revisit those memories.

"How was your day?" she asked, and retrieved the stemmed glasses, which she'd failed to chill, from her cupboard.

"Unfortunately, it was taken up with Chamber activities," Angelica lamented. "Knowing I'm to chair the next meeting, that pain-in-the-butt Eli Meier must have texted me seven or eight times with his ideas for the Chamber. I'm trying to decide if he's harassing me because I'm a woman or if he's reverted to being a pain-in-the-butt teenager."

"What do you mean?" Tricia asked, and retrieved the pitcher from the fridge.

"You know how boys might slug a girl in the arm in middle school thinking it's a show of affection?"

"Thankfully that never happened to me." Tricia poured their drinks.

"It did to me—once! I nearly knocked Kevin Johns off his feet. He thought twice before pulling that move on any other girl in our class." She reached for her glass and sipped her martini before taking another cheese puff. "My, but these are *good*."

Tricia smiled, taking another cheese puff for herself. "Do you think Eli might be interested in you romantically?"

Angelica shuddered. "God, I hope not. How was *your* day?" she asked, changing the subject.

"You'll never guess who I ran into at the bank."

"You're right. I won't. So just tell me," Angelica said flatly.

"Ian McDonald."

Angelica blinked. "Who the heck is that?"

"*Ian McDonald*. The security officer on the *Celtic Lady* cruise."

"Oh, him," Angelica said, and looked thoughtful. "Whatever is he doing here in Stoneham?"

"He's Terry McDonald's long-lost second cousin and staying with him for a few days."

Angelica looked skeptical. "Really?"

"Yes. He kind of . . . sort of . . . invited me to dinner."

Angelica's eyes widened. "When?"

"Soon," Tricia said without conviction. "He said he'd come to visit me at the store in the next day or so."

Angelica's expression soured. "That's hardly a *real* dinner invitation."

"But he *did* mention it."

"How long is he likely to be in the village?"

"Not long," Tricia remarked. "I mean, surely he's only here for a few days before he has to be back on board the *Celtic Lady*, if he's even still assigned to that ship."

"Maybe he's between ships, which is why he had the time to visit Terry. And why didn't Terry mention he was here in Stoneham? Surely Ian had mentioned meeting the whole Stoneham contingent during our cruise."

"Ian didn't seem to remember I was a Stoneham resident. He said he knew I lived in New England but didn't know, or remember, if I mentioned it."

Angelica scowled and reached for another cheese puff. "How convenient."

"Either way, it was nice to see him," Tricia declared.

"I don't know why. He was just as dismissive of your thoughts on EM Barstow's murder as Grant Baker ever was." And then Angelica gasped. The sisters had made a pact not to talk about Stoneham's late police chief. During the months since Baker's death, Officer Henderson had been leading the force. Thankfully nothing more than petty crimes of theft and vandalism had occurred during his tenure. But the Board of Selectmen had been searching for a replacement since days after Baker's death. So far, that search had been fruitless.

Tricia didn't like to think about it. She changed the subject.

"How're things going at Ginny and Antonio's house?" As Angelica had acted as their general contractor to replace their home that had burned to the ground six months before, it was a subject she loved to expound upon.

"They should be able to move in only days from now."

The couple had lost their former home to an arsonist who'd been paid to strike at Tricia's loved ones. Many in the village assumed Antonio was just a friend to the Miles sisters but he was, in fact, Angelica's son. Ginny had been Tricia's assistant at Haven't Got A Clue before she was given the opportunity to work at the Happy Domestic gift and bookshop, one of Nigela Ricita's first business acquisitions in the village. Ginny had since been elevated to head Nigela Ricita's Marketing Department, where she'd excelled. And now she was just weeks away from delivering her second child, a much-anticipated boy.

"What's left to do at the house?" Tricia asked.

"Most of the furniture has been delivered, and the kitchen is in the process of being set up, but they're still waiting for the certificate of occupancy to come through."

"What's the holdup?"

"The person who approves such things went on vacation. In April—who does that?"

"Someone with an agenda. Maybe a first-time granny or a conscientious employee who knows that the village's citizens will need most of her attention during the summer months."

"Oh, you are generous of spirit."

Tricia smiled. "I like the sound of that."

Angelica's phone pinged. She pulled it from her slacks pocket and glared at the screen before rolling her eyes and shaking her head.

"Another text from Eli?" Tricia guessed.

"You got it."

"What's he want now?"

"He's asked me out to lunch tomorrow."

"Wow, that's unexpected."

"Tell me about it." Angelica looked thoughtful. "I'll bet he's just too cheap to spring for dinner—if he doesn't suggest we go dutch treat, that is."

Tricia's eyes widened. "And your answer?"

"It'll be an emphatic *no*!" Angelica scowled. "Except I'll

be much more diplomatic with my reply . . . once I figure out what it will be."

"And when will you deliver it?"

"Later tonight after I've had time to come up with a convincing reply."

"A reply or an outright lie?"

"Take your pick," Angelica said, and swigged the last of her drink. Tricia's glass was still half-full.

"When I first met Eli, I thought he was a nice enough guy, but this past year or so he's become downright scary," Tricia said, and gave a little shudder.

"I agree. According to June"—who managed Angelica's Cookery bookstore and kitchen gadget shop—"his subject matter has radically changed since he first opened for business."

"So I heard."

"She says about all he sells nowadays are books and magazines dedicated to crackpot subjects like how the earth is really flat, that 9/11 never happened, that all visits to the moon were faked, and so on."

"Do you think he really believes all that stuff or is he just pandering to the crowd that does?"

"You've heard him speak. What do you think?"

"That maybe he has a screw loose," Tricia said.

"Or two." Angelica's phone pinged again. She glanced at it and scowled.

"Now what?"

"He wants to know what's taking me so long to answer."

"When you finally do, tell him you were taking a bubble bath."

"And have him imagining me in the buff? No way. Better I should tell him I was cleaning the toilet."

Tricia smiled. She liked her sister's thinking.

THREE

Wednesday morning dawned bright but brisk, typical for mid-April, and Tricia left Haven't Got a Clue for her daily walk more than an hour before she had to open for the day. Since she hadn't arranged the evening before to collect Angelica's dog, Sarge, to accompany her, she made her way through the village alone with her thoughts, stopping at the Coffee Bean to buy a pound of freshly roasted and ground arabica coffee and two dozen butter cookies before returning to her store.

As Tricia hung up her jacket at the back of the shop, she heard a banging on the front door. Dodging the bookshelves, she hurried to the other end of the building and peeked through the blinds to see Mary Fairchild about to knock again. Tricia unlocked the door. "What brings you here?" she asked, allowing Mary to enter.

"Is there something you can do about that darn Eli Meier?" Mary asked, sounding perturbed.

"What do you mean?"

"After the Chamber meeting yesterday, he came straight to my shop and berated me for making the motion to end the meeting."

"Really?"

"Yes. Leona Ferguson called and told me he'd visited

her, too. Someone kept calling my shop's phone all day and then hanging up when I answered—it had to be Eli. As one of the Chamber presidents, can't you toss him out on his ear for harassment?"

Tricia grimaced. "It's not that easy."

"Well, what can be done to stop that kind of behavior?"

"You could report him to the police."

Mary scowled. "A fat lot of good that will do. Since Chief Baker di—" But then she stopped speaking in mid-sentence. A number of Chamber members still walked on tiptoes when mentioning the deceased chief to Tricia. Some blamed her for his death, while others were concerned about bringing it up for fear of causing her pain. "Without a chief, the force has been useless. When are they going to hire someone to take his place?"

"That's something that needs to be taken up with the Board of Selectmen."

"Someone like you, who shoulders some *real* authority in the village, would have more pull than me."

Tricia blinked and stifled a laugh. Being a Chamber co-president gave her no advantage when it came to swaying the Board of Selectmen. Then again, Angelica could probably sweet-talk a shark out of eating her. She'd mention Mary's request to her sister later.

"I still think your best bet is reporting Eli's behavior to the police. If nothing else, it would be on record should his threats escalate."

Mary's eyes widened. "Do you think that's a possibility?"

Tricia shrugged. "Eli *is* a loose cannon."

Mary's expression soured. "If he keeps it up today, I'll consider it. Do you think it's *really* necessary?"

"I do."

Mary gave a shiver. "I have to admit, knowing he's next door to my shop during business hours has raised my hackles."

"He doesn't have any paid help, so that should keep him out of your hair from ten in the morning until six at night."

"Unlike the rest of us, he'll close down if it's a slow day. I don't want him dropping in on me the next time he feels the urge to vent."

"Then file that police report." What more did Mary expect Tricia to do?

"Right. But from now on, I'm bringing my gun with me to the store."

"You've got a gun?" Tricia asked, startled.

"I've got three. A woman alone needs to protect herself."

Tricia had a security system for that, although she had to admit it hadn't kept her safe from intruders and on more than one occasion, but she had never considered obtaining a gun for protection. It would be just her luck she'd either shoot herself or some villain would wrestle it from her and finish her off.

"How will the Chamber deal with Eli the next time he brings up his conspiracy theories?" Mary asked.

As it would be Angelica's turn to chair the meeting, Tricia would be just as happy to let *her* deal with the clod. But that wasn't very sisterly. "We'll be discussing it," she said simply.

"I sure hope so. That said, Eli has a point. We won't be known as a book town if there are more retail and service businesses than there are bookstores."

"If you have any ideas on who to recruit, feel free to invite them."

"That's the thing. . . . I don't have a clue."

That was the excuse most of the Chamber members gave.

"I'd better get back to my shop," Mary said. "Do you mind if I use your back door? I don't want to run into Eli on the sidewalk so he can harangue me in public."

Tricia nodded and escorted her neighbor to the back of the store. Mary gave a wave as she headed down the steps to the alley, and Tricia locked the door once more. While she was in the back of the store, Tricia filled the coffeepots to get them ready for her employees and customers. She made the brew and got the beverage station ready as well, setting out some of the cookies.

Pixie arrived a few minutes early, said a quick hello, and immediately went to the back of the store to hang up her coat. Upon her return, Tricia noted she was dressed in what she called her Snow White–style dress. The top looked like a dark blue blouse, while the skirt was a cheerful yellow. A simple yellow belt separated the two. She wore her auburn-dyed hair in a chignon and looked smart with a white rhinestone butterfly clip to one side. No doubt about it, Pixie had style. The one thing missing was the gold canine tooth she used to sport. After breaking the crown some months before, Pixie had chosen to replace it so that it blended in with her other teeth. The flashy tooth had once irked Tricia, but now that it was gone she rather missed it.

"Have I told you how much I love that outfit?" Tricia said.

"Every time I wear it," Pixie said, but she didn't seem unhappy to hear the compliment once again.

"When you went to lunch yesterday with Mr. Everett, did he mention how he felt about working with a broken wrist? I don't want him to do anything that would risk him getting hurt again."

Pixie's lips pursed. "I think he's feeling a little vulnerable—scared of falling again—but you know him. He wouldn't want us to worry."

"I *do* worry."

"Me, too. But we shouldn't try to baby him, either. You know he'd hate that."

Tricia nodded.

"What did you have for lunch? I'm hankering for something different from my usual today."

Pixie shrugged. "The special. A BLT and the soup of the day."

"That's what I often get, too."

"Mr. Everett does, too, but yesterday he had the salad instead of the soup."

"Salad's good, too."

The bell over the door rang as Mr. Everett entered, wearing his sling over a dark blue cardigan. "Good morning, ladies."

"Good morning," Tricia and Pixie chorused.

"It's a beautiful morning," Mr. Everett said cheerfully.

"You're just in time. The coffee's hot and the cookies are fresh," Tricia said.

"Shall I pour?" Pixie offered.

"Sure."

"Uh, I'll just have a cookie this morning," Mr. Everett said as he headed for his usual seat at the reader's nook.

"Two coffees, it is," Pixie said, and she pulled out the mugs and doctored her own and Tricia's brew just the way they preferred them.

The three of them sat in the reader's nook. After her encounter with Mary, Tricia was glad to have a pleasant few minutes with her employees, who were also her dear friends. It was a nice restart to the day.

Business was good on that Wednesday morning. Not up to summer standards, of course, but it gave Tricia hope that when the tourists returned they'd have a busy, lucrative summer.

As usual, Pixie and Mr. Everett went to lunch first and Tricia followed later in the afternoon. By the time she made it to Booked for Lunch, Angelica was already sitting in their favorite booth in the back.

"What looks good today?" Tricia asked as she sat down, knowing Angelica was well versed on the daily specials she helped plan.

"The soup-and-sandwich special today is—"

But Tricia shook her head. "I want something different. Something exciting!"

"You want excitement? Go climb a mountain. Here you'll get good, old-fashioned but tasty food. If you want to live dangerously, try the fried chicken tenders. We have three different sauces."

Tricia was not amused.

"What's new in your neck of the woods?" Angelica asked.

"I got a visit from Mary Fairchild this morning. It seems Eli paid her a call after the Chamber meeting yesterday and more or less threatened her for motioning for the end of it. He called Leona Ferguson as well for seconding the motion."

"Well, that's not nice."

"I told Mary to report it to the police. But it seems she doesn't have much faith in them."

"She isn't the only one," Angelica muttered.

Tricia leaned in closer and lowered her voice. "But that's not all. Mary says she's going to protect herself with a gun. Even more surprising, she has three of them!"

"Really?" Angelica said, and sipped her water.

"You don't sound all that surprised."

"That she has a gun—or three?"

"Both."

"Because I've got two myself."

Tricia's jaw dropped. "You have two guns? Whatever for?"

"Protection, of course. Although I must admit, they mostly languish in my gun safe. There's no way I'd want Sofia"—Antonio and Ginny's toddler daughter—"to get ahold of them, and they're always kept unloaded."

Molly the waitress arrived with a pot of coffee in hand. "Ready to order, ladies?" she asked, and filled their cups.

"I'll have the half rack of baby back ribs," Angelica said.

"You didn't tell me the special was ribs," Tricia accused.

Angelica merely shrugged.

"I'll have the same," Tricia said.

"Coming right up," Molly said, and turned for the kitchen.

Tricia resumed their conversation as if the interruption had never occurred. "How long have you had these guns?"

Angelica looked thoughtful. "Twenty years thereabout."

"Why didn't you ever tell me about them?"

"It never came up."

Tricia frowned. Close as the sisters were, she found it

astounding that she was still learning new things about Angelica.

"Hey!" a voice shouted. Everyone's heads whipped around and all conversation in the café halted.

Tricia looked over her shoulder to see Eli standing just inside the door, looking angry.

"Uh-oh," Angelica muttered.

Eli stalked toward them, stopping in front of their table. "I thought you told me you had plans for lunch!" he accused Angelica.

"Yes, I did. And those plans were to have lunch here with my sister."

"You can do that any day."

"Yes, and I often do."

"Why don't you want to have lunch with me? Aren't I *good enough* for you?"

"Please lower your voice," Angelica said quietly.

"Don't tell me what to do!"

"I'm not telling you, I'm asking you, and if you can't tell the difference, then you have your answer as to why I decided *not* to dine with you."

Eli's eyes narrowed. "I know about you," he said loud enough for everyone in the still-quiet diner to hear. "I know what you're up to—buying up the entire village."

"I own three establishments and a share in a fourth. I'd hardly say that was the entire village."

"Oh, yeah? Well, I know all about your scheme to take over Stoneham and get rid of anyone who stands in your way. They say you know a lot more about the deal behind the lot where the old warehouse stood than you told us at the Chamber meeting."

"If you will recall, I didn't speak at the meeting."

"Oh, yeah?" Eli challenged, and as though to emphasize his disbelief again said, "Oh, yeah?"

Angelica raised an eyebrow, but otherwise showed no trace of anger or surprise. "If you really believe all of that is true, why were you so eager to have lunch with me?"

"To get you to confess, of course."

Angelica waved a hand in dismissal then picked up her cup and sipped her coffee. "Now, if you've had your say, you're interrupting my lunchtime. Please leave."

"Who's going to make me?" Eli huffed, and drew to his full height.

"I will," came a cold voice from the direction of the kitchen. Tommy, the short-order cook and maker of all the heavenly desserts served at Booked for Lunch, stood with his hands on his hips, the tattoo of a carving knife that ran the length of his forearm looking even more menacing than his baleful expression.

"I suggest that you leave. We wouldn't want to call the police. I don't think it would be good for either of our businesses," Angelica said, her voice so low it was barely audible. But Eli had heard enough. His scowl deepened and he turned and left the café, slamming the door as he exited.

Molly stood nearby, looking dumbfounded. "How about refilling all those empty coffee cups," Angelica suggested.

Molly nodded and headed for the urns behind the counter as the other customers began to chat once more.

"Well, that was an unpleasant start to our lunch," Tricia said quietly.

Angelica merely shrugged. She had handled the situation perfectly.

"Mary wants us to do something about Eli harassing other Chamber members," Tricia said, and heard a bell ring in the kitchen. Molly made a dash for the swinging door.

Angelica looked thoughtful. "Is Eli up to date on his dues?"

"I'm not sure," Tricia said.

"Let's make finding that out a priority—"

And as if on cue, Molly burst through the kitchen door with a tray loaded with ribs and crispy french fries.

"But first," Angelica finished, "lunch."

FOUR

 No sooner had Tricia returned to Haven't Got a Clue when Pixie practically pounced. "What happened at lunchtime?" she demanded. "Everybody in the village is talking about the dressing down Angelica gave to Eli Meier."

"Who's everybody?" Tricia asked, because it wasn't like Pixie to repeat gossip. She listened but didn't often spread it.

"Donna at the bank. The UPS guy. June at the Cookery."

"And they all called here to report this?" Tricia said, shrugging out of her jacket. The incident had happened only some forty minutes before.

"Oh, no. June came over to get some change. She heard it from Donna, who was in the café when it happened. Lots of people have been wanting to put Eli in his place for quite a while now."

Tricia wasn't about to ask who else but guessed it could be just about anyone who ran into the man for the past few years.

She gave Pixie a quick recap—just enough to satisfy her basic curiosity before changing the subject. "Let's not waste any more time thinking—or talking—about the man." She looked around the shop. "Where's Mr. Everett?"

"Oh, he popped over to see Grace at her office"—which

was across the street. "He said he'd be back in a few minutes."

"Oh, okay."

"Right after June left, we had a large cash sale," Pixie said.

"That's great."

"Except that he paid with two one-hundred-dollar bills. After giving June so much change, we're nearly out."

"What about our stash in the basement?"

"I'm pretty sure it's just about gone."

"Oh, rats." Tricia thought about what Pixie had said. If Donna, the bank teller, had witnessed the whole debacle at Booked for Lunch, she'd probably want to rehash the whole thing with Tricia and she was not up to that.

Tricia looked at her watch and sighed. "I guess I should go to the bank. I was just there yesterday."

"I'll go."

"You wouldn't mind?"

"Not a bit. I'll go get my coat."

While Pixie did that, Tricia plucked the two hundred-dollar bills from the register. She looked under the cash desk and found an opened envelope. Taking out the contents, she slid the bills into the envelope and handed it to Pixie. "Don't let Donna bend your ear for too long," she said, trying to hide the beginnings of a smile.

Pixie pulled at one of her pierced earrings. "Me—listen to gossip?" And with a wave, she was off.

Tricia wondered what was keeping Mr. Everett but was soon distracted by the flyer that had been in the envelope. It was from an estate liquidator. She'd been on their mailing list for years and wondered why they hadn't upgraded to an e-mail newsletter. She glanced at the dates and location of their sales for the rest of the month. Two were happening that very weekend. Sundays were Pixie's day off from working at Haven't Got a Clue. She had no problem hitting the sales and looking for merchandise to help keep the store's shelves filled, and Tricia decided to ask if she'd care to visit the sales.

Pixie had been gone only a few minutes when the bell over the door to the shop rang cheerfully. But it wasn't Mr. Everett returning. Instead, it was the scruffy young man who'd given Pixie such a hard time the day before. He'd gathered his hair into a ponytail, looking a little less disreputable. He shuffled up to the cash desk, his hands in his pockets. Was he going to rob the place?

"May I help you?" Tricia asked coolly.

"Excuse me," he said politely. "But where is the lady who was working here yesterday morning?"

"She's out running an errand," Tricia said guardedly. "May I help you?" she asked again.

"You were in the store yesterday morning, too, weren't you?"

"I was."

His gaze drifted to the floor. "Then I guess I owe you an apology as well."

Tricia blinked in surprise, but said nothing.

"I . . . I was a little upset when I left here yesterday. My nana would have been appalled if she knew I'd spoken like that in front of two ladies. I should've never lost my temper—especially over something so incredibly stupid. Things just haven't gone well for me lately."

"In what way?"

"I haven't been able to find a decent-paying job and things are getting a little tight."

"I'm sorry to hear that," Tricia said, although she wasn't sure she meant it. Was this young man just looking for a handout?

"I was wondering if the owner had any work I could do to make a few bucks before I hitch a ride back to Nashua."

"I'm the owner. And what's in Nashua?"

"The homeless shelter where I kind of live."

Was he telling the truth, or really laying it on thick to sucker her in?

"Why would someone your age live in a homeless shelter?" He looked no more than nineteen or twenty.

"That's what happens to you when you age out of the

foster care system. You get a couple of bucks and a pat on the back and you're on your own."

"And how long have you been on your own?"

"Fifteen months. I've had jobs, usually two or three at a time, but I heard about Stoneham being a book town and I wondered if maybe I could sell some books."

"Are you a picker?"

"I've done that in the past. I spent my last twenty bucks buying books at thrift stores thinking I might be able to turn them around for a hundred or so."

Not with the books he was trying to hawk.

"Books aren't really my thing," he explained.

"And what *is* your thing?" Tricia asked.

"My nana was a collector of porcelain and fine china. She liked silver, too, but the bottom kind of fell out of that market years ago—unless you have solid silver, which most people just want to melt down." He sounded sad about that eventuality.

"What do you know about vintage kitchenware?"

"A lot, not that it does me any good. My nana was into that, too."

"I take it your nana is no longer with you."

"She died almost two years ago."

"And that's when you went into the foster care system?"

"No. That happened when I was a baby. I bounced around several families before my nana took me in at thirteen." He laughed. "She straightened me out pretty quick, not that I was a bad kid. I just didn't fit with those other families. Nana, her real name was Helen, asked me to call her that. I'd never had a grandmother before. I was her fourteenth and final foster kid. She meant everything to me. Wanna see her picture?"

Before Tricia could answer, the young man had already whipped out his wallet and extracted a well-worn color photograph of a younger version of himself and an elderly black woman with her arm wrapped around the boy's neck, her smile beatific.

"Very nice," Tricia said, noting the young man's adoring gaze at the photo. But then he sobered and returned the photo to his wallet, stowing it into his back pocket once again.

"Why did you ask about vintage kitchenware?"

"My sister owns the Cookery next door. She's always on the lookout for old kitchen utensils and cookbooks in very good condition."

"I could keep my eye out for that kind of stuff. Be easier once the tag sales start once again. But I don't know where I'll be when the warmer weather hits. I might just hitch my way down to the Carolinas or Florida. It's too cold up here when the shelters are full."

"Are you from around here?"

He shook his head. "Connecticut. Over the winter, I had a job as caretaker at a camp on Newfound Lake, but that ended a couple of weeks ago when the place was sold. The new owners decided they didn't need me, so I'm kind of at loose ends." He shook himself. "Sorry, I didn't mean to dump on you like that. I only came here to apologize to the cool, retro lady. When will she be back from her errand?"

"Maybe ten or fifteen minutes. Her name is Pixie."

"Thanks. I'll come back then."

"And you are?"

"Edward Dowding."

Tricia smiled. "And I'm Tricia Miles."

He nodded. "Nice to meet you." He started for the door.

"Uh, Ed—"

He turned. "Edward," he corrected her.

"Edward. As it happens, I could use someone to move some boxes around in my basement. Why don't you come back around four and I could put you to work for a couple of hours."

"Thank you, ma'am, I'll do that. Only I'll come a few minutes early so I can apologize to Ms. Pixie."

Tricia nodded and watched him go, wondering if she'd just been suckered.

* * *

No sooner had young Mr. Dowding left Haven't Got a Clue than the phone rang. Tricia picked up the heavy receiver of the vintage black telephone that sat on the cash desk. "Haven't Got a Clue, this is Tricia."

"Ms. Miles?"

"Mr. Everett, where have you gotten to?"

"I'm sorry, but Grace has had to leave her office early today and as I'm catching a ride with her—"

"Don't worry. Pixie and I can handle everything here at the store."

"I feel bad to have let you down."

"Nonsense. We'll see you tomorrow morning, won't we?"

"Definitely."

"Let me know if you need a ride."

"Not to worry. Grace can drop me off. I'll see you then."

"Good-bye."

Tricia hung up the phone just as Pixie returned from the bank. She withdrew the envelope now fat with tens, fives, and ones from her purse and handed it to Tricia. "Was I gone too long?" she asked as she headed for the back of the shop to hang up her coat.

"Just a bit."

"Oh, I'm sorry," Pixie said, sounding contrite.

"It's just that you missed getting a well-deserved apology."

Pixie stopped short. "From whom?"

Tricia almost laughed. Pixie wasn't known for speaking grammatically correctly. "From that young guy who tried to sell you books yesterday morning."

Pixie just looked at Tricia for long seconds, the color draining from her face before she turned and resumed her trip to the back of the store.

Several customers arrived and departed before Tricia could tell Pixie that Mr. Everett had gone home for the day.

"Well, we've only got a couple of hours before closing anyway."

The shop door opened and Edward Dowding stepped

inside. He looked at both women and hung his head in shame once again.

"Hello," Pixie said, her expression hardening.

"Hello, Ms. Pixie." He approached the cash desk where Pixie was stationed. "I came to apologize for being so rude to you yesterday." He gave her an abbreviated version of the same story he'd given Tricia earlier, but there were no deviations. Maybe the kid really was sincere.

"I accept your apology," Pixie said, but there was no warmth in her voice.

"Thank you, ma'am."

"With Mr. Everett out of action, I invited Edward to help us shuffle boxes in the basement. The stock on the shelves is getting pretty sparse," Tricia said. She started to walk toward the back of the building when Pixie's voice stopped her.

"I'll show him what to do."

"Are you sure?"

"Dead sure," Pixie said, and quirked a somewhat wicked smile.

There was something in her tone that made Tricia's hackles rise. She watched as the young man and older woman headed for the basement storeroom and wondered just how much she should trust Edward Dowding.

FIVE

Tricia was again hosting happy hour at her place. Since she'd spent the last couple of hours hovering around the back of her shop just in case Pixie needed her, she hadn't had time to prepare anything. When a customer came in, Miss Marple kept watch from the top of one of the bookshelves. It wasn't until a few minutes before closing that Pixie and Edward emerged from the basement. Tricia paid him cash for his trouble, and he thanked her profusely before leaving. She hadn't promised him more work, but she was pretty sure they hadn't seen the last of Edward Dowding.

Feeling just a little paranoid, she kept Pixie behind for a few minutes after the young man had been dismissed.

"So, what do you think of him?" Tricia asked. "Do you think he's sincere?"

"I don't know. He regaled me with tales of his nana. She must have been some lady for him to be preaching her saintly virtues."

"Pixie!" Tricia admonished her.

"Sorry. It's just that he seemed to be pouring it on a little thick."

Although Tricia had thought the same thing, she didn't comment.

Pixie put on her coat and glanced at the clock on the wall.

"Would you like me to drive you home?" Tricia offered.

Pixie squinted at her boss. "Do you think he's going to jump me the minute I walk out the door?"

"Of course not," Tricia protested.

To say Pixie looked skeptical was putting it mildly.

"Okay. Maybe a little. It's just . . . I guess I'm not as trusting as I used to be."

"Ha! With good cause. But don't forget, I'm a kickboxer. I can take care of myself."

And luckily she was wearing another flared skirt that day, so if she had to take on a mugger, she could probably wipe the sidewalk with him.

"I'll be fine walking home. And if someone does follow me, I'll call Fred and he can come and pick me up."

"Well, okay," Tricia said reluctantly.

Tricia walked Pixie to the door, and as she went out, Angelica came in.

"Hello, good-bye," she said to Pixie, who gave the sisters a wave.

Tricia shut and locked the door and then moved to the big bow display window to watch Pixie head north up the sidewalk.

Angelica crowded in behind her. "Why are we watching Pixie walk home?"

"It's a long story."

"Well, why don't you tell it to me over a drink. I've had a rough day."

"Don't tell me, let me guess: Eli Meier."

Angelica pulled down the blind on the window before she turned and started for the back of the shop toward the door marked PRIVATE that led to Tricia's apartment. "That nuisance of a man kept texting me. I finally had to block him. That's when he started calling the Cookery every ten minutes until June was a nervous wreck. I could cheerfully shoot the man."

"Angelica!" Tricia protested as they started up the stairs, with Miss Marple scampering up ahead of them.

"Don't be surprised if he doesn't start hounding you next. And, unfortunately, he *is* up to date with his Chamber dues, so we can't just chuck him out of the organization."

Angelica entered the apartment with Tricia trailing behind her. She hung her jacket over one of the barstools and glanced around the kitchen, where obviously nothing had been started for their snack or dinner. "Are the glasses at least chilled?"

"Sorry. We had a visitor at Haven't Got a Clue this afternoon." While Tricia made the drinks and Angelica cobbled together a snack of cheese and crackers, Tricia relayed the story and her reservations about Edward Dowding.

"Are you getting paranoid in your old age?" Angelica asked as she carried the plate of crackers and cheese into the living room.

Tricia followed with their drinks on a tray. "Definitely. I mean, he was downright threatening the first time he showed up at my store and today he was as docile as a kitten. Talk about the Jekyll and Hyde syndrome."

"Maybe you shouldn't encourage him to keep coming to your store."

"I didn't invite him back—but that doesn't mean he won't show up again."

Angelica reached for a cracker but just stared at it.

"You seem down. Is anything wrong?" Tricia asked.

Angelica frowned. "I've spent so much of the past six months working as a general contractor on Antonio and Ginny's home that the people I hired to take care of my other businesses have more or less taken over."

"Is their work subpar?" Tricia asked.

"Not at all. Every one of them has excelled to the point that I've had to give all of them bonuses."

"Is that a bad thing?"

"No, but it makes me feel as though I don't matter—that I can no longer contribute to make my own businesses prosper." Angelica's mouth trembled and for a moment Tricia wondered if she'd resort to tears.

"The answer seems clear to me," Tricia said.

"And that is?"

"You've always said you hired the right people to take care of your businesses. Let them."

"And am I supposed to just sit back and do *nothing*?" Angelica practically wailed.

"Not at all. Start another business, and one where it's just you, or at least just enough of you to get things going."

Angelica looked skeptical.

"Surely you and Antonio have talked about where NR Associates can branch out."

"Of course, but those plans are projected for the future and only after we reach certain benchmarks. What else could I do?"

"Well, cooking is kind of out as you already own two restaurants and a food truck."

"You've got that right," Angelica said tartly.

"And the village already has a bakery and the Coffee Bean, where Alexa sells her own goods baked on the premises."

"And unfortunately both places have loyal clientele."

"So, what else interests you?" Tricia asked.

"Before my bunion surgery, I would have said shoes. Now I can't in good conscience sell the kind of shoes I used to love because they looked so damn good and are so very bad for feet."

Tricia shook her head. "No, your forte is still food."

"But you've already pointed out that I've already covered that territory."

"Not entirely. You've covered the *retail* aspect of offering food to the citizens of Stoneham. What if you went into the wholesale business?"

"You mean open some kind of a grocery store?" Angelica asked in disbelief.

Tricia let out an exasperated breath. "No. You could think about growing hot-house vegetables."

Angelica rolled her eyes. "Those kind of tomatoes are absolutely tasteless."

"Who says you have to grow tomatoes? And who says what you grow has to be in dirt?"

Angelica's eyes widened. "Hydroponics?"

"It's an option."

Angelica frowned. "My only vegetable experience has pretty much been limited to what I can grow in containers on my balcony."

"Who says that has to be your *only* experience? More and more people want locally sourced food. Not only could you supply your own food outlets, you could do that for all of Stoneham and a pretty big chunk of New Hampshire, too."

Angelica raised an eyebrow, looking intrigued. "I guess I could give it some thought."

"Yes, think about it," Tricia said. She reached for her drink. "And while you do that, I need to think about finding something for our dinner."

"There's nothing started?"

"Uh, no. But isn't that why God created pasta in a box and frozen shrimp?"

"Scampi sounds good to me. Got a frozen baguette?" Angelica asked.

"It'll be perfect for garlic bread."

"A double garlic whammy. I guess it's good we haven't got dates later tonight."

"True enough." Which only reminded Tricia that Ian McDonald had mentioned just that possibility. Now . . . would he actually come through and invite her out?

Angelica emptied her glass and sighed. "You are totally right about one thing."

"And what's that?"

"That I hired only the best people—and Antonio taking over the *Stoneham Weekly News* has turned that business around in only six months. We ran through the numbers this afternoon and ad revenue is up over three hundred percent when compared to Russ Smith's last month of leadership."

"Well, it didn't hurt that Nigela Ricita Associates started advertising again."

"That figure is *without* the Ricita brand's contributions."

Tricia's eyes widened. "To what do you attribute the change?"

"Antonio's leadership, of course. But also that he gave Patti and Ginger the opportunity to blossom. They both got the training they wanted and needed, and Patti is one sharp cookie and a crack at taking care of the books. And—we're thinking about hiring someone else to do more of the editorial work. Poor Antonio is so tied up with Nigela Ricita work that despite encouraging him to take time off and do more writing, he says he feels too loyal to the brand to let anything slip by." Angelica sighed, her smile rather sappy.

"He's a good son," Tricia said.

"I couldn't have asked for better."

Tricia nodded. "I haven't really spoken to Patti since Antonio took over. I'll have to drop in and congratulate her on helping to make the paper a success."

"She's a keeper. And now that we have an online version, we're seeing a lot of hits. People seem to toss their print editions and then suddenly need to refer back to them."

"Really? I had no idea."

"You never *did* read the paper, did you? There's lots of good stuff in there."

"All right. You've convinced me. I'll make an effort to read the next issue."

"Thank you."

Angelica's stomach grumbled. "Now, do you need help with that scampi?"

"I never say no to help in the kitchen."

"Good, and while we work, we can have another round."

The sisters got up and returned to the kitchen. Angelica actually hummed as she sautéed the shrimp. Was she daydreaming about growing lettuce, chard, kale, and cucumbers?

Rats. Now Tricia wanted a salad! But she was happy her sister's melancholy had lightened. Her own thoughts turned back to Edward Dowding and what she might have to do if he resurfaced again.

SIX

Springtime in New Hampshire is fickle. One day it'll be blue skies and soft breezes, and the next thing you know, it's snowing. Tricia awoke early the next morning to gloomy skies and the temperature hovering just above freezing. She bundled up for her morning walk, and as she left Haven't Got a Clue, it began to snow. The tiny flakes hit the ground and immediately melted, but the whole idea of snow when the forsythia was just beginning to bloom was demoralizing.

Tricia hadn't even gone ten feet when someone called her name—and that someone was female and sounded terrified.

"Tricia!"

She turned to see Alexa Kozlov from the Coffee Bean standing on the sidewalk across the street, looking utterly panicked.

Tricia looked both ways before hurrying across the road. "What's wrong?"

Alexa grabbed Tricia's jacket sleeve and nearly knocked her off her feet trying to haul her into the little coffee shop. Once inside, Alexa slammed the door.

"I'm going to be deported. *Ve're* going to be deported!" she cried. "You have to tell me vhat to do. You do dis all de time." Alexa's Russian accent was usually subdued. That it had returned with such force testified as to just how upset she was.

"Do what?"

Alexa threw a look over her shoulder toward the shop's back room, and Tricia could see she was shaking violently. "Find de dead."

Tricia's heart sank. "What? Where?"

"By de dumpster behind our shop. You've got to help me."

"Help you do what?"

"*Hide* it! Get *rid* of it! *Someting!*"

Tricia shook her head vehemently. "Absolutely not. Tampering with evidence *will* get you thrown straight into jail."

Alexa's eyes widened until they looked like they might pop out. "Vhat do ve do?"

"Show me," Tricia commanded.

Again, Alexa grabbed Tricia's sleeve and dragged her into the back room that served as the shop's kitchen and storage space and out the door to the alley. At first, Tricia didn't see anything that looked out of place, but then Alexa moved behind her, giving her a shove. That's when Tricia saw a man's scuffed shoe sticking out by the side of the dumpster.

Tricia's stomach did a kind of flip-flop as Alexa gave her another little shove. Tricia tiptoed up to the dumpster as though not wanting to disturb a sleeping form and took a tentative peek at the body, immediately recognizing the dead man.

Good grief! It was Eli Meier!

"Vhat do ve do?" Alexa asked, wringing her hands—on the verge of apoplexy.

"Call nine one one."

"But dat vill bring the police!" Alexa wailed.

"Yes. That's what happens when you find a body. He *is* dead . . . isn't he?"

Alexa seemed to shrink as her shoulders rose on par

with her neck. "I nudged him vith my toe. He didn't move. I don't tink he's drunk."

Stealing herself, Tricia crouched down and placed two fingers against Eli's neck. His flesh was cold to the touch. He must have been lying in the alley for most of the night. No blood pooled around the body, and there didn't seem to be any visible trauma, but she wasn't about to roll the body over to check, either.

Tricia pulled out her phone.

"Please don't!" Alexa begged.

Tricia tapped the call icon and then the numbers that would connect her with dispatch. "I want to report a body."

"Is that you again, Tricia Miles?" asked a disembodied female voice.

"Yes," she said with chagrin. She'd reported so many bodies in Stoneham that even the dispatchers recognized her voice. "I'm in the alley behind the Coffee Bean with one of its owners, Alexa Kozlov."

"Stay there. Someone will be there in minutes. Would you like to stay on the line?"

"No, thank you," Tricia said because she didn't need to feel guilty by association when it came to a corpse.

The call ended.

"Now vhat?" Alexa asked.

"Where's Boris?" Alexa's somewhat creepy husband reminded Tricia of a stereotypical Russian cartoon character—sinister, with shifty eyes.

"Gone to get supplies for de shop up at the club store up on de highway. He should be back any moment."

Tricia looked around the alley. "Was your camera on last night?"

Alexa's gaze dipped. "It . . . is broken," she sheepishly admitted.

That wasn't helpful.

"It has not vorked for some time," she said, sounding contrite.

Seeing movement to her right, Tricia saw a plain-clothed

figure jogging down the alley toward them. In seconds she recognized the man, who practically skidded to a halt in front of the two women.

"Ian, what are you doing here?" Tricia asked.

Ian bent low and placed his hands on his thighs, trying to catch his breath. "You called for the police. I'm it."

Tricia stared at the ginger-bearded man standing before her and dressed in street clothes. "I beg your pardon?"

"Can you believe it? I've only been on the job for ten minutes and I've already got a body on my hands. Where is it?"

"He," Tricia said as Alexa backed off, her eyes wide with fear and suspicion. Tricia led Ian over to the dumpster. He crouched down to look for signs of life and, like Tricia, found none.

"Who is it?"

"Eli Meier. He owns—owned—the Inner Light bookstore, next to Terry."

Ian stood. "And *you* found him?"

"No. Alexa, here, did. She owns the Coffee Bean." Tricia pointed to the sign above the back door of the business. "She flagged me down when she was—" But then Tricia didn't know what Alexa had been doing when she found the dead man. Probably throwing out trash.

"Alexa, why don't you tell Mr.—er, Officer—er, Chief—McDonald what happened."

"Uh . . . uh . . ." Poor Alexa was tongue-tied.

Tricia heard the sound of a siren and a Stoneham police SUV pulled up in the alley with Officer Henderson behind the wheel. He took his time getting out of the vehicle and when he spoke to his new superior it was apparent he was not happy about the situation.

"Your orders, *sir*?"

"And you are?"

"Officer Paul Henderson, *sir*."

Ian gave him a curt nod. "Looks like we've got a dead body on our hands. What happens in these cases?"

Henderson just glared at Ian.

"Is the coroner immediately called when there's a report of a deceased person?"

"Medical examiner," Henderson corrected his boss, "and yes, *sir.*"

"Fine. You can wait for them to arrive. Keep the curious away while I speak with the witness who found the body."

Henderson's gaze immediately strayed to Tricia.

"It wasn't me this time," she defended herself.

Ian turned away from his subordinate, taking a few steps toward Alexa. "And your full name is?"

"Alexa Kozlov," she barely squeaked.

"Is there somewhere we can speak privately?"

Alexa's gaze traveled to the back door of her shop.

"Let's go," Ian said, and gestured toward the building.

"I vould like Tricia to accompany us," Alexa said, apparently mustering a little courage, but Ian shook his head, his expression impassive.

"I'll speak to her separately," Ian said with authority. Tricia didn't have a chance to tell Alexa that this was standard police procedure.

Alexa shuffled off to her shop like she was heading toward her doom.

Once they were inside, Tricia looked back toward the dumpster where Eli Meier's body lay. She pulled up her collar and huddled inside her jacket.

Eli was dead. Was that surprising considering he'd become such a nuisance to so many people in the village? Including, unfortunately, her own sister. And plenty of people had a beef against the dead man. Tricia could think of three the cops might immediately concentrate on: Mary Fairchild, Leona Ferguson, and even Angelica for the very public encounter she'd had with Eli the day before at Booked for Lunch.

Eli was dead. An autopsy would prove the cause. If he

died by gunshot, Mary or Angelica could become suspects. Of course, ballistic tests could/would establish their innocence . . . but how long would that take?

Tricia was getting ahead of herself. Eli was dead, but lying where he was, there was no apparent cause of death. But in the meantime . . .

Henderson took to pacing the area in front of the dumpster while speaking to someone on the radio attached to his uniform. His expression could be described only as brash— or was it defiant? Had his day started off on the wrong foot or was his beef that he'd lost the designation of interim chief of police and been firmly brought back to the reality of being a lowly officer once more?

Baker had been a good detective and administrator, yet he'd never elevated any of his subordinates to a rank higher than officer. Was it time for that to happen? The members of the Stoneham Police Department were young, with only a couple of years of service under their holsters, but surely one of the six officers under Baker's command had shown a degree of leadership. If they didn't, had it been a calculated move on his part to always be superior and not just in rank but in intelligence and drive? It was a side of Grant Baker Tricia had never considered.

Henderson finally got around to checking out the body. "Eli Meier," he muttered.

Tricia nodded. "Did you know him?"

"He was a familiar face to just about everybody on the force."

"In what way?"

Henderson's gaze hardened. "I'm not Chief Baker. I don't repeat everything that I know about suspects to civilians."

Tricia's eyes widened. So, Eli had been a suspect . . . but in what way? And as she now suspected, Baker hadn't been universally beloved by the officers under his command.

Another cruiser arrived with Officer Cindy Pearson. She and Tricia weren't exactly chums, but she wasn't rude to

Tricia, either. Still, there was no chitchat as Tricia struggled to stay warm, marching in place to keep the blood circulating in her fashionable but not terribly warm boots.

Curious shop owners and their employees had appeared at both ends of the alley, rubberneckers all, although there wasn't much to see.

It was a full ten minutes after entering the Coffee Bean that Ian reappeared in the alley. "Mrs. Kozlov is going to come down to the station to give a statement later this morning. Will there be anyone there to take it?" he asked his officer.

"Polly can do it," Cindy volunteered. Henderson had his back to the new chief.

Ian nodded and looked back at Tricia. "I can speak with you now, Ms. Miles."

Was he calling her that instead of her first name only because he didn't want the other officers to think they had known each other before Meier's death?

"It's cold. I've been standing around here for almost half an hour. Can we take this discussion over to my shop?"

Ian glanced at the officer standing around waiting for the medical examiner. "Any idea on when the coroner will get here?"

"Your guess is as good as mine," Henderson said.

"Keep the area secure. I'll be taking a statement from Ms. Miles over at her shop."

"Whatever you say, *sir*."

Ian ignored the officer's tone. Tricia didn't comment.

Ian gestured toward a break between the buildings. "Shall we?"

Tricia led him across the street, where they entered Haven't Got a Clue. Ian closed the shop door behind them.

"I had hoped to enter your store for the first time under better circumstances," Ian said gravely, looking around.

"Believe me, it's the same for me. Would you like a cup of coffee? Or I can make you a cup of tea?"

"Real boiled water or just hot from the tap?"

"Boiled."

"And milk?"

"It could happen."

"Then tea, please," Ian said.

"For that, we'll have to go upstairs to my apartment."

Ian raised an eyebrow, and for a moment Tricia expected him to make a double entendre, but she was sure his professionalism—and the fact it was his first day on the job—probably prevented him from doing so.

"Lead the way."

Tricia hung up her coat (so much for her morning constitutional!) before leading Ian up the stairs to her home, with Miss Marple scampering up the stairs along with them. Upon entering the apartment, the cat stopped before Ian as though to block his entrance.

"Hello, puss-puss. And what's your name?" Ian asked, bending down to pet her.

Miss Marple leaned into his hand and stood so he could pet her from the top of her head to the tip of her tail.

"It's Miss Marple."

"After the Christie novels?"

"She's got gray hair, after all," Tricia said.

"That she does."

Tricia went into the kitchen and filled the electric kettle while Ian settled himself on a stool at the island, taking a notebook from the pocket of his jacket.

"English breakfast or Earl Grey?" Tricia asked.

"You insult an Irishman," Ian said with faux effrontery.

"Sorry. I do have a couple of herbal teas, but I thought you'd probably prefer the real thing."

"You've got that right. I'll take the breakfast tea and pretend it's Irish—just this once." Ian didn't wait for the tea before he got down to business. "What's your assessment of Ms. Kozlov?"

"Do you mean do I think she killed Eli Meier?" Tricia asked before turning away to get out cups, spoons, and a small pitcher of milk.

"Not necessarily. When a body is discovered, does everyone around here always assume the deceased to be a murder victim?"

"Uh, it seems to happen a lot," Tricia remarked.

Ian shrugged. "Mrs. Kozlov seemed terrified to answer my questions. That could be seen as a guilty reaction."

"Alexa was born in the Soviet Union. She remembers how the KGB treated its citizens. Believe me, there's no way she would want to draw attention to herself from the police by killing someone."

"But she didn't want you to call nine one one, either."

Had Alexa told him that or had he guessed it?

"Alexa asked me what she should do and I told her. It was my civic duty to call."

"More hers," Ian muttered. "How well did you know the deceased?"

"Not well. He was—"

"A crank?"

"I doubt Alexa would have described him as such."

"She claims she never met him."

"That's entirely possible. While they're both Chamber of Commerce members, of which I am one of the co-presidents, I don't believe Alexa or her husband, Boris, has ever attended a meeting. The bulk of their business occurs in the morning when we hold our monthly meetings."

"Couldn't Meier have been one of their customers?"

"And pay more than a dollar for a cup of coffee?" Tricia laughed. "I highly doubt it."

"Did Meier regularly attend the Chamber meetings?" Ian asked.

"Only in the past few months."

"And when was the last meeting?"

"Yesterday." She told him what had occurred and the threats he made against Mary Fairchild and Leona Ferguson.

"Can you give me their contact information?"

She did.

"Would you consider them capable of—"

"Murder?" Tricia asked. "Of course not."

But then Mary was prepared to defend herself—with a gun. Tricia had no clue what caused Eli's death, but what if he'd been shot? Could Mary be considered a suspect? Should she mention Mary's admission to Ian?

Not yet, she decided. She'd wait.

And speaking of suspects . . .

"You ought to know that Eli threw a bit of a temper tantrum at Booked for Lunch yesterday afternoon."

"A tantrum?"

"Yes. And in front of more than a dozen witnesses."

"And the content of his tantrum?"

"He tried to pick a fight with my sister, Angelica. She owns the Cookery next door to me, among other businesses. She's also my co-president at the Chamber."

"And?" Ian prodded.

"He didn't succeed in getting her to respond in kind."

"Why was he angry?"

"He wanted to speak to my sister about the Chamber meeting the day before. Eli could be quite"—Tricia chose her descriptor carefully—"contentious."

"What was he going on about?"

"Eli thought we should discourage retailers other than booksellers from buying or renting space here in the village."

"What can you do about that?"

"Not a thing."

"Depending on what the medical examiner says, I may want to speak to your sister."

"As I said, she owns the Cookery next door and usually works from home. She lives above her store the same as I do."

Ian raised an eyebrow. "And you don't mind living in such close proximity?"

"I couldn't think of anything better," Tricia said sincerely. The kettle boiled and Tricia made the tea.

"Any other potential suspects?" Ian asked. "That is . . . should there *need* to be suspects."

"My sister is *not* a suspect."

"I beg your pardon. Did Meier have any enemies?" he clarified.

Was he beginning to think about this death like everyone else? "Why are you treating this death as a murder?"

Ian's expression was positively dire. "As you said, Stoneham's reputation precedes it."

Tricia went to pour the tea.

"You're not going to serve it now, are you?" Ian accused, sounding panicked.

"Why not?"

"You've barely let it steep."

Tricia cringed. "Sorry."

They looked at each other for long seconds.

The radio on Ian's jacket squawked. "McDonald here."

"*Sir*, the medical examiner has arrived," Henderson said.

"I'll be right there." Ian stood.

"Boy, that was fast. Sometimes it takes hours for her to arrive from Nashua."

"Apparently you would know," Ian quipped.

Tricia did *not* laugh.

"What about your tea?"

"I'll have to take a rain check," Ian said.

Tricia shook her head and grabbed a mug with the store's logo on it. "You can take it with you."

"Police officers aren't supposed to accept gifts."

Tricia thought about all the coffee and doughnuts cops were supposedly famous for accepting from the grateful public.

"I hardly think an old chipped mug could be construed as a gift. Even thrift shops won't accept chipped cups."

"Where's the chip?" he asked suspiciously.

"On the bottom, under the handle." She showed him the flaw.

Ian shrugged and poured milk into the mug and then the tea. He seemed to wince.

"Still not strong enough?"

"It'll do." He picked up the mug and headed for the door muttering, "I could wee stronger than that."

Tricia followed him down the stairs and through the shop. He paused at the exit.

"We'll speak again soon."

Of that, Tricia had no doubt.

SEVEN

 Since all the action concerning Eli Meier's death was concentrated in the alley behind the Coffee Bean, the other businesses on Main Street prepared to open their doors as usual. Death hadn't taken a holiday and neither had the shop owners.

Pixie and Mr. Everett arrived for work simultaneously. Pixie was her usual chipper self, but Mr. Everett seemed just a teensy bit morose, which wasn't like him.

"Is your wrist hurting?" Tricia asked as she poured coffee from the pots on the beverage station for all three, and Pixie hung up the jackets.

"It's not too bad," he said, taking his usual seat in the reader's nook. "It's just frustrating not to be able to do the things I usually do. It has disrupted our whole lives. Poor Grace has had to take on nearly all my tasks, even feeding the cats since I cannot hold the cans and dole out the food. She even has to help me dress and perform other personal duties." At that last statement, his cheeks turned a furious red.

"Well, the good thing is it'll only be for a few weeks," Tricia said.

Mr. Everett looked up, his vivid blue eyes blazing.

"I know that seems like a long time from now, but the older we get, the faster time seems to go," Tricia said.

Mr. Everett made no comment.

"Hey," Pixie called as she grabbed her cup from the beverage station. "I saw the cops parked in the alley on the other side of the street," Pixie said. "What gives?"

"Eli Meier was found dead behind the Coffee Bean."

"Get out! Really?" Pixie asked.

Tricia nodded. "Dropped dead or—" Pixie made a slashing gesture across her throat.

"We don't know."

"Five will get you ten the guy didn't die of natural causes," Pixie said.

"Pixie!"

"Well, he wasn't well-liked. He probably pushed someone's buttons a little too hard."

"Let's hope that's not the case," Tricia said.

Pixie shrugged. "What's on the agenda today?"

Tricia glanced around the shop. "It looks like we need to vacuum and restock the shelves."

Mr. Everett usually pushed the Dyson around the carpet, but he could hardly do that with his right wrist in a cast.

"I'll vacuum," Pixie volunteered, "and you guys can go to the storeroom and choose what you want to put on the shelves. Take your time. I can handle any customers that arrive."

"Sounds good to me," Tricia said. "Mr. Everett?"

"I would be delighted."

"I'll carry our mugs," Tricia said, and gave Mr. Everett a hand to rise from his chair before they started downstairs.

As always, work came first for Mr. Everett, and though on the injured list, he did his best to fulfill his duties by collecting a box cutter and, though he struggled awkwardly, slit the tape on a box of books, pulled the carton's flaps open, and lifted out the first title, *The Mirror Crack'd* by Agatha Christie.

Tricia set his coffee near his workstation as the sound of the vacuum roared overhead. Before she could take a sip from her own cup, the shop's landline rang and Tricia picked up the extension on her desk. "Haven't Got a Clue. This is Tricia—"

"Tricia, it's Mary Fairchild. I just heard that you found Eli's body behind the Coffee Bean!"

Tricia sighed. She just knew she was going to spend the rest of the day—week?—clarifying what happened.

"Alexa Kozlov found him. I merely called nine one one. And how did you find out about it?"

"Everybody's talking."

And just who was everybody?

"Wow. Eli dead," Mary said wonderingly. "Well, I'm sure there won't be many mourners at the funeral—if there *is* a funeral." Mary definitely wouldn't mourn the man's loss.

"I also heard that they hired some foreigner with no police experience to be the new chief."

"I wouldn't say that. But you've already met Chief Mc-Donald."

"I have?" Mary sounded astounded, to say the least.

"Yes, on the *Celtic Lady*. He was the security officer you dealt with after your accident."

"Him? Why on earth would he come to Stoneham and take the job?"

"He's Terry McDonald's cousin. I assume that's how he found out about the opening."

"Wow. Talk about a small world. But why didn't the Board of Selectmen just hire Officer Henderson for the job of police chief? He's been with the force since its inception."

"Lack of experience?" Tricia suggested. "The former chief was a sheriff's deputy for decades before taking the position."

"So was Larry Harvick. Couldn't he be convinced to come out of retirement to take over the job?"

"Who do you think should have mentioned it to him?"

"Well . . . somebody in authority. Someone like you."

"I am *not* anyone with authority," Tricia reiterated for

what seemed like the tenth time. "It's pointless to even discuss the matter. They've hired McDonald. I doubt they'd take the job away without giving him a chance to prove himself."

"I suppose you're right. He did make sure that dreadful Arnold Smith was arrested when we docked in New York."

"Yes, and I'm sure he'll work just as hard for the citizens of Stoneham. At least . . . if we all give him the chance."

"You're right," Mary begrudgingly said.

Tricia heard a little bell ring in the background.

"Customer. Gotta go," Mary said, and the connection was broken.

Tricia replaced the receiver and wondered how many times during the next few days she was going to have to repeat the information she'd just given Mary. If past experience was a guide, it would be far, far too many.

Thursdays were Tricia's days to have an early lunch at Booked for Lunch with her former assistant manager, Ginny. That she was now Tricia's niece by marriage made their relationship even better.

As this was to be their last lunch before Ginny left on maternity leave, Tricia called ahead and asked if Tommy, the short-order cook, could make something special.

"How about lamb shanks? I got a couple from my meat distributor." Who also happened to be Pixie's husband, Fred Pillins. "I thought I might try them out. You can be my guinea pigs."

Tricia wasn't pleased to be described as such, but as she was a big fan of lamb, she took the chance that Ginny might like it, too, and gave him a firm *yes*! She reminded him of the timing of their lunch.

"Don't worry. I'll make sure they're ready when you are."

"Perfect."

As usual, Tricia arrived first at Angelica's little retro café, taking the table their waitress, Molly, had reserved for them. There were definitely perks to being the owner's sister.

Only five minutes late, Ginny practically waddled to the table and struggled to sit in the booth. Tricia moved the table closer to her side to accommodate Ginny. "Hey."

"Hey, yourself. How are you feeling?"

Ginny stuck out her tongue like an overheated dog and slumped in her seat. "Ready to pop. Don't get me wrong, although I'll miss our lunches while I'm off work, I will welcome my old body back."

"Who says we have to end our Thursday lunches? I can always bring a take-out order to your house and we can eat around the chaos of a toddler and a newborn and enjoy someone else's cooking."

Ginny's eyes welled with tears. "You'd do that for me?"

"Of course," Tricia said.

Ginny reached across the table and clasped Tricia's hand, giving it an affectionate squeeze. "Thank you," she managed, obviously trying to keep her composure, "I felt so isolated after Sofia was born. I don't want that to happen again."

"Well, then, I'll make it my mission to see that you have all the help and company you need. If you want people to stay away, I'll bar the door. And if you need a break, you know Grace and Mr. Everett will leap at the opportunity to cuddle the new baby as well as amuse Sofia. And you won't need to entertain them, either. If you need your space, they won't be offended if you say so."

"There's nothing those two dear people could ever do to crowd me. I love them as much as I loved my own grandparents, and Sofia has no clue they aren't her biological grandparents. We're all so lucky to have them in our lives."

"Yes, we are," Tricia agreed.

"I haven't seen Mr. E since he broke his wrist. How's he getting on?"

"Okay," Tricia said, although her voice did rise just a little at that fib.

Molly arrived to take their drink orders. "That baby

must be coming soon," she said, her gaze lowering to Ginny's swollen belly.

"My due date is two weeks away, but I'm thinking my little guy will come sooner than that."

"Have you picked out a name yet?"

Ginny shook her head. "I peruse the baby book just about every day, but Antonio and I haven't come to a mutual decision."

"Well, if I may make a suggestion—"

Ginny flashed Tricia a chagrined look.

"It should be something well out of the ordinary. How about Aloysius?"

"Al-lew-what?"

"It was my German great-great-grandfather's name. It means 'clever and filled with strength.' Anyone would be honored to be called that."

Except that Tricia knew neither Ginny's nor Antonio's ancestors were from Germany.

"We're still discussing it," Ginny said diplomatically. "We may even wait until our little one arrives to see what name will fit him."

"Well, if you think that's best," Molly said, sounding unconvinced. "Now, what can I get you ladies?"

"Uh, I ordered in advance," Tricia volunteered.

"Oh?" Ginny asked.

"Lamb shanks. Tommy's making it especially for us."

Ginny's eyes widened in delight. "Oh, I always wanted to try them but was afraid. I mean . . . *lamb*."

"Yes, but we had it for Easter and you said it was good. So, trust me. You'll love it." They ordered their drinks.

"Lamb shanks and coffee—decaf for you," Molly said, indicating Ginny, "it is." She retreated to get the pots, giving the friends back their privacy.

"So, what's new with you?" Ginny asked Tricia.

"Way too much. But if I'm honest, I'm bummed about Eli Meier's death."

Ginny frowned. "I heard about that. I mean—my office

overlooks the alley. Had I cared to, I could have watched them take him away." She shuddered. "I closed my blinds. That said, my experiences with the man were pretty unpleasant."

"Oh?"

Ginny nodded. "He came into Haven't Got a Clue more than once not asking—but demanding—that I make change for him. My impression was that he was a misogynist pig."

"Really?" Tricia asked, feeling dumbfounded.

"Oh, yeah. And he always made a point to come into the store when you weren't around because I'm pretty sure he knew you wouldn't have stood for him treating me that way."

"Why didn't you mention it to me at the time?" Tricia asked, both concerned and puzzled.

Ginny shrugged and took a swig from her glass of water. "I was your assistant. You trusted me to handle things when you weren't in the store. It was a learning experience." She smiled. "Although, there were a few times when Eli insulted me that I actually had to restrain Mr. Everett from clocking him."

Ginny may have thought it was funny, but the idea of one of her employees being abused by a fellow shop owner gave Tricia a sour stomach. Additionally, Tricia had thought Eli's behavior change was a recent development. Ginny's experiences told a different story.

"I wish you would have told me about that at the time."

Again, Ginny shrugged. "Just one of the hazards of working in retail. But it toughened me so that when I got to manage the Happy Domestic, I was practically fearless."

"And are you still?"

"Well, not when Sofia takes a tumble and skins her knee. Then I fly into total Mom Panic Mode. Soon I'll have two little ones to worry about, but I'm ready." She looked down at her bulging waistline. "Believe me, I'm *more* than ready."

It was Tricia's turn to laugh.

Molly arrived with the coffeepots and filled their cups. "The shanks will be out in a minute."

"Thanks," Ginny said. Once Molly had gone, she turned back to Tricia. "What's new in your world?"

Tricia sighed. "It seems like everybody I know owns a gun. Isn't that weird?"

But instead of looking perplexed or sympathetic, Ginny looked nonplussed. "Not really."

Tricia blinked in surprise.

"Who are you talking about?" Ginny asked.

"Angelica, for one. She told me she has *two* guns. How could that be without my knowing?"

"I've got two guns, too. Just about everybody I know owns at least one."

Tricia's jaw fell, but she quickly recovered. "You, too?"

Ginny nodded. "I got my first gun when I hit twenty-one. It was a gift from my dad. He took me to a shooting range and taught me gun safety. I bought the second—more powerful—one after Brian."

Brian had been Ginny's boyfriend since high school . . . until she found out that not only had he cheated on her, but had killed without remorse.

"I was scared living all alone at my little cottage in the woods. Having that gun made me feel safer."

"And you still have them—with Sofia around?" Tricia asked, astounded.

"Sure. But I keep them locked in a safe. There's no way she can get at them. And I'll keep their existence from her, and the new baby, for as long as I can—maybe forever."

Tricia wasn't sure how that could be accomplished. And now she wished she'd never brought up the subject.

Molly arrived with a tray and set the plates in front of them. The lamb shanks were nestled on a bed of mashed potatoes, smothered in luscious gravy with a side of petite peas. "*Bon appétit.*"

"Oh, wow—this smells delicious," Ginny said, and picked up her fork.

"Wait 'til you taste it."

They sampled the lamb. Tommy had outdone himself. The lamb tasted even better than it smelled.

Ginny tucked in, reminding Tricia that she was eating for two. But Tricia found her appetite had waned. Even Ginny owned firearms.

Tricia was feeling distinctly outgunned.

EIGHT

While Tricia felt satiated by her dinner-worthy lunch, her mind was preoccupied with the fact that so many of her fellow citizens were armed to the teeth. Pixie noticed her distraction. "Is everything okay?" she asked when Tricia returned from hanging up her jacket.

"Oh, sure. I'm just a little rattled."

"After the morning you had, I'm not surprised."

The phone rang.

"I'll get it," Tricia said. "Haven't Got a Clue—"

"Tricia."

"Angelica. What's up?"

"You tell me. I just heard that it was *you* who found Eli Meier's body."

Tricia let out a sigh. Considering how fast news traveled around the village, Angelica must have been out of the loop to find out so late in the day. "I did *not* find him. Alexa did."

"Whatever. You were there. Am I right?"

"You're right," she said wearily.

"Why is it always *you*?"

"I wish I knew."

"Anything else to tell me?"

"I'll tell you tonight over a martini. But if you're making a feast for dinner, count me out. Tommy made the most amazing lamb shanks for lunch and I won't need anything except for a snack."

"I suppose I could dig something up for myself and just enjoy your company. I want the whole story about finding Eli—"

"I did *not*—!" Tricia began.

"—and your lunch with Ginny," Angelica plowed on. "Okay?"

"Okay."

"Talk to you later. Tootles!"

Tricia hung up the phone, feeling frustrated. She took a breath to center herself and noted that the store was devoid of customers. Not a surprise, considering the time of year.

"Ready to get some chow?" Pixie asked Mr. Everett.

"Yes, indeed," he said from his seat in the reader's nook. He shooed away Miss Marple, who'd been keeping his lap warm, and struggled to his feet.

Pixie grabbed her coat and purse and the two of them left the shop to get their later-than-usual lunch. In their absence, Tricia puttered around the store, but finally gave up trying to find busywork and settled into the reader's nook for a few minutes to catch up on book reviews in the latest edition of her favorite online mystery magazine, reading from her phone.

It was nearly two when the shop's vintage phone rang. Tricia shot out of her chair and charged across the store to answer it. "Haven't Got a Clue—"

"Tricia? It's Ian. I know it's rather late in the day to be asking, but would you be free for dinner tonight?"

"Uh . . ." After that gigantic lunch? Dinner was the last thing on Tricia's mind. Still . . . "I suppose I could be. I usually have dinner with my sister. Let me check and get right back to you."

"Certainly."

Tricia made a quick call to Angelica. "Do you mind if I take a rain check for happy hour?"

"Why, what's up?"

"Ian McDonald just called and asked me out."

"Of course you should say yes. You haven't dated in an eon."

"This is *not* a date. It's dinner."

"And you know what dinner can lead to," Angelica said with an impish lilt to her voice.

"Very funny."

"Don't worry about me. Go. Have *fun!*" It almost sounded like a command. "And I want to know all about it tomorrow— plus everything that happened today. Promise."

"I promise," Tricia said wearily, and said good-bye. She immediately called Ian back. "What time do you want to pick me up?"

Pixie and Mr. Everett chose that moment to return from lunch.

"Uh, seven o'clock?"

"Perfect." That would give Tricia a chance to figure out what she was going to wear, apply a new coat of nail polish, and do something with her hair. And maybe she'd walk a mile or two on her treadmill to work off a portion of that lunch. "I'll see you then."

"Someone's got a hot date," Pixie practically sang.

"You're as bad as Angelica," Tricia chided her employee.

"I just want to see you as happy as Fred and I am."

"And Grace and me, too," Mr. Everett chimed in.

"That's very nice of you to say so." But why did everyone assume Tricia had to have a man in her life to be happy? So far, the men in her life had brought nothing but unhappiness in the long run. Some might think she and Angelica lived in a rut, but it was a comfortable rut. They enjoyed each other's company and Tricia enjoyed the fact that they made excellent sounding boards for each other.

Still, escaping that existence for one night couldn't hurt. Could it?

Ian knocked on the door to Haven't Got a Clue at precisely seven that evening. Tricia wasn't about to admit that she'd been standing near the cash desk peeking through the blinds for at least five minutes before in case he arrived early. But since Ian had to walk only a few feet from his temporary digs, it wasn't likely he'd be late, either.

Tricia was ready with her coat and purse. "Right on time," she greeted him. Since there was no car at the curb, Tricia had a pretty good idea where they'd be dining.

"Is the Dog-Eared Page okay with you?" Ian asked. "I had lunch there earlier and it's brilliant."

"I love it there, too."

Ian offered her his arm and they headed down the sidewalk until they stood opposite the pub and then jaywalked across the street.

Bev, the waitress, greeted them warmly and guided them to a table in the back with a RESERVED sign on it. She set a couple of menus down on the table and turned to Ian. "What can I get you?"

"A Guinness, if you've got one."

"Coming right up."

Bev turned away.

"Wait!" Ian called, but Bev stayed on course, leaving them behind. "I'm so sorry she ignored you. When she gets back with my drink, I'll—"

But Tricia waved a hand in dismissal and leaned in closer. "So, you're Stoneham's new police chief."

Ian smiled broadly. "I've got my green card and, as you know, I'm already on the job. As I recall from speaking to the former Stoneham police chief"—Had Ian been told about the circumstances surrounding Chief Baker's death?—"your extensive knowledge of crime, fictional and otherwise, made you a sounding board to law enforcement."

"That's a polite way of putting it," Tricia admitted. "I'm afraid my input wasn't always welcome or appreciated."

"I'll always encourage citizens to report any suspicious activity," Ian promised.

Well, we'll see how long that lasts, Tricia thought.

Bev returned sooner than expected with a tray, setting down a dry gin martini with olives for Tricia and the foamy-head Guinness for Ian. "There you go. Shall I give you a few minutes to think about what you want to order?"

"Yes, thanks," Tricia said.

Bev winked and turned to check on some of the pub's other patrons.

"Did you know she was going to get you a martini?" Ian asked.

"Let's just say she's brought more than a few to me in the past," Tricia remarked.

Ian lifted his beer and held it up. They clicked glasses. Ian took a sip and shook his head. "It's just not as good as draft."

Tricia smiled and sipped her martini. Yoshi the barmaid made a good martini, but Angelica made a great one.

"How was your first day on the job?" Tricia asked.

"I'd be lying if I didn't admit it was a bit of a challenge. I've met with some resistance among the ranks, but nothing I can't handle. I've spent most of my time looking into Eli Meier's last few days."

Tricia sipped her martini.

"I've heard several accounts of what happened at the Chamber of Commerce meeting the other day. Would you give me your take?" Ian asked, and took another sip of his beer.

Tricia decided to answer honestly. "Eli was a gigantic pain in the butt."

"So I've heard."

Tricia related the events of the meeting as she remembered them—and in greater detail than she'd reported them to Ian earlier that day.

"That's pretty much what I've been told. Tell me more about the altercation between your sister and Meier at Booked for Lunch on Wednesday."

"Altercation?" Tricia repeated. "I'd hardly call it that, at least from Angelica's perspective. Eli burst into the café in a foul mood."

"Because your sister wouldn't date him," Ian stated.

"She wouldn't have *lunch* with him. And who could

blame her? Angelica never raised her voice. She was the epitome of calm, and after a brief discussion, she politely asked him to leave."

"And when he wouldn't, her bouncer threatened Meier with a knife."

Tricia's jaw dropped. "Bouncer? Knife?" And then Tricia remembered Tommy's tat. "The so-called bouncer was Angelica's short-order cook, Tommy, who never came within ten feet of Eli. And the knife was a tattoo on his arm. I hardly think that could be construed as a weapon. And who told you such nonsense, anyway?"

"A Mr. Dan Reed."

Tricia closed her eyes and let out a weary breath.

"So, you know him?"

"Oh, yes. Were you aware that Dan wasn't even *in* the café at the time?"

Ian looked perturbed. "No, I wasn't."

"So what he told you was only hearsay. If you want to know what *really* happened, you should talk to someone who was actually there. Like me."

"You're biased."

"Because Angelica is my sister?"

Ian nodded.

But then, Donna from the bank, who'd been at the café, had told June at the Cookery a rather sensational version of the facts. Or was it that June had just interpreted what Donna *said* as sensational? Tricia did, however, give him a list of people who had been in attendance. He didn't write it down, so she figured he might have already sought them all out.

Tricia decided to change the subject. "Has the medical examiner determined the cause of Eli's death?"

"Meier was shot at close range."

"That's not surprising," Tricia said, although the thought made her feel uneasy.

"Apparently not—in a state where the gun laws are so lax. People in your country have far too easy access to firearms."

"You won't get an argument from me."

"And many American big-city police forces have armored personnel carriers, provide their officers with assault rifles and flash-bang grenades and launchers, just to mention a few of their offensive tools of the trade."

Tricia couldn't refute that statement. She'd seen such displays of force on the TV news far too many times.

"That said," Ian continued, "perhaps the cities *should* be well armed when their citizens often outgun them."

Tricia sighed. "I really don't want to talk about it."

"You don't think there are too many guns in this country?"

"Oh, I fully agree with that, but there's nothing I can do about it."

"No? Too many of your countrymen—especially those in leadership roles—don't wish to discuss it, either."

"Must we spoil the evening by talking politics?" Tricia asked.

"Dealing with the gun situation here in New Hampshire will be a big part of my job. There are no laws against carrying a loaded concealed weapon and no permits required. Quite frankly, with so many of its citizens packing heat, I'm surprised the state ranks as high as it does for safety. But then, most New England states have lower crime statistics than many other parts of the country—perhaps because of their size and lack of urban areas."

Tricia listened politely through his speech, but Ian finally seemed to notice her discomfort. It wasn't just the fact that he wouldn't drop the subject, but that what he said had such a sobering effect on her.

Ian forced a smile. "I'm sorry. What would *you* like to talk about?"

"Well, for one, what made you decide to go into police work in the US of all places?"

Ian brightened. "I've visited this country many times and I love it. Terry and I didn't just discover each other. We'd been corresponding for nearly five years. When he told me of Chief Baker's death—"

Tricia winced.

If Ian noticed, he plowed on anyway. "And that there might be an opportunity for me to apply for the job."

"But I thought you enjoyed working on the *Celtic Lady*."

"I always knew my life at sea would be my *first* career, but not my only one. I have several degrees in law enforcement and security. Working for the Celtic cruise line was a way for me to see the world, albeit in small chunks at a time. Have you traveled far and wide?"

"I've traveled through most of Europe, but not so much these past few years. Although I did go to Ireland last fall. I must admit, I thought of you quite often during that trip."

"Really?"

"Yes. Not like I was obsessing, or anything, just that I had no friends or acquaintances in the country, but I did know you, and heaven only knew what part of the world you were in while I was in your home country."

"And your assessment of it?"

Tricia smiled. "Ireland is very green."

Ian laughed. "That it is. Anything else?"

"I love it. The food, the people—"

"The whiskey?" Ian asked with a raised eyebrow.

Tricia let the ghost of a smile settle on her lips. "I wouldn't say no." But then she wasn't about to order a wee dram at that moment, either. "Now that you've got the job, will you be staying with Terry for the foreseeable future?"

Ian shook his head. "It was very kind of him to invite me to stay with him, and he says I can do so as long as I like, but we have different lifestyles."

"You mean he stays up half the night playing video games?" Tricia suggested.

"Well, there is that. But now that I've got the job, I'm eager to have my own place." He smiled. "It's been quite a while since I rented a flat. I've lived on ships for the past twelve years, so I don't need a big place. I understand there's a flat over one of the buildings along here that might be available."

Tricia knew that apartment all too well. "Oh, please don't rent it," she said with dread.

"Why not?"

"Because the last two men who did died tragically and I wouldn't want that to happen to you."

Ian looked skeptical.

"I don't know if you've heard, but I'm known around here as the village jinx."

"I've heard," he said simply.

She didn't ask from whom. Probably Polly Burgess—the police department's receptionist—who seemed to take every opportunity to besmirch Tricia.

"My ex-husband, Christopher, lived there. So did Marshall Cambridge."

Ian nodded. He'd at least heard about Marshall. "Do you have any suggestions on where I should look?"

"NR Realty often handles rentals, as well as selling properties. I know the manager, Karen Johnson. I could ask."

"If you wouldn't mind. I'm so busy during the day, it's going to take me months to get up to speed with the new job."

"I'd be glad to."

"Thank you."

Bev ambled over to the table. "Are you ready to order?"

"We've been catching up with each other and haven't even looked at the menu," Ian admitted.

"I'll give you a few minutes," Bev said. "Can I get you another round?"

Tricia hadn't even noticed that she'd finished her martini—and eaten both queen olives.

They consulted their menus and ordered. Ian had the fish and chips and Tricia braved a calorie overload by deciding on the Scotch eggs. After her large lunch, she didn't really need any more food.

While they ate and drank, they passed an hour or so in pleasant conversation, with Tricia expounding on the joys and drawbacks of living in a small village, forgetting that Ian himself was from such a place across the pond.

Afterward, he walked her back to Haven't Got a Clue,

saying good night and giving her a chaste kiss on the cheek. For some reason, Tricia felt a stab of disappointment that he hadn't offered just a little bit more.

As she readied herself for bed, Tricia thought back on a portion of her conversation with Ian. It had given her more than a little food for thought. She was adamantly against citizens armed with assault rifles and automatic handguns that fired large-capacity clips. And that there weren't more safeguards to keep guns out of the hands of people who would misuse them to threaten, maim, and kill innocents.

But what if . . .

What if someone she loved was in danger? What could *she* do to protect them? Would her ideals implode if there was a possible lethal threat to any of them—or even a stranger? Say one of her customers was taken hostage?

Suddenly her firmly held beliefs seemed to stand on shaky ground.

The problem was . . . you couldn't tell the good guys with guns from the bad guys, and that terrified her.

She couldn't put such thoughts out of her mind and grabbed one of her comfort reads, *Pride and Prejudice*. It wasn't a mystery, but sometimes Tricia felt the need to escape even the fictional world where murder was an everyday occurrence. Sadly, too many days the nightly news was filled with senseless violence, and far too often those deaths were attributed to guns.

It took a long, long time before sleep claimed Tricia that night.

NINE

 Daily routines could be such a bore, but after the trauma she'd endured emotionally some six months before, Tricia found that everyday practices brought her comfort. Beginning each morning with a brisk walk gave her time to pull her thoughts together, plan the day—and possibly the evening meal—and seeing the village's familiar landmarks brought her pleasure. Especially the gazebo in the village square and, when in season, the gardens in front of the Stoneham Horticultural Society.

Her store's landline began to ring just as Tricia was about to head off for her walk. She picked up the vintage phone's heavy receiver but before she could utter a word—

"Hi, Tricia. It's Becca Chandler."

Becca Dickson-Chandler, the former world tennis champion who had invaded Tricia's life after Marshall Cambridge's death. Becca had been Marshall's ex-wife . . . from a time when he was known as Eugene Chandler—an accountant for a racketeer. He'd lived under a false identity after testifying against his former boss and had met his maker from a street accident just six months before. Now retired from the game due to a leg injury, Becca had moved to the area to assume ownership of Marshall's shop, the

Armchair Tourist, and she had her eye on becoming the next Nigela Ricita of Stoneham.

"What are you doing for lunch later?" Becca asked.

No Hello, how are you? Tricia thought. "Eating," she replied simply.

"Very funny. I missed the last Chamber meeting on Tuesday and was hoping you could fill me in on everything that happened."

"There's not much to tell," Tricia said.

"Ooh, that's not what I heard. I'd like your perspective. Shall we meet at the Brookview at one?"

"Well, I—"

"Great, I'll see you then." And the call was cut short.

Tricia hung up the receiver and frowned. She and Becca were not friends. Wary acquaintances was perhaps a better descriptor. Tricia wasn't sure she could trust Becca, not that she'd overtly lied to her or had done anything to hurt her. It was more Becca's motives that always seemed just a bit off. Why should she care what happened at the Chamber meeting? None of it concerned her or her business.

With a shake of her head, Tricia headed for the door remembering she'd promised Ian to touch base with Karen Johnson. Figuring she could kill two birds with one stone— get in her morning walk and speak to the village's top Realtor—she returned to the shop's cash desk, picked up the phone, and dialed the number.

"Hey, Karen, it's Tricia Miles. Are you busy this morning?"

"I've got an appointment at eleven, but I'm free until then. What's up?"

"What if I came by with a take-out cup from the Coffee Bean in, say, ten minutes?"

"I'll be waiting."

Tricia asked how Karen liked her brew.

Ten minutes later, Tricia walked into the offices of NR Realty. The place had undergone quite a change from the last time she'd entered the premises. Before, it looked like it could have passed for a satellite DMV office, but after Angelica's intervention, it now looked a lot more professional and welcoming. The two agents who shared the office with Karen now had their own tiny offices where they could speak with clients in privacy, and each had been given the choice of art they wanted on the walls. A big bulletin board had also been erected that held color pictures of the outsides of the properties for sale or rent. Tricia was glad to see there were several listed under the for-rent category.

After hearing the door buzz, Karen emerged from her office. She'd changed her hairstyle since the last time Tricia had seen her. It was now cropped short with tight curls, but though her hair was now a more casual style, she still wore a sharp business suit and low heels. That day, the suit was navy blue.

"Hey, Tricia."

"Hey, yourself. Here." Tricia handed Karen the tall, insulated paper cup. "When I told Alexa it was for you, she made it just the way you like it."

"She's a gem. Thanks. Come on into my office for that chat you suggested."

Tricia followed Karen, taking one of the chairs in front of her desk. Karen's office was still the same as it had been the last time Tricia visited—filled with French provincial charm.

"What brings you here?" Karen asked, taking the lid from her cup.

"Have you heard about our new chief of police, Ian Mc-Donald?"

"I heard he's got a charming accent."

"He does. And he's interested in renting an apartment here in the village."

Karen nodded. "And you're running interference for him?"

"I guess you could say that. I see there are several."

Karen sipped her coffee before answering. "There's the one over—"

"No!" Tricia said emphatically.

Karen nodded. "I get that reaction a lot. How big a place is he looking for?"

"He's been used to a tiny cabin on a cruise ship, so he's not opposed to a small space."

Karen nodded. "There's a two-level apartment over the Bee's Knees. It's so small, I haven't been able to find anyone who'd even look at it once I tell them the square footage."

"Which is?"

"About six hundred feet."

"That's small."

"No smaller than a tiny house. And I've got one coming up for rent on the village outskirts in June."

"I don't think he wants to wait that long. Do you have pictures?"

Karen set her coffee down, pulled a keyboard out from under the table that served as her desk, tapped a few keys, and then turned her monitor so Tricia could see it. She picked up her mouse and clicked on the seven or eight pictures that showcased the apartment.

"It's small," Tricia agreed, "but it's actually quite functional. I don't suppose it comes furnished."

"As a matter of fact, it does. It was being used as a short-term rental, but the owner grew tired of dealing with the cleaning routine every couple of days."

"And is too cheap to hire someone?" Tricia guessed.

"You didn't hear it from me. The owner would be very happy to rent it out and is pushing for at least a one-year lease."

"That seems fair. What's the price?"

Karen told her.

"Wow, that's quite reasonable."

"It's been empty for more than a month. The owner is eager to get some cash coming in on a regular basis."

"When would you be able to show it?"

"Anytime this afternoon. If I can't do it myself, Jess or Rob can do it. We're pretty much available from nine to nine every day. We need to accommodate our clients when *they've* got the time to look."

"That's great. Can you e-mail me the URL for the listing so I can send it to Ian? If he likes it, he can get in touch with you about it."

"Sure." And with a couple of keystrokes, the deed was done.

"Thanks," Tricia said, and toasted Karen with her own cup.

"What else is new?" Karen asked.

"Of course you heard about Eli Meier."

Karen shook her head. "It's been the talk of the village ever since the Chamber meeting earlier this week."

"Did the new owners of his storefront ask you about listing it?"

"Yes. But it was contingent on them getting Mr. Meier out. That said, I did walk a potential client there on Tuesday."

"Rick Lavoy?"

Karen nodded. "The place needs a total gut for his purposes, but he didn't flinch at the idea. That space would make a great tasting room. And there's space for one or two apartments above that would also need total renovations."

"Would you say the building's owner was in a hurry to get Eli out? I heard he owed four months' rent."

"Eviction papers were in progress," Karen admitted. She scrutinized Tricia's face. "Are you thinking someone wanted to hurry Meier out and killing him was a fast track way to do it?"

"It's a possibility."

Karen's expression darkened. "I never like to think ill of my clients."

"But you must have run into more than a few shady people during your career."

Karen opened her eyes in wide innocence. "Never."

Tricia suspected Karen was lying through her teeth. She rose from her seat. "I'd best get back to my walk."

"Keep in touch. Maybe we can do lunch some day before long."

"I'd like that. Talk to you soon."

Tricia left the office. She drank the rest of her brew as she walked. Since she was on the opposite side of the village, she departed from her usual route, finishing her coffee and disposing of the cup in one of the municipal trash containers along the way.

As soon as she returned to Haven't Got a Clue, Tricia forwarded the information Karen had given her about the apartment to Ian before she began her day by filling the pots for coffee in the beverage station. She'd just hit the on switch when the bell over her door rang. Tricia was surprised to see it was Louise Griffin who entered, sporting an ear-to-ear grin.

"Louise, how nice to see you."

The two women hadn't exactly hit it off when they'd met some six months before when Tricia found out that the man who'd asked her to marry him had been carrying on with Louise as well. That wasn't Louise's fault and Tricia had decided to take the high road when dealing with the woman.

"What brings you to Haven't Got a Clue?"

Louise held a blue folder in one hand, the kind schoolkids keep their science or English notes in. "I looked for you this morning on your walk, but you didn't pass my studio at the usual time."

"I took another route. What's up?"

Louise's grin widened. "You're the second to know." The first probably being Karen at NR Realty, who'd been a friend of Louise's since college days. "It's taken me months, but I can finally use my own name on my photographic works. I've officially changed the name of my business and I'd love for you to mention it in the next Chamber of Commerce newsletter." She plucked a business card from the folder and handed it to Tricia, who studied the card.

"Louise Griffin Photography."

Louise's eyes positively sparkled. "Yes."

"And you've taken back your maiden name, too."

"I should have never changed it." Louise let out a sigh. "This is a monumental step for me."

Yes, it was. Louise's late husband, Mark Jameson, had held the copyright on all her work under his LLC protection—or exploitation, depending on how one looked at it. Now that she was on her own, Louise had finally been able to take control of her life, which pleased Tricia.

"And more good news. I was able to sell Mark's dental practice. I wanted to personally thank you for your help in lining up another practice to move into the office. Mark had signed a five-year lease and I would have been liable for those payments if you and your sister hadn't intervened on my behalf. You saved me hundreds of thousands of dollars. I don't know how I can ever repay you."

"Knowing you're on your way to success is repayment enough for us." Although Tricia was sure Angelica wouldn't complain if Louise took a few free photos of the newest member of the family when he was born in a few weeks.

"I wish collecting what was owed Mark was as easy to navigate," Louise remarked.

Tricia had heard from a number of Mark Jameson's patients with the same complaint: while he may have done good work, his prices could be obscene. Pixie herself had visited him on an emergency basis and had been handed a whopping bill for his services.

"I'm sorry to hear that," Tricia said.

"People assumed that when Mark died their obligation to pay for his services would be forgiven. Unfortunately, I can't afford to do that. Worse, now I'll never get a nickel of what that deadbeat Eli Meier owed Mark."

Tricia's eyes widened. "A lot?"

"Four fillings and two crowns. I've been sending him invoices for months and had just turned his account over to a collection agency."

"When was the work done?"

"That's just it. Some of it was done over a year ago."

"And Mark didn't hound him for payment?" Mark wasn't known to be softhearted. Tricia couldn't believe he'd fall for any kind of sob story. That he would continue to work on Eli's teeth when he was owed so much money seemed out of character.

"I found that puzzling, too."

"Were they friends, is that why Mark gave him a break?"

Louise shrugged. "Not that I know of. Mark didn't have many of them," she added under her breath. It wasn't surprising, considering his unpleasant personality. *Obnoxious* some might have called him—including Tricia, although she didn't like to speak ill of the dead.

"Had you ever met Eli?" she asked.

"Oh, yes," Louise said with chagrin. "I was taking photos of the rebuilt gazebo in the village square at sundown last spring to get some ideas before I had my own built on the new property north of the village. He happened to be sitting on a bench nearby and threw a conniption fit threatening to sue me if I included his likeness in any photo I displayed or sold. He wasn't anywhere near the gazebo. It almost seemed like he just wanted to pick a fight with me."

"Did he know you were Mark's wife?"

"I don't think so."

Tricia mulled over what Louise had said. Why would Eli be afraid to have his photo taken? What did he have to hide?

"I'd better get going," Louise said. "I have five appointments today."

"Sounds like business is booming."

"And may it continue," Louise said. She headed for the door and gave a wave before departing.

Tricia's phone pinged. She took it out and glanced at the screen and saw Ian had sent her a reply.

The place looks just about perfect. I spoke to Ms. Johnson and she's going to show it to me this evening. If it's as nice in person, I can sign the lease tonight. Thanks.

Tricia wrote back: What are friends for?

She put her phone down and glanced at Louise's pretty new business card. Eli had owed money to his landlord *and* dentist. How many other people had been annoyed or inconvenienced by Eli Meier . . . and was that ill will enough to shoot the man to death?

TEN

 Since Tricia usually had lunch with Angelica, she figured she had better call and let her know she'd be eating lunch alone that day.

"Again?" Angelica lamented. "But I had to have dinner alone last night, too."

"She never gave me a chance to refuse."

"Then you don't have to show up."

"That would be rude."

"It was rude of her not to give you a chance to decide whether you wanted to have lunch with her."

Tricia sighed.

"Oh, all right," Angelica relented. "I'll see you tonight. But we seriously need to catch up. You still haven't told me about your date with Ian."

"Well, don't get your hopes up for a juicy story," Tricia warned.

"Oh, pooh."

"I'll see you tonight," Tricia said firmly.

"You'd better."

They ended the call and Tricia hung up the phone and finally started her workday.

Fridays were Mr. Everett's day off, but Pixie arrived right on time, brimming with good cheer. That day she'd chosen to wear a perky dress with a full red skirt with black polka dots. The bodice was black with a skinny black belt and a matching red sweater. It was what Tricia called one of her "Barbie" dresses from the doll's original incarnation, not the suntanned blondes little girls played with these days. While still girly as all get-out, the dolls now had careers as astronauts and nuclear scientists and had multicultural friends. But Tricia felt nostalgia for the Barbies she played with as a child. She'd imagined her Barbie reading books to children and working in a library or a bookstore while still being stylish. And her Barbie book dream had come true.

"That's a big smile," Pixie commented.

Tricia blushed. "Just thinking about something from the past." She cleared her throat and sobered. "I've got a big favor to ask."

"Shoot," Pixie said, and took the cup of coffee Tricia offered her.

"Could you take your lunch break early today? Becca Chandler called and wants to have lunch with me at one. Before I got a chance to even reply she hung up."

"So it looks like you're stuck. Where are you going?"

"The Brookview Inn."

"I'd like to be stuck going there," Pixie muttered, and drank some of her coffee.

"How about I bring you one of their decadent desserts as a thank-you?"

Pixie grinned. "Bribery usually works for me."

Her smile, however, was short-lived when the bell over the door rang and, instead of a customer, it was Edward Dowding.

"Good morning, ladies," he called with the shadow of a smirk on his face.

"Edward," Tricia said evenly in acknowledgment. Pixie said nothing, her expression wary. "To what do we owe the pleasure?"

"I wondered if you might need more help today. If so,

I'm available." He flexed his muscles, not that they could be seen under his jacket.

Tricia gave her employee a sidelong glance, but Pixie shook her head ever so slightly.

"Well, thank you for the offer, but we're all caught up."

"There's several estate sales this weekend. I was hoping Ms. Pixie might want to take me along when she goes hunting tomorrow or Sunday."

Pixie's eyes narrowed. "And how did you know I go to estate sales?"

"I figured one of you had to, and Ms. Miles here probably has to take care of her store seven days a week. Besides, how else would you find so many great vintage clothes? That's a very pretty dress."

"Thanks," Pixie said, her voice devoid of inflection.

"Do you think you might have some work for me to do next week?" Edward asked, sounding hopeful.

With Mr. Everett physically out of commission, it was likely they might need some help. But then, between them, Tricia and Pixie were usually able to handle the boxes that arrived and move the stock around, thanks to the dumbwaiter and the sturdy dolly Tricia kept at the back of the store.

"Why don't you call before you come? That way you won't have to make the trip all the way from Nashua if we don't need your services," Tricia suggested.

"I don't mind hitching a ride. Besides, the shelter kicks us out pretty early. I've got to be somewhere during the day."

He was playing the guilt card, but it wasn't Tricia's fault the young man was homeless. Still, it kept her from feeling bad for Edward's situation, even if she felt wary about him. For some reason, her gut was telling her not to trust him. She'd learned to listen to those inner warnings.

"Do you have a card or something? Maybe I can call from the shelter. Some of the guys there have phones."

"You don't even have a phone?" Pixie asked, sounding mildly interested.

"They cost money. I'm running kinda lean right now."

Still, neither of the women offered him a cent.

"I'd better hit the road—literally," Edward said sadly.

"Thanks for stopping by," Tricia said, feeling a little guilty for her insincerity.

Edward looked at Pixie. "I'll be seeing you." It almost sounded like a threat.

Pixie said nothing.

They watched as Edward left the store.

Once he was gone, Pixie let out a long breath. "That kid makes me nervous."

"Me, too," Tricia admitted.

"He sure laid it on thick about being broke."

"I feel bad for him. Bad enough that I'm going to make another donation to the shelter."

"But not give him actual cash?" Pixie asked.

"We don't know if he told us the truth or a pack of lies." Tricia shrugged. "I don't know what the answer is, but rather than do nothing, I'd feel less guilty knowing I help support a place that takes care of homeless people."

Pixie nodded. She made no mention of making such a donation. Tricia wasn't about to judge her. She knew that Pixie and her husband, Fred, had overextended themselves when they'd bought their little house. They lived frugally. Pixie had a big heart. That she wasn't able to show it to Edward Dowding didn't mean she wasn't moved by the plight of others like him.

Pixie sipped her coffee and grimaced. "Cold." She headed toward the washroom to pour it down the sink and start again.

Tricia was as good as her word. Once the store was officially open to the public, she went down to her basement office, fired up the computer, and sent an online donation to the Nashua homeless shelter Edward had mentioned. Hitting enter on her keyboard, the transaction was complete.

Tricia found herself staring at the computer's monitor and feeling troubled by Edward's most recent visit. Why did he keep returning to Stoneham? And why did his every appearance fill her with such dread?

Tricia arrived at the Brookview Inn just before one o'clock. Since the Chamber meeting four days before, the lobby's décor had undergone a subtle change from Easter to simply seasonal décor. A large floral display sat on a table in the middle of the room, featuring forsythia, pussy willows, and daffodils in a large verdigris vase. The cheerful blooms made her smile.

Tricia crossed the lobby and stood before a podium waiting for Yvonne, the restaurant's hostess, to appear.

"Hey, Tricia, a table for one?" Yvonne asked.

"No, I'm meeting someone. Becca Chandler."

"Oh, yes. She's already seated. Please follow me."

Somehow, Becca always seemed to commandeer the best seat in the house, overlooking the brook. She'd changed her hairstyle since the last time Tricia had seen her some three or four weeks before, gaining long blonde locks thanks to extensions. She'd donned a navy pantsuit with a crisp, white blouse, looking very businesslike. She'd claimed she wanted to be more like Nigela Ricita. Was this her attempt? Not that anyone in Stoneham had ever laid eyes on the mysterious woman behind Nigela Ricita Associates. Or at least they *thought* they hadn't, since Nigela was Angelica's pseudonym. In comparison, Tricia's pink sweater set practically screamed *casual Friday*.

"Ah, there you are," Becca said, and motioned for Tricia to sit.

Tricia took the opposite seat—the one with the view of the front lawn instead of the tranquil woods and brook. "You summoned me. Here I am," she said without rancor.

"Darlene will be your server. Can I have her bring you anything to drink?" Yvonne asked Tricia.

"We'll have coffee," Becca said with authority. The hostess nodded and left them. Becca already had a glass of something with a cucumber slice in it—probably her favorite cucumber water.

Tricia wriggled out of her jacket, settling it on the back of the chair, and placed the linen napkin on her lap. It would have been nice had Becca allowed her to answer for herself. But then, as a former world tennis champ, Becca was used to getting what she wanted.

Becca leaned forward, a sly cast to her eyes, and lowered her voice conspiratorially. "So, what's this about you being romantically involved with the village's new police chief?"

Tricia's eyes narrowed. "What gave you *that* idea?"

"Everybody says so," Becca said, her tone changing chameleonlike to innocence.

"Who's everybody?" Tricia demanded.

"*Everybody*," Becca said, and took a sip of her cucumber water. "They say you met this guy several years ago. I assume this was before you and Gene got together." Becca's ex-husband and Tricia's former lover—although she knew him as Marshall.

Tricia took a calming breath before commenting. "I met Ian McDonald on the *Celtic Lady* cruise ship, a trip sponsored by the Chamber, and yes, it was before Gene and I were close. But I never had a relationship with Ian."

Becca leaned back in her chair, looking disappointed. "That's too bad," she said offhandedly. "But you *were* on a first-name basis, right?"

"Only since he came to the village," Tricia said firmly.

Becca looked thoughtful. "I wonder if he's open to a new relationship. . . ." Had Becca even set eyes on Ian?

Becca shook herself. "Now, what was the ruckus about at the Chamber meeting with Eli Meier, God rest his soul?"

Tricia sighed. "He seemed to think there's some underhanded business going on with the sale of the old warehouse property on Main Street where the Chamber met briefly last year."

Becca's eyes widened. "Is there?"

"Not that I know of. Nobody knows who bought it, but it's not all that unusual."

Becca's mouth tightened. "They say Nigela Ricita owns half the village."

"She doesn't," Tricia said, and swirled the ice in her water glass. "She owns this inn, the Dog-Eared Page, the Happy Domestic, the *Stoneham Weekly News*, the Eat Lunch food truck, NR Realty, and a half interest in the Sheer Comfort Inn. That's hardly half the village."

"It's a good chunk of it. She and your sister are the big players in the village."

"I suppose," Tricia said, trying to sound bored by the subject—which she was.

Becca placed an elbow on the table and rested her chin against her cupped palm. "The whole business fascinates me. I'd love to have a nice long chat with Nigela Ricita, but I get the runaround every time I've tried to contact her."

Tricia feigned interest. "Oh?"

"They say she lives out of town. That Antonio Barbero runs the shop. There's no way I want to talk to *him*."

Becca and Antonio had had a run-in some six months before. Sparks had flown—and even landed on and burned Tricia. She had no plans to attempt to reconcile the two.

"Do you think your sister would speak to me?"

"Why don't you ask her?" Tricia scrutinized Becca's face. "Are you still planning to buy a second business?"

"Well, it wouldn't be the worst thing I could do."

"What did you have in mind?"

"An operation like what I've got with the Armchair Tourist. Ava manages the store, leaving me free to do other things."

"Like what?" Tricia asked.

"Like looking for something much more interesting to do."

Aha! Tricia had predicted Becca would be bored living in a small town. "You could write a memoir."

Becca waved a hand in dismissal. "I've been working on and off with a ghostwriter on it for years. I thought I'd let things calm down after Gene's death before I started on *that* chapter."

"I'm sure it would get you on all the late-night talk shows in Hollywood and New York. You might even get paid a cool million or more from a publishing house to spill the beans."

"I've got more beans to spill than you could possibly know," Becca deadpanned, "but now's not the time."

"I would have thought the further from your glory days the less the interest." If Tricia thought that barb would wound, she was mistaken.

"Possibly," Becca said offhandedly. "Obviously, I *will* emphasize my relationship with Gene. That should be salacious enough for the tabloids. The thing is . . . I have other people to think about who could be hurt by the revelations."

Tricia felt catty. She hadn't thought Becca capable of such compassion.

Darlene, the waitress, arrived with a steaming pot of coffee, pouring for both of them. "Would you like to order now?"

"I'll have the grilled chicken salad."

"The same," Tricia echoed.

"I'll be back in a few minutes," Darlene promised, and left them alone again.

"So, you wanted to know about the last Chamber meeting, right?"

Becca nodded.

"One of the topics was bringing in more booksellers. Have you thought about opening a bookstore with a sports theme?"

"No. Go on."

"Well, you could sell new and used books about sports and sports celebrities. I'm sure with your star power you could lure big-name sports figures in to sign who've got books out—whether they wrote them or not." She couldn't help the little dig. It was an open secret that most celebrity books were as-told-to narratives, and Becca had already admitted to working with a ghostwriter.

"What else?" Becca asked, her tone thoughtful.

"Well, you could sell sports equipment—or at least knee braces and liniment for weekend warriors."

Becca scowled. "Ha ha." She wasn't laughing, but she did look intrigued. "How does one source used books?"

"Ah, that's the problem. In my case, starting out, I hired a picker—someone who scoured flea markets and yard sales—and I did so for a couple of years before I went into business. I rented a climate-controlled storage unit in a little town in upstate New York where the cost was a heck of a lot cheaper than in the city."

"Smart move."

"My husband—at the time—thought it a frivolous waste of money, but I saw it as an investment. It eventually paid off. I was in the black within a year, and that included paying two assistants a living wage."

"Do you still employ a picker?"

"My assistant manager, Píxie, is an avid bargain hunter and has the knack for finding salable mysteries to keep my sales shelves stocked year-round. We usually find the more rare volumes online or at estate sales."

"Sounds dreadfully dull to me," Becca said with a sniff, and took another slug of her cucumber water.

"That's the beauty of hiring a picker. They do the dirty work for you."

"And probably charge the moon."

"Not in my experience. Most just love to rescue things. In Pixie's case, she's out there looking for vintage clothes and fabrics. It's a bonus for me that she knows what it takes to keep the store stocked. And she's come up with a few really valuable pieces."

"For which you rewarded her handsomely."

"Of course. Why wouldn't I?"

Becca raised an eyebrow and shrugged. She drained her glass. "What are your thoughts about owning rather than renting a property on Main Street?"

"It's not often a storefront goes up for sale around here."

"You bought yours. And your sister owns several buildings as well."

"Yes, but those properties only went up for sale because the owner was sent to jail."

"For murder. Yes, Gene mentioned that to me."

Tricia wasn't about to talk about Bob Kelly, his relationship with Angelica, and Tricia's mistrust of the man from the moment she met him.

Tricia continued. "The man couldn't run his empire with a twenty-five-year-to-life sentence, so the buildings were sold to pay for his legal defense. I'm sure whatever money is left is languishing in bank accounts. But who knows if the man will ever see the light of day outside a prison cell?"

"You never thought of suing him in civil court?" Becca asked, ever mercenary.

"No."

Gene must have told Becca the circumstance surrounding Tricia's ex-husband's death. She had no need for blood money, as she was more than capable of taking care of herself. And, upon Christopher's death, Tricia inherited all his worldly wealth. Once probate was complete on Chief Baker's death, she would inherit half of his estate as well. She'd already decided which charities would benefit from that bounty as she had no need—nor wanted—his money.

Darlene arrived with their salads, setting them on the table. "Let me know if you need anything else."

"Just the check," Becca said.

No dessert, then.

Darlene left them once again and Becca dove into her lunch.

Tricia picked up her fork and poked at a piece of lettuce, remembering her conversation with Ian the evening before. "Just out of curiosity, do you own a gun?"

"Of course I do. It's Gene's Glock."

Tricia blinked. "You kept it—knowing it had killed more than one person?"

Becca shrugged and laughed. "It just goes to prove how well it works, huh?"

Tricia didn't think it was funny.

Becca sobered. "Glocks aren't cheap. I wasn't going to throw it away." Becca was a multimillionaire. What did she care about the cost of a gun? "I inherited his estate, it's mine."

"Do you know how to use such a powerful weapon?" Tricia asked.

"I've taken lessons at a firing range so, yeah, I feel comfortable with it. And it turns out I'm a pretty good shot. I have an eighty-nine percent accuracy rate."

No doubt thanks to the hand-eye coordination so necessary in her former career as a tennis star.

"From your tone, I take it you don't own a gun," Becca commented.

"I never felt the need," Tricia said.

Becca scowled. "Are you kidding me? The way *you* constantly stumble over dead people? This quiet little village is New Hampshire's murder capital."

"I wouldn't go that far," Tricia said sourly, and stabbed a grape tomato with her fork.

"Wasn't it *you* who found Eli Meier?"

"No. Alexa Kozlov found him. I merely called nine one one."

Becca waved a hand in dismissal. "Same difference."

"It is not!" Tricia protested. "And besides, it hasn't been announced if Eli was murdered." At least it hadn't been yet made public—but then Tricia hadn't watched the news that morning.

"I'm betting there are plenty of potential suspects right along Main Street," Becca predicted.

Tricia couldn't argue with that assessment. But for once, she was glad she wasn't in the running.

That said . . . it worried her that some might think her sister could be.

It worried her a lot.

ELEVEN

It was a little after two when Tricia returned to Haven't Got a Clue, feeling less than happy. That was her usual reaction after spending time with a woman she considered her frenemy.

She handed Pixie a little white bakery box.

"You remembered my surprise dessert!"

"Of course," Tricia said without enthusiasm.

"Uh-oh, what's up?" Pixie asked, but then answered her own question. "You didn't have a good time lunching with Becca what's-her-name, huh?"

"You've got that right," Tricia said, taking off her jacket. She wasn't about to discuss the bulk of their conversation, but she was curious about one aspect of it.

"Pixie, do you have a gun?"

Pixie shook her head violently. "Not a chance. I'm a convicted felon. If I had a gun, they could send me back to the joint on a one-way ticket."

Tricia let out a breath, glad to hear that.

"But that doesn't mean I haven't *had* a gun in the past. In my line of work"—Pixie had been a lady of the evening—"a girl has to protect herself."

"Weren't you afraid one of your customers might get hold of it and use it against you?" Tricia asked, aghast.

"I may have been a"—but then she didn't say the word—"but that didn't mean I didn't know how to take care of myself."

"Did you have a permit?"

"For the first one."

The first one?

"The laws have changed and that's all water under the bridge now. But that ain't to say I wouldn't have a gun now if I could. Poor Fred had to give up his guns when we moved in together—else they might construe them to be mine."

"What happened to them?"

"He sold them at a gun show." No rules or regs in New Hampshire for that, either.

Something Pixie had said jarred Tricia. "Um, I thought that . . . that your crimes were classed as misdemeanors."

"Uh . . . most of them were," Pixie said quietly, and didn't volunteer any more information.

"Is there something I should know about?" Tricia asked.

Pixie's eyes narrowed. "Have you been unhappy with my work?" she asked, her voice tight.

"No."

"You've trusted me in your home, taking care of your business, and most of all your cat."

"That's true."

"Then is it really necessary for me to go into all that?"

Tricia wanted to say *yes!* but refrained from doing so. "I guess not."

Pixie's gaze dipped to the floor, her cheeks flushed and her lips pursed. She stood there, silently, for long moments before she said, "I'd better get back to work." She left the front of the store, heading for the back of the shop, where she disappeared down the stairs to the office below, leaving her dessert behind.

Tricia was about to call her back but thought better of it. Pixie was right. Whatever she'd done in the past was just that—in the past. She'd proved to be an exemplary employee and had never given Tricia cause for mistrust.

Tricia slogged over to the cash desk and sat down on the stool behind it, feeling like she'd failed as a boss and wondered how long she would have to work to gain Pixie's trust once again.

The atmosphere inside Haven't Got a Clue was strained for the rest of the afternoon, and Tricia found herself counting the minutes until she could close for the day. When the time came, Pixie mumbled a barely audible "See you on Monday," and hightailed it out the door.

Angelica was in charge of happy hour and dinner that evening, and Tricia had a feeling being with her sister would be the highlight of her crummy day.

Well, maybe.

Tricia locked her store and headed over to the Cookery. June must have left a few minutes early because Tricia had to unlock the door and let herself in. She found herself trudging up the stairs to Angelica's apartment, but the cheerful sound of Sarge's greeting did help to lift her spirits at least a little. His legs seemed to have springs attached as he bounced up and down before her.

"Welcome, *bienvenue, accogliènza!*" Angelica called, standing behind the kitchen island and stirring the glass pitcher of martinis.

A simple "Hi" was all Tricia could muster. She shuffled over to one of the stools and sat down, taking the lid off the crystal jar that held Sarge's biscuits and tossing one to the dog, who instantly quieted, taking his treat to his bed to enjoy in comfort.

"What smells so good?" Tricia asked.

"Good, old-fashioned clam dip. The recipe called for canned clams, but I bopped over to the clam shack up on the highway and bought some fresh ones. I was going to make clam fritters, but then decided it would be too much before dinner. Get the crackers out, will you?"

Tricia slogged over to one of the cupboards and removed a box of butter crackers, placing ten or so on a plate.

"Boy, you look down," Angelica observed as she pivoted to the fridge to retrieve the chilled glasses.

"I had a terrible day."

"Oh, dear. Well, tell all," Angelica encouraged, and set the pitcher, glasses, and crackers on a tray before she retrieved the dip from the oven.

"As you know, I had lunch with Becca Chandler at the Brookview Inn."

"Yes, while I sat in front of my computer monitor mindlessly eating leftovers on the verge of going bad that I found in my fridge," Angelica lamented, and picked up the tray, carrying it into the living room. Tricia followed.

"If you didn't want it, you could have thrown it away and gone to Booked for Lunch."

"And toss more food into a landfill?" Angelica asked.

Tricia wasn't about to argue with her sister on that account.

"Anyway, I learned a couple of interesting things during our encounter," Tricia said.

"'Encounter' sounds more like a confrontation than a lovely lunch."

"The food was fine; the company, not so much."

"Well, name one of the things you learned," Angelica retorted.

"First of all, Becca says she's been trying to connect with Nigela Ricita to talk tactics on acquiring businesses. Have you been avoiding her?"

Angelica looked uncomfortable. "Well, yes. Nigela only responds when she absolutely has to—and, as you know, only with a voice-altering program on the computer. I haven't even spoken directly to Becca as myself since the time I met her last fall when she and Ginny played tennis—not even at the Chamber meetings she's attended."

"Why won't you speak to her as Nigela?"

Angelica straightened haughtily. "One does not associate with the rabble."

"Oh, come on. Becca is hardly rabble. She's an international tennis star."

"*Former* international tennis star," Angelica clarified.

"Granted," Tricia conceded.

Angelica looked pensive. "I wasn't impressed with Becca as a person. She treated Ginny pretty poorly."

"Which didn't faze Ginny in the least. Becca also mentioned she'd like to speak to you as your real self, too."

Angelica sighed. "I suppose as co-president of the Chamber of Commerce I would be required to do so, but she hasn't contacted me in that capacity, either."

"Yet. I encouraged her to reach out to you. What will you do when she does?"

Angelica shrugged. "I'll speak the truth." She gave a little shudder. "But I'm not sure she'll listen. It seems to me that Becca has her own agenda."

Tricia nodded. She felt the same way.

"What was the other interesting thing you learned?" Angelica asked.

"It seems some in the village think I'm romantically involved with Ian McDonald."

Angelica's brow furrowed. "After one date?"

"It wasn't a date."

"He kissed you, didn't he?"

Tricia hadn't discussed her dinner with Ian with Angelica, but she answered honestly. "Well, yes . . . but only on the cheek."

Angelica shook her head. "Too bad. So what's the scuttlebutt on you two?"

Tricia took a sip of her martini and shrugged. "Thanks to the Authors at Sea cruise, a number of those who traveled with us remember my speaking with Ian multiple times during the voyage."

"Such as who?"

"I have no idea. But I know Ian has spoken to both Mary and Leona and goodness knows how many others."

"Well, we *did* have quite a Stoneham contingent on that vacation."

"Indeed," Tricia agreed. "Ian's tenacious. I'm sure he's already contacted most of them to check out both of us."

"Yes, we spoke this morning by phone. It was a short conversation," she said dismissively. "Do you think he suspects you?"

"Of what? Eli's death?" Tricia shook her head. "But if he's looking for suspects, I don't think he'll count you out."

"Why on earth should I be considered a suspect?" Angelica asked, affronted.

"That rather loud discussion the two of you had at Booked for Lunch."

Angelica frowned. "I kept my cool and have an abundance of witnesses as the chief well knows."

"Yes, but as both Ian and Becca pointed out to me, Stoneham itself doesn't exactly have a sterling reputation. Nashua typically only has one murder a year. Stoneham has double that rate, sometimes more every year."

"That's still a lot less than most metropolitan cities," Angelica pointed out.

"Stoneham is hardly a metropolis," Tricia said.

Angelica's expression soured. "I'm not going to give that vile man's death another thought until or unless they deem it a murder."

"Too late. Ian told me he was shot to death."

Angelica blinked and then took a gulp of her drink.

Tricia gouged some of the dip from the bowl and spread it on a cracker, taking a bite. "Becca has a gun. Marshall's gun," she added.

"Eww!" Angelica said, wrinkling her nose in revulsion. "Knowing it had killed so many people?"

Tricia nodded.

Angelica let out a breath. "I'm not surprised she has a gun, only that she'd kept one with such a tragic history."

"Well, guns *are* for killing."

"Shooting," Angelica corrected. "That said, I'd never keep a gun that had killed someone. I'd have it destroyed."

Tricia sighed. "It's because of Becca's gun that Pixie and I are on the outs."

Angelica frowned. "What happened?"

Tricia took a fortifying sip of her drink before answering. "I was a little upset after my conversation with Becca and I asked Pixie if she had a gun."

"I certainly hope not. That could land her back in jail."

"That's what she said. Because in order for that to happen, you have to be a convicted felon."

Angelica looked puzzled. "And?"

"Prostitution isn't a felony."

It took a long moment before Angelica realized the significance of that statement. "Oh, dear."

"I asked Pixie to tell me about it and she refused."

"Out-and-out refused?" Angelica asked.

"Not exactly, but she asked me if I trusted her."

"And you do."

"Yes, but . . ."

Angelica shook her head in what seemed like disappointment. "Oh, Tricia. You at least apologized, didn't you?"

"Well, I—"

"Oh, no! How are you going to fix this?"

"I don't know," Tricia said sadly. "I just don't know."

TWELVE

Tricia slept fitfully, tossing and turning so much that Miss Marple jumped from the end of her bed at some point during the night, choosing to sleep elsewhere. However, the cat did turn up for her breakfast but made it plain that she planned to nap on the couch as soon as she'd finished her morning ablutions. Tired as she was, Tricia was determined to stick to her morning routine, hoping that during her walk she would come up with the right words to apologize to Pixie. She didn't want that conversation to take place on the phone or via text. But then she remembered it was Saturday and Pixie had weekends off. She would have to live with the guilt for at least forty-eight hours.

The sky looked more than a little threatening when Tricia stepped outside Haven't Got a Clue, locking the door behind her. Well, April showers were supposed to bring May flowers, and she was all for that. Still, she was glad she'd brought along her cheerful, floral umbrella—just in case.

As Tricia started north up an empty Main Street, she was surprised to hear footfalls coming from behind. She turned to see Ian McDonald hurrying up to meet her.

"Good morning," he called.

"Good morning. I wasn't expecting to see you out so early."

"I'd be lying if I said the same. I know you usually take a walk every morning."

"Spying on me?" Tricia asked, and started off again with Ian dropping into step beside her.

"No. I asked Terry."

Tricia had run into her nearest neighbor on many of her morning constitutionals. "What did you want to talk to me about?"

Ian shrugged. "Just about some of the people here in the village."

"Why don't you just ask the officers under your command?"

"I'm new here. They don't yet trust me."

"Why shouldn't they?"

"I'm a foreigner. I didn't rise through the ranks, and more than a few people I've run into think the Board of Selectmen should have been more transparent in hiring a replacement chief of police."

Just as she'd thought. "Welcome to life in a small village in New England," Tricia said with amusement.

"I'll admit it, I'm still waiting for some of that Yankee hospitality."

"What can I do to help you get it?" Tricia asked.

"Not much, I'm afraid, but I'm hardly likely to make any headway on investigating Eli Meier's murder unless more people start opening up to me."

"It's not that the people here are unfriendly, but they do tend to be reserved."

"If you say so."

"I do. I've lived in the village for seven years and I'm still considered an outsider." And a jinx, to boot. She didn't tell him that.

They crossed the street at the light. "What do you want to know?" Tricia asked.

"Talk to me about Eli Meier," Ian said.

"We've already had this discussion," Tricia pointed out.

"Tell me again."

She shrugged and they started up Locust Street. "Eli was much less interested in conspiracy theories when I first arrived in Stoneham. He was much nicer back then, too." She considered what Ginny had told her. "Well, to me at least. It's almost as though he went through a complete personality change."

"That's probably because the man suffered from a brain tumor."

Tricia stopped dead, her jaw dropping. "Good grief!"

Ian nodded. "The medical examiner estimated he probably would have lived another six months to a year—maybe a little longer if he'd had medical care."

Tricia found her hand clutching the handle of her umbrella in a death clamp. "Poor Eli. We all just thought he was a major pain in the butt."

"He was more than that. A lot more," Ian said.

Tricia's brow furrowed. "What do you mean?"

"Naturally, I had Meier's fingerprints checked to see if he'd ever been arrested."

"Makes sense," Tricia said, and started walking once more.

"You see, Eli Meier's paper trail is only about thirty years old, and he was obviously twice that age."

"You mean missing are high school or college records—things of that nature?"

"Exactly."

Tricia looked thoughtful. "Do you think he was living under an assumed identity?"

Ian raised an eyebrow. "Not unlike your friend Mr. Cambridge?"

"Eli Meier was never a member of the Witness Protection Program," Tricia declared.

Marshall had probably been a criminal. He was unindicted, but had turned on his former employer and was whisked into the WPP after testifying.

Tricia pursed her lips. What were the odds that two duplicitous men would live in such a small village tucked away in New England? It was just Tricia's luck that she'd had to deal with both—and now both were dead.

Perhaps honesty really *was* the best policy.

"I've now heard from the FBI. Fingerprint records identified Meier as a radical from years before. His name was Joseph Martin."

The name meant nothing to Tricia.

"He was a member of the Crimson Nine," Ian added.

Tricia's eyes widened. That name *did* stir a memory. Back in the 1960s, the Crimson Nine was a group of radical college students bent on anarchy.

"It turns out Martin was the only surviving member and was never brought to justice," Ian continued. "It was thought he died in an explosion that took out a couple of houses in Boston."

Tricia began to walk again, albeit slowly. "Surely DNA evidence would have proved he didn't."

"This was back in the early days of genetic testing."

"How did he manage to evade the law for so long?" Tricia asked.

"By keeping his head low and living under a false ID. The real Eli Walter Meier died as an infant. In years past, assuming the identity of a deceased person was a common way of evading the system. I'm sure there are probably still hundreds if not thousands of felons out there living a lie in the same way."

Tricia remembered reading a story about a felon who had assumed the identity of a dead infant, living undisturbed for more than three decades, and was found out only when he applied for a renewed passport. That he'd fooled the government (local, state, and federal) for so long was considered unprecedented, and yet here was another example of an individual who'd successfully ghosted the system.

"So Eli's whole life in Stoneham was a sham," Tricia said, thinking how he was not unlike Marshall, both fleeing a dangerous past. "Do you think knowing about Eli's past can help you solve his murder?"

Ian shrugged. "That remains to be seen. I don't have a lot of leads. It seems many villagers disliked the man, but did they feel annoyed enough to kill?"

Tricia thought about how the new owner wanted to evict Eli from the building. And Louise, who was owed thousands of dollars. But each had taken the usual steps to pin Eli down, through eviction proceedings and a collection agency. Would Tricia be a tattler or a tipster by revealing that information?

"You're thinking something," Ian remarked.

"Just trying to decide if saying something makes me a good citizen or a bad friend." She reconsidered. "Okay, maybe acquaintance."

"You mean people Meier ticked off?"

Tricia nodded.

"Who has to know you spoke to me?"

Tricia stopped once again. "We're walking in plain sight of everyone in the village. Believe me, there are *no* secrets around here."

"For you, maybe," he retorted.

Tricia frowned and resumed walking. She spent another minute or so wrestling with her conscience before she told Ian about Becca and Louise. "It's not Becca I mind so much, but I don't think Louise told anyone else about her problem trying to shake money out of Eli. If you confront her, she's going to know it was me who told you so."

"You said she'd turned his account over to a collection agency, right?"

Tricia nodded.

"It's standard procedure to look at a victim's credit report. I can tell her I found her through it."

Tricia let out a relieved breath. "Thank you."

They'd made it back to Main Street and paused on the sidewalk.

"Well, I need to get to work," Ian said.

"Me, too."

"Thanks for helping me get up to speed on this case."

"You're welcome."

Ian gave her a warm smile. "I'll see you soon."

"I'll look forward to it."

He gave her a nod and started north up the sidewalk. Tricia watched him for a few seconds before turning for home. She hadn't gotten even half her ten thousand steps for that day.

Upon reaching Haven't Got a Clue, Tricia hung up her coat and headed down to her basement office. Of course, she'd learned about the Crimson Nine while in high school, but she didn't remember much about them other than the barest of information. She decided to do her own Internet sleuthing and fired up her computer. In the search box, she typed in the words "the Crimson Nine." In seconds she got more than a thousand hits, knowing she would find most of what she needed to know with just the first page of links. She skimmed the premier article.

As Ian had mentioned, the Crimson Nine were a bunch of college students who'd dropped out to change the world—and not in a peaceful way. They'd been radicalized by one of their professors, a John Winthrop. Their goal: to disrupt government at all levels. They saw laws as a restriction of their personal freedoms and against the laws of nature.

The gang of nine were somewhat successful during their first forays into anarchy by the placement of pipe bombs and tossing Molotov cocktails into the storefront offices of small-time politicians. Four of their members were caught in a sting operation but pledged allegiance to their colleagues who'd escaped capture and urged them to fight on. Among those still at large at the time was Joseph Martin. He was their explosives expert, a chemistry major who apparently wasn't as good as he thought he was. The apartment complex where the five remaining members hid out was virtually destroyed when their stock of chemicals ignited.

Only one of them survived, with burns over 50 percent of her body. Gloria Berry had once been a pretty coed with strawberry blonde hair, but after the explosion and fire, her facial features were so distorted that all pictures of her dur-

ing the period of her trial showed a woman so scarred she
wore a surgical mask and head covering to hide her appearance. She died in prison less than five years after her conviction, found hanging from a bedsheet in her cell. It was
said she suffered from depression because of her injuries
and the fact that she knew she'd never see the outside world
again. Those who knew her said she couldn't bear the
thought of spending the rest of her life behind bars and
razor wire.

It was thought that Martin died in the explosion along
with his comrades. Had he set the fire that caused the blast,
or had he had the good luck to be away when it happened?
They'd probably never know. One thing was for sure, Eli
Meier had kept a low profile for more than fifty years. And
then he'd started coming to Chamber of Commerce meetings, where he was anything but discreet. As far as anyone
knew, he'd never married, wasn't outgoing, and seemed to
have no friends. Was the lonely life he'd led as a fugitive
any better than the years he would have spent in prison?

Yes! But he had to have been a prisoner within his own
mind, and surely that was almost as bad—worrying every
day if he'd be caught.

But Eli had never been caught. Or had he? Could someone he'd harmed—or the loved one of someone he'd
harmed—have tracked him down and taken revenge?

It was too early in the investigation to make such as-
sumptions.

*And there you go . . . trying to insinuate yourself into the
inquiry. Stop it!*

That was Tricia's problem. She was too curious and it
hadn't always served her well.

Miss Marple appeared out of nowhere and jumped onto
the desk, startling Tricia.

"You couldn't give your mom some warning?" Tricia
chided the cat, her heart thudding.

"*Yow!*" Miss Marple said, and rubbed her head against
Tricia's chin.

Glancing at the clock, Tricia decided she had better head

upstairs. Mr. Everett would be arriving soon and she needed to get the beverage station stocked and ready to go.

As she climbed the stairs, she thought about her confiding to Ian about Becca and Louise, and her problem with Pixie and wondered what kind of terrible friend she was turning out to be.

No sooner had the coffee begun to drip when a car pulled up outside Haven't Got a Clue. It was Grace, dropping off Mr. Everett. He was able to extricate himself from the car, closed the door, and waved good-bye to his wife before turning and entering the shop.

"Good morning, Ms. Miles," he called as he crossed the threshold with the door's little bell chiming cheerfully as though to greet him.

"Good morning. And how are you today?"

"Fine, fine," Mr. Everett assured her. He wore a dark blue cardigan—no jacket—but went to fetch his hunter green apron with the store's logo emblazoned on it, letting Tricia settle it over his head and around and under his sling and tie the strings in the back.

"There you go. Ready for a cup of coffee to start the workday?" she asked.

"None for me, thank you. I had doubles at breakfast."

"Very well." Tricia poured herself a cup of coffee just as the first customer walked through the door. "Welcome to Haven't Got a Clue. Please let us know if you need help choosing a title."

"Thanks," said the older man in a blue windbreaker and a Red Sox baseball cap.

Seconds later the bell over the door rang again, but this time instead of a customer, it was Betty Barnes, of Barney's Book Barn. As far as Tricia could remember, Betty had never set foot in Haven't Got a Clue. She was short, dressed in a khaki raincoat that was far too long, with a plastic rain hat covering her magenta curls, which also didn't suit her rather chubby face.

"Good morning," Betty said rather sharply. Tricia couldn't see how this brusque woman would relate to small children. Betty clutched a ring-bound notebook in one hand, her expression businesslike. Tricia had a feeling she wasn't going to enjoy the encounter.

"Hello, Betty," she said. "I'm surprised to see you here so soon after opening."

"I have an assistant. Imogene is quite capable of taking care of my store when I need to be away."

O-kay.

"What can I do for you?" Tricia asked.

"I haven't been able to track down a single member of the Board of Selectmen. It's almost as though they've gone into hiding to avoid speaking to their constituents."

"Really?" Tricia asked.

"Yes, because otherwise, they'd have to justify their latest ill-advised decision."

"And that is?"

Betty looked around the store, took in the customer perusing the shelves, and Mr. Everett wielding his beloved lamb's wool duster. "Can you tell me why they felt they had to hire a—a—*foreigner* for the chief of police job? There must be plenty of qualified lawmen right here in New Hampshire who could have filled the vacancy," Betty fumed, her cheeks going pink.

"Because no one wanted the job?" Tricia suggested.

Betty's lips pursed, her expression souring. "Perhaps you're right. The murder rate around these parts has sure skyrocketed during the past seven years," she grumbled. She glanced at Tricia, her eyes narrowing.

It was yet another veiled jibe that Tricia's presence had somehow been responsible for that statistic.

"Why wasn't there a press release?" Betty demanded. "It shows a total lack of transparency from the Board of Selectmen."

"They must have had their reasons," Tricia mused. Yeah, because people like Betty would only want to complain about it.

"That got me to thinking. . . . Someone should start a petition to get rid of him," Betty said. "That person is *me*. If we could get enough signatures, maybe they'd fire McDonald."

You wouldn't get mine, Tricia thought. "For what reason?"

Betty shrugged. "Because he isn't one of *us*."

And neither am I, Tricia thought, but again didn't voice it because, come to think of it, neither was Betty, who'd relocated from Delaware to open her store. Tricia may not have had many conversations with Betty during her time in Stoneham, but this one conversation was more than enough. Luckily, the man who'd entered just before Betty wandered up to the cash desk with a couple of books in hand.

"If you'll excuse me, Betty, I have a customer. I really need to get back to work," Tricia said in her most pleasant voice.

"Will you sign my petition?"

"I believe in giving someone new to a job more than just five days to prove their worth."

Betty scowled. "Well, I'm going to canvass the rest of the booksellers on Main Street to see what *they* think of my idea."

"You do that," Tricia said, and turned to her customer. "May I ring that up for you?"

Betty turned on her heel and left the store.

Tricia wasn't sorry to see her go.

THIRTEEN

 Mr. Everett and Pixie usually had lunch together on the days they both worked, either by going to Booked for Lunch, the Bookshelf Diner, or buying something from the Eat Lunch food truck and having their meals in the store's basement office, which doubled as a break room and Tricia's home gym—if that's what you could call it. She had a treadmill, several sets of weights, and that was about it. On days when Pixie was off, Mr. Everett usually had lunch with his wife—as he did on that day.

There were no customers in the store when he returned to Haven't Got a Clue, and it was time for Tricia to go for her lunch with Angelica at Booked for Lunch. Mr. Everett settled himself in the reader's nook and Tricia gave him a quick wave good-bye and rushed out the door.

As usual, Angelica had arrived before her and was seated in their usual booth.

"Well, hello, stranger," Angelica said in greeting as Tricia settled behind the other side of the table and shrugged out of her jacket.

"Oh, hush," Tricia said, mimicking what Angelica usually said to chastise her dog.

"I will not. We've hardly spoken in days. I feel as though you've abandoned me," Angelica lamented, sounding pitiful.

"You're a big girl. Suck it up," Tricia advised.

As though realizing she wasn't going to receive any pity, Angelica changed the subject. "I've had a perfectly disheartening couple of days."

"Doing what?"

"Investigating commercial hydroponics—known as horticultural engineering in the trade," Angelica said knowledgeably.

"I thought you were doing that earlier in the week."

"Real life intruded," Angelica explained simply. "I feel like I have a good idea of what it would take and have a video conference appointment on Monday to talk to someone about the kind of space needed for a start *and* expansion, the technicalities, the kind of workforce needed, and the varieties of vegetables that would be most salable."

"What do you mean by the latter?"

"I mean if there's another commercial grower nearby doing tomatoes, I don't want to be in direct competition."

"Would these experts know what's going on here in New England?" Tricia asked, looking around for Molly the waitress. She was hungry.

"I imagine they probably helped set up anything that's around. I'll also be speaking to someone at the New Hampshire Department of Agriculture."

"Wow, you're not wasting any time."

"Time is money."

"Yeah, and it sounds like setting up a business like this could cost a *lot* of money. Can you afford it?" Tricia asked.

"I can afford something—but I need to find out how big I have to go to make the whole idea practical. The beauty is—as everything is grown indoors, it'll be a year-round operation."

"Do you think you should have been doing all this under your"—Tricia lowered her voice to a whisper—"Nigela Ricita persona?"

Angelica sighed. "Probably. But then if Nigela can do it better than me, she's welcome to have my research."

Molly suddenly appeared before them. "Hello, ladies. What can I get you today?"

"What are the specials?" Tricia asked.

Nothing was as delightful as the lamb shanks Tommy had made two days before, so Tricia settled for half an egg salad sandwich and the soup of the day: beef barley. Angelica had the same. Once Molly left with their order, Angelica spoke again. "How about you? What's going on in your world?"

Tricia shook her head sadly. "I'm just as disheartened as you, although for a different reason." She told her sister about her encounters with Ian and Betty Barnes. "I can't believe how many people have commented on Ian being hired as police chief and how upset they are about it."

"People don't like change, and Ian being Irish is a change from"—Angelica stopped midsentence—"from what they're used to."

"Not to mention the fact he's still a *man*."

Angelica squinted at her sister. "As I recall, you weren't fond of a certain *woman* sheriff," she remarked.

"Sheriff Adams seems to have changed—and for the better. At least that was my experience the last time we spoke," Tricia remarked.

"Surely you didn't think the Board of Selectmen would hire Officer Cindy Pearson for the job. She's only been a cop for a couple of years—and probably has no administrative experience."

"No, I didn't think they'd hire Cindy. They were *always* going to pick a man. And I have no problem with Ian being the chief. He seems perfectly capable and I hope he does a wonderful job and stays in the position for decades to come."

"Now you're being facetious," Angelica said sourly. "It doesn't suit you."

"I'm sorry."

"Just who besides Betty is annoyed by Ian being hired?" Angelica asked.

"Mary Fairchild, for one, but it was Betty who wants to do something about it."

"I don't think I've ever spoken with the woman," Angelica said.

"I wish I hadn't."

"Anything else happening?"

Tricia leaned forward and lowered her voice to a whisper. "It seems that Eli Meier was living under a fake ID."

Angelica, too, leaned in closer and whispered, "What?"

Tricia nodded. "Apparently he was a radical with the Crimson Nine."

Angelica's eyes widened and her jaw dropped. As she was five years older than Tricia, the name of the group obviously had more meaning for her. "Wow."

Molly arrived with their lunches. "Thanks," the sisters muttered.

Tricia waited until Molly had left the area before speaking again. "What do you think this means?"

Angelica blew out a breath. "A PR nightmare for the village."

Tricia nodded. "I suppose that means the Chamber should come up with a statement. And as I'm the newsletter editor, I suppose that should be my job."

"And as I have such a natural presence, *I* should be the one to field any press requests."

Tricia had dealt with that kind of responsibility far too many times in her role at the nonprofit. She was more than willing to cede that task to her sister.

"We'd better eat up and get back to work," Angelica said, her expression somber.

When they'd taken on the job of co-presidency the sisters hadn't counted on the kind of troubles they'd inherited by doing so.

This wasn't the first time Tricia was sorry she'd taken on the responsibility.

Tricia blew in from lunch just before two thirty and found Mr. Everett sitting in the reader's nook. Miss Marple sat on his lap. It looked like he hadn't moved since she'd left the store almost an hour before.

"Everything okay?" she asked as she headed for the back of the store to hang up her jacket.

Mr. Everett didn't answer.

Tricia walked through an aisle between shelves and stopped by the side of the big square coffee table in the reader's nook.

"Did we have any customers while I was gone?"

Mr. Everett shook his head but didn't look at her.

"It's that time of year," Tricia said wistfully. "Things will start to pick up in May—and by June we'll be wishing for the calmer days before the summer rush."

Still Mr. Everett said nothing, just idly petting Miss Marple's fluffy back. It was then Tricia realized that her employee and friend's gaze seemed unfocused and he was just staring at nothing.

"Mr. Everett?" No reaction. "Mr. Everett!" she said louder, and reached over to give his shoulder a little shake.

Mr. Everett seemed to rouse himself. "Oh, I didn't hear you come in."

Tricia's brow furrowed. "Are you all right?"

"Well," he began, but then didn't elaborate.

Miss Marple suddenly rose and jumped from his lap to the carpeted floor. Mr. Everett rubbed a shaking hand across his face before he tried and failed to get up from the chair. Taking a breath, he made another attempt, but when he got to his feet he swayed. It was only Tricia's fast reflexes that allowed her to grab his good arm that kept the old man on his feet.

"You'd better sit down again," she said, and practically forced him back into the seat. "Are you all right?" she asked, alarmed.

"Just a little dizzy," he muttered, and closed his eyes. He looked quite pale, too.

"I'm going to call nine one one," Tricia said, her panic escalating, and turned to head for the phone on the counter, but Mr. Everett caught her hand.

"No, please don't. I'm feeling much better already."

Tricia squinted at her dear friend, not believing a word. "What can I do? Can I get you something to eat or drink?"

"I'll be fine. I just need to sit here for a few more moments. But perhaps it would be wise if I went home a little early today. Would you call Grace and ask her to bring the car around to the front of the store? I'm not sure I want to walk all the way to the municipal parking lot."

That statement was tantamount to a complete confession that the old man was feeling downright ill.

"Stay here," Tricia said.

Tricia called Grace and explained the situation. She could hear the concern in Grace's voice as she said she'd immediately leave her office and get the car. It was less than five minutes later when she parked at the curb outside Haven't Got a Clue and hurried inside.

"William, dear," she said, and bent down to kiss the top of his head. "No fever," she said worriedly. "But we're going straight to urgent care in Milford."

"I don't need—"

"No arguments," Grace said firmly.

Mr. Everett looked to Tricia for help but found her solidly in Grace's camp.

"You should get checked out. You've had a very stressful week. We don't want anything else to happen to you," Tricia said solicitously.

Mr. Everett looked from Tricia to his wife and frowned. "Well, if you really think it's necessary."

"We do," Tricia and Grace said in unison.

Mr. Everett made his displeasure known, but only by the set of his mouth. It wasn't like him to make a show of any emotion, and rarest of all was anger. Arm in arm, he allowed Tricia and Grace to lead him to the car and settle him into the passenger seat. Grace buckled him in.

"Please call or text me later this evening, won't you, Grace?" Tricia asked.

"I will."

Mr. Everett turned dry eyes on Tricia. "Please don't worry about me, Ms. Miles. I assure you, I'm fine."

"Good night," Grace called, and hit the button for the passenger side window to close.

Tricia gave Mr. Everett a wave, which he acknowledged by a nod, and Grace drove away from the curb. Arms folded for warmth, her heart heavy, Tricia continued to watch until the car was out of sight. She didn't cry . . . but it had taken all her resolve not to.

FOURTEEN

It was again Angelica's turn to host happy hour and dinner that evening. Tricia let herself in and began climbing the stairs to Angelica's apartment. Instead of feeling cheered by Sarge's happy greeting, Tricia found herself wishing the little dog would just shut the heck up! Upon entering the apartment, she didn't even bother making a fuss of Sarge and quickly tossed two biscuits into his bed. The barking stopped like a switch being thrown.

Angelica was taking what looked like meatballs out of a large slow cooker, placing them in a bowl, and threw a look over her shoulder. "No hello?"

"Hello," Tricia said, her voice low as she sank onto one of the kitchen island's stools. "What smells so good?"

"Grape jelly meatballs. I found the recipe online, but I seem to remember Grandmother made it once."

"That's an awful lot of meatballs for the two of us," Tricia commented.

"I like to make a recipe as written before I start taking liberties. As it is, this recipe uses frozen meatballs—which I'm sure won't be nearly as good as my own. It's an experiment. If we approve of the taste, I might just concoct my own version. And what we don't eat tonight, I'll freeze."

Tricia sighed. "That's sounds like a plan."

Angelica scrutinized her sister's face. "Do I detect more than a note of the usual weariness in your tone?" Angelica asked, and retrieved a box of toothpicks from the cupboard.

"Not only did I have a perfectly dreadful morning, but to top off the day, Mr. Everett nearly fainted. If I hadn't been nearby to steady him, I shudder to think what might have happened to him."

Angelica's mouth dropped. "What's wrong? Is he okay?"

"I don't know. I called Grace and she immediately left her office at their foundation and came to pick him up. She took him to urgent care in Milford. She said she'd call and give me an update this evening."

"When did this happen?" Angelica asked, concerned.

"Right after I came in from lunch."

"Oh, the poor man. I hope he's going to be feeling well enough to attend our family dinner tomorrow."

"Me, too."

Not only would Tricia miss him at dinner, but she depended on him for help at her store, not that he could physically do much with his dominant arm in a sling, but he was a font of knowledge and beloved by the customers as well. Not only that but Tricia would be stuck alone for the entire day. She'd endured many a Sunday by herself in the shop before Mr. Everett had come to work for her. They weren't miserable but could be either harried or lonely, depending on the season.

"Let's talk about something else," Tricia said, hoping for a distraction. "Something cheerful."

Angelica collected the martini pitcher and glasses from the refrigerator. "I got a call from Antonio this afternoon. He and Ginny went to see the obstetrician today. The baby hasn't yet begun to turn, so it looks like she's got a little more time to go before Sofia becomes a big sister. Once that happens, I'll be a gramma times two," she said happily.

"You're really looking forward to this, aren't you?"

"Of course. Then I'll have two bambinos to spoil." She looked positively gleeful.

Tricia wished she could share that euphoria, but she kept

thinking about Mr. Everett's well-being and the rift between her and Pixie.

Tricia's phone rang. She quickly checked her screen and saw it was Grace. "Hello," she answered anxiously.

"Hello, Tricia. I've called to let you know that William is feeling much better. We're back at home and he's resting in front of the television with two cats on his lap demanding attention. I'm about to fix us some dinner."

"Would you like me to come over and help?"

"Oh, no, dear. I'll just make some scrambled eggs and toast. That's what dear William requested."

"What happened to him?"

"It seems he was dehydrated. The urgent care staff gave him an IV and instructions to take in more liquids. We stopped at the store to get a few bottles of those sports drinks that elevate your electrolytes. I'd prefer him to stay home from work tomorrow, but he insists he's feeling fine."

"If you think he should stay home then—"

"He's a stubborn man," Grace said, cutting her off. "It's hard to dissuade him once he's made up his mind. I do think he'll be fine by morning, but if not, he *will* stay home. We'll just have to see how it goes."

"Please tell him I'm thinking of him and that I only want what's best for him. He shouldn't feel obligated to—"

"I will," Grace interrupted. "Good night, dear."

"Good night." Tricia ended the call and let out a weary breath, feeling dispirited.

"And?" Angelica asked anxiously.

"Dehydration."

Angelica let out what seemed like a relieved breath. "Thank goodness it wasn't something worse. I take it he's insisting on coming to work tomorrow."

"Yes, but I'm going to make sure he doesn't overdo it. He can sit in the reader's nook with a good book all day. He can advise customers about titles and locations without leaving his seat."

"Good idea. And lots of liquids. Maybe you should go to the store and buy some of his favorite things."

"As far as I know, he likes coffee and iced tea."

"You could get that and maybe a few of those flavored seltzers. They're quite refreshing."

"That's a great idea. I've got a lot to do tomorrow morning. Would it be okay if I just bought a dessert for dinner instead of making one?"

"Of course. What were you thinking?" Angelica asked, and poured their drinks, handing one to Tricia.

"I don't know. Cake—something. I'll figure it out at the store."

"I'm sure it'll be fine," Angelica said, although from her tone, Tricia wasn't sure. "Or I could order something from the Patisserie."

"I'd prefer you didn't." Since the business had changed hands, the quality had dipped.

"Store-bought whatever it is, then," Tricia said.

Tricia sipped her drink. Buying dessert for their Sunday dinner was the least of her worries.

"With everything that went on this afternoon, I never got around to writing something on Eli's alias."

"I picked out an outfit, but that's as far as I got," Angelica remarked.

"I haven't had a chance to check the news to see if reports about Eli have been released but we'd better be ready for it when it hits."

"Right." Angelica got up and strode to her desk, where she came up with a couple of pads of paper and some pens. She returned and handed one to Tricia. "Let's start brainstorming."

FIFTEEN

There were no more martinis that night as Tricia and Angelica worked on the Chamber's announcement should the need arise. Tricia quizzed her sister with possible questions the press might ask and they polished her presentation. They were ready.

Although Tricia kept checking the news that evening and the next morning, both online and the major networks— nothing appeared on Eli Meier/Joseph Martin's death. Yet.

Since Haven't Got a Clue opened two hours later on Sundays, it gave Tricia time to catch up on cleaning and laundry. Still, accomplishing those chores wasn't going to keep her from her daily constitutional, and after that, she'd still have time to hit the grocery store to get a variety of liquids for Mr. Everett and dessert for the family dinner— and be prepared to duck the press if it was disclosed she was the one who'd called 911 to report Eli's death. Was Mr. Everett going to be up to the task? She might just have to close the store for the day. She'd wait and see.

The sky was overcast, but a warm breeze blew in from the south and Tricia set out at a brisk pace. In addition to Eli's death, she had a lot of other things preying on her mind, particularly worrying about Mr. Everett. And she still hadn't figured out what she would say to Pixie when she showed up for work on Monday.

Still pondering her options, Tricia entered the village square, intending to cut through to Locust Street. Up ahead, a woman sat on one of the hunter green benches, huddled in a pink jacket and sniffling. Tricia paused, wondering if she should retreat, walk past without commenting, or offer the woman a tissue.

"Excuse me," she said upon approaching the woman, "but are you okay?"

The woman looked up, her eyes bloodshot. She dabbed at her nose with the back of her right hand but nodded.

"Would you like a tissue?" Tricia always carried a little pack of them in her pocket, as sometimes a strong wind would disperse pollen and she'd find herself having a sneeze attack.

"Yes, thank you," the woman said, and Tricia proffered the package. The woman took it.

"I don't think we've met before. I'm Tricia Miles. I own the mystery bookstore on Main Street—Haven't Got a Clue."

"I'm Nadine."

"Nice to meet you. Are you from around here?" Tricia asked, not to be nosy but to be friendly.

"No. I'm originally from Lake George, New York. My parents owned a little burger joint on the lake." She gave a halfhearted laugh. "It's hard to make a living in a place that's only alive when the tourists are in town."

"Not unlike Stoneham?" Tricia asked wryly.

Nadine wiped her eyes. "Yeah." She took another tissue and offered the package back to Tricia and stood. "Pity party over for today. Time to get back to work. Thanks for the tissues."

"You're welcome. Anytime."

Nadine gave a nod and started off in the direction Tricia had come and Tricia continued on her way, idly wondering if the stranger she'd just met was a citizen of Stoneham. If so, she hadn't seen or met her in the nearly seven years she'd lived in the village. Maybe the woman was just passing through.

As Tricia continued walking through the square, something caught her eye near one of the blooming forsythia bushes. She bent down to take a closer look at what appeared to be . . . a wallet? She retrieved the worn, brown leather billfold. Inside were a few dollars in cash, a few black-and-white photos encased in crusty plastic, and in a side pocket a number of cards. She pulled out the first, which was a New Hampshire driver's license. She immediately recognized the man in the color photo.

Eli Meier.

Tricia didn't bother calling 911 and turned on her heel and started straight for the Stoneham Police Department. She hadn't graced its doors in six months and found herself feeling just a little nervous at the prospect. The department's administrative assistant, Polly Burgess, had always treated Tricia with disdain. Polly, an older woman of about sixty, wore her dull, gray hair scraped back into a tight bun at the back of her head. She always wore a somber-colored suit and a starched white blouse with no jewelry to embellish her stark attire. Polly had always—and erroneously—blamed Tricia for causing Chief Baker heartache by breaking up with him. *Piff!* His heart was *so* broken that he'd almost immediately found himself another lady friend—a high-powered attorney who was also the former governor's daughter. Would Polly be as protective when it came to Chief McDonald?

There was only one way to find out. But then—it was Sunday. Surely someone else would be manning the reception desk.

Tricia pushed open the door to the police station. As she entered the rather barren room, there was Polly, seated at her desk. She looked up from her computer, her expression twisting into a sneer. "What do *you* want?" she asked, her tone derisive.

"Do you work seven days a week?"

"It's called overtime," Polly grunted. "Now, why are *you* here?"

"I'd like to speak with the officer in charge, please," Tricia said, keeping her voice level.

Instead of arguing with Tricia, which was her usual stance, Polly simply pushed the intercom button. "Tricia Miles to see you, Chief McDonald, *sir.*"

Tricia cringed at the way Polly had addressed her new boss. Not the word, but how she said it: with as much disdain as she spoke to Tricia.

"Send her in, please," Ian answered.

Polly nodded toward the office. "You know the way," she said, and turned back to her computer.

The door to Ian's office opened and he ushered Tricia in with a wave of his hand. "What brings you here?" he asked as Tricia took one of the chairs in front of his desk.

All the awards, pictures, and personal effects Tricia had seen under the office's previous owner were long gone. Had they been given to Chief Baker's ex-wife, Mandy, or had they been tossed away? Somehow, Tricia didn't believe that scenario. Polly was such a Chief Baker devotee that she would have never allowed that. And Ian had taken residence less than a week before, so he hadn't had an opportunity to apply his own imprint on the cramped office's walls.

"What brings you here today?" Ian asked again, leaning forward on his desk, hands folded on the blotter before him, looking and sounding so sincere.

Tricia pulled the wallet she'd found out of her pocket and handed it to the new chief of police. "I found this in the village square not ten minutes ago while on my morning walk."

Ian took custody of the billfold and opened it, scrupulously examining its contents. Tricia studied his facial expressions during the procedure but wasn't sure what to make of them.

After several minutes, Ian spoke. "Thank you for bringing

this to our attention. I hope you'll be able to show me where, exactly, you found this."

"Definitely. Because of its location, I wonder if Eli was attacked—possibly killed—in the village square before the body was moved to the alley behind the Coffee Bean."

"Was there any sign of blood nearby?" Ian asked.

"Not that I saw."

Ian nodded. "There were indications on the victim's clothes and body that he'd been dragged, but no grass stains were visible on his clothing or skin."

"It seems likely he was killed on the square and then planted behind the Coffee Bean," she stated, knowing it was the most reasonable explanation.

"Yes," Ian agreed with a nod.

"That really doesn't help in your investigation, though, does it?"

Ian shook his head. "Not really."

"What have you unearthed so far?" Tricia asked.

"It's not something I'm willing to talk about to the public at large."

Tricia frowned. "Is that what you consider me?" He'd asked her—twice—for her insights.

"Yes!" Ian said emphatically. "You may have had a cozy relationship with the man who occupied this office before me—"

"Believe me," Tricia interrupted, "Chief Baker and I may have once been *cozy*, but when it came to investigating crimes, we were anything *but*."

Ian's expression was bland. "So you say."

If Tricia had a more mercurial nature, she might have slapped him for that rebuke.

Tricia stood. "Would you like to see where I found the wallet?" she asked, her tone clipped. She'd had to endure the same kind of official derision from Baker and his predecessor. It made her wonder why she was willing to help them solve criminal cases in the first place.

Ian placed the wallet in his right top desk drawer, locked

it, and rose from his seat. He waved a hand in the direction of his office door. "Lead the way." He grabbed a jacket with the words *Stoneham PD* embroidered on the back, shrugged into it, and held the door as Tricia exited the office.

They walked in silence the block or so to the village square and Tricia led the new police chief to the spot where she'd found the wallet. She pointed. "Right there, almost under the bush."

"I wish you'd thought to take a picture before you disturbed the evidence," he grumbled.

"How was I supposed to know it *was* evidence? It could have been anyone's lost wallet."

Ian merely shrugged.

"Have you come up with any next of kin?" Tricia asked.

"Martin's parents died years ago. They'd made it known even before his supposed death that they wanted nothing to do with the son who'd brought shame to their family. He had an older brother, but he's gone now, too. I doubt his children would want anything to do with the family's black sheep, but we will ask."

Tricia nodded. "Have you poked around inside Eli's store?" she asked.

Ian nodded. "Just for a cursory glance. Why?"

Tricia shrugged. "Maybe you'd get a better feel for the man if you scoped out his workplace. I'm sure you could tell a lot about me from walking through my store."

Ian offered a half smile. "I'm sure I could. Would you like to go there now?"

"My store?"

"No, the Inner Light."

Tricia glanced at her watch. If she ditched doing the laundry and cleaning, she would still have time to hit the grocery store before Haven't Got a Clue opened for the day. "Sure, why not?"

They left the village square and started down Main Street at an easy pace.

"What do you think I'll find at Meier's shop?"

"Eli was into conspiracy theories. But perhaps he was paranoid enough to hide things in his shop instead of his home."

"Things that could incriminate him?" Ian asked.

"Maybe . . . maybe not. As he was a fugitive from justice, there might be a load of books about felons who got away with their crimes."

"Such as?"

"The Zodiac Killer in Northern California. The Alphabet Murders in Rochester, New York. The Colonial Parkway killer in Virginia."

"You seem to know a lot about serial killers."

"My former"—Tricia paused and chose her descriptor carefully—"friend Marshall sold true crime books before he bought the Armchair Tourist."

"And did you share his interest in that subject?" Ian asked, his gaze sharpening.

Tricia shook her head. "I've read a few, but I prefer the crimes I read about to be fictional. That way no real person is ever hurt."

"If only we lived in such a world," Ian muttered. "Is it likely, though, that Meier would carry such books in a store that was supposed to be inspirational?"

"That was his *original* intent. Perhaps when he first opened the shop he was trying to find redemption for the crimes he committed," Tricia suggested to the newly minted lawman.

"Possibly."

They crossed the street at the light and headed past the still-closed shops. All except the Patisserie, where the lights were on and the aroma of fresh-baked bread permeated the area.

Less than a minute later, they were standing in front of the Inner Light. Ian produced a key on a ring and unlocked the door.

"Were you planning on visiting the store today?" Tricia asked.

Ian's expression was bland. "I may have been." He entered first and switched on the store's main lights. Tricia followed and wrinkled her nose. The shop emanated more than a faint whisper of mustiness. Sometimes used bookstores had their own distinctive scent, rather like some thrift stores around the clothes racks that bore a whiff of must or dried sweat. Tricia wasn't sure if it was the books that smelled or if the roof leaked and mold was the culprit. But then if the latter was the case, surely the tenant above the shop would have complained to the owners. The odor spoke to her of neglect.

While Ian meandered through the store, checking out the stock on the shelves, Tricia noted the worn, stained carpet, the dust throughout the place, and the poor lighting. Did Eli's store have a web presence? She'd have to check once she returned to her own shop, and if so . . . was it enough to attract the people who lived their lives steeped in either religion or conspiracy theories?

Tricia moved to stand in the middle of one of the three aisles and tried to envision the store's typical customer. It wasn't a pretty picture. Folks who thought the government was out to get them, or perhaps that the Lord might smite them, neither could be very happy individuals. But then her customers enjoyed books that revolved around murder.

Tricia retreated to the wooden lectern that served as the store's cash desk. On top was a rather dated register that she surmised to be two or three decades old. It would give a customer a cash receipt but wasn't sophisticated enough to be tied to a computer. That meant that Eli had no digital inventory.

She noticed a small cabinet beside the podium that brandished a tiny brass lock hanging from a hasp. A yellowed sticker with faded blue ink said *restricted*. She thought about the Restricted Section in the library at the fictional Hogwarts School of Witchcraft and Wizardry. Was Eli's cache of such books as dangerous?

Ian returned to the front of the shop.

"Well, what do you think?" Tricia asked.

"That this place should have closed years ago. It looks

like many of the books have stood in the same dusty place for years."

Tricia nodded. "Sad, really. Were there other keys on Eli's ring?"

"A couple. Why?"

She showed him the cabinet. Ian retrieved the small ring from his pants pocket and sure enough, a key just the right size for the little lock hung from it. Ian crouched down to open it. The cabinet's hinges creaked as he pulled it open. It contained a stack of books. Well, manuals, really. Some of them looked like they had been printed on an old-style mimeograph machine, with grimy covers, and were crudely stapled. The titles were enough to turn Tricia's stomach. *Construct Your Own Bombs*, *A Patriot's Guide to Anthrax*, *The Ricin Horizon*, and *Building a Strong Militia* were just a few of the titles.

Ian frowned. "I can see why Meier wouldn't want these out on display. Look at the prices."

"They look pretty dated. I'm sure if you know where to look, you can get all this information for free on the Internet," Tricia remarked. "What does this tell you about Eli Meier the victim?"

"That I wouldn't have wanted him as a friend."

"I don't know that anyone in the village considered him a friend."

Ian eyed the seedy surroundings. "And he wasn't a good tenant, either. Did you know he was months behind on his store's rent?"

"Yes. Karen at NR Realty said so, and I can't say I was surprised, either. His views had changed—and so had the products he sold," Tricia reiterated.

"Yes, with more and more Americans identifying as having no religion, I can see why his original customer base might have dwindled. How would you describe the man's personality?" It was a question he'd asked before. Had he doubted her first response?

"Cranky."

Ian nodded. "That seems to be the consensus. Those

types of individuals have a tendency to end up like Mr. Meier—dead."

"Lately he ruffled a few feathers," Tricia said, eager to change the subject.

"And he was about to be evicted."

"Do you know who owns the building?" Tricia asked.

"Apparently it was quietly sold about four months ago."

"At the same time Eli stopped paying his rent."

"That's right. He may have thought he could get away with it for a while, but the new owner wasn't going to have it."

"You still haven't told me who owns it."

"A holding company owned by Rebecca Chandler."

Tricia blinked. "Becca Chandler?"

Ian nodded. "The same person who's going to build an indoor tennis court on that empty piece of property up the road."

How did Ian find out of all this when she, Angelica, Antonio, and everyone else she knew—including Karen Johnson at NR Realty—hadn't been able to track it down? She asked him.

Ian's smile was enigmatic. "I'm a cop. I know how to unearth information."

He hadn't been a cop until just days before. But he certainly was one now.

SIXTEEN

After returning to Haven't Got a Clue, Tricia wasted no time in calling Becca.

"Hello."

"Hello, Becca. It's Tricia. I've got a question for you."

"Shoot."

"Why didn't you tell me you were the owner of the old warehouse property on North Main Street?"

Silence.

"Becca?"

"Uh, who told you that?" Becca asked quite innocently.

"Police Chief Ian McDonald."

"The blabbermouth," Becca growled.

"Well?" Tricia demanded.

"Who says I was obligated to mention it?"

"You've pressed me for ideas on opening businesses for months. You might have at least let me know you were already investing in the area."

Becca laughed. "Oops. Caught."

Tricia wasn't amused. "I thought you weren't interested in exploiting your tennis years by teaching."

"Who says *I'm* going to teach? I can hire people to do that. But I wasn't about to put my name on a franchise without owning the biggest piece of it. If this first iteration flies,

I'll open up a chain of them and then either sell franchises or auction the company off to the highest bidder."

Wow. Tricia knew Becca could be cold, but now she suspected she could be ruthless as well.

"I also heard you were in the process of evicting Eli Meier from the Inner Light."

"The former owner of the building warned me that guy would be a deadbeat. He said Eli would often pay him late and catch up just in time not to be evicted, but he didn't reckon with me!"

"How so?"

"Once the store's cleaned out it'll be the perfect location for a craft brewery tasting room."

"You've already gotten a commitment from Rick Lavoy?"

"Yes. A darling man, but unfortunately very married."

So Becca was prowling for another romantic victim. Lavoy should be counting his lucky stars Becca couldn't sink her fangs into him. Then again, if monogamy wasn't his thing . . .

"And yes, NR Realty is handling the paperwork."

As Karen had mentioned days before after liaising with Becca's holding company.

"The inside of the Inner Light is a pit," Becca continued. "The floors are old and warped, the walls are scarred and pitted, but the original tin ceiling is in good shape and gives the perfect ambiance for a tasting room. I've seen some of Lavoy's sketches, and the property is ideal for them. And now that Meier is dead, we can move ahead with the renovations. I've got my lawyers working on it now. I might have to keep Meier's stock in a storage unit until I can run down any heirs, but it'll be worth the cost if I can move the Lavoys in there by the end of the summer."

That was a pretty ambitious timeline, but if anyone could pull it off, it was Becca.

"When will you start clearing it out?"

"As soon as legally possible. Hopefully in the next week or so."

She really was eager to get her new tenant in. That said,

her plans might just be blown out of the water when the news of Eli's association with the Crimson Nine made the headlines.

"Why are you upset about all this anyway?" Becca asked, sounding perturbed.

"I'm not upset."

"You sure sound it. Admit it, you didn't like Eli Meier, either."

Much as she would like to agree, Tricia wouldn't—if only to annoy Becca.

"Think of it this way," Becca continued, "instead of a dying business, the tasting room will bring in a new customer base—and likely *younger* ones. People who have more to do than just sit around and *read* all day," she stressed.

Tricia's jaw dropped. "Thank goodness the entire world isn't hardwired to their phones and the Internet. May I remind you that readers are the ones who brought this village back to life. And not all of them are old, either."

Silence greeted her mini rant. Tricia could just imagine Becca yawning while inspecting her nails.

Finally, Becca spoke. "Was there anything else you wanted to chat about this morning?"

"No," Tricia answered succinctly.

"Well, until next time," she said cheerfully, and ended the call.

Tricia set down the phone, unhappy with the direction the conversation had taken. She was still angry, but there was nothing she could do about Becca and her land acquisitions. One thing was clear: Becca was to be a permanent fixture in Stoneham.

And apparently a permanent pain in Tricia's butt.

Tricia only just had time to get to the grocery store in Milford and pick up an assortment of flavored seltzers for Mr. Everett as well as dessert for that evening, returning to her store just ten minutes before opening. She wasn't happy about the sweets she'd bought—they weren't up to her usual

standards, but they'd do. Soft oatmeal cookies the manu-
facturer advertised as just like homemade, but Tricia
thought of as almost baked, and a frozen pound cake with
containers of frozen strawberries and raspberries and a
large can of whipped cream. She had just enough time to
put the seltzers in the basement fridge and the rest of the
items in her own refrigerator, quickly scooting back down
to her shop to get the coffeemaker going.

When Mr. Everett appeared a few minutes later, a shopping bag hung from his good wrist as he wrestled with the
door to enter Haven't Got a Clue.

"You gave me quite the scare yesterday," Tricia said,
resisting the urge to throw her arms around the old man.
Mr. Everett was not keen on outward shows of affection
unless it involved little Sofia. That was when he showed he
really was an old softy.

"I'm sorry. I didn't realize how parched I was."

"Yes, Grace told me you were dehydrated. Well, we
won't let that happen again. Come and have a nice hot cup
of coffee and a couple of cookies."

Mr. Everett set the bag down on the reader's nook's big
square coffee table. "I'm to have some of this sports drink
during the day as well. It helps balance one's electrolytes."

"So I've heard."

Mr. Everett's lips pursed. "I must say I'm not very fond
of it."

"I've filled the fridge downstairs with several flavors of
bottled seltzer. Feel free to help yourself throughout the
day."

"Thank you, Ms. Miles. You're very kind."

"It's my pleasure."

Tricia poured their coffees and they retreated to the
reader's nook to enjoy them. Tricia didn't want to harp on
Mr. Everett's difficulties the day before, and since Eli Meier
seemed to have taken up permanent residence in her
thoughts, she decided to bring up that subject.

"I was one of the last booksellers recruited to Stoneham,
but you were here before any of us arrived."

"Yes, I was. I did stock some paperbacks in my store"—
Everett's Grocers—"before it went under, but I never could
have competed with the incoming booksellers. What makes
me sad is that if I could have hung on another five or six
months, my store would have survived."

"Oh, I'm so sorry. I never realized that."

Mr. Everett nodded sadly and sipped his coffee.

"Were you acquainted with Eli Meier?"

Mr. Everett's gaze dipped down to his good hand, which
held his cup. "Acquainted? Yes. Did I know the man personally? No."

"How were you acquainted?"

"I don't like to speak ill of the dead, but his abrasive
personality was known to many so I would hardly be the
first—or the last—to discuss it."

"And?" Tricia prompted.

"He had a habit of coming into my store to squeeze the
bread, dent cans, and bruise the fruit before asking for a
discount."

Tricia's eyes widened. "Did you catch him at it?"

Mr. Everett shook his head. "I was either behind the
butcher counter or in the office for a good part of the day,
but more than one of my employees reported him to me."

"Did you give him the discount?"

Mr. Everett nodded sadly. "The goods weren't going to
be purchased after he manhandled them. I could at least get
back the cost of the item if not make a profit."

Mr. Everett had always been a more-than-generous man.

"I'm sorry you had to put up with that."

"Just another of the many reasons why my store failed," he
said matter-of-factly. It had been nearly seven years since the
grocery store had gone under. He'd accepted the loss.

"Had you spoken to Eli since those days?"

Mr. Everett shook his head. "Never." But then he seemed
to think things over. "He would sometimes come into Haven't
Got a Clue demanding Ginny make change for him."

"Yes, she told me about it. I believe she said she had to
restrain you from *clocking* him."

"Just once or twice," he said with the barest hint of a smile. "Mr. Meier was not a nice man."

As an avowed anarchist, he'd destroyed property and killed. Saying he was not a nice man was putting it mildly. But then, Mr. Everett was the epitome of nice.

Mr. Everett drained his cup and stood. "I'd best get to work. These shelves aren't going to dust themselves."

Tricia smiled and stood. "And I have things to do as well."

While Mr. Everett went to the back of the store to retrieve his lamb's wool duster, Tricia moved to look out the window south down Main Street. Just another quiet Sunday early afternoon. But how busy would it be when the networks sent their reporters and vans with uplinks?

She shuddered at the thought.

SEVENTEEN

 On Sundays, Tricia usually ate a late breakfast and skipped lunch so that when closing time came and it was time for their makeshift family's weekly dinner, she was usually starved. Angelica didn't always mention what she had planned for the meal, so it was often a lovely surprise.

"What do you think your sister will make for dinner this evening?" Mr. Everett asked once Tricia had fetched her dessert from her refrigerator and she and Mr. Everett left Haven't Got a Clue, dodging raindrops as they walked the several feet to the Cookery, where Tricia let them in with her key.

"I wouldn't mind roast chicken. It's one of my favorites."

"The leg of lamb she made for Easter dinner was fabulous," Mr. Everett said. High praise, but then Mr. Everett was an expert, not only when it came to vintage mysteries, but as a former butcher, for cuts of meat and the best ways to cook them.

The rest of the family had already arrived, and as they ascended the stairs to Angelica's apartment they could hear Sofia's childish laughter while Sarge barked joyfully.

"Yay! The whole family's now here," Ginny called, and

waddled over to give Mr. Everett a kiss on the cheek. "Come—come sit next to me," she encouraged, leading him by the hand to the big sectional couch that could comfortably seat six.

Angelica popped out of the kitchen. "Mr. Everett, how are you feeling? I was heartsick when Tricia told me you were ill yesterday."

"I'm much better now, dear lady." He helped Ginny to sit before he sniffed the air. "And I shall be even better when we sit down to the delicious dinner you've prepared for us."

Angelica waved a hand in dismissal. "Oh, it's only a couple of roast chickens, mashed potatoes, gravy, and most of the trimmings of a Thanksgiving dinner," she said, and laughed. She'd probably spent the entire afternoon preparing for the meal and reveled in every step of the operation.

"It's just what I was hoping for," Tricia said.

"How you spoil us," Mr. Everett told Angelica sincerely.

"It's always my pleasure. I so look forward to spending these evenings with our dear little family. Now, what can I get you to drink?"

Mr. Everett took in a shaky breath and sat between Ginny and his wife, who reached over to give his hand a squeeze. "I do believe I shall wait until we sit down to your wonderful dinner to imbibe."

It almost sounded like he was going to accept wine or spirits, but Mr. Everett was a staunch teetotaler. That didn't stop the rest of the party—apart from Ginny, who was counting the days until she could drink alcohol once again—from sharing a bottle or two of vino.

"Does anyone need anything?" Angelica asked.

"I could use a glass of wine," Tricia said.

"Then come into the kitchen and pour yourself one."

Tricia did so, but also absentmindedly poured a glass of iced tea—what Mr. Everett usually drank—and brought it to him. He accepted with a rather grim smile and a quiet "Thank you."

Ginny wiggled around on the couch, looking distinctly uncomfortable.

"How many more days until the baby arrives?" Grace asked.

"Supposedly eight. An absolute *eternity*," Ginny said with chagrin.

"That's if the baby comes on time. It could go a week or two either way," Antonio said, and Ginny shot him a murderous glare.

"Have you got your certificate of occupancy for the new house yet?" Grace asked.

"No! I will be *so* upset if we have to bring the new baby home to that cramped little rental apartment. But I'll handle it—*if* I have to."

Angelica arrived in the living room with a big silver tray. "Swedish meatballs?" she asked, offering one of the appetizers scored by a toothpick to the first person she encountered.

"I haven't had one of these in years!" Tricia said, wondering why her sister hadn't served the grape jelly meatballs she'd made the day before.

"Whatever caused you to make Swedish meatballs?" Grace asked. "They used to be very popular."

Angelica held the tray out for Grace to try one. "Lately, Tricia and I have been making some of our grandmother's favorite appetizers. They're old-fashioned but are *so* good and ought to be enjoyed by a new generation!" She offered the tray to everyone before leaving it, along with a small bowl for the used picks, and headed back to the kitchen.

Ginny took another meatball, smiling as she ate it. "I'd never turn this appetizer down." She discarded the pick and turned to Tricia. "Hey, the word on the street is you're helping our new police chief to investigate Eli Meier's death," she said as Sofia raced by with Sarge hot on her heels, the little girl shrieking with joy while the dog barked with just as much glee.

"Sofia!" Antonio called, and bounded after his daughter.

"I wouldn't say that," Tricia replied, her voice rising to overcome the clamor.

Antonio must have caught up with his tot because the screeching ceased, as did the barking.

"I've heard you're dating him," Grace added.

"My dear!" Mr. Everett admonished.

"We are *not* dating, We simply had dinner the other night to catch up on our lives since we met on the *Celtic Lady* cruise."

Antonio reappeared with a giggling Sofia tossed over his shoulder like a sack of flour. "Rumor has it that you found a vital piece of evidence related to the crime."

All eyes turned toward Tricia, looking at her expectantly. How had that piece of information already made it to the village's gossip mill? Or was it Antonio's journalistic prowess that had unearthed the fact?

"I found Eli's wallet on the ground in the village square while on my walk this morning."

"And its significance?" Antonio asked.

Tricia shrugged. "I speculated Eli might have been"—in deference to Sofia, she mouthed the word *killed*—"there and the body moved. It'll be up to Chief McDonald to prove it."

"As I recall, the new chief *is* rather dashing," Grace commented. "Rather like a pirate with that beard," she continued with amusement.

"He's pleasing on the eyes," Tricia said neutrally. "But we're only friends. Well, not even that, really. Acquaintances."

"Who could become more than that?" Grace asked all wide-eyed with the hint of a smile.

"Don't bet on it," Tricia said.

Now that the conversation had turned to talk of romance, Antonio lost interest and wandered over to the windows that overlooked Main Street.

Grace asked Ginny for more details on the new house and Tricia picked up her glass and rose, crossing the room to join her nephew.

"Hey, there. Angelica was telling me about how proud she is with the way you've turned around the *Stoneham Weekly News*. Congratulations."

Antonio ducked his head in modesty. "It has been a group effort. It would not have been possible without Patti and Ginger. They are two very creative and hardworking women."

Tricia was glad he not only knew of their contributions but told others. But then, she wouldn't have expected less of her nephew. "She also said that your sense of obligation to Nigela Ricita Associates is keeping you from fulfilling your journalism dreams." Okay, she hadn't come right out and said it so blatantly, but Tricia could read between the lines.

A flush rose up Antonio's neck and he looked decidedly uncomfortable.

"Is something wrong?" Tricia asked.

Antonio seemed to squirm. "Eh . . ."

"Antonio?" Tricia pressed.

He looked chagrined. "Please do not tell Angelica this, but while I enjoy writing the main editorial for each issue, I prefer the work of running the day-to-day operations of our brands."

Tricia frowned. "But I thought you wanted to be a journalist."

"Yes," he said with a nod. "That is what I thought."

"Oh. And what does Angelica think of that?"

Antonio's lips flattened in embarrassment. "Uh, I may not have mentioned it to her."

"Don't you think you should?"

The blush grew darker. "Perhaps."

"Sooner rather than later?" Tricia suggested.

"Perhaps," he said once again.

"What does Ginny think?"

A ghost of a smile touched his lips. "That I work too much."

Tricia rolled her eyes. "So says the other workaholic in your marriage."

"*Sì*," he agreed, and the smile broadened.

"Ms. Miles," Mr. Everett called, and approached them. "May I have a word with you?"

"Excuse me," Tricia told Antonio, and let Mr. Everett draw her aside to the other window that overlooked Main Street.

"Ms. Miles, I completely forgot to mention earlier that I have an appointment for physical therapy on Tuesday. When I found out the date, I tried to change it to my day off, but the receptionist said they couldn't accommodate me. Would it be an imposition if I work tomorrow instead?"

"Of course not," Tricia said, and gave a mental sigh of relief. Mr. Everett's presence was just the balm to make the uncomfortable situation with Pixie easier to endure. He had such a calming manner, which was one of the reasons Tricia treasured his friendship. It especially helped when Haven't Got a Clue was filled with anxious customers eager to get back to their tourist buses before they took off without them. That said, Pixie and Mr. Everett usually arrived within minutes of each other. Perhaps she'd ask Mr. Everett to come to work fifteen or twenty minutes late so she'd have an opportunity to speak to Pixie alone. But then she'd have to explain to him *why* it was necessary for him to come in later and she wasn't sure she wanted to do that, either.

She gave him what she hoped was a warm smile.

"Tricia!" Angelica called. "Could you come in here and give me a hand?"

Tricia reached out to touch the old man's good hand. "If you'll excuse me."

"Of course."

Tricia hurried to the kitchen. Angelica handed her a spoon and pointed to the pot of gravy on the stove. "Stir, please."

Tricia immediately set to the task, but Angelica didn't move. "Any news on the Eli development?"

"Not the last I looked. Perhaps the networks are waiting until Monday. Who wants to unveil a major news story on a Sunday afternoon? Ratings, ratings, ratings."

Angelica nodded.

Nobody mentioned Eli's name during the dinner. Everyone seemed to be having such a good, relaxed time visiting that neither Tricia nor Angelica wanted to spoil the mood.

The pound cake, berries, and whipped cream for dessert were a big hit.

EIGHTEEN

Tricia was up early the next morning, her stomach tied in too many knots to even have coffee. She'd checked the news and sure enough, the story of Eli's death and his association with the Crimson Nine was splashed all over the Internet. It wouldn't be long before crews from all the major news networks showed up in Stoneham. She hoped Ian was ready for the onslaught.

In addition, she dreaded facing Pixie but was determined to apologize and crossed her fingers that they could work out the little glitch between them.

Thinking that sticking to her normal routine of a brisk walk might make her feel better, she started off, but when she was halfway through her usual route, she turned back for Haven't Got a Clue.

Once again Tricia cut through the village square and headed for the same bench where she'd first met Nadine. This time the woman wasn't crying, but she'd buried her nose in a small paperback book.

"Penny for your thoughts," Tricia called as she approached.

Nadine looked up. "They aren't worth even that much." She closed her book, and Tricia saw the title: *Don't Sweat the Small Stuff . . . and It's All Small Stuff* by Richard Carlson.

"We meet again," Tricia said brightly.

"It seems so."

Tricia indicated the volume. "I've read that title a couple of times myself—when things got a little overwhelming," she admitted. "My favorite quote is: 'Ask yourself the question, Will this matter a year from now?'"

Nadine forced a laugh. "It's a good one." She sighed and her expression turned dour once again. "I wish I could say it wouldn't."

"I'm sorry to hear that," Tricia said sincerely.

"If I had more courage"—Nadine laughed—"if I had *any* courage, I'd make a change and then I wouldn't have to sweat *any* of the crap I'm going through ever again."

"I'm sorry to hear that," Tricia repeated.

"That I'm going through crap or that I'm a coward?"

Tricia blinked and Nadine laughed again. "Now it's me who's sorry. That wasn't very nice of me."

"Is there anything I can do to help?"

"You want to help a total stranger?" Nadine asked in surprise.

"We *have* spoken before," Tricia pointed out. "We know each other's names, so we're at least acquainted."

"Yeah, I guess you're right. And no, you can't help, but it was kind of you to ask."

"Well, if you ever need to talk—my shop is just up the road." She nodded in the direction of Main Street.

"Haven't Got a Clue," Nadine remembered. "And do you?"

"Have a clue?" Tricia asked, and gave what she hoped was a wry smile. "I sure hope so. I'll see you around."

"I'll probably be here," Nadine said with a sigh.

Tricia headed for Main Street and was glad to see there was still no sign of the upheaval yet to come when the big-city press came to get the story on Eli Meier.

Although it was twenty minutes until Haven't Got a Clue opened, Mr. Everett had arrived while Tricia was gone, letting himself in, and had already commandeered the shop's lamb's wool duster and was attacking the tops of the books and shelves with left-handed vigor.

"You're here early," Tricia said in greeting.

"Grace had an appointment and dropped me off. I hope my being here before opening isn't an imposition."

"Not at all. I'll get the coffee started." By the time both pots were dripping their brews, the door opened, admitting Pixie, who was almost ten minutes early herself. But instead of her usual chipper self, she was visibly upset— apparent not only by the anxious expression on her face, but also evidenced by the fact that she was dressed in widow's weeds: a black suit jacket over a black silk blouse, black skirt, black tights, black pumps, and a black pillbox hat. Her bloodred lipstick was her only concession to color.

"Pixie, what's wrong?" Tricia asked, her own distress inching up.

"I spent almost three nerve-racking hours with Edward Dowding yesterday."

Mr. Everett wandered up to listen. "That young man who helped us out last week?"

"The same."

"Come, sit down in the reader's nook. I'll get us all coffee and you can tell us all about it," Tricia said.

Pixie nodded, looking grateful.

A minute later, Tricia handed the cups around and took her seat. "Now, tell us what happened."

"Well, after Edward showed up on Friday, I had a feeling I might run into him at the estate sales he mentioned. And by the way, I scored a boatload of 1950s Nancy Drew and Hardy Boys books for the store, in mint condition and for a really nice price. Fred will bring them around on his lunch hour."

"That's great," Tricia said, "but tell us what else went down."

Pixie took a gulp of her coffee, as though to fortify herself before speaking. "I usually go to these sales by myself, but this time I asked Fred to come with me. I admit I was feeling kinda nervous. I only ever go to these sales on the last day because that's when you get the best deals—when the liquidators are desperate to get rid of the stuff."

And Tricia was grateful that Pixie's thrifting hobby had scored so many vintage books for her store and for prices that would insure a profit.

"So, what happened?" Tricia asked.

"When Fred pulled up to the curb at the first sale, there was Edward standing outside the house looking wet and bedraggled. Fred felt sorry for him."

"And how did you feel?" Tricia asked.

"To be honest, kind of freaked. I said hi, but that was about all. Then the kid shadowed me as I walked through the sale. And wouldn't you know it, because I was rattled, he actually saw a few things I'd missed. You know I also look out for stuff for not only Angelica for the Cookery, but for Brittney at the Happy Domestic, too."

All of which Tricia knew. "And?"

"Well, Edward got to talking to Fred and kind of charmed him."

That didn't sound good.

"And despite my nervousness," Pixie continued, "Fred invited Edward to come with us to the next sale. I could have *killed* him."

Fred, not Edward, but Tricia wasn't sure Pixie wasn't speaking of both men.

"And how did that go?" Tricia asked.

"Just as before. The three of us walked through the house and we all saw different things—and I ended up with tons more stuff than I ever would have found on my own, which makes me think I'm losing my edge. Maybe I need to get glasses." Pixie shuddered. "Me—in glasses?" It sounded like she'd rather be buried in quicksand.

"What happened after you were done with the sales?" Tricia asked.

"Fred is pretty softhearted. We ended up at Mickey D's and had lunch. And then we wound up taking the kid back to Nashua so he wouldn't have to hitchhike."

"Did you drop him off at the homeless shelter?" Tricia asked.

Pixie shook her head. "They don't open until six o'clock. But I saw Fred slip the kid some money before we left. We had a big fight about that on the way home."

"Why?" Tricia asked.

"Because . . . it feels like that kid is stalking me."

"Why would he want to do that?" Mr. Everett asked.

Pixie shrugged. "Uh . . . probably because I wouldn't buy those crappy books he had the first time he came to Haven't Got a Clue."

"Well, I'm truly sorry about that," Tricia said.

Pixie looked like she wanted to say something more, but then she shook her head. "I just don't feel safe around him."

"He hasn't threatened you, has he?" Mr. Everett asked, concerned.

Instead of answering, Pixie stared at Mr. Everett. "What are you doing here today. It's your day off."

"I have physical therapy tomorrow to keep my arm and shoulder from getting too stiff from nonuse."

"Oh," Pixie said, and nodded, but she hadn't answered Mr. Everett's question, either.

Though Tricia wasn't happy to hear about Pixie's weekend troubles, at least they'd diverted her from acknowledging the tension that had occurred between her and Tricia three days before. They would eventually have to address it. Tricia knew it was cowardice on her part, but she had so much on her mind she was content to let it slide . . . for now.

Pixie drained her cup. "Anything happen over the weekend? What did I miss?"

Tricia sighed and glanced toward her other employee. "Mr. Everett gave me quite the scare Saturday afternoon."

Pixie's eyes widened. "How?"

"By nearly keeling over. I called Grace and she took him straight to urgent care in Milford."

"What was wrong?" Pixie asked, her concern escalating.

"Dehydration."

Pixie nodded wisely. She'd been an EMT at some point in her past. "That can be bad for a man your age, Mr. E."

"It was my own fault. I feel like I'm overcompensating for my broken wrist. I lost track of things for a while. But I'm back in the pink now."

"Well, we'll just make sure you stay hydrated through the day, won't we, Tricia?"

"You bet."

The little bell over the door rang cheerfully and Ian McDonald entered the store.

"Ian," Tricia said, and rose from her chair, crossing the store to meet him. "Welcome back to Haven't Got a Clue. What can I do for you today?"

"I thought I'd stop in rather than phone or text to say thank you for helping me find my new flat."

"All moved in?"

"Just about. There are a few things I need to make it a bit more of a home, but it can wait until my days off."

"Are you finding it too small?"

He laughed. "After living aboard ships for more than a decade, it seems positively luxurious."

"I'm glad it's working out for you."

"I wondered if I might impose upon you to help me find some of the things I need to better outfit the place."

"Such as?"

"The kitchen is adequate, but is low on the utensils one needs to pull off a decent meal."

"Such as?"

"A potato peeler."

"There isn't one?"

"There is but it doesn't really work."

"Wow."

Ian looked off to his left. "I'm supposed to have weekends off—that is, subject to whatever is happening locally, of course."

Tricia nodded.

"But it would be helpful to me if I had someone to guide me when I came to the finer points of establishing my new home."

They looked at each other for long seconds before Ian

cleared his throat and began again. "Would you have time to help me in that regard?"

Tricia was both flattered and bummed by the question. She worked seven days a week, month after month, year after year with very few breaks.

"Well, I . . ."

"Of course she would," Pixie piped up.

Tricia rounded on her assistant manager, but she was afraid to dispute the claim because she didn't want to damage their working relationship any further. She turned back to Ian.

"Of course I'd like to help. When and where were you thinking?"

"There's a big-box store up on the highway. I thought we might walk through the housewares section and you could advise me. I mean, after you've looked at my kitchen."

Tricia hesitated. "I could do that. When do you want me to go with you?"

Ian shrugged. "Whenever you're free. I can always hit the diner or the pub for my meals, although it does get a bit pricey to do so."

Did that mean the Board of Selectmen had hired him and were paying him less than a living wage? Was it because he *was* an outsider?

"I'd be delighted. When do you want me to do a walk-through of your apartment?"

"Would this afternoon be too soon? My lunch hour is from twelve until one."

Tricia looked back toward her employees, who usually had their midday meal at that time."

"We can go later," Pixie chimed in.

"Yes. It wouldn't be at all a problem," Mr. Everett agreed.

"Great. We'll do a walk-through today at noon to assess what needs to be acquired."

"That sounds doable," Tricia agreed.

"Brilliant. Shall we meet at my flat at noon, then?"

Tricia managed a smile. "I'll see you there."

Ian nodded, flashed a smile, and headed for the door. "Until then."

Tricia watched him go. Pixie moved to stand beside her.

"Seeing him twice in the space of a week. Does *this* constitute a date?"

"Of course not." But it might just indicate friendship.

Of course, as most people misquoted the poet Robert Burns, "the best-laid plans of mice and men often go awry," and thus it was so with Tricia's visit to Ian's apartment, for as she'd anticipated, a fleet of competing news vans from various news networks descended upon Main Street with pert reporters dressed in topcoats against the brisk temperatures and seeking out anyone they could nail down for an interview.

"What's going on?" Pixie asked, rubbernecking to look out Haven't Got a Clue's big display window. Mr. Everett approached and Tricia gave them a fast recap of what she knew about Eli Meier's previous life.

Pixie looked appalled. "What a fink! Blowing up innocent people."

"Apparently they weren't all innocent," Mr. Everett muttered. "Still, no one deserves to die in such a fashion."

"Yes, well, it's likely they're going to eventually track me down and I really don't want to talk to any of them," Tricia told Pixie as she crowded next to her employees and peeked out the window.

"Ya really think they'll come looking for you?" Pixie asked.

"Alexa isn't going to want to talk to them, and since I'm the one who called nine one one, I'll probably be a target."

"Can't you just say 'no comment' and let it go at that?" Pixie asked.

"Reporters can be tenacious."

"You could hide out in the office or in your apartment. Mr. E and I can handle things here."

"Yes, Ms. Miles. We certainly can."

The phone rang. Tricia picked it up. "Haven't Got a—"

"Tricia? It's me," Angelica said. "I've already been

asked to give a statement by one of the national TV networks. Would you like to be there with me?"

"Where are you being interviewed?"

"On the sidewalk outside of the Cookery."

"When?"

"In about ten minutes."

Tricia looked out the window once again and saw a female reporter with a cameraman in tow heading up Main Street.

"No, thank you. And if they ask if they can speak to me, tell them I'm not available."

"I can't speak for you."

"I give you my permission."

"What are you going to do?" Angelica asked, sounding alarmed.

"Hide."

"Now, is that the *adult* thing to do?"

"I don't owe these people anything. I did my civic duty and I want my privacy."

She heard Angelica give a heavy sigh. "Very well. I'll talk to you later. And I'll let you know when I'm going to be on TV. I'll turn this fiasco into a great PR opportunity. You just watch!" And with that, she ended the call.

Tricia's cell phone pinged. She looked at the message, saw it was from Ian, and quickly read it.

Rain check on the apartment tour. I've got some interviews to give. Later.

Pixie took a guess. "Me and Mr. E can go to lunch at our regular time, huh?"

Tricia frowned. "Yes."

NINETEEN

 Tricia didn't mention her invitation to visit Ian's apartment to Angelica that afternoon at lunch, where she'd arrived wearing a hat and sunglasses, feeling like some kind of chickenhearted spy. Instead, she listened as Angelica relayed—in great detail—her interviews with four different TV stations and two networks, in addition to the conference call conversation with the state agricultural people. Setting up the whole vegetable-growing operation sounded incredibly complicated and Angelica seemed discouraged about the possibility of establishing such a venture.

"If your talks went well, how come you're so bummed?" Tricia asked.

Angelica frowned. "I thought there'd be plenty of land around the north side of the village that would be perfect for such an operation. It's pretty much trees. But I spoke to Karen Johnson at NR Realty and she said most of it's been bought up."

"Most?" Tricia asked.

"The choice parcels."

"And what constitutes choice land?"

"Flat."

"What's left?"

"Hills."

"And that's bad?"

"When it comes to a large agribusiness, it is."

"Who would buy such plots?"

"I have no idea, but I wish I'd thought of it first." Angelica shook her head sadly but then seemed to shake off her disappointment.

"Anything interesting happen to *you* this morning while you hid in the shadows?" Angelica asked, giving Tricia a look of disapproval.

Tricia shook her head. "Not a thing."

"You mean *no one* was clamoring to interview you?" Angelica asked with more than a hint of sarcasm.

Tricia picked up her sandwich and bit into it. Even Angelica knew it was impolite to speak with your mouth full.

Back at Haven't Got a Clue, the early part of the afternoon was pretty quiet—for a bookstore. Other businesses in the area seemed to be having a tremendously satisfying day, what with all the newspeople in town looking for places to eat, drink, and find someone—anyone—to interview. This peaceful respite gave Tricia's staff a chance to catch up on their reading, while she stayed in her basement office to catch up on paperwork. After a couple of hours, however, she got lonely and returned to the sales floor just as Pixie closed her book. "I need another John D. MacDonald to read that I haven't gone through in the last year."

"There are several down in the storeroom," Mr. Everett volunteered. "Shall I get one for you?"

"No need, I'll be right back," Pixie said, and replaced the book she'd carefully been reading—she and Mr. Everett were always careful not to crease the bindings—on one of the shelves. Pixie disappeared into the basement.

"Did anyone come looking for me?" Tricia asked innocently.

"Why no, Ms. Miles. It's been quiet all afternoon."

Tricia nodded, not sure how she felt about the situation. She *was*, after all, a witness of sorts in finding the body of a major criminal who'd been on the run for decades. The fact that she wasn't in demand for a quote both pleased and annoyed her, which she found unsettling.

With nothing better to do, and feeling like a cur with its tail between its legs, Tricia decided to check the shelves, as often customers looked at books and weren't careful to replace them in alphabetical order by author. Pixie was back in less than five minutes. "I brought you another bottle of water," she said brightly, handing the liter bottle to Mr. Everett. "You've got to stay hydrated."

Tricia looked up as Mr. Everett let out a heavy sigh. "I really don't wish for any more."

"Now, now, now, Mr. E. The doctors know what's best for you," Pixie chided him.

"Yes, but—" he said, and bit his lip as though not to say more. "Thank you," he said rather tersely. Pixie stood over him until he'd opened the bottle and took a sip. He forced a smile and stood. "I'd better get to dusting the back of the shop. We wouldn't want the customers to be able to write their names on the shelves."

As if that could happen. Not a day went by when Mr. Everett didn't dust the shelves, and he was particularly dedicated to the task after his days off. Besides, he'd already attacked them earlier in the day.

Although it was late in the afternoon, they saw more than their usual amount of customers for a Monday afternoon in late April. They seemed to have been drawn to the village because of Eli's death, for they peppered Pixie and Mr. Everett with questions about the case. Tricia stayed out of the conversations entirely. But at least ringing up customer sales helped to pass the time. It was just after four thirty and a few customers still lingered in the store when Tricia realized that if she didn't go to the bank before opening the next day, they would be short on change. Unlike Eli Meier, she didn't like to bother her neighbors to help her out, although she could always depend on June at the Cookery to come to her rescue—and vice versa. Pixie had noticed the register's lack of bills as well.

"I can handle things here if you want to go to the bank," she volunteered.

Tricia looked at the clock on the opposite wall. Still twenty-five minutes until closing time. "If you're willing to go, you can head straight home afterward. What do you think?"

Pixie seemed delighted. "Great."

"Okay, I'll pull things together and you can head out."

Pixie nodded and went to the back of the shop to grab her dark suit jacket. In no time, Tricia had the bank bag ready and they made a discreet transfer of it to Pixie's rather big purse.

"I'll see you tomorrow," Pixie said, and headed for the door. She opened it and tentatively stuck her head outside. Was she looking for Edward Dowding? Finally, she gave a brief wave and was on her way.

Tricia handled a customer, who appeared to have cleaned out the bargain section. They'd have to restock before re-opening in the morning. As the man left the shop, she glanced at the clock once again. It was just ten minutes until closing, with only a few stragglers left browsing the shelves.

One of them, a woman who looked to be about forty, approached the cash desk with a grim-faced eight- or ten-year-old girl tagging behind her. "Excuse me, ma'am, but is the washroom out of order?"

Tricia blinked. "Uh, no. Why?"

"The door has been locked for some time and my daughter"—she nodded toward the girl and lowered her voice to a whisper—"really needs to go."

"Mom!" the girl wailed, embarrassed.

"I'll check," Tricia said.

"Thanks."

Tricia rounded the counter and walked briskly to the back of the shop and stopped at the washroom door. The mother and daughter were not far behind. She knocked. "Is anyone in there?"

No answer.

Tricia rattled the door handle and found it was indeed locked. "Excuse me, but there's a little girl here who needs to use the restroom."

Still no answer.

It wasn't the first time the door had been locked by someone—and usually a child—and needed to be opened. "I'm afraid I'll have to go to the front of the store to get a screwdriver," Tricia told the woman. "It may take a few minutes. Might I suggest you go next door to the Cookery and use their restroom? Just tell the manager that Tricia sent you and they'll be happy to accommodate you."

"Thank you," the woman said, and turned to her daughter. "Come on, Charlotte."

Tricia followed them to the front of the store, where she retrieved a slender flatheaded screwdriver. Mr. Everett had shown her how to unlock the door from the outside after it had happened several times.

Armed with the appropriate tool, Tricia sidled past the shelves and again halted in front of the washroom door. She inserted the screwdriver into the little hole, found the slot and turned it until it wouldn't move, grasped the handle, and pulled. The door opened a crack but it was abruptly yanked shut once again, and she heard the lock click.

Tricia rapped on the door sharply. "Excuse me, but it's almost closing time. Would you please vacate the washroom?"

"Go away," came a muffled-yet-familiar voice.

"Mr. Everett . . . is that you?" Tricia asked, aghast.

"Yes, please go away."

"Do you need help?" she asked, concern gripping her. "Should I call Grace?"

"I . . . no. Not yet. I just need a little time."

Tricia looked at the clock on the wall. The store was due to close in another seven minutes.

"Please," came his voice once more, sounding distressed.

"Very well," Tricia said, and backed off. What in the

world was wrong this time? Did he have a stomach upset? He'd seemed fine an hour before, if a little preoccupied.

Tricia returned to the front of the store to wait on the final customers, finding her gaze traveling to the back of the store between each one. Waiting on the customers would have gone faster if she'd had some help, but the last of them was out the door only three minutes after the official close of business.

Tricia turned the store's OPEN sign to CLOSED, locked up, and headed to the back of the building once more. She knocked on the washroom door. "The store is now closed. Can you come out now?"

"Grace should be out front to pick me up at any moment. Could you please ask her to move the car to the alley? I'd prefer to leave through the back door."

Tricia heard a honk and saw through the front display window that Grace's car had just pulled up. "All right." She retreated to the front of the store and exited the building. Upon seeing her, Grace lowered the passenger side window and Tricia conveyed Mr. Everett's message.

"Whatever for?" Grace asked, sounding puzzled.

"I don't know, but I'm worried. He locked himself in the washroom more than half an hour ago and wouldn't come out."

"Oh, dear," Grace muttered, looking chagrined.

"Do you know what's wrong?"

Grace's expression darkened. "I have a good idea. Do you have any large trash bags?"

"Yes," Tricia answered, rather surprised by the question.

"Perhaps you should get one out. I'll drive around the block and meet you at the back of your store."

A strange request. "Okay."

The window went back up, Grace steered the car away from the curb, and Tricia hurried back inside her store. She returned to the back of the shop and rummaged in the cabinet where they kept cleaning supplies and other miscellanea and pulled a tall kitchen bag from the box.

Tricia unlocked the back door and waited until Grace's car appeared. She parked and, keys in hand, mounted the steps to intercept Tricia, who led the older woman to the washroom door.

"May I have the bag?" Grace asked, and Tricia immediately handed it over.

Grace rapped on the washroom door. "William, dear, I'm here."

They heard the washroom's lock click, and the door opened a crack. A portion of Mr. Everett's face appeared in the narrow aperture.

Without asking, Grace thrust the plastic bag toward the door and Mr. Everett grabbed it, slamming the door once again.

Tricia turned to Grace. "What's going on?"

Grace shook her head. "This is something we anticipated but hoped wouldn't happen."

Tricia raised her hands in supplication, not understanding.

Grace frowned. "William is a *very* proud man."

"And?"

"Without full use of his hands, he's found bathroom rituals difficult to maintain."

Tricia's brow wrinkled in confusion, and then she realized the problem. "You mean he can't handle the zipper on his pants?" she whispered.

Grace nodded.

Oh, the poor man. And all day long Tricia and Pixie had been pushing liquids on him. "Why didn't he ask me to help? I would have gladly done so."

Grace shrugged. "As I said, William is a proud man."

Seconds later, Mr. Everett emerged from the washroom with the trash bag hanging from his waist to his knees, looking like he wore a white miniskirt over his trousers and covering his shame. Somehow he mustered his dignity, head raised high, though his gaze did not meet Tricia's.

"Good night, Ms. Miles," he said succinctly.

"Good night, Mr. Everett."

"Come, William," Grace said, and took her husband's

hand. Together, they exited the shop and descended the stairs, headed for her car. They got in and Grace started the engine. She gave Tricia a halfhearted wave but Mr. Everett's gaze was leveled straight ahead, his body rigid.

And suddenly Tricia was afraid she might never see her dear friend again.

TWENTY

 A heavy-hearted Tricia practically trudged over to Angelica's for dinner that evening. Even Sarge's jubilant barking couldn't lift her spirits. She tossed him a biscuit, which cut the noise, and flopped onto one of the stools at the kitchen island.

"Well, don't you look like you've just lost your best friend," Angelica quipped as she held a glass spoon and stirred the matching pitcher of martinis.

Tricia hung her jacket over the back of the stool. "What if I told you I might have done just that?"

"Uh-oh, I hope you're going to spill all."

"I don't know if I should. It's rather personal."

"For whom?"

Tricia's gaze dipped. "Mr. Everett."

Angelica frowned. "This sounds like it might be a three-queen-olive story."

"It sure is," Tricia said as Angelica poured their drinks. Angelica had thawed some of the grape jelly meatballs, which sat steaming in a shallow bowl. She set the dish on a tray along with their drinks and they retreated to the living room. Upon settling in, Tricia told her sister what had happened.

"Oh, poor Mr. Everett," Angelica simpered. "Why didn't

he just ask you or Pixie for help? It's not as though you haven't seen a guy's"—she paused—"equipment before."

"As Grace said, he's a very proud man."

"Well, it's only *you* who knew about it."

"Yes, well, now it's you, too. And I really should mention it to Pixie. We were both guilty of pushing him to drink more liquids than he was comfortable with. I dread bringing up the subject, but I am going to have to talk to him about it. But the last thing I want to do is embarrass the poor man."

"Do you think he'll show up for work tomorrow?"

"Well, that's the good thing—if you can call it that. He usually has Mondays off but he worked today as he has to go to physical therapy tomorrow. He should be back to work on Wednesday. How did the rest of your afternoon go?"

Angelica sighed. "After all the excitement this morning, it turned out to be just as depressing as yours, I'm afraid. You wouldn't have wanted to speak to me several hours ago. I was so, so angry!" Angelica practically spat.

"Why?"

"You'll never guess who bought up all the available land in the area."

Tricia closed her eyes and sighed. "Don't tell me: Becca Chandler."

"Yes! Why should she do such a thing?"

"Because, dear sister, she wants to be the next you?"

"What?"

"She so admires what Nigela Ricita has done in Stoneham that she wants to be just like you."

"You mean usurp me."

"Well, that, too."

"Well, because of *her*, I had a long conversation with Antonio. I've made a decision about the whole agriculture idea."

Tricia had a feeling she knew what was coming. "And?"

"It's not something I or even Nigela Ricita Associates should take on. I mean, if it was the only operation I or NR brands would handle, then it would be viable, but we're too diversified. We specialize in retail and the hospitality trade, and we think that's where our focus should be."

"Your businesses excel at both," Tricia pointed out.

Angelica nodded. "Are you terribly disappointed in me? I mean, it was you who suggested the idea."

"Of course not. I have lots of great ideas—that doesn't mean any of them will ever come to fruition. I merely thought it was something that might interest you."

"Oh, it does. A lot. In fact, I may invest in such a company, but there's no way I could take on a project like that."

"It's a smart woman who knows her limitations," Tricia said, proffering her glass as though in a toast.

"Oh, you're so profound—or should that be profane? Speaking of which, did you apologize to Pixie today?"

"Uh, no. With everything that happened she was more concerned with Edward Dowding."

"Why?"

"Oh, didn't I mention that she thinks he's stalking her?"

"No, you did not. Surely she could handle the likes of him. She *is* a kickboxer."

"Among her many talents. But it's worrying. She genuinely seems afraid of him—and that's not like her."

Angelica shook her head. "And anything new on Eli's murder?"

"You mean that hasn't already been blasted on the airwaves? Not that I heard."

"Not even when you spoke to Ian McDonald this morning?"

"You heard?"

Just then, the sisters heard a ping. They both reached for their phones, but it was Angelica's phone that had made the sound. She tapped the message icon, read the message, and frowned.

"What's up? Is something wrong?"

"Not wrong. Weird."

"Who's it from?"

"My literary agent, Artemis Hamilton. He wants to know if I've heard from Eli. He's been trying to contact him."

"What? Is he living in a cave? He hasn't looked at the news?"

"Obviously not."

"What did he want to talk to Eli for?"

"About his memoir."

Tricia took over the dinner prep while Angelica caught up with her agent. Not only did she need to bring him up to speed with Eli's murder, but on her own life—and why she hadn't finished her third cookbook. They'd long finished their second martini and Tricia had set places for them at the kitchen island when Angelica finally got off the phone. Tricia had deliberately tried not to listen in on the conversation because now she wanted a moment-by-moment recap.

"How on earth did Eli connect with Artemis?" Tricia asked.

"From the acknowledgments in my first cookbook. He tracked him down and pitched his book idea."

"So, Artemis knew Eli was really Joseph Martin?" Tricia asked.

"Yes. He hadn't heard about his death and the big reveal about his true identity. He said he tries not to look at the news or social media when he's working. It's too tempting to fall into that time sinkhole."

Tricia did the same. "Did he ever once consider turning the guy in to the FBI?" she asked.

"Are you kidding? The publisher was supposedly going to pay Eli a hundred-grand advance for a book they were sure could reap them a lot more in return."

"From what I understand, Eli was broke," Tricia remarked.

"Well, technically, they didn't actually have a signed contract. Eli had written an outline and a few chapters, but it was evident they were going to need to bring in someone to help assist with polishing the manuscript. Artemis was quite upset to hear Eli had died. But there were supposed to be journals or something like fifteen or sixteen chapters' worth of material, so he's hoping they can still pull off a book and pay the estate."

"And where are these journals?"

"That's the thing. He doesn't know."

"You need to talk to Ian and report this. It could be a motive for his murder," Tricia said.

Angelica didn't seem excited at the prospect. "I did think of that."

"When will you tell him?"

Angelica looked at the clock. "Not tonight. I want to think about it first."

"What's to think about?"

"That's it. I need to think of every possible contingency."

"Maybe Ian could help look for the journals."

"Didn't you tell me he's already been through the store's contents?"

"Yes, but he didn't know what to look for. Of course, they could have been in Eli's apartment—wherever he lived."

"The same horrid apartment building that Pixie's Fred used to live in on the edge of the village."

Tricia remembered that awful little complex. "How do you know this?"

"Silly, it's on the Chamber address list."

Oh, yeah.

"Come on. We'd better eat dinner before it's as dry as the desert," Angelica said, taking back her duties as hostess.

Tricia was just as happy to resume her part of the evening as a guest—albeit not an attentive one. She had far too many things on her mind: Mr. Everett, Pixie, Eli's death—and now a missing manuscript attributed to him. What else could occupy her mind that evening and keep her from sleep?

She was afraid to find out.

TWENTY-ONE

To assure getting any sleep at all that night, Tricia took a melatonin supplement, washing it down with some hot cocoa, read until she felt thoroughly drowsy, and ended up in the land of nod until the alarm went off the next morning. Finally feeling rested, she decided to face the day with a more optimistic outlook, and she always felt invigorated after a brisk walk through the village.

Halfway through her constitutional, Tricia decided to make cutting through the village square a part of her daily walk just in case she ran into Nadine. The woman had seemed so sad the other times they'd met.

Sure enough, Nadine was sitting on the same park bench. This time, the tome she held was titled *Divorce and Money: Everything You Need to Know* by Gayle Rosenwald Smith. So, her marriage *was* the cause of Nadine's unhappiness. Maybe Tricia could give her a few pointers on her problems after having been divorced herself.

"Hi, Nadine," she called.

"Hey, Tricia." Nadine closed the book. She turned it over so that the title wasn't visible, but she had to know Tricia had already seen it. "Another lovely morning."

"It's actually starting to feel like spring," Tricia agreed. She gestured to the bench. "Do you mind if I sit?"

Nadine moved aside. "Be my guest."

Tricia sat and gave her new acquaintance a smile before sobering. "I saw the title of your book."

Nadine looked away. "I figured you did."

"Divorcing?"

"Not yet. I need to gather as much information as I can get before I do anything."

"What does your husband think?"

"That he's the greatest, smartest bully in the world and that he can manipulate me and our kid in order to shut us down."

"I'm sorry to hear that."

Nadine shook her head sadly. "I never thought I'd even consider divorce." She gave a mirthless laugh. "Maybe I should just shoot the bastard. That would solve all my problems."

So, Nadine had a gun, too? Shooting her husband would only create a new set of problems for the woman. Tricia didn't want to talk about that.

"I never considered divorce, either," she said. "It was my ex who instigated the separation."

Nadine raised an eyebrow.

"He needed to find himself."

"And did he?"

"Oh, yes. After everything he put me through he found that what he needed in life was me."

"And are you together now?"

Tricia's gaze dipped. "No, he died." Surely Nadine had to be new to Stoneham if she hadn't heard about Christopher's murder. "But at least we were friends when he passed."

"That's nice. I'm at the stage where if my soon-to-be ex died I'd do a jig on his grave," Nadine deadpanned.

"I never got to that stage. Oh, I was angry with him, but I never wanted to see him dead." Tricia sighed. "But then his leaving gave me the courage to change my life. I quit the job I had loved but felt I'd moved beyond. I used my settlement money to move here and open my store. I got a whole new life in six crazy months."

"Do you ever regret it?"

"The divorce?" Tricia frowned. "At first I was devastated, but I honestly think it may have been the best thing that could ever have happened to me."

"I'm thinking that way already and I haven't even told the bastard I want out."

"He hasn't got a clue?" Tricia asked, remembering Nadine's dig during their last conversation.

Nadine smiled—a real grin this time. "No."

"When are you going to break the news to him?"

Nadine's flash of pleasure was short-lived. "That's a good question. Until I have my financial ducks in a row . . ."

"The prudent approach," Tricia approved.

"As it is, most of our assets are in *his* name and I'm sure it wasn't by accident. And New Hampshire *isn't* a community property state."

"I hear you," Tricia said in commiseration. She didn't understand the notion that what a couple built over a marriage shouldn't be split down the middle. Surely both spouses had contributed to a household and often the burden of keeping a home was deemed less worthy than the heavier financial contribution that one spouse might give.

When Tricia worked for the high-profile nonprofit in Manhattan, she'd had to parse the duties of keeping house to a number of others. Her job had been totally fulfilling but left her exhausted. She had no time to cook and clean, and she'd had the luxury of being able to afford to farm those duties out to women who were far more capable in that regard. When she'd moved to Stoneham and set up housekeeping, it had been a rude awakening to find herself on the other end of a toilet brush in her home and business, something she'd never had to contend with in her former privileged life.

"Have you thought about speaking to a marriage counselor?" she asked.

Nadine gave an exasperated laugh. "And where would I find the money to do that?"

Yes, all the advice columnists glibly told their readers to

seek out that kind of help, but unless insurance would pay for it—which was doubtful—how were these women supposed to access such help? The whole mental health care system in the US was quite frankly a joke. If you couldn't pay for it—and at hundreds an hour, how could regular working people do so?—they were out of luck.

Tricia's own experience with a counselor hadn't been at all helpful. She'd consulted a psychologist at her primary care physician's recommendation. She'd stopped seeing him after the second session when he'd asked her how she'd caused her husband's dissatisfaction in their marriage.

"Can you talk to your clergyman?" Tricia asked.

Nadine shook her head. "I left the church years ago when I was told I needed to submit to my husband's every whim. Now I happily work Sunday mornings so I don't have to listen to that point of view."

"What did your husband think of that?"

"Oh, he never went to church. He didn't think he needed it."

"Did *you* think he did?"

"Let's just say that most sinners never recognize themselves," Nadine said. "Either that or they only concentrate on the Old Testament and not the texts that encourage a love for our fellow men—or women."

"Are there other resources you can utilize?" Tricia asked, playing devil's advocate.

"If there are, I haven't been able to find them. I feel so isolated."

"A woman's shelter?" Tricia suggested.

"I'm not ready for that step. Yet." Nadine offered a wan smile. "Over the years, my husband has done a good job isolating me from everyone I care about. How sad is it that you're the closest thing I have to a friend?"

Tricia touched the woman's arm. "I'm glad you consider me so. Is there *anything* I can do to help you?"

"Just show up here every so often and listen. That's worth a lot."

And hardly what Tricia considered to be of much help.

Nadine looked at her watch. "I'd better get back to work before my husband misses me."

"So, you work together?"

Nadine nodded. "I've only been able to sneak out this past week or so because he had regular online meetings with his crazy friends."

"Friends?"

"You bet. It's like a cult. He's into all kinds of conspiracy theories."

Tricia's stomach tightened. "Did he know Eli Meier from the Inner Light bookstore?"

"Know him? My husband had to be his best customer."

"You never did tell me your last name."

"It's Reed. My husband, Dan, owns the Bookshelf Diner. I'm the chief cook and bottle washer."

Tricia was still trying to absorb that nice Nadine was married to that big bossy bore Dan Reed when she turned onto Main Street. No news vans were parked on the road that morning, but up ahead she could see a moving truck parked outside the Inner Light, and several men were unloading cardboard cartons.

"What the heck?" she muttered, and quickened her pace.

"Hey, what's going on?" Tricia asked the bigger of the burly movers.

"Gotta clean out this store today."

"Under whose authority?"

"The building's owner." He reached into his pocket and pulled out a set of keys. "See? All nice and legal."

But Becca had said it might be a week or more before she'd have permission to do so. It must have come sooner than she thought. Did Ian know about this?

Tricia pivoted and started back to her store, taking out her phone as she walked. She tapped the contacts icon and scrolled down to Becca's name. She answered right away.

"Hello, Tricia. What's up?"

"There are moving men outside of the Inner Light."

"Oh, good. They wasted no time in starting the job."

"What's going to happen to all Eli's merchandise?"

"I told you. It'll go into storage until I can find an heir. And if I can't—the dumpster."

"But—but . . ." She wasn't about to tell Becca about the journals, but she thought she had better strongly encourage Angelica to tell Chief McDonald about them.

"Have you been looking for an heir?"

"I asked the new cop in town to keep me posted. Legally, I only have to keep my tenant's property for seven days after abandonment."

"Eli hardly abandoned his store."

"Well, he ain't coming back to occupy the space, either," Becca said sarcastically. "I suppose you want a chance to poke through the contents to look for *clues*," Becca said, sounding amused.

"Well, I—" It might be best if Tricia oversaw the operation.

"You're a regular Miss Marple, aren't you?" Becca accused.

"No, that's my cat," Tricia said flatly.

Silence. Apparently she had never mentioned the feline Miss Marple in a conversation with Becca.

"If you want to poke around—be my guest," Becca said.

"You'd better tell that to the movers."

"It'll have to come from my admin. The fewer people know I control the whole operation, the better."

"Could you have him or her call them?"

Becca sighed. "I guess. I'll text you when it's a done deal."

"Thank you."

"Later," Becca said, and ended the call.

Tricia let herself into her store. She had half an hour before it was due to open and she busied herself with setting up the beverage station and writing a quick note for Pixie. It was ten minutes to ten when Becca's text came through giving her the all clear. Tricia left the note on the counter and scooted out the door.

By the time she entered the Inner Light, the guys had already assembled a mountain of small book boxes and were about to start emptying the shelves.

"You Tricia Miles?" the biggest guy asked. The name on his coveralls said *Mike*.

"Yes."

He gestured, taking in the entire store. "We're supposed to let you poke around while we work. We're on the clock, so please don't get in our way."

Well, at least he said "please."

"I'll do that."

Tricia stepped away from the men at work and took in the shabby retail space. Becca was right. It was a pit. She didn't even know what she was looking for. Journals. That could mean books with nothing written on the spines, but there were thousands of books in the shop. The two men could empty a bookcase faster than she could look through the titles, but she had to give it a go.

Tricia moved to the bookshelf behind the movers and started scanning the spines, knowing it was probably a futile gesture.

Eli had organized the titles by subject. Those books devoted to the world's top religions were in the front of the shop. Was it likely he'd hide his journals among them? She didn't think so. She moved around the store, looking for oddities instead—there weren't many. If she had run the store, she would have added a gift line, such as angel figurines, religious and inspirational placards, greeting cards, jewelry—but apparently Eli wasn't that marketing savvy.

As Tricia watched the men pack, she thought again about the best place to not so much hide the journals, but keep them from getting mixed in with the regular stock. The logical place would be where Eli spent most of his time: at the front of the store near or behind the podium he used as a cash desk. She moved to stand behind the lectern and did a more thorough search, but the only oddity was a faux leather box filled with cassette tapes. She glanced at the eclectic titles on the plastic cases. They were a strange mix of old country-western artists, classical music, and show tunes. Eli's taste in music was certainly diverse. Beside the box on the tower's shelf was a small cassette player, but no sign of any journals. There was, however, a grubby little spiral notebook, but it looked like it contained a list of items and prices for things he'd purchased for the store over the years.

The shop's distinct odor was starting to get to her and Tricia coughed into the elbow of her jacket sleeve. She saw that the movers were breaking out masks. It made sense. Who knew what kind of cooties were circulating in the air—or on the books themselves? Feeling dispirited, she decided she had better turn her attention to her own store and her employee.

She thanked the movers and gave the shop's horrible interior one more look before she turned and left the building.

TWENTY-TWO

 Pixie had arrived in Tricia's absence and was puttering around the cash desk when Tricia returned to Haven't Got a Clue. "Morning," Pixie practically sang. If she was still angry at Tricia for their strained conversation five days earlier, she didn't show it.

"It seemed weird enough that Mr. E was here at work yesterday. Now it seems weird that he's not here today," Pixie said.

And would he show up the next morning? Only time would tell.

Tricia hung up her coat and returned to the front of the shop.

"Coffee's hot," Pixie said, indicating the cup before her on the cash desk.

"Great. I could use a cup," Tricia said, and stepped over to the coffee station to pour some into one of the store's mugs. Several people had asked about buying them. She'd ordered a few from a specialty house just for herself and staff but thought she might put in a bigger order and offer them to customers as well. Such a souvenir might remind them to return to the store more often.

Tricia's phone pinged. She looked at her screen. A message from Ian McDonald.

Are you free at noon for that tour of my apartment?

She was.

Great. See you then.

Tricia put her phone away, smiling.

"Can I take a wild guess at what that was about?"

Tricia frowned. "Go ahead."

"The new top cop has called in that rain check to scope out his crib."

"You've got that right." Tricia raised a hand to her head. "I forgot that you'll be here alone. I'll have to cancel so you can have your lunch break."

"Not a problem," Pixie said. "I brought my lunch. It's in the fridge downstairs. If there're no customers, I can eat it up here, and when you get back from lunch with Angelica, I can take a break."

"Are you sure?" Tricia asked.

"Absolutely."

It seemed like now was the time for Tricia to apologize to Pixie, but then the shop door opened and a customer came in. "I'm looking for some old Nancy Drew books for my granddaughter. Can you help?"

"Can we ever," Pixie said, and cheerfully led the woman to the store's children's section. The truth was, children very rarely were interested in the old Nancy Drew, Hardy Boys, Trixie Belden, et cetera, section—but luckily their elders were eager to introduce those characters to a younger generation.

Tricia glanced at the clock on the wall. She had about an hour and a half until she met Ian for the apartment tour. She found herself counting the minutes.

Despite the traffic from the plethora of news trucks and increased foot traffic the day before, the excitement had died down and another story now dominated the news cycles, which was no doubt why Ian had time to show Tricia his new digs.

Tricia didn't even need to knock on the apartment door that faced the street next to the Bee's Knees, leading her to believe Ian had been standing right behind it, waiting for her.

"Come on in," he said, and gestured for her to follow him up the stairs, which were steeper than she'd anticipated.

Knowing how small the retail space was below it, Tricia had been prepared for the tiny space. She'd already seen pictures of it online, but they must have been taken with a wide-angle lens, for the combination living/dining/kitchen area could only be called compact—like it had been designed for a hermit crab, but the bones were good and there was a certain heartwarming charm to the place. Oak hardwood throughout graced the floors, with a dark area rug in the living room, no doubt chosen to hide any stains guests might make.

The furnishings in said living room consisted of a love seat, a chair, a hassock that doubled as a coffee table, and a TV mounted on the wall. A five-by-seven-inch framed picture of a smiling family of four was the only personal item on display—probably Ian's sister and her family. The kitchen consisted of an apartment-sized fridge, stove, and tiny porcelain sink, but no dishwasher. The counter barely housed a small microwave and coffeemaker. A short bar divided the apartment with just enough room for two stools.

"Tight quarters," she commented, looking around the stark white walls that bore no ornamentation.

"It'll do. Well, actually, it won't. There doesn't seem to be enough of anything to actually prepare a meal. There's one pot, a coffeemaker—not that I drink it that much—and nowhere to store much. I could use some help in that direction. Would you be willing?"

"Sure." Tricia indicated the kitchen beyond. "May I look through the cupboards and drawers?"

"Be my guest."

There was barely enough room for one person. Tricia had been on sailboats with bigger galleys. She pulled out a drawer under the counter and found four settings of silverware, a serving spoon, a can opener, one paring knife, and a set of measuring spoons. Anyone staying here probably wouldn't want to stay for very long—either way they'd likely have planned to eat most meals out. Tricia checked the cupboards and found all-white matching dishware consisting of four dinner plates, four glasses, four soup bowls, and four plain mugs, but not much else, despite the fact that two shelves were completely empty. The stove housed a frying pan and one saucepan. Ian wouldn't be entertaining lavishly.

"Well, what do you think?" Ian asked.

"It's sparse." Tricia looked around the space. "How much do you want to spend?"

"Not a lot. I mean, it's a rental."

She nodded. "Then I think a visit to the dollar store should be in order. You can buy pot holders, dish towels, kitchen utensils, glasses, and even dishware. You could probably outfit the whole kitchen for less than thirty bucks. There's one up on the highway just outside of the village."

"I think I saw it when I drove in the other day. I'm not much into decorating, but this place could use a bit of personality."

"My assistant knows all the thrift shops in a fifty-mile radius and hits every estate sale she can find. I could ask her for her advice."

Ian nodded. "My mother was a regular visitor to the charity shops in our village and beyond. I used to go with her when I was a lad. I had to travel light for a lot of years. I'm actually looking forward to acquiring a few things."

"I'll ask Pixie and get back to you for the best places to go, but I'm betting they'll be in Nashua or Concord."

"It might be a fun way to get to know a little about the state." He frowned. "If my first week on the job proves to be the norm, I might not have time to do more than hit that dollar store."

"If you give my assistant a budget and a list of items, I'm

sure she could help you out for a song and have you all set up by next Monday."

"Oh, but that would be such an imposition, as we've never even been introduced," Ian protested.

Tricia shook her head. "Pixie's a picker in her spare time."

"A what?"

Tricia explained. "She likes to visit estate sales on the last day to get the best prices."

Ian looked in the direction of the kitchen. "I could sure use a teapot."

"I'll speak to her."

Ian nodded.

Tricia nodded in return.

Ian gave her a smile.

Tricia smiled back.

"Would you like to see the bedroom?" Ian asked.

Tricia blinked.

"I mean, you may as well get the whole tour as long as you're here."

Tricia shrugged. "Lead the way."

The stairs to the third floor were just as steep as those she'd ascended minutes before. The bedroom seemed considerably roomier than the living area below. The bathroom was small, but updated, with a picture of a goldfish in a bowl gracing the wall above the toilet. Its one salute to the past was the multicolored stained glass window, which overlooked the alley below.

The bedroom boasted a queen-sized bed, double nightstands, and a small seating area with a reading lamp, but nothing in the way of decoration graced the stark white walls. A tiny closet held what clothes Ian possessed. A small bookshelf housed a few paperbacks, along with tourist information printed by the Stoneham Chamber of Commerce. On the top was a blue-and-white porcelain bowl, presumably a place for the flat's occupant to toss their keys and/or change.

"It could use some personality," Tricia said. "I take it there's no laundry?"

"I'll have to hit the launderette," Ian remarked.

Tricia nodded. She had never had to darken the doors of a laundromat and was grateful for it.

"I guess this concludes the tour of my humble abode," Ian said.

"I guess," Tricia said.

Ian seemed rather embarrassed.

"How did your interviews go yesterday?" Tricia asked.

"You mean you didn't watch the national news programs?" Ian actually seemed hurt.

"No. To tell you the truth, I didn't want to visit all the hype surrounding Eli's death. I suppose the federal government will be taking over the investigation."

"I haven't been told not to investigate, but there are a number of federal agents who've taken rooms at the Brookview Inn." Angelica would no doubt be pleased by that bit of news. "They'll be poking around, but they seem more interested in investigating Martin's past, under-the-radar life than his recent death. Of course, they'd be very interested to know if he was killed as an act of revenge, but that doesn't seem likely."

Once again Tricia nodded.

"Well, as you aren't really interested in Martin's death—"

"Oh, I didn't say that. I'm just not interested in the drama surrounding it. I'm glad the news crews have left the area—although I suspect not all the merchants feel that way."

"No doubt."

An uncomfortable silence fell between them.

"Uh . . . how can I thank you for advising me on what to get to make this little flat more of a home? Would you like to go to lunch?"

"You mean now?" Tricia asked.

Ian nodded.

"That's very kind, but I have a standing lunch date with my sister over at Booked for Lunch."

"Do you ever deviate from that routine?" Ian asked.

"Occasionally," Tricia admitted.

"If you're free on the weekends maybe we could go to lunch and a few charity shops?"

Tricia shook her head. "My store is open seven days a week."

"And you have to be there each and *every* day?" he asked.

"Pretty much. Pixie works another job on Saturdays. I don't know if you noticed, but my other employee Mr. Everett recently fell and broke his wrist. I wouldn't feel comfortable leaving him on his own for any space of time during the next few weeks. I would worry about his safety."

Ian nodded. "You're a conscientious manager. But what's that saying about 'all work and no play'?"

"Makes Tricia a very dull woman."

"I wouldn't say dull, but perhaps in desperate need of some time off?" Ian suggested.

"Definitely. But then . . . if you're anything like your predecessor, you'll end up working most weekends anyway."

Ian's gaze hardened. "I don't suppose I'm *anything* like my predecessor."

Tricia scrutinized Ian's face for a long moment. "No, you're not."

TWENTY-THREE

 Tricia just had time to scoot across the street to meet Angelica and was in fact there before her sister, settling at their usual reserved table. But Angelica didn't keep her waiting long and was there before Tricia could do more than take a sip from her water glass.

"Hello!" Angelica announced as she sat down. "What a busy morning."

"Do anything special?" Tricia asked.

"Just working on Chamber business. I want to get it out of the way so that I can concentrate on other things. Like my new grandbaby," she said with relish. "He could arrive any day now." She giggled in anticipation. "How about you?"

Tricia considered telling Angelica about her visit to Ian's apartment and decided she would—before someone else did.

"Well, I—"

The café's door was wrenched open and an imposing figure stopped, looked around, and advanced toward Tricia and Angelica's table, bumping against it and jostling their cups so that the coffee sloshed onto the table.

"Do you mind!" Angelica said, perturbed, and grabbed her napkin to mop up the mess.

"I've left messages since six this morning and no one has gotten back to me," Dan Reed shouted at the sisters, and all conversation in the café quieted, just as it had when Eli had disrupted their lunch a week before.

Angelica heaved a sigh and looked pained, but Tricia raised an eyebrow and shrugged, content to let her sister handle the bully.

"Dan, you know the Chamber has no clerical help as of yet. The presidency is an unpaid, part-time job with absolutely no perks."

"As there are two of you, I'd have thought *one* of you could be bothered to check voice mail once in a while."

"We do. *After* our own business hours. Now, what is it you need to have answered that's so dire you couldn't have waited until tomorrow morning for a callback?"

Dan's face crumpled into a vicious sneer. "What in God's name are you doing, *woman*"—he practically spat the last word—"to fulfill Eli Meier's dying wish to bring in more booksellers to Stoneham?"

"It was hardly his dying wish," Tricia pointed out. "That is, of course, unless you think he killed himself."

Dan turned a murderous gaze on her and Tricia remembered the man's wife's tearstained cheeks and how he'd driven her to the brink of divorce because of his bullying nature, and suddenly she wished she hadn't spoken to further antagonize the man.

"You shut up!" Dan growled.

"Don't you talk to my sister like that," Angelica snapped, rising. It was a pity she'd given up wearing stiletto heels because she was at least three inches shorter than Dan. Still, she was an imposing figure when her ire was aroused.

Dan took a step back.

"We are looking into every possible way to bring in new booksellers and will fully update you *and* the rest of the organization at our next monthly meeting. Can I count on *your* being there to hear our report?" she asked pointedly, never raising her voice even a halftone.

"Well, yeah," he answered, backpedaling.

"Fine. Now, would you mind letting me eat my lunch in peace where I will also be discussing Chamber news with my co-president, all to the benefit of our membership?"

"Well, I guess so," Dan said.

Maybe Nadine should stand up to him a little more, Tricia thought, because he sure backed down quickly enough. Then again, he'd been abusing his wife—at least verbally—for years. Like water dripping on a stone, that kind of treatment had worn her down.

Dan hadn't moved, so Angelica raised her arm and waved her hand as though to shoo him away before she sat down and turned to Tricia. "Now, where were we before we were so rudely interrupted?"

"About to order lunch," Molly the waitress said, creeping up from behind Dan, order pad in hand, coming in late for the rescue.

"I'll have the fish taco," Angelica said as Dan inched away.

"Make that two," Tricia echoed, watching as Dan backed his way to the exit.

"Coming right up," Molly said, and turned to go to the kitchen.

Once the door closed on Dan's back, the murmur of voices could be heard once again.

"What is it with people—men," Angelica clarified, "interrupting us at lunch?"

"Just the crappy ones," Tricia pointed out. She lowered her voice. "And speaking of crappy, I spoke to Dan's wife again this morning."

"Oh? I didn't know he had one."

"I've met her while on my morning walk. I've spoken to her a few times."

"What did she have to say about her less-than-charming husband?"

"That Dan was Eli Meier's best customer."

Angelica shrugged. "That doesn't surprise me. People who believe in conspiracy theories often feel like victims, and not getting his way makes Dan feel like a victim."

"Well, you sure shut him down."

"I've had far too much practice in that regard," Angelica said, sounding just a tad weary of it.

"And speaking of Eli, I got another walk-through of his store this morning."

"Yes, I heard it was being cleared. Did you find anything that resembled a journal?"

Tricia shook her head. "You would have been the first to know. Speaking of which, have you spoken to Ian about the missing manuscript?"

Angelia looked away. "It may have slipped my mind."

"Why don't you want to tell him?"

"I don't feel comfortable being the one to break the news. Why don't you do it?"

"Because I only heard about it thirdhand." She glared at her sister. "Do you want me to tell him?"

"Well, no. It's my responsibility, I suppose."

"Or you could just text Artemis and have *him* call Ian, that way it isn't your responsibility at all."

Angelica sighed. "Okay. I'll get around to it."

"See that you do—and sooner rather than later."

"Yes, Mother," Angelica grated.

"And don't you dare call me *Mother*," Tricia snapped. Although she and her mother had made some kind of peace, they would never be close. And Tricia thought of herself as being a much kinder person than the woman who'd given her life. She doubted Angelica would argue about that, either.

Angelica didn't acknowledge the rebuke and picked up her water glass, taking a sip.

Molly arrived in record time with their entrées, setting the plates before the sisters. "*Bon appétit.*"

Tricia looked down at her lunch, grateful it was a small taco with a few blue corn chips, a small container of sweet salsa, and a little dab of guacamole on the side. After their encounter with Dan, her appetite had certainly waned.

Angelica shook her napkin over her lap before picking up a chip and dunking it into the salsa. "The word is you toured Ian's apartment before you came here."

There really *were* no secrets in Stoneham.

"Who told you that?" Tricia demanded.

"June. Who got it from Brittney over at the Happy Domestic. At least, they assume you toured it. You were in there for just about an hour."

Tricia's cheeks burned. "I swear, there's a whole spy network here on Main Street. No one has *any* privacy." Which was why Tricia found it astounding that Angelica had been able to keep her Nigela Ricita persona relatively quiet.

"Why didn't you mention it to me?" Angelica asked.

"We've had so many other more pertinent things to talk about it didn't seem important."

Angelica scowled, apparently unhappy with that answer. "So, what's Ian's apartment like? Did you check out the bedroom?" she asked coyly.

"Yes, it was a part of the scheduled tour. It's small but comfortable."

Angelica waggled her eyebrows. "Did you try out the bed?"

"No. And it's rude of you to ask, anyway."

Angelica shrugged. "I was just trying to show you how much interest I have in your daily life."

"I cleaned the toilet in my apartment this morning, did you want to know about that, too?"

Angelica glowered at her sister.

"If you must know, Ian asked me there to help him figure out how to properly outfit the place."

"I thought it came furnished."

"For short-term stays. Not for someone who wants to heat up a pot of sauce to go with their spaghetti." Tricia savagely bit into her taco. It tasted great.

"Do you have the time to help right now?"

Tricia chewed and swallowed. "Not really. I suggested what he might get from the dollar store and said I'd get Pixie looking at her estate sales this weekend for the larger things."

"If anyone can sniff out a bargain, it's Pixie," Angelica remarked.

Tricia nodded. She picked at her chips, realizing that so much had already happened that day that she felt suddenly exhausted—and the day was only just half over.

She let Angelica take the conversational lead for the rest of the meal. It wasn't often that she'd be eager to cut short her lunch dates with her sister. That day was one of those rarities.

Ian McDonald was an enigma. He seemed to vacillate between friend and foe and Tricia wondered if that was a trait most lawmen displayed. If he showed the same tendencies as his predecessor, then he'd never be more than an acquaintance . . . and why would she even think he could be more?

The idea was unsettling. After all, what was wrong with just being a friend to a person of the opposite sex? Why did Angelica and Pixie seem to want to push her into what might be yet another doomed relationship? After what she'd experienced with Harry Tyler, Christopher Benson, Russ Smith, and Grant Baker, Tricia felt the need to protect her heart. For the most part, the men in her life hadn't seen the need.

"Time to go back to work!" Angelica said cheerfully, disrupting Tricia's reverie. She'd lost all track of time.

Molly was already clearing away their dishes.

Tricia grabbed her coat. "Thanks for lunch. It's my turn at the stove tonight."

"Maybe you won't be so distracted," Angelica said, rising from her seat.

"Maybe," Tricia said, but that was only if the rest of her day didn't turn to crap.

TWENTY-FOUR

 Upon entering Haven't Got a Clue, Tricia asked Pixie if she'd be okay helping the village's new police chief to outfit his apartment. Pixie did not look thrilled. Tricia had forgotten her aversion to men in blue.

"But do you think you could help him out?"

"Would I actually have to, you know, talk to him?" Pixie asked, sounding apprehensive. "Could I just text him and then he could come here to pick up whatever I find?"

"I think he'd find that satisfactory."

Pixie heaved a sigh of relief. "Okay then. I'll do it." She said the words, but the trepidation in her voice was evident.

"I'll give the chief your number and he can send you a list."

"Fine." And with that, Pixie found something else to do to end the conversation.

The rest of the afternoon dragged, making Tricia's feeling of exhaustion multiply exponentially, and her head began to pound. She rarely got headaches, but this one was a doozy. There was no way she could face a happy hour of martinis and small talk. So when she closed the shop for the day, she texted Angelica, begged off their usual dinner, promising to host her sister the next evening, and went straight upstairs and crashed on her bed, falling asleep almost immediately.

It was nearly two in the morning when Tricia awoke, feeling better, and decided to take a hot bath, knowing that afterward she'd fall right back into bed and sleep until the alarm went off. It was a plan that worked to perfection.

Since she hadn't had anything to eat since lunch the day before, Tricia got up, fed her cat, and headed out on her walk, at the end of which, she decided to treat herself to breakfast out. That meant patronizing the Bookshelf Diner, but she wanted to check out where Nadine worked.

Hildy, who'd been the morning-shift waitress ever since Tricia came to Stoneham, picked up a menu and led her to a booth in the middle of the diner. "Haven't seen you in forever, Tricia," she quipped.

"I've been watching my calories," Tricia lied. The last time she'd dined in the place had been with the former chief of police. She didn't like to revisit that time.

"Will you start off with coffee?" Hildy asked, placing the plastic-covered menu on the table within Tricia's reach.

"Yes, please."

Hildy nodded and set off for the coffee urn behind the counter.

Tricia glanced at the menu. She hadn't had French toast in forever. When Hildy returned with the pot, she ordered it with a side of bacon. "Is Nadine around?" she asked.

"Who?"

"Nadine. She's married to Dan."

"Oh, you mean Nan. Lately, she's been taking a break around now."

"What's her job?"

"She's the cook." Hildy shook her head. "Tough job behind that stove all day. I sure wouldn't want it."

"Then who's in the kitchen right now?"

"Her assistant, Jeremy. Don't worry. It's pretty hard to screw up French toast."

"Where's Dan?" Tricia asked.

Hildy rolled her eyes. "Probably in the office scrolling

through his social media accounts. He likes to keep up with what's happening in the world. Or at least what he *thinks* is happening in the world."

"I understand he's interested in 'alternative facts,'" Tricia said.

"That's putting it mildly. He likes to pontificate to all of us on all his latest discoveries. I hear, but I don't necessarily listen."

"And the rest of the staff?" Tricia asked.

Hildy shrugged.

"How about the customers?" Tricia tried again.

"Dan's got his fans. I'll put your order in. It won't take long," Hildy said, apparently eager to move on from the conversation.

"Thanks."

Hildy gave a nod and started for the kitchen.

Tricia wished she'd brought along something to read, but then she hadn't planned on a sugar-and-starch-filled fatty breakfast when she'd left her home, either. With no distractions, it gave her time to think. Why hadn't Nadine introduced herself as Nan when obviously it was the familiar form of the name that the staff at the diner knew her by? If she got the chance, Tricia decided she'd ask. Would she catch Nadine—or Nan—in the village square that morning?

She'd just have to wait and see.

As it turned out, Nadine had already left the square—if, indeed she'd been there at all that morning—by the time Tricia finished her breakfast and walk. It was later than she'd thought, and Haven't Got a Clue had already been open for more than a quarter of an hour when she returned to the shop.

Tricia entered the building, removed her jacket, and looked around the store. "Good morning," she said.

"Morning, Tricia," Pixie said from behind the cash desk, where she'd settled with a book and a mug of steaming coffee.

"Where's Mr. Everett? Down in the office?"

Pixie shook her head. "It looks like he's AWOL."

Oh, dear.

Tricia glanced at the clock. Mr. Everett was usually early—and *never* late. That he hadn't arrived by ten twenty was not a good sign and Tricia wasn't sure what to do. If she called him directly, would he answer? And if he didn't . . .

She decided to wait for a while before doing anything. Pixie wasn't as eager to do so.

"Polite as he is, you'd think Mr. Everett would call if he was going to be late," she said, craning her neck to look out the display window. Grace had been dropping him off at the door, but Tricia suspected it wouldn't be happening that day.

"I don't know that he'll be back anytime soon," Tricia said quietly.

"Did something happen on Monday after I left?" Pixie asked, concerned—or was she thinking of Tricia's impertinent question directed at her the Friday before and wondering if she'd offended Mr. Everett, too?

Those were Grace's words.

"I'm not sure Mr. Everett would like me to discuss it."

"How bad could it be?" Pixie asked, although her expression betrayed her true feelings.

"Pretty bad. At least for Mr. Everett."

Pixie looked thoughtful, and then it seemed as though a lightbulb went off over her head. "Uh, we were pushing hydration on him pretty heavy. Did he—?"

Tricia's gaze dipped and she nodded.

Pixie looked crestfallen. "Oh, poor Mr. E. He's such a proud man."

"He barricaded himself in the washroom. I'm pretty sure he made it there in time, but with his broken wrist . . ." She didn't feel the need to continue.

Pixie nodded. "Well, why didn't he just ask for help?"

"As you said, he's a proud man."

"It's just a zipper. And he hasn't got anything either of us hasn't seen. And in my case . . ." But then she didn't continue with the sentence. "What do you think we should do—because we *have* to do something."

Discretion was said to be the better part of valor. So instead of calling him directly, Tricia took out her phone and tapped the contact list until she scrolled down to Grace's name, calling her personal number instead of that of the Everett Charitable Foundation. She answered almost immediately.

"Hi, Grace. It's Tricia."

"What can I do for you?" Grace asked, her tone neutral.

"Is everything all right?" Tricia asked tentatively.

"Of course."

"Grace," Tricia said gravely, "Mr. Everett didn't show up for work today."

"Uh, if you remember, he had physical therapy yesterday."

"Did it take a lot out of him?"

"Yes. More than he would have liked."

"Oh, well, I'm sorry to hear that. Shall we look forward to seeing him tomorrow?"

"Perhaps," Grace said succinctly, but something about her tone sounded off.

"Is everything all right?" Tricia asked again.

"Yes. Excuse me, dear, but I have an appointment. I really must go. We'll speak again soon. Good-bye."

Tricia never even got the chance to say *good-bye* before the call ended. She set her phone on the counter and frowned. Grace's words were all perfectly correct. So why did it feel like there was something she *wasn't* saying?

"Well?" Pixie demanded.

Tricia let out a weary breath. "Grace wouldn't say if he's coming back to work tomorrow."

"Damn." Pixie was quiet for a long moment. "Do you think we need to do an intervention?"

"You mean kidnap him and haul him into the store? I hardly think the state employment office would approve."

Pixie shrugged. "It was just a thought." She looked thoughtful. "Mr. E and I have shared a lot of confidences over the years." She thought better of it. "Okay, *I've* shared a lot of confidences with him. I know you've got a different kind of special relationship with him and Grace. Maybe it would be easier for me to talk to him about it. I mean, I was an EMT and let me tell you, someone pissing their pants ain't nothin' compared to what I've seen."

"I hope you won't couch it in quite those terms," Tricia said, appalled.

"I can be diplomatic," Pixie assured her.

Tricia thought it over. Again, was she being cowardly if she allowed Pixie—who hadn't even witnessed Mr. Everett's embarrassment—to talk to him? But Pixie was right. She and Mr. Everett *did* have a different rapport.

"Could you visit him and not mention his little mishap?" Tricia asked sheepishly.

"You mean to see if he brings it up first?"

Tricia nodded.

"Sure. But what if he doesn't want to talk about it?"

Tricia's shoulders slumped. "Then we have to come up with another idea."

"And that would be?" Pixie asked.

"I haven't got a clue."

Tricia frowned. She seemed to be saying that phrase a little too often of late.

TWENTY-FIVE

Between customers, Tricia and Pixie brainstormed ideas, finally deciding that Pixie should pick up a take-out order from Booked for Lunch and surprise Mr. Everett by showing up at his home. She'd take a third order just in case Grace came home for lunch, too. Her presence might actually help resolve the situation. At least, Tricia hoped so.

Around eleven o'clock, Pixie called in her take-out order. Forty-five minutes later, she gathered her coat and purse and paused before the cash desk.

"Take as much time as you need. If you're not back by the time I head out for lunch with Angelica, I'll just close the store," Tricia said.

"Are you sure?" Pixie asked, concerned.

"Hey, at this time of year it's not likely we'll have a crowd beating down our door. It'll be much better for us to reassure Mr. Everett that we're here for him—no matter what it takes."

Pixie nodded. "Okay. Cross your fingers this goes well."

"I'll cross my toes, too," Tricia said.

Because there were no customers during the noon hour, Tricia found herself watching the clock. When Pixie hadn't returned by one thirty, she turned the OPEN sign to CLOSED and locked the shop's door before crossing the street for Booked for Lunch.

As usual, Angelica was already there.

Tricia shrugged out of her jacket and took her seat. Angelica had a notebook in front of her, as well as a gold pen, making notes—she was always doing that.

"Sorry I'm late," Tricia said.

"What's a minute or two?" Angelica said without looking up. She closed her notebook. "What's new?"

"Mr. Everett didn't turn up for work."

"Oh, dear. Just as you feared."

"Pixie went to talk to him. He must not have thrown her out, otherwise she would have been back an hour or more ago."

"Let's hope that's good news."

"And on your end?"

"I had breakfast at the Bookshelf Diner this morning."

"That's not like you."

"I didn't have any dinner last night. I was starved. Anyway, it turns out that Dan Reed's wife is their short-order cook. He always seems to be out front in the diner."

"And this has to do with us because?" Angelica asked.

Tricia leaned in closer and lowered her voice. "I think she's thinking of divorcing him."

"Well, who could blame her? The guy is *not* a shining example of manhood. Are you two friends?"

"No, but . . . I kind of feel sorry for her simply because I've been exposed to her husband on way too many occasions."

Angelica laughed. "You make it sound like he's got a virus."

"There's something wrong with that man, but apparently he has his fans."

"What?" Angelica asked.

Tricia explained about her breakfast at the Bookshelf Diner and speaking with Hildy. "How do you feel about people calling you Ange?" Tricia asked.

"I loathe it. I only allow *you* to call me that because I love you."

"That's what I thought. Nadine introduced herself to me with that name, but it seems everyone at the diner calls her Nan. I wonder if she feels the same as you about it."

"Why don't you ask her."

"I will."

Tricia looked for Molly. She wanted to order and get back to Haven't Got a Clue to hear what Pixie had to report. "Do you know what the specials are today?"

"The soup is chicken corn chowder. The sandwich is egg salad. We're trying out a different lemonade, it's a little more tart than what we've sold in the past."

"Sounds like a totally yellow lunch."

"It's spring," Angelica said mildly.

"I'm going for it as soon as Molly shows up. I want to get back to my store ASAP."

"Have you and Pixie patched things up yet?"

"Well, we haven't spoken about it, but things seem to be back to normal."

Angelica shook her head. "If you don't address it, it's going to fester, and then one day—*pow*! It'll blow up in your face—and it could destroy your friendship with Pixie."

"It'll happen," Tricia assured her sister, not quite sure she believed it but she didn't offer a timeline because Molly arrived and they ordered.

"I heard Becca's already finished clearing out the Inner Light," Angelica mentioned once their meals had arrived.

"The guys who did it seemed extremely good at their jobs. I wish I could have found those manuscripts."

"Why? So the man could justify his actions before he met his maker?"

"Maybe he was going to apologize."

Angelica didn't look convinced.

"Did you contact Ian yet about the possibility of a missing manuscript?" Tricia asked.

"Not exactly," Angelica said, and sampled her soup. "Mmm, this is good!"

"Don't change the subject," Tricia chided her.

"I'll get around to it."

"When?" Tricia pressed. "It's already been two days."

"Soon."

"This afternoon?" Tricia pressed.

Angelica spooned up more soup and blew on it to cool it. "Maybe."

Tricia wasn't sure she believed her.

Pixie had already returned and reopened the store by the time Tricia arrived back at Haven't Got a Clue. Fortunately for the shop, she was with a customer who seemed to want a complete history of the mystery genre and was prepared to listen at length. Of course, Pixie was just as much an expert as Tricia or Mr. Everett and she loved to pontificate, but after ten or so minutes, she seemed to sense Tricia's exasperation and cut short her lecture. Still, the woman bought almost a hundred dollars' worth of merchandise, and Tricia was only too happy to wrap it while Pixie rang up the sale. It was hard to remain patient until the customer was out the door.

"Well, what happened with Mr. Everett?" Tricia asked anxiously.

Pixie sighed. "I *think* I convinced him to come to work tomorrow. I may have pulled a bit of a guilt trip on him. Telling him how much we *really* need him."

"Well, we do."

"He would prefer no mention was *ever* made again of his dilemma."

"That's a given. But what can we do to make sure we don't have a replay of the problem?"

"Mr. E would prefer to take several breaks a day and go visit Grace across the street so she can help him with whatever he needs."

"Well, that works on Fridays when she's at her office, but what about the weekend when she's off work?"

"We discussed it."

"Oh, then Grace *was* there, too?"

"Yes, and she loved Tommy's soup. So did I, come to think of it."

"And will Grace come to Haven't Got a Clue to assist him on the weekends?"

Pixie nodded. "That way she can run errands and he can keep working. He made a point of saying just how important it is to him to keep his job here."

"Like you, he's a valued member of the team."

Pixie looked like she wanted to say something—perhaps question that statement after their painful discussion the week before—but then the moment passed.

The bell over the door rang and another customer entered the store. "Hi, I'm Pixie and this is Tricia. Let us know if you need any help finding a title or want a recommendation."

The man gave a brief salute and turned to peruse the shelves.

The door opened again, but instead of a customer, Becca Chandler strode in, looking as self-assured as ever. "Hello, Tricia!" she called amiably. For some reason, that tone made Tricia's hackles rise. But she gritted her teeth and smiled anyway. She owed Becca for letting her go through the Inner Light one last time.

"What's up?"

"I just happened to be passing by and thought I'd drop in." She looked around the shop. She'd already made her disdain for the written word quite apparent and probably thought genre fiction to be the lowest of the low. "Did you find whatever you were looking for in the Inner Light the other day?"

"Uh, no."

"And just what *were* you looking for? Evidence of Meier's involvement with the Crimson Nine?"

"That's it exactly," Tricia said, although until word about the manuscript—or lack thereof—came out, she wasn't about to discuss the topic in detail. "Is his stock all snug in a storage unit?"

"I paid to store it until May thirty-first. After that, I'll sell the contents to the highest bidder."

Knowing how decrepit and dated most of the stock was, Tricia doubted Becca would break even.

"How's your empire-building going?" Tricia asked.

Becca smiled sweetly. "Wonderful! Now that the Inner Light is all cleared out, I've had my contractor in. Rick Lavoy is using him as well, so I'll get the building back up to code, and then it's up to Rick to pull off the changes he wants to make for his tasting room." Tricia had had the same kind of deal with Bob Kelly when she'd first leased the building that held her shop and home.

Becca sighed and looked out the window. "I just wish Stoneham was a little more . . ."

"Cosmopolitan?" Tricia ventured.

"Well, yes. But I suppose I'll eventually get used to having to make do with a more simple life."

"What *is* your attraction to Stoneham?" Tricia asked. "Was it just because Gene"—Becca's ex-husband—"lived here? If it doesn't suit you, why don't you just go home?"

"To an empty mansion? Well, for one thing, it's damn lonely. All those empty rooms. All that empty time." Becca shook her head. "Plus it was a security nightmare. You have no idea how many people hate me for winning so much over the years—including some of the players I bested because my talent was far greater than theirs."

And did she let them know it, too?

"I find my condo in Milford to be a snug haven," she continued. "I don't have to employ a fleet of house- and groundskeepers, either. Despite the drawbacks, I feel so much safer in a smaller environment."

Tricia pitied those who'd lost their jobs when she'd made the move. Then again, whoever bought the mansion would need to hire as many people to maintain that kind of excess. But Tricia could also understand Becca's desire to have more control over the space in which she lived. Did she have to rent additional storage space for her decades' worth of trophies and other awards?

"Have you been stalked?" Tricia asked. She *had* been stalked and it had been a debilitating experience.

"Are you kidding? I can't count the number of trolls who've threatened me over the life of my career—and even after. Crazies who saw me on TV and read interviews and believe I should be accessible to them twenty-four/seven. Men—and sometimes women—who sought to be my lover. Once you're a public figure, a certain portion of the public thinks you belong to them. That there should be no boundaries. That they *own* you. Believe me, coming to small villages like Stoneham and Milford has been a godsend."

Although Tricia had never experienced it herself, she did appreciate the difficulties of celebrity.

"Well, what can I do for you today?" Tricia asked, figuring there had to be some kind of motive for the visit.

"I understand Ginny Barbero used to work for you."

"Yes. She was my first assistant manager."

"And you let her go because . . . ?" Becca asked.

"No! She was offered a better opportunity—a chance to manage the Happy Domestic."

"Didn't you at least try to keep her?" Becca asked, sounding rather proprietary.

"You mean offer her more money to stay?"

Becca nodded.

"No, because I knew she'd have an opportunity to grow while managing a store of her own. I taught her what I knew, set her free, and she soared."

Becca frowned. "But then she married the man in charge of Nigela Ricita Associates and was made their marketing guru, which sounds like pure nepotism."

"That's *not* the case. Ginny has excelled in the job."

"When we played tennis last fall, she told me she didn't even have a college degree."

"That's true. But Ginny has used her innate smarts and what she's learned in the retail world to help her succeed." Tricia scrutinized Becca's bland expression. "Why are you asking about her?"

Becca shrugged. "I was remembering that she was a

half-decent tennis player. I just wondered what else she was half-decent at."

As far as Tricia was concerned, Ginny was far better than half-decent at everything she chose to do.

"Ginny's an excellent employee, a dedicated mom, and a loyal and trustworthy friend. Again, why are you asking?" Tricia pressed.

Becca gave a meager shrug. "I'm bored. I haven't made a lot of friends in this area. I thought I might ask her out to lunch. We got along pretty well last fall."

Yeah, but Ginny had also mentioned how Becca had castigated her as being an inferior tennis player despite the fact she'd given the former sport-of-kings star a run for her money on a couple of occasions. That kind of criticism wasn't likely to engender a positive response.

"I've read of studies that say the older one gets the harder it is to make friends," Tricia said.

"They aren't wrong," Becca agreed. "From all I've heard, you aren't overwhelmed when it comes to friendship, either. They say you and your sister are practically joined at the hip. That you prefer her company to almost everyone else."

Tricia was taken aback. Just who was saying such things? Not that it wasn't true. She did depend on Angelica—much more in adulthood than they had ever done in their childhoods.

"I assume you never had a sibling," Tricia countered.

"No. I was an only child. A child who was schooled at an early age to learn to love the game of tennis—even if it wasn't my own idea."

Well, then both women might have shared a similar unhappy childhood. Still, Tricia didn't think she owed Becca an explanation when it came to her past or present relationship with Angelica.

Thankfully, Pixie and their single customer approached the cash desk laden with several books each.

"If you'll excuse me," Tricia told Becca, "but I need to get back to work."

Becca's lips flattened and she looked distinctly unhappy.

"We'll talk again soon. Perhaps we could do lunch once again."

"I'd love it," Tricia lied. "Call me when you've got an opening in your schedule."

"I'll do that," Becca said, and gave Tricia a wan smile. Then she turned and sauntered toward the exit. The bell over the door jingled as she left the building.

Tricia rang up the customer's order, and Pixie carefully placed each book in the brown paper bag with string handles that sported the store's logo printed in green.

"Thanks for shopping with us," Tricia said as the man headed for the exit.

"Come back soon," Pixie encouraged him. Once the door closed, Pixie turned to Tricia. "I heard some of what that woman said about Ginny. What do you think she really wanted?"

Tricia looked toward the door where Becca had disappeared just a minute or two before. "I have no idea." And to be honest, it worried her.

TWENTY-SIX

As Tricia was hosting happy hour and dinner that evening, she left her shop an hour early to get things prepared. Pixie texted that she was locking up and that Angelica had just entered so Tricia opened the door to the stairwell to await her sister's arrival. Miss Marple stationed herself at the top of the stairs, giving Angelica a much more quiet reception than Tricia received from Sarge.

"Hello!" Angelica called.

"In the kitchen," Tricia replied.

Angelica had changed out of her business attire and wore a pink jogging outfit, complete with her sparkling sequined sneakers and her hair caught up in a short ponytail.

"Don't you look sweet," Tricia said, and she removed the chilled glasses from the refrigerator.

"I do." Angelica took a seat at the breakfast bar. "I can't believe I wore heels for all those years. I feel much freer in flats."

"I tried to tell you so—for years," Tricia reminded her.

"Yes, you did. I should *always* listen to you. And I'm particularly interested in hearing what happened with Pixie and Mr. Everett this afternoon."

"She says he's coming back to work tomorrow. I'm going to cross my fingers and hope really hard."

"Is that it?" Angelica asked, sounding disappointed.

"He doesn't want any talk of what happened and we're going to honor his request."

Angelica nodded and sighed.

"However, that wasn't the most interesting thing to occur," Tricia teased.

"Oh?"

Tricia opened the door to the oven and removed a tray.

"Ooh. Grandma's cheese straws?" Angelica gushed.

"Hopefully they'll taste just like she used to make them."

"I'm so liking these gastronomic visits to yesteryear with Grandma's treats. I need to start getting Sofia to help me in the kitchen. I want her to have the same happy memories."

"A toddler in the kitchen? Is that a good idea?" Tricia said, dumping the straws onto a platter. The recipe called for them to fully cool, but she didn't think they could wait that long.

"She could stir dry ingredients and maybe dump in some wet ones if I measured them into little ramekins first."

She probably could, at that.

Tricia placed the pitcher and glasses and the platter on a silver tray and carried them into the living room. "I've got something bigger to tell you—or perhaps warn you about."

"That sounds ominous," Angelica said as she followed Tricia to the seating area.

Tricia poured their drinks and passed a glass to Angelica.

"What should we drink to?"

"Our staffs."

Angelica blinked. "That's an odd toast." Nevertheless, they clinked glasses. Angelica sipped her drink and smiled. "Just as good as I make them."

"I learned from the best," Tricia agreed.

Angelica sat back in her chair. "Now, explain what you mean about my staff."

"I got a visit from Becca Chandler this afternoon."

"Oh, that must have been fun," Angelica deadpanned.

"You'd better watch out. I think she aims to poach your employees—and one in particular."

"Who?"

"Ginny."

Angelica's mouth dropped. "Why?"

"She came in asking a lot of questions about her background, her education, et cetera."

Angelica took a gulp of her drink, her expression hardening. "Ginny would never leave me."

"I agree—under normal circumstances. But what if Becca makes her an offer she couldn't—or wouldn't want to—refuse?"

"Like what?"

"I don't know. But I don't trust that woman as far as I can spit—and I can't spit far."

Angelica reached for a cheese straw and sat back in her chair, looking decidedly unhappy. Tricia sipped her drink. "I'm having lunch with Ginny tomorrow afternoon at the new house. I could ask if she's heard from Becca."

"Please don't. I don't want her to think . . ." But then she didn't finish the sentence.

Tricia eyed her sister. "What *would* you do if Ginny left Nigela Ricita Associates?"

"You mean besides cry?" Angelica crunched her cheese straw, chewed, and swallowed. "I don't know. I just don't know."

Tricia wanted to welcome Mr. Everett back the next morning with a special treat. He wasn't a fussy man and was always grateful for anything Tricia baked (or bought) as a treat for her staff or customers. So she got up early and baked some carrot cake muffins, based on Angelica's famous carrot cake recipe with maple icing, before she left for her morning walk.

The park bench where Tricia had found Nadine Reed on several occasions was empty once again. Perhaps it was because Tricia had started out late that morning. Or . . . had her husband found out she'd been fraternizing with the enemy? Tricia didn't consider him to be an enemy, but Dan might have thought *she* was an enemy by proxy since he did nothing but disparage Angelica and her dining establishments whenever he had an audience.

Tricia decided to wait for a few minutes just in case Nadine was late, and sat down on the bench. She also wished she'd stopped to pick up Sarge before taking a walk. She'd let the little guy down of late by not taking him on her daily walk as they both enjoyed each other's company.

She glanced at her watch. She'd give Nadine another few minutes.

Down the sidewalk, a tall, dark-haired boy walked beside an energetic beagle. Tricia had a soft spot in her heart for the breed after her encounter with the Pets-A-Plenty Animal Rescue. On that frosty April morning, the boy wore jeans and a light jacket that was unzipped to reveal a Godzilla T-shirt.

The boy drew closer, letting the retractable leash go so that the dog could run ahead a ways. It trotted right up to Tricia.

"Hello, little guy." She looked up at the boy. "What's his name?"

"Indy. You know, like Indiana Jones."

"He's an archaeologist?" Tricia asked, amused.

The boy laughed. "No! He's just Indy."

Tricia held out her hand for the dog to sniff it. He did, sat down, and then offered his paw to shake.

She shook.

"My name's Tricia," she offered.

"I'm Ian."

"Really? Did you know Stoneham's new chief of police is named Ian?"

"Wow—that's cool. I've never met anyone with the same name as me before. It's kind of rare."

Not in Ireland.

"Would you like to meet him?"

"Cool," he repeated.

"Do you know where the police station is on Main Street?"

"Everybody does."

"Drop in and tell him Tricia sent you. I'm sure he'd love to meet you, too."

"Do you think he's there now?"

Tricia glanced at her watch again. "He should be."

"Crap. I have to drop Indy off at home and get to school. But I could go after."

"I could text the chief and find out if he'll be there later," Tricia offered.

"Go for it." Ian told her what time he got out of class. While Tricia texted, young Ian let Indy wander around the grass for a while to have a good sniff. Within a minute, Tricia was rewarded with a reply.

"It's all set. Unless something comes up, he'll be waiting for you in his office. He'll even give you a tour of the station."

"Awesome! Thanks, book lady."

"How did you know I sell books?"

"Lots of ladies sell books here in Stoneham." Young Ian reeled the dog in. "I gotta get to school. Thanks for setting me up with the chief."

"You're welcome."

"See ya!" the boy called cheerfully, and started back down the sidewalk once again.

Nice kid, Tricia thought. He wasn't that much younger than Edward Dowding, but a few years made a vast difference in maturity. Then again, Edward hadn't shown much maturity by his explosive temper and his near stalking of Pixie.

Tricia gave Nadine another five minutes before she rose from the bench and started off on her walk once again. What could have happened to the woman? It bothered her that she hadn't shown up. Did that mean Dan was punishing her for dereliction of duty during the Bookshelf Diner's breakfast rush? But then Hildy the waitress had said Dan was preoccupied with his fans, no doubt other conspiracy theorists.

Nadine was the least of her worries. If Mr. Everett had a change of heart and didn't show up for work, Tricia was tempted to do just what Pixie had proposed: kidnap him and bring him back to Haven't Got a Clue. It was a fun thought, but not practical. And Tricia found herself crossing her fingers for the rest of her walk.

It was only nine twenty when Tricia returned to her store to find Edward standing outside the door, his arms wrapped around his chest to ward off the cold. The jacket he wore was better suited for a cool summer day than a raw April morning.

"What are you doing here? I thought you were going to call before you came back to Stoneham."

"*You* decided I should call," he remarked.

Yes, she had.

Tricia unlocked and entered her store with Edward right behind her. "Pixie told me you did well picking out items not only for Haven't Got a Clue, but the Cookery and the Happy Domestic," she said, and shrugged out of her jacket, placing it on the glass case.

Edward practically beamed. "Thanks. Do you think maybe you could put in a good word for me with any of the other businesses in the village?"

"I don't know," Tricia said honestly. "I'm sorry, but I can't help but think back to my—and Pixie's—first encounter with you."

A blush of what Tricia hoped was shame—not anger—rose to color Edward's cheeks. "I was having a bad day," the young man defended himself.

"And is that how you typically react on a bad day?"

Edward hesitated before answering. "It's something I've struggled with . . . but not for the reasons you might suspect."

Tricia waited for him to elaborate. When he didn't explain, she tried again, wondering if testing him might bring back the surly young man she'd first encountered.

She took the chance.

"I can't in good conscience recommend you to anyone until I'm sure that side of your personality won't explode to frighten or intimidate my fellow merchants, whom I also consider to be friends—or at least fond acquaintances."

Edward nodded. "I can see that. But I wasn't really angry at Ms. Pixie because she wouldn't buy those crappy books I offered her."

"And what made you act like a deranged soul?" Tricia asked, crossing her arms over her chest. She hoped he could read her body language and figure out that she wasn't about to budge.

Edward's gaze dipped. "Because . . . because she didn't recognize me."

"And why should she? Had you ever met before?"

"Not in nineteen years. You see, I'm her biological son."

Tricia blinked. "Excuse me?"

"Ms. Poe is my mother. The woman who gave me up. I spent my entire childhood in foster homes. Terrible places. Homes where all I meant to the people there was a steady income. Money that was almost never spent on me," he said bitterly.

Despite the surprise of his announcement, Tricia felt she had to defend her employee and friend. "Did it ever occur to you that what Pixie did was done out of love, knowing she couldn't properly take care of you?"

"Not really," the young man answered, and probably honestly.

Tricia felt umbrage on Pixie's behalf. "How could you make such a judgment without knowing her circumstances at the time of your birth?"

"You mean because she was just a common whore?"

It was Tricia's cheeks that turned crimson at hearing that description.

"Why did you come to Stoneham?" she asked, her voice cold. "After many years of struggle, Pixie has worked damned hard to turn her life around. She's got a good job, a stable marriage, and she doesn't need someone to intrude on that life with an intent to destroy it."

"That's not why I tracked her down."

"Then why did you come here?" Tricia demanded.

"I wanted to meet her."

"And?"

"She's not what I expected," Edward admitted. "She's actually a pretty cool lady."

"You've got that right. She *is* a lady. And I don't ever want to hear you—or anyone else—use that dreadful word to describe her past life. Because that's what it is—her past."

"How generous of you to cut her such slack," Edward said just a tad snidely.

A flame flickered amid Tricia's smoldering anger. "If you thought disparaging my assistant manager was the way to get a job recommendation, you are sadly mistaken, mister. I'd appreciate it if you'd leave my store. Now!"

Edward appeared to think over her request and for a tense moment, Tricia thought he might revert to his angry persona. But then he turned and left the building without a word.

He didn't even slam the door.

TWENTY-SEVEN

With only minutes to spare before her employees showed up for work, a rattled Tricia banged around the shop, getting ready for the day's customers. The coffee was made, and the muffins were waiting under a domed cake plate. If only she could get her hands to stop shaking—she was that angry with Edward Dowding. And no way was she going to bring up his visit to Pixie, but Edward's announcement did explain a lot when it came to Pixie's strained silences and uncomfortable looks during the previous days.

The shop door opened, the little bell ringing cheerfully, and Pixie and Mr. Everett arrived together. "How cool is this that we ran into each other on the sidewalk?" Pixie called brightly. However, Mr. Everett's gaze was fixed on the carpet.

Tricia took a couple of calming breaths before speaking. "Good morning. How are you guys?"

Mr. Everett didn't look up. "Very well, thank you," he said quietly.

Pixie removed her coat, slinging it on the cash desk. "I'm walking on air," she gushed.

She wouldn't be if she knew that Edward had left the premises only minutes before—or what he'd revealed to Tricia.

"I made some carrot cake muffins. Shall we sit down and have some?" Tricia asked.

"I would like that very much," Mr. Everett said.

"I made them especially for you."

"You're too kind."

"Nonsense. Would you like coffee?"

"None for me, thank you," Mr. Everett said.

"I could go for a cup," Pixie said. "I'll pour."

"Thanks." Meanwhile, Tricia and Mr. Everett selected muffins, setting them down on paper plates before heading for the reader's nook.

"Shall we sit?" Tricia asked Mr. Everett.

"Yes, thank you," he said, and the two of them took their usual seats. As Mr. Everett had requested that the incident of days before shouldn't be mentioned, Tricia felt bound by that request. But what *could* they talk about to break the ice? She waited for Pixie to arrive with their coffees.

"I'm having lunch with Ginny today at her new house," Tricia began.

"That's nice," Pixie said. "Those last pictures you showed me were wonderful. I can't wait to see how she decorated, although if it was me, I'd have chosen art deco."

Ginny's rebuilt house was to be more French country in style. Very relaxed. "She isn't getting around all that much and will probably be stuck at home for the next couple of months."

"Babies tend to do that to a mom," Pixie said, and laughed before peeling the wrapper from her muffin and taking a bite.

Pixie hadn't been homebound with Edward but Tricia wasn't about to bring up her encounter with him, at least not yet.

"I promised I'd get her some of that wonderful beeswax lip balm from the Bee's Knees. Do you mind if I run over after we finish here and get it for her?"

"Not a bit. We've got everything covered, haven't we, Mr. E?"

"Indeed we do," he said, sounding more like his old self.

"Great."

The three of them chatted for another ten minutes, finishing their muffins and coffee before Tricia retrieved her jacket from the back of the shop and grabbed her purse from under the cash desk. "I'll be back in a few minutes."

"We'll be here," Pixie said.

Tricia hurried down the sidewalk and entered the Bee's Knees. As she had hoped, it was Larry Harvick who stood behind the register taking care of the shop's only customer, who seemed to have purchased a number of items if the large shopping bag Harvick handed her was any indication. "Come back anytime," he said with a smile, and the woman nodded and headed for the door. Tricia stepped up to the register.

"Hey, Tricia. What can I do for you today?"

"I stopped in to get some lip balm for my niece. She's out on maternity leave and I didn't want her to have to struggle with a two-year-old and a newborn to come to your shop to get some."

"You're a nice aunt." A cardboard display stood next to the register. "How many do you want?"

"I'll take three."

Harvick laughed. "The poor woman must have a really bad case of chapped lips."

"Only two of them are for her. My own tube is getting pretty low."

Harvick deposited them into a small paper bag with the shop's logo. "Was there anything else?"

She did have another reason to be there, after all.

"Well, I was wondering what you thought about the Board of Selectmen hiring Ian McDonald as the village's new chief of police."

Harvick shrugged. "Doesn't bother me, although the rank and file seem pretty upset about it."

"Yes, I heard some of them think someone more local should have been hired."

Harvick met her gaze. "You mean someone like me?"

"Well, I did hear your name bandied about."

He nodded. "Yeah, they asked me if I wanted to interview for the job. I gave them an emphatic *no!*"

"And why was that?"

"There's a reason I retired from the county Sheriff's Department."

"And that is?"

"I was ready to move on. I found beekeeping to be a lot less stressful than police work. Eileen"—his wife—"had never really approved of me being a deputy. When I mentioned retiring, she couldn't have been happier. And now we have this business to keep us occupied. We get to spend a lot more time together on a project we both enjoy."

"I'm glad to hear you say that. How's the business doing?"

"It's been lean since the holidays," he admitted, "but web sales have kept us reasonably afloat. Eileen is better at managing that end of the business so she takes care of processing the orders and shipping them out and I'm more the face of the retail operation. It's worked out well. And if what everyone says is true, we'll have a great summer of sales and won't be as stressed next winter. For me, I'm hoping we can expand to a bigger footprint. This place is cozy, but if we get more than three or four customers in here, it feels like a sardine can."

Tricia nodded. Her store's footprint was at least three times bigger than the Bee's Knees'.

"Do you have any insights into Eli Meier's murder?" Tricia asked, hoping she sounded innocent, and fully knowing that Harvick was aware of her reputation as an amateur sleuth and the village jinx.

He shook his head. "The news media tried to interview me, but I didn't have anything to say to them. What did I know about the guy? That he was a felon on the run was news to all of us. I've heard what the locals are saying at the Dog-Eared Page, and I've spoken to Chief McDonald, but you have to remember, I was never a detective for the Sheriff's Department. I was only ever a patrol officer."

But surely he had to have *some* opinions. Tricia asked.

"Meier—or Martin—was an unpleasant man with a nasty past. His present life was hardly better. He ticked one person off one too many times, and that's the person who killed him."

Talk about oversimplifying the situation.

Tricia was pretty sure that was all she was going to get out of Larry Harvick. She completed her transaction. He handed her the small paper bag.

"If I might offer a bit of unsolicited advice," he began, and then continued before Tricia could give an answer. "Leave the detection work to Chief McDonald. That's what he gets paid for."

"I am not detecting."

Harvick raised an eyebrow. "Thanks for stopping in."

Tricia didn't reply and left the shop without a backward glance.

TWENTY-EIGHT

 Ginny's car was parked in the driveway of her grand new home, which looked nothing like her little cottage in the woods. Tricia got out of her Lexus to take in the structure. Of course, she'd seen the plans and then visited often with Angelica as the house was constructed. Acting as the general contractor, Angelica had been on the site more than anyone else. It was her vision, and sometimes Tricia thought Ginny and Antonio may have let her have a little too much control over the project. But that had been *their* decision.

Most of the landscaping had been installed since she'd last seen the house. The sod would be laid before the end of the month. It really was beginning to look like a home.

The front door opened and a very pregnant Ginny called for Tricia to "Come inside, where it's warmer."

"Coming!" Tricia crossed to the other side of the car to retrieve their lunches and hurried to join Ginny.

Once inside the foyer, Tricia looked around at the beautiful marble tile floor and the sparkling chandelier overhead. Angelica had done well. The house was the epitome of good taste—and she'd spent lavishly on the home she'd spent months preparing for her son, daughter-in-law, and grandchildren.

"Wow!"

"Yeah, it is a little overwhelming, isn't it?" Ginny said sadly. "I miss my little cottage, but I think I could get used to living here."

"At least you still have most of the woods."

"We'll have to take out more of the trees for the tennis court, but I think I can live with that, too. You have to promise you'll play with me this summer." She patted her tummy. "It's going to take a lot to get back into shape."

"I don't think I'm up to your standards," Tricia protested.

"Don't be silly. I've seen pictures of your trophies."

"Angelica had far more than me. And where did you see such pictures, anyway?"

"Angelica had some squirreled away."

That was news to Tricia. She hadn't thought anyone in her immediate family had taken snapshots of her awards and trophies. Even she didn't have such photos. She'd have to ask her sister about that.

Ginny eyed the large brown paper bag in Tricia's hand. "Um, is that lunch?" she asked hopefully.

"Oh, I'm sorry. Are you starved?"

"I'm *always* starved, especially since I've been home for *four long days* with not much to do. Come on, I'm dying to show you the kitchen now that it's set up," she said, and waddled off in that direction.

Tricia followed her through the beautiful dining room and into the large white kitchen, with marble counters, where all the appliances were hidden behind doors that matched the white cabinetry. The last time Tricia had seen the room, it had been in a state of chaos. Now it felt clean and completed. Pretty dishes lined the shelves of the cabinets with glass fronts. The utility room beyond was still stacked with boxes. Out of the window that overlooked the patio and spacious backyard, Tricia could see a stack of collapsed cartons.

"You've been busy unpacking."

"You got it."

"You haven't been carrying anything heavy, I hope," Tricia admonished.

Ginny shook her head. "No." She took one of the stools at the combination kitchen island and breakfast bar. "Angelica offered us movers, and I accepted for the larger pieces, but I didn't want someone to arrange our personal stuff." She gave a halfhearted laugh. "Not that much of it is personal. When you've lost everything you own, you don't have much feeling of attachment to the new things you've accumulated. In fact, I'm kind of worried that I may never value anything again, because why should I get attached to things that might be taken away from me. Does that sound weird?"

"No. I had a friend in college who lost her home to fire. She felt the same way. She was determined not to feel owned by possessions ever again. But I know she was sad about losing all her photographs and other personal treasures."

"I'm glad most of our photos are stored in the cloud somewhere. But I worry that something could happen to them, too, which is why I've copied them on a flash drive and have them stored in our safety deposit box. I try to update it once a month. I'm also having the photographer who took our wedding photos put together the same package we bought so we can have an album here at home."

Looking around, Tricia noticed that there were more smoke detectors distributed through the house than she'd ever seen in a residential dwelling. It probably made the family feel safer, despite the fact that they'd lost their home to arson and not an electrical problem or an act of God.

Ginny eyed the paper sack that sat on the island. "What did you bring for lunch?"

"Oh, I'm sorry. You said you were starving."

She unpacked the biodegradable cartons, setting them on the counter. "The soup of the day is vegetable beef. And the sandwich is chicken salad."

"One of my favorites," Ginny said. She got up to get plates and cutlery. "What do you want to drink?"

"Water is fine."

"I could make tea."

"All right," Tricia said, remembering how Ian had quizzed her on whether she'd actually boil the water. But Ginny reached into a cabinet and brought out an electric kettle, filled it, and plugged it in. Next, she reached for several pretty bone china teacups from one of the glass-fronted cabinets.

"My, that's a pretty pattern," Tricia said.

"They were a present from Grace. She seemed almost timid when she offered them to me as a housewarming gift. They were part of a set she received when she was a new bride."

Tricia admired the design of a halo of black lace on a white background and a pink rose. "They're absolutely gorgeous."

"I like them a lot," Ginny said, sounding pleased.

Tricia unpacked the lunch while Ginny made the tea, using loose leaves and an infuser. "I had to learn to make tea the proper way when I ran the Happy Domestic," she explained. "My customers expected me to know all kinds of rituals and homemaking tips. It was fun to learn them—even if I haven't had much of a chance to actually use them myself."

Maybe she'd found that kind of research enjoyable, but there was something about the set of Ginny's mouth and a tightness around her eyes that made Tricia feel uncomfortable.

"Is anything wrong?" she asked as Ginny poured the boiling water into the teapot.

"Well, I wouldn't say wrong. Just . . . odd." She settled a tea cozy over the pot and brought it over to the island. She pulled open what looked like a large cabinet that proved to be the nearly empty refrigerator. She removed a quart container of milk and poured some into a small jug that matched the teacups before returning to the island and taking her seat. "I had a rather strange call just before you arrived."

"Oh? From whom?"

"Becca Chandler."

Tricia's gut tightened at the sound of the name. "What did *she* want?"

"To offer me a job."

Tricia's eyes widened, just as she'd suspected. "Now? When you're nine months pregnant?"

"Yeah, odd timing. But the position doesn't open until the fall, anyway. She wanted to give me a heads-up."

"And what job was she offering?"

"To run her new tennis facility."

"The one that hasn't even broken ground yet," Tricia asked, awed.

"That's the one."

"Did she know you're on maternity leave?"

Ginny nodded. "Word gets around about these things."

It certainly did.

"Are you considering it?"

"Sure, I considered it. For about ten seconds, although . . ." The wistful tone in that one word made Tricia wince. "There's no way I could ever leave NR Associates. I owe Angelica far, far too much for all the breaks she's given me professionally, and the love, respect, and support she's given me personally. We started off on the wrong foot and she could have held that against me, but then she gave me the chance to prove myself." Ginny shook her head. "No, I'm sticking with my job—and I already miss it." Just four days into her leave. "That's why I've spent so much time here at the house. I want to get to know it. To make it a real home for Antonio and Sofia—and our new baby, too. I'll have to show you the nursery. It's absolutely adorable."

No doubt.

"Will you mention the job offer to Angelica?"

"Of course. I'm going to call her as soon as we're done with lunch. I don't want the rumor mill to get started. I spent quite a bit of time with Becca last fall. I can't say I entirely trust her."

And another one who felt that way.

Ginny opened her soup container. "Sorry, but I haven't unpacked all our new everyday china yet. I have no idea where the bowls are, so this is going to have to be it." She gestured to the other end of the kitchen and the utility room beyond.

They unwrapped their sandwiches. "Once we're settled and get a new routine with the baby, we're going to have a big party here for our friends and family, including my staff, and Pixie and Fred, and Tommy and Molly from Booked for Lunch, and the ladies at the *Stoneham Weekly News*, and some of the staff from the Brookview Inn. Wow! Maybe we should have it in June when the weather's fine and we can rent a tent."

Tricia laughed. "That sounds like a plan."

Ginny's eyes were wide with delight. "Yeah. After this past year—the fire and all—it feels good to be planning for the future."

Tricia gave her a warm smile. She raised her teacup. "Here's to the future—may it be bright and happy for all of us."

They gently clinked their china cups and took a sip, while Tricia crossed the fingers on her other hand.

It was after four and Tricia was in fine spirits when she returned to Haven't Got a Clue, glad she and Ginny could continue their weekly lunches for the foreseeable future. She was a lot later than she'd planned but she couldn't resist taking a tour of the house and helping Ginny move some of the heavier boxes to the kitchen island to unpack— including the missing soup bowls, which went straight into the dishwasher.

"Did you have a nice time?" Mr. Everett inquired.

"Wonderful. The house is beautiful and Ginny seems very happy."

Mr. Everett's lips curled into a shy smile. "I'm so pleased."

"I want to know all about the house," Pixie said from her station behind the cash desk.

Tricia removed her jacket, hung it over her arm, and moved closer, about to launch into a detailed account when the shop's door opened, admitting Ian McDonald.

"Well, hello," Tricia greeted him.

"Hello." He paused in front of the cash desk. "I was on my way back to my apartment after a long day at work and thought I'd stop in for a moment."

"I'm always glad to see you," Tricia said. Tricia gestured toward Pixie. "This is my assistant manager, Pixie. Have you guys connected?"

"We texted earlier," Ian said. "Very nice to meet you in person, Ms. Poe."

"Call me Pixie." The words were correct, but her tone was wary.

"And this is Mr. Everett."

"Sir," Mr. Everett said, and nodded. Ian did likewise.

"So, what brings you back so soon?" Tricia asked.

Pixie and Mr. Everett drifted away from the front of the store, giving the two some privacy.

"You sent a boy to visit me this afternoon," Ian remarked.

"I did. And how did that go?"

Ian nodded. "He's a smart kid. He aspires to be a marine biologist."

"And?" Tricia asked again.

"There's nothing wrong with that. I told him about the dolphins, whales, sharks, and sea turtles I'd seen while working for Celtic Cruises."

"And what did young Ian think of that?" Tricia asked.

Older Ian smiled. "The boy was entranced."

"And how did that make *you* feel?"

Ian's smile was grudging. "Pretty darn good. We need kids who want to save our oceans and the creatures who inhabit them. We've abused our world. The only hope *for* our planet is kids like him."

It was a sad testament and it pained Tricia to think that the fouled world—with climate change and the oceans filled with plastics—was being left to future generations to correct. If they could.

They smiled at each other and Tricia wondered if she ought to be upfront with the village's new chief about her activities earlier in the day. She didn't want it getting back to him that she'd been snooping—as Harvick seemed to believe.

"I dropped in at the Bee's Knees this morning. I understand Larry Harvick spoke to you about Eli Meier's death."

Ian's expression flattened. "I met him at the pub and he introduced himself to me."

"So, you didn't talk about Eli's murder?"

"Is it important to you if I did?"

Tricia was taken aback. "I—I'm merely curious." She decided to make a joke about it. "I guess I should have chosen journalism as a career instead of bookselling."

"I understand your former work was as the director of a large nonprofit in Manhattan."

"It was. Who said so?"

Ian shrugged. "Someone."

Tricia hadn't made her former occupation a secret, so it could have been anyone.

"Why would you want to leave such a high-powered job to become a bookseller?"

"For the same reason Larry Harvick left the Sheriff's Department. For a more peaceful life."

"And you've found that here in Stoneham?" Ian asked.

Tricia answered honestly. "Not really. But it sure beats the commute."

"I'll bet."

"Was there anything else on your mind?" Tricia asked.

"I wondered if we might have dinner again sometime."

Tricia liked Ian—a lot. But did she want to get involved with another lawman? Then again, who said it had to be more than dinner? Ian had few (any?) friends in the village. She was a familiar face. Why not go out to dinner . . . as a friend?

"That would be nice. Thank you."

"Are you free this weekend?"

"I'm booked for Sunday, but free tomorrow and Saturday evenings."

"Shall we say Saturday? I can pick you up at seven."

"Fine. I'll see you then."

Ian nodded, sketched a wave, and headed for the door. Tricia watched him go.

Yeah. She could have dinner with a friend.

Just a friend.

TWENTY-NINE

 Since Tricia had been tied up most of the day, she was glad that Angelica was once again hosting her for happy hour and dinner. She would volunteer her services for the next evening.

She arrived at Angelica's apartment just after six and could smell the aroma of fresh-baked bread wafting from the kitchen. Greetings and salutations were exchanged, Sarge was soon happily ensconced in his dog bed with his biscuit, and Tricia settled herself on one of the stools at the kitchen island.

"You're baking bread?" she asked.

"Oh, just a baguette or two," Angelica said flippantly, and turned to the refrigerator, opened it, and pulled out a large wooden tray—a charcuterie board—filled with meats, cheeses, and an assortment of grapes and olives.

"Ooh, I haven't had such a treat in a long time," Tricia said gleefully.

"I thought it might be fun to just graze this evening. Especially since you had such a late, *late* lunch." Angelica eyed her sister critically.

"The lunch wasn't late—*I* was late getting back to the store after giving Ginny a hand with some of the boxes."

"Thank you for that. Uh, how *did* your time with her go today?" Angelica asked in all wide-eyed innocence as she retrieved a crystal pitcher from the fridge and stirred the mixture.

Tricia had an idea Angelica knew exactly what went on during her visit, but she decided to play along.

"As I thought, just before I arrived, Ginny got a job offer from Becca Chandler."

"Mmm. So she said," Angelica said diffidently. She seemed a lot more confident about Ginny's future employment than she had the evening before.

"And what do you think about the offer?" Tricia asked.

"Of course, I'd never stand in Ginny's way when it came to her professional life"—Angelica began as the timer went off and she checked her bread—"and it would be one heck of an opportunity. But I wonder if Becca would offer her a job of that scope just to see her fail."

"Do you really think she'd do that when it's her financial future that's on the line? The way she spoke about it to me, Becca seemed determined to make sure the facility succeeded so she could either franchise it or sell it outright *when*—not if—it became successful."

"That would be the prudent approach," Angelica agreed.

"But you'd sure be upset if Ginny actually *took* another job."

"Perhaps." She removed the baguettes from the oven and set them on the counter to cool.

"Perhaps, my butt! You'd be terribly upset."

"Yes, but Ginny assured me she had no plans to *ever* work for Becca. Like us, she doesn't trust the woman."

Tricia nodded. "I hate to speak ill of another businesswoman, but for some reason, I wouldn't put it past Becca to deliberately try to cause trouble among our friends and families."

"Why do you think that?"

"I don't know. Maybe because she doesn't appear to have any family or close friends of her own. Jealousy is a powerful motivator."

Angelica's mouth drooped. "I often think about how we aren't close to our parents and how it didn't have to be that way."

"Mother made her choices," Tricia said simply. Yes, like choosing a ne'er-do-well man for a husband and then trying in vain to control him. Flawed as they were, Tricia *did* love her parents. She just didn't like them all that much and suspected Angelica felt the same way. That was why they had embraced Grace, Mr. Everett, and Ginny so fiercely. These were people they could trust implicitly and love unconditionally.

Tricia picked up a piece of cheese and nibbled on it. "Lunch with Ginny was probably the high point of my day, but there were others."

Angelica took the glasses and garnishes from the fridge and finally poured their drinks. "Such as?"

Tricia told her sister about her encounters with young Ian, Larry Harvick, capping off the topic with her invitation to dinner with the new police chief on Saturday.

"But that's not the biggest news," Tricia added.

"There's more?" Angelica asked, popping a seedless green grape into her mouth.

"I suspect that Edward might be Pixie's biological son."

"Why do you say that?" Angelica asked, taken aback.

"Well . . . because he told me so."

"Then why use the word 'suspect'?"

"Because if he is, I'm not sure Pixie is emotionally ready to admit it—to him or anyone else."

"Whyever not?"

Tricia directed a scowl at her sister. "I imagine for the same reason *you* aren't."

A deep flush rose to color Angelica's cheeks. "I'm in a complicated situation."

"And you don't think Pixie was?"

Angelica had the decency to look embarrassed.

"I'm sure plenty of prostitutes end up pregnant," Tricia remarked. "The easy answer to that is to end the pregnancy. For whatever reason, Pixie didn't."

"And why do you think that was?"

"I have no idea." But that was a lie. Pixie was a loving, giving person. Perhaps she'd wanted a child, longed to have someone to love, to add a stabilizing force to her earlier, troubled life. If so, giving up such a child would have had to be a devastating thing.

Then again . . . maybe it was just convenient.

But Tricia couldn't believe that of her assistant manager. Pixie had the biggest heart in the world. That may have been at the center of her problems.

Tricia returned to her home and was warmly welcomed by Miss Marple, who seemed unusually clingy that evening. If Tricia wandered into another room, her cat followed, waiting patiently as Tricia performed a task, or stridently demanding attention, which Tricia was more than happy to provide.

Maybe Miss Marple sensed the tension Tricia felt. It wasn't Larry Harvick's intimation that she was a nosy so-and-so, but remembering her encounter earlier in the day with Edward Dowding.

It was apparent that the young man was not going to go away anytime soon, and Tricia wrestled with the idea of confronting Pixie with his assertion that she was his birth mother.

Should Tricia have mentioned it earlier in the day? But then where was the opportunity? So much had happened, from her encounters with young Ian, welcoming Mr. Everett back to the store, speaking with Larry Harvick, and her prolonged lunch date with Ginny. There had never been a time during the day when Tricia and Pixie had been alone long enough to have a private conversation. But the next day was Mr. Everett's day off. Theoretically, they should have hours of time to talk privately since they had relatively few customers at this point in the retail year. But how could she bring up the subject? She had no doubt that Edward would soon force a confrontation. What if Pixie was blind-sided by the young man's assertion? And Tricia had not been presented with any real evidence that what Edward had said about her was even true.

It was a very delicate situation, and one Tricia struggled with. Would she be overreaching to even bring up the subject, especially as she hadn't apologized for their tense conversation a week before? And yet Tricia had a feeling Edward meant to make her store the battleground in which to confront Pixie with his version of the truth.

Tricia couldn't concentrate to read and went to bed early, but then she couldn't fall asleep because the whole Edward-Pixie dilemma preyed on her mind.

In desperation, she ended up going down to her basement office and inventorying the rest of the stock Pixie had acquired the weekend before. Dressed in her nightgown and robe, she even found herself stocking the shelves in her bookstore by the faint security lights and finally crept into her bed well after two o'clock.

Tricia slept through her alarm, and it was after eight when she awoke the next morning. She still had plenty of time to take her usual walk and complete her other morning rituals, but on that day she just didn't feel up to it. Instead, she indulged herself and made some mini walnut scones to share with Pixie and her customers. Just the regimentation of measuring and mixing the ingredients and then waiting for the oven timer to chime was a balm to her troubled soul.

She couldn't really supply whipped cream (a poor substitute for clotted cream) or butter for her customers, but she could put enough of both items in mini ramekins for herself and Pixie to enjoy before the (hoped-for) onslaught of customers arrived.

She settled the scones on a domed plate, along with the ramekins, and headed down to the store, where she set up the beverage station for the day and anxiously waited for Pixie's arrival.

As it happened, Pixie arrived ten minutes early for work, intending to start inventorying the books Tricia had taken care of in the wee hours.

"Wow. You're Ms. Efficient," she said after hanging up her coat.

"More like Ms. Insomniac," Tricia said as she poured coffee for the two of them.

"What's on your mind?"

"Let's sit down," Tricia said, and gestured toward the reader's nook.

"Uh-oh, this sounds like bad news," Pixie said, sounding wary.

"We have a situation," Tricia said.

"Why do I feel like I want to run away?" Pixie asked as she took her seat. But then she took a deep breath. "Okay, you're firing me, right?"

"What? No, of course not. But . . . yesterday morning I had a visit from Edward."

A shadow seemed to cross Pixie's face and Tricia could see her entire body tense. "And?"

"He said some pretty startling things."

"Like what?" Pixie asked, her voice sounding flat—dead.

"He's under the impression that you . . . could be his birth mother."

Pixie's eyes widened so that they looked like they might pop out of her head. "What?"

Tricia gave a little shrug. "That's what he said."

Pixie sprang up from her chair and began to pace.

"It's none of my business . . . but is it true?" Tricia asked.

Tight-lipped, Pixie made a circuit around the reader's nook, her brow furrowed. She was obviously extremely upset.

Tricia picked up her cup and took a sip of her coffee, which seemed particularly bitter on that chilly spring morning. She waited, not sure if Pixie was going to answer or simply run out the door.

Pixie kept pacing, and with every step seemed to grow more and more distraught. Finally, she spoke.

"I recognized him—the minute I saw him," she began, her voice catching. "A girl *never* forgets the face of her rapist."

Tricia's mouth dropped. "Are you saying . . . ?"

"That Edward is the spittin' image of his father? Yeah."

Tricia fought the urge to ask who that was. Pixie seemed to sense her reluctance.

"He was my . . ." She paused and took in a hiccuping breath as tears filled her eyes. "My pimp."

"Oh, Pixie," Tricia lamented, but Pixie held up a hand to stave off such sympathy.

"Al Dowding was a horrible man. He hit me—he hit all the girls in his stable. He had his way with all of us, which is such a quaint expression for rape. And he got most of them hooked on drugs—including me. We blotted out—but not nearly enough—the worst of our lives."

"Oh, Pixie," Tricia said again, the weight of her colleague's words seeming to crush her own soul. "What happened when you found out you were pregnant?"

Pixie took her seat once more, looking shell-shocked. "I knew better than to tell Al. He must have caused a lot of unwanted pregnancies and knew how it would impact his business model and that's just what he called it. So he made sure to fix the problem. I was lucky . . . for a while. I got away from him. I escaped to Connecticut and I got straight, which was a hell of an ordeal. But I was determined to deliver that baby even though I was sure I could never love it. I only ever saw a fleeting glance of him before he was taken away and I surrendered him to social services. As I recovered, I knew I had a shot at a real life. That's when I signed up for EMT training. I got a job as a paramedic with a fire company." Her expression softened. "Not to brag, but I was *good*. I got to help so many people. I had a studio apartment. I had a *real* life. Something I could be proud of. And nobody had to know what I'd been before."

"And then?" Tricia asked.

Pixie exhaled a long breath and her mouth trembled. "And then Al found me," she said bitterly. "He'd never stopped looking for me—to punish me. And he did. He injected me with heroin and I found myself hooked all over again and back in his stable," she said with a sob.

"Oh, Pixie," Tricia said for a third time, feeling helpless.

"Al was murdered, and me and a bunch of the other girls thought that would be our ticket to freedom, but another meaner guy just stepped up to the plate."

"Did you ever wonder what happened to your baby?"

"Every day of my life. I hoped to God he would be adopted and live a happy life. But I guess the kid was just as cursed as me."

Pixie had never spoken so much—well, really at all—about her past, and her confessions were painful to hear, but Tricia hoped that relating them might lighten the burden on Pixie's soul.

"The minute Edward walked in here I knew there'd be trouble. And that he was so mean to me . . . Well, I was pretty sure the apple hadn't fallen far from the tree."

"And now what do you think?"

Pixie braved the ghost of a smile. "Maybe that there might be just a little bit of me in him."

"If nothing else, he seems to have your eye for vintage finds," Tricia said.

Pixie's smile broadened. "Yeah. But that doesn't change the past—and I don't want him screwing up my life. There's a reason a lot of us don't want adoption records to be opened. I didn't know he'd never found a home and I feel bad about that, but his life would have been a lot worse if he'd ended up with me."

"After speaking with me, he had to know you and I would talk about it," Tricia said. "What do you think he really wants?"

"If he wants a relationship, he's going to be very disappointed."

"How are you going to discourage him?"

Pixie let out an exasperated breath. "I dunno."

"Does Fred know who Edward is?"

"Yeah, we don't have any secrets. And he thinks I should make nice with the kid. This could really shake up our marriage—which is the best thing that ever happened to me. Oh, and working here, of course," she backpedaled.

"Of course," Tricia said, amused.

Pixie didn't have to ponder the problem for long, as the shop door opened and Edward Dowding stepped across the threshold.

THIRTY

"Hello," Edward said, his penetrating gaze fixed on Pixie.

Tricia stood and moved between Edward and his quarry. "What are you doing here?"

"I came to talk to Ms. Pixie."

"Well, Ms. Pixie doesn't want to talk to you," Pixie said with authority. "Why don't you just leave?"

"Tricia, could you give us some privacy?" Edward asked, but his words sounded more like a command.

"No!" Pixie retorted. Was she afraid to be left alone with the child she had given birth to? Pixie, who was a kickboxer, who had proved she could take care of herself, apparently didn't want to be alone with her progeny. Not that Tricia could protect her from violence, but to have moral support—and possibly a witness—was obviously important to Pixie, and Tricia could at least do that. She stood her ground.

"So, talk," Pixie told Edward.

"You dumped me into foster care," Edward accused, his voice laced with anger.

"I couldn't take care of you."

"And you didn't want to, either."

"You're right about that. You were conceived because I was raped. I was afraid you might turn out just as bad as your sperm donor—and I may not have been wrong about that."

"How dare you accuse me of that!" Edward shouted.

"You look just like *him*," Pixie stated, "and you're acting just like *him*."

"You don't know me," Edward accused.

"I only know what you've shown me."

"I'm a good person," he insisted.

"Good people don't threaten others," Pixie said.

"I haven't threatened you."

"Oh, no? Showing up here at the store, throwing me the finger, yelling at me? Stalking me at estate sales? You don't think that constitutes a threat?"

"I wanted to get to know you."

"Yeah, well I don't want to know you."

"Please, please," Tricia interrupted. "Let's lower our voices and—"

"You stay out of this," Edward commanded.

Pixie finally stood. "No, *you* should leave. This is a place of business. We could have customers walk in here any minute."

"Well, then, I'll just wait for you to leave."

"And then what?"

Edward's lips moved, but he didn't seem to have an answer.

Pixie pointed to the door. "Go. Now!"

Edward's glare was filled with malevolent anger. "We're not done."

"Oh, yes, we are. Now get out!"

Edward stared at his mother for long seconds and then turned and stalked out of the store, slamming the door behind him.

Long seconds passed before Pixie groped for the back of one of the upholstered chairs and sank into it.

"That was rough," Tricia commented.

"Tell me about it."

"What are you going to do? It sounds as though Edward isn't going to back off."

Pixie let out a shuddering breath. "I can take care of myself—and I've got all day to think about how to do it."

So did Tricia. And . . . to worry.

Throughout the morning, Pixie jumped every time the bell over the door rang, her anxiety rising exponentially.

"Why don't we order lunch in?" Tricia suggested. "Or we can go together to Booked for Lunch. I don't want to leave you alone here in the store."

Pixie sagged with relief. "I don't know why I'm letting that kid get to me."

"Because he's been volatile twice already. I've been thinking, you might want to talk to someone at the Stoneham Police Department. You might want to consider taking out a restraining order against Edward."

"It's been my experience that those things aren't worth the paper they're printed on," Pixie said bitterly.

Tricia had to agree. In many cases, it only seemed to provoke the person it named into causing more harm to the person it was meant to protect.

As Tricia's lunch hour approached, she decided the best thing to do was simply join Angelica. She texted her sister saying that something had come up and Pixie would be joining them, with an explanation to come—later that evening.

The more the merrier, Angelica texted back.

So at one o'clock, Tricia hung her seldom-used GONE TO LUNCH sign with a little clock indicating the time they'd return, then locked the store. Pixie kept looking all around as they crossed the street for Booked for Lunch, as though expecting Edward to pop out of one of the sheltered doors along Main Street. She seemed relieved, too, when they entered the little café and didn't find him among the patrons.

They took off their jackets and sat down.

"Hello, you two," Angelica said in welcome. "It's nice to see you, Pixie. It's been too long."

"Thanks," Pixie said, looking over her shoulder to glance at the exit.

"Tricia said that young man who's been trying to become a picker has been bothering you. I'm so sorry you're having problems, Pixie. Is there anything I can do to help?" Angelica asked sincerely.

"Uh, not really," Pixie hedged, "but I appreciate your letting me crash your lunch with Tricia. I know how tight you girls are."

"I consider you a friend, and I'm always happy to see you," Angelica assured her. "Now, I've got something for you," she told Tricia, and reached beside her to bring out a copy of the *Stoneham Weekly News*, handing it to her sister. "You assured me last week that you were going to start reading the paper so I made it my business to pick up a copy of the latest issue fresh out today."

Tricia sighed. She had never been a fan of the village's weekly rag. She'd tried to read it in the months since Antonio had taken its helm, but she'd been so soured on it from dealing with the paper's former owner that she rarely looked at anything except Antonio's editorial. However, the top (well, only real) story in the current issue was an interview Antonio had conducted with the village's new chief of police. Tricia found herself scanning it while Angelica and Pixie chatted.

The article charted Ian's background, his former life as a cruise ship security officer, and his education. Yada yada yada. It was the paragraphs about the investigation into Eli Meier's—aka Joseph Martin's—death that really drew her attention. And yet, he hinted at suspects but didn't name names. Tricia, however, could read between the lines. She mused that Ian's list of suspects was, at best, superficial—and apparently all women: Angelica, Mary, Leona, Louise, and Becca.

To Tricia's mind, only Becca had ever shown an unrelenting passion for something—her tennis career. Could she have channeled that kind of single-mindedness to removing the obstacle that kept her from renting out the space occupied by the oh-so-shabby Inner Light bookstore to Rick Lavoy for his beer-tasting room and go from a tenant who was constantly behind on his rent to someone who'd pay top dollar for it and on time, too?

No, despite Becca's less-than-cordial outward appearance, Tricia couldn't see someone of Becca's talent and stature going to the trouble of risking life and liberty to remove a pesky renter.

Sure, Louise was passionate about her art, but now that she had access to the assets of her marriage, the few thousand dollars Eli Meier had owed her late husband could be considered a mere pittance. She wasn't likely to risk her old and new business ventures to rid herself of the man— especially since that would mean she'd never see a penny of what was owed her.

To think that Mary, Leona, or Angelica had credible motives for murdering Eli was ludicrous.

Tricia frowned. Could Eli—Joseph Martin . . . whoever— have had a local enemy? He'd been supported by Dan Reed at the last Chamber meeting, but that could have been just one good old Yankee championing another. Tricia hadn't paid attention to who else might have raised a voice in support of Eli's protests.

It seemed far more likely that Eli's cover had been blown and someone harmed by his actions—or those of his former comrades—had decided to take justice into their own hands.

The only person new to the village, at least that Tricia knew about, was Rick Lavoy. But he was half Eli's age. Say one of Lavoy's family members had been harmed by Joseph Martin or another of the Crimson Nine, he might— and that was a pretty big leap in logic—have been motivated to take revenge.

Her ruminations were interrupted when Molly the waitress finally showed up at their table to take their orders.

"Order anything," Angelica said. "This lunch is on me."

"Oh, you don't have to do that," Pixie said.

"It's my pleasure."

Tricia had grown tired of the soup-and-half-sandwich special and opted for a salad instead. Angelica ordered a Reuben. Pixie skipped lunch altogether and ordered two pieces of chocolate cake, showing just how upset she was and presumably acting under the notion that chocolate could solve just about all life's problems.

The three of them conversed amiably, but Pixie kept looking over her shoulder the whole time and twice nearly spilled her cup of coffee—she was that rattled.

By the time they finished their meal, Pixie seemed to have calmed down just a little and she and Tricia headed back to Haven't Got a Clue, with Pixie keeping a sharp eye out for her tormentor. But they hadn't been inside the shop for even a minute when the door opened and once again in walked Edward Dowding.

Pixie backed in to stand behind the cash desk, pulling the vintage—and extremely heavy—black telephone closer.

"I asked you to leave," Tricia reminded Edward.

"And I did."

"Do I have to call the police to make that *more* than a simple request?"

He let out a sigh. "I just want to talk."

"You've had that opportunity."

"This isn't about my personal situation," Edward said quietly.

Tricia threw a glance toward Pixie, but her gaze was riveted on the young man who stood before them.

"Then what is it?" Tricia said.

"I think I may have seen the prelude to a murder."

THIRTY-ONE

 Tricia gazed at the young man before her, crossing her arms over her chest and scowling. "And I'm the Queen of England."

"No, really. I saw something, the night Eli Meier was killed," Edward said, his voice subdued.

"How do you even know about him?"

Edward pulled a wrinkled copy of the front-page story from that day's issue of the *Stoneham Weekly News*.

"Where did you get that?"

"In the newspaper office. It was cold out and I was bored. Some lady, Ginger, said it was okay if I sat down for a while and read the paper."

It sounded plausible for a guy hanging around with nowhere else to go.

"So, what did you see?" Tricia asked.

"A couple of guys arguing in the park."

"You mean the village square?" Tricia asked.

He shrugged. "If that's what you call it."

"What were they arguing about?"

"I couldn't really tell. Their voices were low."

"And you think one of them was Eli Meier?"

Edward shrugged. "I don't know for sure."

"Would you recognize his face if you saw a picture?"

"I doubt it. It was pretty dark."

"What were you doing in the park at that time of night anyway?" Pixie asked.

"Sleeping—or trying to, at least. I have a sleeping bag. The bushes are good cover—at least until spider season."

Was the sleeping bag the extent of his possessions? And what about critters bigger than spiders? Skunks, ground-hogs, and rodents? The thought of sleeping that close to nature made Tricia shudder. But as she thought back, Edward *had* first shown up at Haven't Got a Clue before Eli was found dead. If he was hiding out in the village square, he *could* have witnessed Eli's encounter with his killer.

"Have you told Chief McDonald about this?" Tricia asked.

"What for? I told you, I can't identify anybody."

"But you said it was a man Eli was arguing with. If so, that would clear all the women on McDonald's suspect list."

"He suspects a bunch of broads?" Pixie asked, sounding skeptical.

"Pixie!" Tricia admonished.

"Okay, *ladies*," she acquiesced.

"That's what the story in the *Stoneham Weekly News* intimates," Tricia explained.

"Yeah, right. How could a woman have carried that tub of—" Pixie stopped short. "He was no pixie, if you'll pardon the term."

Eli hadn't been morbidly obese, but Pixie was right. He was no skinny Minnie, either.

"I'm just telling you what I saw," Edward reiterated. "It creeped me out."

"Why did you choose me as the person to tell your story to?" Tricia demanded.

Edward shrugged. "People around here say you solve a lot of crimes."

Tricia would bet they didn't say it that nicely, either.

"Was that all? You saw two people arguing."

"Yeah . . . and then I heard the shot."

Tricia's eyebrows rose to the top of her forehead. "And you're only mentioning this *now*?"

Edward shrugged again. "Who's going to believe me?"

"The police." Unless he had a criminal record, but Tricia didn't want to mention that, as it was the basis of the uncomfortable conversation she'd had with Pixie the week before.

"What do you expect me to do about it?" Tricia asked, unable to keep an edge from creeping into her voice. Just like Alexa, Edward didn't want to take responsibility for talking to the authorities about what he'd supposedly seen.

"Talk to somebody in authority."

"He'll want to talk to the source, not hear it thirdhand. Will you be available to corroborate what you want me to report?"

Edward didn't look her in the eye. "I guess."

"That's not good enough."

"Then, yeah. But you talk to the cops first because they have a tendency to dismiss anything a homeless person says."

Tricia didn't doubt it.

She let out a breath. "Okay. I'll tell Chief McDonald what you've told me. How can he get in touch with you?"

"I'll be around," he said slyly.

Pixie threw Tricia an uneasy glance.

Tricia crossed her arms over her chest. "I've got a caveat."

"A what?" Edward asked.

"A condition. While I'm away from the store, you need to stay away, too."

"What do you think I'm going to do? Rob you?" He turned to glare at Pixie.

"Take it or leave it," Tricia said.

Edward scowled. "Oh, all right."

"In fact, why don't you follow me to the police station. You don't have to go inside until after I've spoken with the chief." If he was even in.

"I guess."

"Good."

As Tricia retreated to the back of the store to grab her jacket, she kept glancing over her shoulder to see Pixie glowering at Edward. She didn't trust him, and neither did Tricia. What made her think McDonald might?

Edward preceded Tricia out the door of Haven't Got a Clue, not walking with her, but several steps behind. It unnerved her, so much so that during the walk to the police station, Tricia considered what, exactly, she'd tell Chief McDonald. What if Edward had another reason for coming up with his supposed eyewitness account of Eli Meier's death? What if he was trying to deflect suspicion away from himself?

Oh, yeah, and why would he do that?

It seemed awfully convenient that he had the tale to tell and yet waited nine days after the murder to think to tell someone about it.

Then again, what was his motive for murder? Tricia had found Eli's wallet intact, so obviously robbery hadn't been the catalyst. Still, it bothered her that Ian was apparently considering only women on his list of suspects. On average, women murderers were outnumbered by men more than three to one in the US. It made more sense that a man could have moved the body to the alley behind the Coffee Bean.

As Tricia approached the station, the footfalls behind her ceased. She glanced over her shoulder and didn't see Edward. He'd probably dipped into one of the other storefronts. She opened the station's door and entered, glad to find that Polly Burgess wasn't sitting behind the receptionist's desk. Instead, it was Officer Cindy Pearson. Were they shorthanded again? "Hi, Tricia," she said blandly.

"Hi, Cindy. How's it going?"

"Okay. I suppose you want to see the chief about something wildly important." She couldn't have sounded more bored, but at least she wasn't hostile, as Polly often was.

"If he's in. It's about the Eli Meier murder."

Cindy keyed the intercom. "Chief, Tricia Miles is here to help solve another murder."

Tricia frowned.

"Send her in."

Cindy gestured toward the door. "Be our guest."

Tricia stepped over to Ian's office and let herself in, closing the door behind her. Since her last visit, Ian had installed a large framed picture of the *Celtic Lady*, along with several framed certificates. It didn't look all that much homier, but better than it had.

Ian stood. "Sit," he encouraged. He took his seat once she'd taken hers. "What brings you back to visit so soon?"

"I read the interview you did with the *Stoneham Weekly News*."

"You're at least the fifth person who's mentioned it to me. I'm surprised so many people have felt the need to comment on it."

Tricia was surprised more than five people had actually read it, but she didn't feel the need to voice that. "I was wondering why you thought a woman killed Eli Meier."

"From now on, the department is only referring to the deceased as Joseph Martin," he clarified.

Tricia nodded, waiting for an answer.

"Long hairs were found on the victim's body and caught on a ring he wore. He apparently tussled with his assailant, ripping out a few hairs."

"What if I suggested it wasn't a woman with long hair, but a man?"

"Have you got someone in mind?"

Tricia felt like a snitch, but she had convinced herself that she was actually trying to be a good—helpful—citizen. "A homeless man has been hanging around the village lately."

Ian raised an eyebrow, looking distinctly interested. "Do you have a name?"

"Edward Dowding. As a matter of fact, he came to me this afternoon to tell me that he had witnessed an encounter between Eli and another man in the village square the night of Eli's death. He's waiting out on the street somewhere."

"Why do you think he may have killed Meier?"

"*He* has long dark hair."

"I didn't specify the color," Ian remarked.

"Well, if it's dark, it could be Edward's."

"And just how do you know this young man?"

Tricia sigh. "It's rather a long and complicated story."

"I've got time to listen," Ian said.

Tricia sat back in her seat and relayed everything she thought she knew about the crime, adding that Edward had a volatile temper and had stalked Pixie. Ian listened patiently, his expression betraying nothing.

"Well?" Tricia asked.

"It's not the worst theory I've heard. Where did you say I can find this young man?"

"He lives in a homeless shelter in Nashua, but he's been hanging around the village quite a lot lately. As I said, he followed me here but ducked into one of the storefronts before I got to the station."

Ian leaned back in his chair. "Is it possible you suspect this character because he's been threatening your assistant manager?"

"Are you asking if I'd make up a story like this to get Edward to stop bothering Pixie? The answer to that is no! You can ask Pixie."

"Why should I believe her—or you, for that matter?"

Tricia considered her words carefully. "If I find Edward upon leaving, I'll send him in and you can ask him yourself."

Ian sat back in his chair. Was he going to be as obstinate as Chief Baker had been—refusing to look into what could be a credible piece of information simply because of who had relayed it to him?

They stared at each other for long moments, as though it was a contest to see who'd look—or skulk—away first. Tricia had no intention of skulking. She'd leave with her head held high.

She stood, making another decision. "The other reason I came by is to let you know that I won't be available for dinner on Saturday after all."

"And why is that?"

"I think we'd both be wasting our time. I'm sure you have better things to do."

Ian stood. "I'm sorry you feel that way."

Tricia almost smiled. "You have no idea how sorry I feel about it."

And with that, she left the office.

THIRTY-TWO

Edward must have changed his mind about speaking with Chief McDonald, for when Tricia left the police station, he was nowhere in sight. She hurried back to Haven't Got a Clue, hoping Edward hadn't broken his word and gone back to harass—or worse—Pixie. But when she arrived, Tricia found the store empty of customers and Pixie sitting behind the cash desk, reading.

"How did it go?" Pixie asked, and slid a bookmark between the pages.

Tricia decided not to tell Pixie that she suspected Edward of lying—or perhaps something even more unpleasant. "Not very well."

"The chief didn't want to speak to Edward?"

"He said he would, but then Edward was nowhere around when I left the station."

Pixie nodded knowingly. "Why do you look so sad?"

Tricia sighed. "I felt like I was speaking to Chief Baker's clone. Like nothing I had to say would be taken seriously." Tricia didn't often confide in Pixie, but this was one time she felt she could. "We were supposed to have dinner tomorrow night."

"You and the chief?" Pixie asked.

Tricia nodded. "I told him I was no longer available."

"And left it at that?"

"No, I told him why, which pretty much closed the door on . . ."

"A relationship?" Pixie offered.

Tricia hadn't wanted to say it so plainly, but that was exactly what she meant. "Am I just a busybody trying to nose in on crime because I think I'm—"

"An amateur sleuth?" Pixie supplied.

Tricia nodded.

"As I recall, it was Edward who sent you down that road. Those Dowding men seem to foul up everything and everyone they come in contact with," she said bitterly.

"I don't seem to do much better," Tricia remarked. She glanced down at the floor, making another decision, before looking up once again. "I want to apologize for what I said to you a week ago."

For a moment Pixie looked confused, and then understanding dawned. She shrugged. "It's okay. I did a lot of thinking about that and . . . the way you stood behind me with all this Edward trouble, I figured I should level with you about my past."

"No, if you're uncomfortable discussing it, then you—"

"It wasn't like I went out of my way to become a felon. I guess you could say I was in the wrong place at the wrong time."

Tricia was interested in hearing the tale, but she wasn't about to prod Pixie into telling it.

"See, I had this friend who needed a lift to the store. His car had broken down and he said he needed to pick up a few things at the 7-Eleven."

That didn't seem like a crime.

"Only . . . he didn't buy the items. He didn't buy a thing. He robbed the joint and shot the kid behind the counter, making off with a lousy hundred and fifty bucks."

"Oh, my word!" Tricia cried. No wonder Edward had made a big deal out of glaring at Pixie when he'd asked if Tricia thought he might rob her. He'd obviously known about Pixie's conviction.

"Yeah. They called *me* the getaway driver. It was winter. I had the car running to keep warm. I was listening to the radio, an oldies station—you know that's my thing—and there was Bing Crosby and the Andrews Sisters belting out 'Pistol Packin' Mama' and I was singing right along. Then Benny comes flying out of the store, jumps in the car, and screams, 'Drive!'"

"What happened to the clerk?"

"Shot in the arm, but he recovered and testified against Benny, who got twelve years for armed robbery and attempted murder."

"And you?"

"I got eight years, but they let me out early for good behavior. In a way, it was a good thing. Being away from my old way of life got me clean again, and well read, and they let me move away from Boston so I *couldn't* fall back into that life. I got a lot of breaks. Like when Grace hired me, and then Angelica convinced you to take me on. I know we started out on the wrong foot," she said, echoing Ginny's rocky beginning with Angelica, "but I figured with all the breaks you've given me, you deserved to know the truth."

"Have you ever heard from your friend Benny?"

"He's no friend of mine," Pixie declared.

Tricia swallowed and nodded. "Thank you for sharing that with me."

"It clears the air," Pixie said matter-of-factly.

Tricia would have liked to have agreed but she still felt guilty about not apologizing earlier. It really wasn't like her.

"What do we do now?" Pixie asked. "I really don't want Edward in my life. I made that decision before he was even born, and dealing with him this last week has only made that feeling stronger."

"I'm sorry. I don't know the answer to that."

Pixie shrugged. "I guess I'll have to deal with it on my own."

"Do you mind if I share your story with our little family

group? Maybe we can come up with an answer. We could rally around you—protect you."

"Uh-uh," Pixie said, shaking her head. "And put you guys in danger? Ain't gonna happen."

Tricia thought fast. "Then . . . what do you say about me hiring a bodyguard for you?"

"Are you kidding me?"

"No, I'm not kidding. It might take a day or so to arrange. I can call my lawyer to get some leads—or even talk to Chief McDonald."

"Yeah, like *he's* going to want to help."

Tricia felt the same way, but the police ought to be prepared to come if they were called to deal with Edward's stalking.

Tricia looked at the clock. She couldn't let Pixie walk home alone. She'd drive her. But the weekend meant she'd be on her own. She had her nail appointments at Booked for Beauty, which she wouldn't want to cancel, and her estate sales and thrift store visits on Sunday, which she wasn't likely to want to give up, either.

Pixie seemed to read her mind. "I could just stay home all weekend. But then . . . I'm sure Edward knows where I live."

"You and Fred could go away for the weekend. I'd be happy to pay for it. Edward doesn't have a car. It's not likely he'd be able to follow you."

"I dunno. I'd have to talk to Fred. Don't forget, he doesn't see Edward as any kind of threat. He's actively encouraging me to have a relationship with him."

That did present a very big problem.

"Well, you let me know. In the meantime, I think we should close up shop early and I'll drive you home." Where Edward might already be waiting. Tricia had no plans to just abandon Pixie, however. If Fred wasn't already there, she would wait with her friend and employee until he came home from work. It was the least she could do. That said, it felt like not nearly enough.

* * *

The west side of Main Street was already bathed in shadows as Tricia stepped out of Haven't Got a Clue, looked around, and gave Pixie the all clear to exit. Together, they walked up the sidewalk, heading for the municipal parking lot to fetch Tricia's car.

As they drew closer to the lot, Dan Reed approached them from behind, holding a clipboard in his hand. "I'd like to talk to you, Tricia," he said.

"Sorry, Dan, but we've got an appointment."

"Where?" he demanded, stepping in front of the women to halt their progress.

"That's really none of your business."

Pixie's head swiveled from side to side, looking for Edward.

"I'll tell you what's my business," Dan said, moving so that Tricia couldn't get past him. "I'm collecting for Eli Meier's burial."

Tricia's mouth dropped. "Are you kidding me?"

"Why would I do that?"

"Haven't you been reading the news? Eli was a felon on the run who hid out here in Stoneham for years."

Dan waved a hand in dismissal. "Oh, that. Yeah. That was a long time ago. Eli was a solid citizen who contributed to the success of Booktown and he deserves to have a decent burial. I've been calling around and it seems like no one is going to claim the body anytime soon. The Sheriff's Department said he'd be held in the morgue for a time and if no one claimed him, he'd be buried in a pauper's grave."

"Did the man deserve any more?" Pixie asked, taking a moment away from her visual search of the area.

"He was a human being," Dan asserted.

"Who'd killed half a dozen people. That made him a mass murderer," Tricia said.

"You're talking about my friend," Dan grated.

Tricia sighed. "It's commendable of you to want to give

the man a final resting place, but you can't expect others to pay for it."

"You don't think *I* have that kind of money, do you?" Dan blurted.

"You have a thriving business," Tricia pointed out.

"No thanks to *your* sister stealing my lunch crowd," he blurted, "and her B-and-B business partner who owns that pub that's also stealing my lunch and dinner crowds."

Tricia knew she shouldn't engage further with the man, but she just couldn't help herself and crossed her arms over her chest. "According to a study commissioned by Nigela Ricita Associates, this village could actually use more dining establishments. I had breakfast in your diner the other day and it was packed—and it isn't even tourist season yet."

"It must have been a fluke," Dan groused.

"You wouldn't know because you weren't there," Tricia pointed out.

"I have important duties outside my work at the diner," Dan boasted.

"Attending meetings to talk about the latest conspiracy theories?" Pixie asked. So she'd heard the same thing as Tricia.

"That's none of your business," Dan growled.

"Look, we need to go," Tricia said.

"Just give me a couple of bucks for Eli's send-off," Dan said, and gestured to an envelope under the clipboard's clasp.

"No, thank you," Tricia said, and tried to step around him once more.

"What is wrong with you?" Dan demanded.

"I could ask you the same question," Tricia said.

"I'm saner than most of you sheep. Now, give me some money and I'll leave you alone."

Tricia's ire rose. "That sounds like a threat!"

"Take it any way you want."

Once again, Tricia tried to step away and Dan reached out and pushed her hard, so she fell flat on her bottom, the rounding jolt practically shaking her brains.

"Hey!" Pixie yelled, and without warning she hiked her skirt and lashed out with her right leg, giving a resounding grunt that rose to a howl as her shoe went flying and her foot collided with Dan's jaw, sending him sprawling.

"Pixie!" Tricia cried, shocked and awed by the older woman's physical prowess.

Pixie seemed to shake herself, smoothed her skirt back into place, and reached out a hand to pull Tricia to her feet, while Dan writhed on the ground.

"I think you broke my jaw," he said, the words coming out just a little garbled.

The sound of running feet advanced from across the street: Edward.

"Holy crap!" he hollered. "I saw what you just did!"

Pixie jumped back, looking ready to attack once more.

Edward came to a halt, holding out his arms as a defensive gesture. "Whoa—whoa!"

"Don't come any closer!" Pixie warned, and moved as though to get a better angle for an all-out assault.

"I saw what happened," Edward repeated. "That creep pushed Tricia. I'm willing to tell the cops about it, too."

"Somebody call me an ambulance," Dan wailed, still rolling around on the sidewalk in apparent agony.

Tricia brushed the dirt from the back of her slacks. "Why are you willing to talk to the police now, but disappeared after I went to talk to Chief McDonald on your behalf?"

Edward had the decency to look sheepish. "I got scared. Can you blame me?"

"Yes!"

Pixie glared menacingly at her son but said nothing. Perhaps she was afraid to say anything. She retrieved her wayward shoe.

The sound of a siren broke the late-afternoon quiet and one of the Stoneham police SUVs rolled up to the sidewalk and Officer Henderson jumped out of the vehicle, grasping a wooden nightstick in one hand, his other resting on his holster. "What's going on here?" he demanded.

Everyone started talking at once.

"Stop! Stop!" Henderson commanded, waving his truncheon in the air for emphasis, and the cacophony immediately subsided. "You!" He pointed at Tricia. "Start talking."

It took only a few moments for Tricia to bring the officer up to speed.

Henderson glared at Dan. "Did you push her?"

"I'm a witness, I saw him do it!" Edward said.

"Me, too," Pixie agreed.

Now sitting on his butt, Dan still held a hand to his sore jaw. "I only gave her a little shove. It's not my fault she's not steady on her feet. And then that one"—he pointed to Pixie—"went all Jackie Chan on me."

"She was defending me!" Tricia asserted. She felt like kicking Dan herself.

"Okay, everyone, just calm down. Ladies, why don't you wait over there. I'll call the EMTs and get this guy seen to, and then we can all go down to the station and straighten this out."

"Do *I* have to go, too?" Edward asked, appalled. Had he forgotten he'd volunteered to tell all just moments before?

Henderson turned on him. "You *said* you were a witness."

Edward swallowed hard, his face going a shade whiter. He really didn't want to talk to the cops, which made Tricia feel all the more suspicious of him.

Henderson radioed for the firefighter EMTs and planned to wait with Dan for them, giving Tricia, Pixie, and Edward permission to start off for the station two blocks ahead. Pixie showed as much enthusiasm for that little jaunt as Edward, and it was a silent trek to the small but formidable brick building that had but one small cell to house rowdy suspects until the Sheriff's Department could take them into custody. As Henderson had radioed ahead, Chief McDonald was waiting for them, looking as intimidating as Tricia had ever seen him.

"Ms. Poe," Ian said, sizing Pixie up. With shoulders hunched and looking small in her vintage skirt and jacket,

Tricia wondered if Ian could picture Pixie knocking hefty Dan Reed to the ground with one vicious kick. "We'll start with you." Ian indicated the conference room. Pixie threw a panicky glance over her shoulder before slinking into the room.

Tricia and Edward took seats on the ugly plastic chairs that lined the south wall of the reception area.

"So, have you ever been arrested?" she asked, her tone neutral.

Edward glared at her. "Not that it's any of your business," he snapped, "but no."

"Neither have I. But why are you so nervous about talking to the chief?"

"It comes with the homeless territory."

"Just speak the truth and you'll be fine."

"What about Pixie? What if they arrest her for assault?"

"I have a very good lawyer I can call. And Dan admitted to the officer that he shoved me. If he pressed charges, I'll press my own," Tricia said authoritatively.

They sat in awkward silence for a good twenty minutes before Ian opened the door and Pixie stepped out of the conference room. She didn't look half as scared as she had when she'd gone in.

"Tricia," Ian said, and Tricia got up. "Would you escort Ms. Poe to her home? Then you can come back and give me your statement."

Pixie gave Tricia a quick nod.

"Of course."

The two women left the station.

"Why did the chief ask me to take you home?" Tricia asked once they'd hit the sidewalk.

"I told him Edward was stalking me." Something he already knew. "The chief is going to have him driven back to the homeless shelter with a warning not to bother me anymore."

"Do you think that will do any good?"

"Not a chance," Pixie said bitterly. "But at least he'll be out of my hair tonight. And if Edward shows up at the day spa tomorrow, I'm to call the police to have him removed. The chief also advised me to ask for a restraining order, and we both know that ain't gonna happen."

They started back for the municipal parking lot. The police SUV was gone and there was no sign of Dan Reed, either. Perhaps he'd been taken to the urgent care center in Milford—Tricia really didn't care.

But why had Dan insisted Eli had been his friend? Why was he so loyal to a man who'd killed multiple people? Was he enamored with Eli's real persona—and the fact that he'd acted against a government Dan no longer trusted?

Tricia wasn't sure she wanted to know the answers to those questions.

THIRTY-THREE

"He pushed you?" Angelica asked, her voice filled with shocked anger.

Tricia wiggled on her sister's kitchen barstool. "Yeah. And does my tailbone hurt!"

"Do you think you should get it checked out?"

"It'll be fine. I'll sit on a heating pad when I get home."

"I think I've got one here," Angelica said. "Let me go look for it—"

"Don't bother," Tricia said. "I'm fine. But I can't get over how pushy Dan was about collecting money for a funeral for Eli. As if anyone around here would want to go to one."

"I doubt Dan will collect much of anything—*if* anything." Angelica stirred the mixture in the martini pitcher. "And none of this intrigue brings the police any closer to catching Eli's killer."

"You're right about that. If I didn't know Ian McDonald—"

"And, honestly, you don't," Angelica pointed out.

"I'd wonder if looking for his killer would be that much of a priority. I mean, killing all those people and running away from his crime for over half a century . . . some might say karma stepped in."

Angelica set the pitcher and chilled glasses on a tray, along with a plate filled with crackers and a mound of hot, runny brie. "Let's go in the living room." She picked up the tray and Tricia followed. They took their usual seats and Angelica poured the drinks. "What would you think about Dan being a suspect in Eli's murder?"

"Dan? But he's done nothing but defend Eli. And harassing people to give money for the man's funeral would be hypocritical."

"Not if he's putting up a front."

Tricia shook her head. "Besides, Dan's wife said Dan was Eli's best customer."

"What if," Angelica began, and grabbed the knife on the plate to spread some brie on a cracker. "What if Dan found out his friend was the infamous Joseph Martin? Let's face it, Dan's a nutcase. What if finding that out pushed him over the edge?"

Tricia wrinkled her nose. "Sounds far-fetched to me."

"I don't suppose you'd want to ask that question of his wife. It sounds like she's not all that into him anymore."

"Having him framed for murder would certainly get him out of her life. But"—Tricia shook her head—"not a chance."

"When you think about it, Dan *is* a big guy," Angelica said. "He could probably carry a dead body from the square to the alley behind the Coffee Bean."

"I dunno," Tricia said, shaking her head.

"How about in a wheelbarrow?" Angelica suggested.

"A flat dolly?" Tricia countered.

"We have one each at Booked for Lunch and the Dog-Eared Page, and several at the Brookview Inn. I really do wish the Board of Selectmen had allocated the funds to install cameras around the village just for safety's sake."

"People around here want to live free of Big Brother or die," Tricia reminded her sister. "And speaking of the dead, Ian hadn't heard from you about Eli's so-called memoir. I gave him your agent's name."

Angelica blinked innocently. "Gosh darn, I forgot to do that, didn't I?"

"No, you didn't. You *deliberately* didn't tell Ian about it."

"Well, he knows now. And if you believe that Eli and Dan were actually pals, you should ask *him* about the manuscript. If Dan truly was the closest thing Eli had to a friend, he might have mentioned it at some point."

Angelica had made a good point. But how could Tricia ask Dan such a question? She'd have to think about it.

"After dinner, I think I'll call Randy over at Booked for Beauty and ask him to watch out for Edward while Pixie's doing nails tomorrow."

"Good idea. For someone with no reliable transportation, Edward seems to get around just fine."

"You wouldn't think people would pick up hitchhikers in this day and age. I mean, it seems like there's a crazy person around every corner just waiting to pounce."

"I just hope Ian was able to convince him to stop bothering Pixie." Tricia sipped her drink and eyed her sister. "Now that Pixie's come clean about her son, isn't it time you did, too?"

"She came clean to you—not the world at large. And let's be clear, I'm not the only person in that equation," Angelica said pointedly.

"Have you ever spoken to Antonio about your refusal to acknowledge him as your son?"

"We've discussed it," Angelica said stiffly. "He understands my position."

"Yes, but what's *his* position?"

"He's okay with it. He has a great job, we have a great relationship, and we've acknowledged our relationship with everyone who matters."

"You've never clarified it with Grace and Mr. Everett, and they've become like family to us."

"Are you trying to shame me? Because that's the whole reason I never acknowledged Antonio—because our family would have shamed me *and* him by association."

"I hope you're not counting me among that crowd."

"Mother let us—or at least *me*—know that any kind of shame we brought to the family would have been dealt with by total rejection."

Tricia shuddered, remembering her mother's vehement threats of the past. "If you *ever* brought that kind of shame to us, I'd disown you" was still enough to cause a flush to rise and color her cheeks. It had been why Tricia sought out birth control as soon as she'd entered into her first serious relationship.

"Besides," Angelica continued, "Nigela Ricita is a much more important, accomplished person than me. I should think Antonio would be proud to be the son of such a stunning success."

"That sounds like a cop-out. Have you ever asked him about it?" Tricia persisted.

Angelica took rather a long moment to answer. "Kind of."

"What does that mean?"

"We've spoken about it and I don't think I need to go into it with you. Are we clear on this?"

Tricia shook her head, sighed, and played with the frill pick in her glass. "I guess."

"Fine. Now, if you'll excuse me, I'm going to check on our entrées."

"What are we having?"

"Baked chicken. It's simple, nourishing, and easy." Angelica picked up her glass and took it with her into the kitchen. She'd calm down in a few minutes, but Tricia thought her question concerning Antonio had merit. She knew how she felt all those years in Angelica's shadow when her mother barely acknowledged her existence. Despite having come to some kind of understanding with her mother, Tricia knew she would probably never truly get over the pain of rejection. Antonio seemed a lot more forgiving.

Tricia tried to put the conversation out of her mind. She had other things to think about. Like talking to Dan about the missing manuscript. How in the world was she going to speak to him civilly after what had happened that afternoon? Should she start with Nadine? Yes, maybe that was the approach. That is, if Nadine showed up in the village square the next morning. Tricia would get there early and wait even if it meant she wouldn't get in her walk.

It was the best—the only—thing she could think to do.

Angelica had definitely not been happy with the turn in their conversation, and while she wasn't cold toward Tricia during dinner, there was definitely a bit of a chill in the air.

Once back in her apartment, Tricia berated herself. Why did it matter if Angelica wanted to keep her identity as Antonio's mother such a secret when she was obviously proud of him, the work they'd done together, and of the extended family he'd given her?

As she got ready for bed, Tricia vowed not to bring up the subject ever again. She and Angelica had had a brief spat six months before and Tricia didn't want a repeat of that unhappy time. She loved her sister too much to provoke her.

Tricia awoke the next morning with a new mission: to talk to Nadine Reed.

Dressing warmly despite the bright day, Tricia waited until after eight to head for the village square and the bench where she'd usually found Nadine. She was there, all right, bundled up against the chill air, but there were no tears that morning. Instead, she looked annoyed.

"Tricia," Nadine said in greeting. "I'm surprised to see you here—after what happened yesterday."

Tricia wasn't sure how to interpret that statement. "Oh?"

Nadine shook her head. "In case you were wondering, Dan's jaw wasn't broken. Just badly bruised."

"Well, thank goodness for that."

"Are you going to press assault charges?"

Tricia spoke the truth. "Only if Dan presses charges against my assistant manager."

Nadine shook her head again. "I talked him out of that. We can't afford to hire a lawyer. And let's face it, you've got deeper pockets than we do."

It was probably true.

"Is that why you showed up today?" Nadine asked.

"No. But I do have a question for you about Dan."

Nadine frowned. "So?"

"From what he said yesterday, I got the distinct feeling he and Eli were a lot closer than either of them let on?"

"You mean bosom buddies?"

Tricia nodded.

"No," Nadine said flatly. "Eli just tried to bleed Dan dry by selling him garbage on any cockamamie conspiracy theory that came down the pike. He had"—she made air quotes—"'special' publications that were pure drivel and he sold them for astronomical prices."

Tricia hadn't seen anything like that in Eli's shop, but she had seen the volumes in his restricted area.

Nadine studied Tricia's face. "Why did you ask about Dan and Eli anyway?"

"I wondered if Eli confided in Dan about a book he was writing?"

"*Conspiracy 101* or *Conspiracy 202* by a former terrorist?"

"Something like that," Tricia remarked.

"Not as far as I know."

Tricia nodded. "I've got a question for you."

Nadine looked intrigued. "Go on."

"I had breakfast at the diner the other day."

"Yeah, I heard about that."

"Everyone there refers to you as Nan."

Nadine actually winced. "They sure do, even though I've asked them to call me by my given name."

"Why don't they?"

"Because Dan doesn't like it. That's why *he* calls me Nan. I hate it. I've always hated it, but lately, it's really gotten to me. I'm my own person and I resent being called by someone else's name."

"I don't understand. Why would Dan insist on calling you by a name you—"

"Because he's a bully. Surely you've figured that out by now."

Yeah. She had.

"I'm sorry. Have you figured out what you want to do about . . . your future?"

"The outcome? Yes. How to get there? I have no idea," Nadine said, sounding frustrated.

"I'm sorry," Tricia said again. "If there's anything I can do to help, please—"

But Nadine cut her off. "It's sweet of you to offer, but we both know how empty an offer that is." Nadine stood. "I'm a pragmatist. I'll figure something out—and soon—so don't worry about me. I'll be 'shaking the dust of this crummy little town off my feet and I'm going to see the world.' See ya." And with that, Nadine turned and headed back toward Main Street, going north.

Tricia thought about the words Nadine had said. They had a familiar ring to them. She started walking south toward Locust Street to pick up on one of her usual walking routes. She'd gone about a block when it hit her where she'd heard those words before: the movie *It's a Wonderful Life*. George Bailey had uttered that sentence, which had ended up being an omen instead of a declaration of independence. He never left Bedford Falls, but his life *had* improved. When he thought life was at its worst—he'd found the greatest gift of all. Love. Somehow Tricia didn't think that would be Nadine's fate.

What *was* in store for her?

THIRTY-FOUR

Tricia felt more than a little depressed as she continued on her walk through the village and definitely had no pep in her step. As she rounded Cedar Avenue and circled back to Main Street she headed north to return to Haven't Got a Clue. Up ahead she could see Mary Fairchild on her way to By Hook or By Book with a grocery bag in hand.

In contrast, Mary seemed in fine spirits and waved cheerfully to Tricia. "Hey there! How are you on this fine morning?"

Tricia paused outside of Mary's shop to chat. "Oh, fine."

"Boy, you don't sound it."

"I'm waiting for the warmer weather," Tricia fibbed.

"The weatherman says we might see seventy next week. Of course, that could change in a heartbeat and we might have a spring blizzard."

"Don't even think that!" Tricia warned.

"Hey, what do you think about the latest Eli rumor?" Mary asked.

Tricia's eyebrows rose. "And what's that?"

"That he was writing a tell-all memoir about his life as

a terrorist!" Mary seemed more than a little intrigued by the idea.

"I heard," Tricia said neutrally.

"I didn't think Eli could even type, but then again, he used to sit in front of that ridiculous little lectern he used as a cash desk, microphone in hand, when he was alone in his shop."

Tricia blinked. "He what?"

"Oh, sure. I saw him do that all the time. At first, I wondered if he was doing karaoke to while away the hours when he had no customers, but people usually look happy when they sing, and I swear that man didn't know the meaning of the word."

Tricia's mind flashed back to the box of cassette tapes she'd found when poking around in Eli's store. Was he too cheap to buy new ones and recorded over the tapes from the odd mix of musical genres that he'd either had for years or picked up at a yard sale?

"That's really very interesting," Tricia said, but she needed to get on the phone and call Becca to see if she could get into the storage unit to find the tapes. Or should she tell Ian McDonald and let him find them? Either way, whatever the tapes contained wasn't likely to solve Eli's murder.

Still, she saw it as her duty to say something about them.

"Great seeing you, Mare, but I need to get to my store and get ready for the day."

"Talk to you soon," Mary said, taking out the keys to her store and entering while Tricia pivoted to go back to her store. But upon entering, it wasn't Becca or Ian she called.

"Hi, Tricia. What's up?" Angelica asked.

"I think I know where Artemis can find Eli's missing manuscript."

"Oh, yeah?"

"He taped his memories."

"What?"

"I just spoke to Mary Fairchild. She saw him talking

into a tape recorder on numerous occasions and I found a box filled with tapes while I was poking around the Inner Light."

"Artemis will be so happy," Angelica gushed. She loved to please her agent.

"There's only one problem. They're in a storage unit in one of a couple of hundred boxes."

Angelica's joy was short-lived. "Oh, dear."

"Yeah. Becca said she was going to hold on to the stuff for a month before dumping it, but Artemis had better figure something out before they end up in a landfill."

"I'll call him right now. Thanks for the heads-up. Would you call Becca and get permission for Artemis to go through or have someone else go through the boxes?"

"Were you thinking of doing it?"

"Heavens, no! I was only in the Inner Light once, and it *smelled*. I don't need to be reminded of that odor while poking through all that junk!"

"I figured as much," Tricia said, amused. "And I will call Becca to ask for permission to look through the stuff."

"Thanks. Talk to you later."

Tricia ended the call and immediately checked her contacts list and tapped Becca's name.

"Hello, Tricia. What now?" Did she sound just a little annoyed?

"Just calling to chat."

"Well, let's make it brief. I need to arrange to have some garbage people come and clean out that storage unit."

"What? I thought you said you paid for a month."

"I did. But thanks to that new chief of police, my attorneys were able to contact Joseph Martin's next of kin—who wanted nothing to do with him or the crap from his store. They've signed off on it and I'm free to unburden myself of the whole mess."

"Well, I think you'd better be prepared for a fight over the contents."

"I told you—they signed off."

"That was before they—or you—knew about something very valuable in that storage unit."

"Oh, yeah? And what's it worth?"

"Not much. Just about a million dollars."

After explaining about the tapes and the almost-signed book deal between Eli and the publishing company, Becca wasn't about to let anyone else near that storage unit. She hung up and told Tricia she'd call back later. Tricia immediately got back on the phone to tell Angelica of the new complication.

"Oh, no! Artemis isn't going to be happy to hear that. This will certainly complicate matters."

"Yeah."

"I'd better call him back right away. Boy, am I going to need our happy hour martinis tonight!"

Tricia felt the same way.

Mr. Everett showed up for work a few minutes early, with Grace checking in just long enough to say she'd be back in time to take her husband to lunch at noon.

"Would you like some coffee?" Tricia asked. She could sure use a cup after the morning she'd had.

Mr. Everett looked toward the beverage station, which hadn't been set up for the day. "It appears you've been busy this morning."

Tricia sighed. "You don't know the half of it."

"Would you like to talk about it?" Mr. Everett offered.

Tricia wasn't sure she should—at least about Eli's tapes, but he deserved to know what was going on with Pixie and the trouble Edward and Dan had caused the afternoon before. She explained as she set up the beverage station for the day.

"Oh, my. Poor Pixie." He looked at his useless right arm in the sling. "I wish there was something I could do to help."

Before she could commiserate, Tricia's cell phone rang. It was Becca.

"I've spoken to my lawyer and he assures me, I now own *everything* in that storage unit."

Good for her.

"But I don't trust anyone else to deal with the contents—except you."

"I'm flattered," Tricia deadpanned, although she was pretty sure she knew what was coming next.

"I pulled some strings—dropped a few names—and arranged to pick up a rental truck later this afternoon. Will you help me look for those tapes and also help me load the truck to take the rest of that junk to the dump?"

"Becca, I have a business to run."

"Ms. Miles," Mr. Everett called, waving his good hand in the air. "If you need to leave, I can take care of the store. That is, if Grace will give me a hand."

"Tricia?" Becca called.

"Hold on." Tricia turned to Mr. Everett. "I couldn't ask her to do that. Becca will simply have to wait until I'm available."

"I heard that," Becca said. "When *can* you be available? This evening?"

"I have plans," Tricia told her.

"Drinks and dinner with your sister? You do that *every* night. Couldn't you make an exception for just *one* evening? Or better yet, ask her to help us."

Tricia felt trapped. But why should she? Becca and she were not friends. They were acquaintances at best. And Angelica had already expressed her opinion about going through the contents of the storage unit. But would she feel an obligation to Artemis to help get his million-dollar deal back on the table?

"I'll ask my sister."

"Good. Then I can pick her successful business brain while we search through the crap."

"I said I'd ask. I didn't promise she'd come through."

"I'd appreciate it." Did Becca actually sound sincere?

Tricia sighed—for what seemed like the thousandth time that morning. "I'll get back to you."

"Thanks."

Becca ended the call.

Tricia frowned and set her phone on the cash desk.

"Honestly, Ms. Miles, I'm sure that Grace won't mind helping out at the store."

"It isn't fair to ask her. Besides, I don't know how long it would take to—to . . ." Much as she trusted Mr. Everett, she didn't want to talk about the favor Becca had asked of her. "It could take hours—or even a day or so."

Mr. Everett nodded and Tricia sensed his frustration caused by his temporary handicap.

"It was very kind of you to offer to help, but in this instance—"

Mr. Everett held up a hand to interrupt. "I'll only be in this cast for a few more weeks and then we can all get back to normal."

Normal? What in Tricia's life came under that category? But she didn't argue with her friend. "Exactly."

Tricia didn't feel comfortable leaving Mr. Everett in charge of the store, so she decided to just call Angelica from the sales floor instead of going to the basement office. She wasn't looking forward to the conversation.

Before she could face speaking to her sister once again, Tricia poured herself a cup of coffee. This time, Mr. Everett agreed to join her. He settled with a book in the reader's nook, while Tricia stood behind the counter and took a fortifying gulp from her mug before she called Angelica again.

"What's up now?" Angelica asked upon answering.

"It seems that Becca wants my help to empty the storage unit. She doesn't trust anyone else to help—except you, that is?"

"Me? I told you, I want nothing to do with the stinky stock from the Inner Light."

"And I told Becca the same thing." More or less. "She wants to do it this evening since I told her I couldn't be available during the day."

"She's started her own company. Surely she trusts at least *one* of her employees."

"Apparently not."

"Why on earth would I want to help *her* after she bought the old warehouse and all the decent land outside the village just to spite me?"

"To spite Nigela Ricita, not you personally."

"It's the same thing."

"No, it's not, because she thinks you're two distinct people."

A long silence fell before Angelica spoke again. "I suppose you feel an obligation to help her."

"Well, I—"

"Tricia, Tricia, Tricia," Angelica chided her. "You need to learn to say no. That's always been part of your problem."

"I didn't know I had such a problem," Tricia said sarcastically.

"Well, you do. And if I know you, you'd stick to doing the job until it's done—even if it takes all night."

"I don't know about *that*," Tricia protested.

"Well, I do." Angelica let out what sounded like an exasperated breath. "If it weren't for my own sense of obligation to Artemis, I wouldn't lift a finger to help that woman."

"Then you'll help us clean out the unit?"

"I'm not willing to budge from my home until I've had a decent dinner. I won't be available until at least seven thirty—and you won't be, either."

"Artemis will thank you."

"I'm not doing this for anyone's thanks. I doubt Becca even includes the word in her vocabulary."

"Well, then *I* thank you."

"I'll see you at closing. I'm having at least one martini, too. But I'll make something simple for dinner. We don't want to be lifting boxes with too much in our stomachs."

"Good point."

"All right. Talk to you later."

"See you."

Tricia ended the call and glanced at the clock. It was

only ten thirty in the morning, and already she felt like she was ready to pack it in for the day.

She drank the rest of her coffee, stowed her mug under the counter in case she decided to have another cup, and finally began her workday.

It was going to be a long one.

THIRTY-FIVE

Angelica wasn't kidding when she said she would have her martini that evening, but she was also dressed in her rattiest jeans and sweatshirt and clad in a pair of sensible shoes. And dinner *was* a simple affair of two-egg omelets and toast.

The sun still had another twenty minutes before it set when Tricia and Angelica left to meet Becca. Still, Tricia's hackles rose as the sisters walked to the municipal parking lot. She felt as though someone was watching her. Edward Dowding? Earlier, Pixie had texted her that she'd seen no sign of him and that her boss at the day spa, Randy Ellison, had personally driven her home to ensure her safety. Perhaps Ian's little talk with Edward had done some good. Or . . . he was still on the loose and had taken care not to show himself.

And, of course, it could be that Eli's killer was watching her—although why he would seemed unfathomable. She hadn't told anyone but Becca and Angelica about the tapes, and it was unlikely Artemis had contact with anyone in Stoneham but Angelica. Tricia was just being paranoid.

Five minutes later, Tricia drove up to the self-storage yard and found a U-Haul van parked outside the business, with Becca behind the wheel. Tricia parked nearby and she and Angelica joined Becca, hopping into the van's cab.

"Thanks for coming—both of you," she said.

Tricia eyed her sister as though to say, *See, she does know how to say thank you.* Angelica merely scowled.

"Let's get this over with," Angelica said.

"Right." Becca started the van, drove up to the gates, and used a key card to gain entrance. Then she drove them to the unit she'd rented. It was triple the size of the one that had held Becca's former husband's excess stock from his—now her—shop, the Armchair Tourist.

The place was deserted. Its management seemed to have upgraded the security systems—which had not been working upon Tricia's previous visits—and the lights around the buildings had already begun to pop on.

The women got out of the truck and stood before the unit, which had a double garage door. Becca took out a key and advanced upon it. "Let's hope we don't find a dead body this time," she said, and laughed.

Angelica was not amused.

Tricia helped Becca pull up the door and saw the entire space was filled with boxes, none of them marked as to the contents.

Becca turned on the lights. "There are gloves, dust masks, box cutters, and trash bags in the back of the van. I'll go get them," Becca said, and left Tricia and Angelica to stare at the disheartening amount of cartons they would need to go through.

"I hate the thought of just trashing all those books," Tricia said.

"Yes, well, the state they're in, I'm sure no one else would have bought them and no reputable charity would have accepted them."

Tricia nodded sadly. Still, it pained her to know the books' fate.

Becca returned with a box of big black trash bags, along with the other stuff.

"Does this mean we aren't going to reuse the boxes the books are already packed in?" Angelica asked. "Surely bags will break with the weight of all that paper."

"I'm sure we'll reuse most of them," Becca answered.

"Any instructions?" Tricia asked.

"Find those tapes," Becca said simply.

"Do we need to empty every box?" Angelica asked.

"Until we hit pay dirt, yeah, just in case they're buried at the bottom. By the way, Tricia, what exactly are we looking for?"

Tricia had come prepared for the question. She took out her phone and tapped the gallery icon. She'd looked up and copied a picture of a cassette case similar to the one she'd seen at the Inner Light.

"What if Mary was wrong?" Angelica asked. "What if those tapes are just filled with the ramblings of a man whose income depended on the repetition of conspiracy theories—or worse, singing."

"I for one will be *really* pissed off," Becca said.

"We won't know until we find them," Tricia said reasonably.

Becca and Angelica turned annoyed glances on her and donned their masks and gloves.

"Start unpacking," Becca ordered, and each woman grabbed a box.

Angelica had been right. Despite the mask, the Inner Light's peculiar odor had impregnated each of the tomes that had lived there for at least half a decade. After carefully unpacking several boxes and then repacking them, Tricia and Angelica followed Becca's lead by slashing the tape with the box cutters and dumping the contents.

"I wish you'd hung around the store long enough to see when the movers packed those tapes," Becca groused as she repacked one of the cartons, folding in the flaps.

After they'd gone through twenty or more boxes, their workspace was getting cluttered and Becca ordered her minions to start loading them into the truck.

Tricia removed her mask and climbed into the back of

the van. As Becca and Angelica hefted the boxes onto the van's deck, Tricia moved them toward the front. It wasn't long until her back started to protest.

The sky had darkened and the stack was getting pretty high when Tricia heard the sound of an engine advancing down the lane, but stuck in the back of the truck, she couldn't see the vehicle. The engine cut off and she heard the sound of a car door slam.

"Hey, what's going on?" said a familiar voice. It took a moment for Tricia to identify it. Nadine Reed.

"Just clearing out my storage unit," Becca said, sounding just a little annoyed.

"Why so late?" Nadine asked, stepping into Tricia's line of sight.

Becca pulled down her mask. "I have a day job," she answered simply.

"You look familiar," Nadine said.

"I have common features," Becca lied, apparently not in the mood to tangle with yet another of the fans from her years as a tennis star.

Tricia scrambled from the back of the truck and called, "Nadine!"

Nadine pivoted, clutching a hand to her chest. "My God, Tricia—you scared me!"

"Sorry. What brings you around?"

"We've got a storage unit here, too. Just around the corner. We keep extra stuff for the diner. Tables, chairs, the odd coffeemaker."

It seemed plausible.

Angelica ambled up to the truck with another box, shoving it into the cavernous cavity. Nadine ignored her. "I came to drop off some cases of coffee. Dan overordered them and the distributor won't take them back without a huge hassle, but I can't get my car past your truck."

Becca's expression darkened.

"How many boxes are we talking about?" Tricia asked.

"Two."

"I'll help you carry them to your unit," Tricia volunteered.

"Aw, thanks, Tricia."

"Meanwhile, Angelica and I will continue to go through the boxes," Becca said.

Angelica glowered at her. Perhaps she'd wished she'd volunteered to help Nadine instead of working with Becca.

"Come on," Nadine encouraged Tricia.

Nadine's car was just what Tricia expected—a junker that was rust-pocked and dented. She knew that Dan drove a late-model SUV. Nadine opened the trunk and handed one of the boxes to Tricia. It must have weighed a good ten pounds. Nadine hefted a box for herself with what seemed like little effort, holding on to it with one arm and slamming the trunk lid. "Follow me."

The women walked past Becca's rental truck and the unit where Becca and Angelica were hard at work sorting through the boxes.

"What's going on?" Nadine asked. "Why are they emptying boxes?"

"Becca lost something."

Nadine stopped. "Becca?"

"Becca Chandler."

"Becca Dickson-Chandler? The tennis player?" Nadine asked.

Tricia nodded.

"I heard she lived around here," Nadine said, sounding wary.

"Yes. In fact, she owns the property that Eli Meier rented for the Inner Light."

"I hadn't heard *that*," Nadine said, and began walking again.

"It isn't well known. Nor that she's going to build a tennis center in the village."

"*In* the village?"

"She bought the site of the old warehouse on Main Street."

"She's really making herself at home here in Stoneham. And she's your friend?" Nadine asked.

"It's getting to look like it," Tricia remarked.

Nadine paused in front of one of the smaller storage units, set her box on the tarmac, and extracted a key from her jacket pocket. She unlocked the unit and pulled up the door, then turned on the light. Inside were cases of canned tomatoes and other vegetables, a well-used kayak, and in the corner what looked like a weight-lifting station with a press bench and a bunch of barbells—from small and light to big and heavy—scattered on the floor.

Nadine retrieved her box and took the one from Tricia, stacking them on top of some other cartons. "Thanks for your help," she said, and gestured toward the unit's door. Tricia stepped outside and watched as Nadine locked up.

"Will you be in the square tomorrow morning?"

"Maybe. Maybe not," Nadine said. "I suppose you will."

"I cut through there most days. If you're there, I'll see you tomorrow."

"Yeah. And thanks again," Nadine said as Tricia stopped in front of Becca's unit once more. Nadine gave a wave and walked purposely toward her car.

Tricia joined Angelica and Becca, who stared after Nadine. Becca and Angelica had opened seven or eight boxes during her absence. As she began repacking one of the cartons, Tricia heard the sound of a car engine roar to life and then recede into the growing darkness. Becca kept looking toward where the sound had been.

"Anything wrong?" Tricia asked, and straightened.

"That woman," Becca said, nodding into the darkness. "How do you know her?"

Tricia shrugged. "She and her husband run the Book-shelf Diner."

"Really. I've never seen her there, and I've eaten a lot of meals there," Becca remarked.

"She's the short-order cook. Her husband runs the front of the house."

Becca looked thoughtful. "She said she thought *my* face looked familiar."

"Yeah?"

"Well, her face looked familiar to me, too."

"Why didn't you say so when she first showed up?" Angelica asked.

"Because it took me a while to remember where I saw her."

"And where was that?" Tricia asked.

Becca looked thoughtful. "At the Olympics."

Tricia blinked. "Which one?"

Becca looked thoughtful. "It was a long time ago—maybe twenty years."

"Was she a tennis player?"

"No," Becca said, and shook her head, looking pensive. "The thing is, you don't really hang around with other Olympians outside your sport. And you usually leave after your events. But one year I hung around to do promotional work for one of the networks and interviewed a number of other women athletes. I swear I met that woman before—only, she's lost a lot of weight since then . . . or maybe it's muscle."

"Did you meet at a party?" Tricia asked.

Again, Becca shook her head. "No, she was wearing some kind of clingy shorts that emphasized her really *big* thighs." She snapped her fingers, her eyes widening. "She was a powerlifter."

"How come no one in the village knows we have a former Olympian living in our midst?" Angelica asked.

"Maybe because her husband's a misogynist jerk. According to Nadine, Dan won't even let the Bookshelf Diner staff call her by her given name because *he* doesn't like it. And there were barbells in her storage unit. Souvenirs or does she still lift?"

Tricia pulled out her phone and tapped on the Google icon, looking for an Olympic powerlifter named Nadine. Bingo! Nadine Barton hadn't won a medal at the one and only Olympic games where she competed, and her specialty was the dead lift.

"Dead lift? How much weight are we talking about?" Angelica asked.

Tricia consulted her phone. "As much as six hundred pounds."

"Wow—that's a lot of weight," Angelica said. "About the weight of three men."

Tricia blinked. They'd been wondering who could have lifted Eli's dead weight. Could it have been . . . ?

No! Becca said that Nadine had lost a lot of weight—and had at one time had mighty thighs. So even if she still worked out—and she possibly did—could she lift a dead man's weight and carry it a block to the Coffee Bean?

"Are you thinking what I'm thinking?" Angelica asked her sister.

"You bet."

"What?" Becca asked.

"Uh, nothing," Tricia said.

Becca gave Tricia a sour look. "You're thinking something important. Spill it."

Tricia looked to her sister for guidance, but Angelica merely shrugged.

"We know that Eli Meier was shot with a handgun and his body was moved. We've been speculating who could have carried him from the village square all the way to the alley behind the Coffee Bean."

"And you think it was Nadine Barton?" Becca asked.

"Reed," Tricia insisted.

"Whatever!"

"And why would she want to kill the guy?"

"That's a good question. But like so many other citizens of Stoneham, she *does* own at least one gun," Tricia muttered.

"For protection," Becca reminded Tricia.

"So you say."

Becca eyed the inside of the unit, which still housed three quarters of the boxes. "I wouldn't worry about her."

"You have to admit, Nadine fits a lot of Chief McDonald's criteria for Eli's murderer," Tricia said.

"So do I," Becca said. "Let's get back to work. The sooner we finish, the sooner I'll treat you ladies to a round at the Dog-Eared Page."

"Throw in a burger and you've got a deal," Angelica said.

"I'll even splurge for fries," Becca said.

The women wielded their box cutters and attacked more boxes, slitting the taped sides. Tricia opened hers and there, sitting on top of several large books, was the grubby little cassette tape recorder and beneath that the vinyl carrier of tapes. "I've got it!" she shouted—louder than she'd meant.

Angelica and Becca scrambled to her side as Tricia removed the player from the carton. She hit the play button and could see the little spindles move. "It's still got batteries."

"Shove in a tape and let's listen," Becca urged her.

Tricia selected a plastic case heralding CHARLEY PRIDE GREATEST HITS, removed the cassette, and slipped it into the player, pressing play. At first, all they heard was a hiss, which went on for long seconds, and then Eli's voice issued from the tinny speaker.

"It was April fourth, and the gang and I were meeting to talk about—"

Tricia hit the stop button and glanced up at Becca, who smiled widely. "I think I've got myself a million-dollar book deal."

"I hope you'll at least mention us in the acknowledgments," Angelica deadpanned.

A phone pinged. The three women all pulled out their phones to check, but it was Angelica who spoke, her eyes wide in delight. "I just got a text from Antonio. Ginny's water broke and he's taking her to the hospital. He wants to drop Sofia off at my place. I need to leave right now."

"Go!" Becca said. "Tricia can help me clean up here."

"I drove her here," Tricia said.

"You'd leave me here all alone when we just spoke to a potential murderer?" Becca practically wailed.

"You didn't think she was all that threatening a few minutes ago. Besides, there're security cameras all over the place," Tricia pointed out.

"Yeah, and they weren't working the night we found Mark Jameson, were they?"

"I'm sure they've been fixed by now."

"And you want to bet my life on it?" Becca asked.

"We need to go!" Angelica said. "Sofia needs me."

"Can't her daddy drop her off at the gate?" Becca asked.

"No, he cannot. My little granddaughter is not going to be hanging around a self-storage facility in the dark!"

A shot rang out, and the globe on one of the surrounding cameras on the building across from them exploded. The women ducked in terror as another shot took out the camera across the way. They scrambled into the storage unit and Becca and Tricia clambered to grab the bottom of the door to yank it closed, when Nadine stepped out of the shadows.

"Hold it right there," she ordered, brandishing a handgun that James Bond might have used.

"Nadine, what are you doing?" Tricia asked, hoping she sounded astounded.

"You know damn well. I knew it, I knew *you'd* figure it out eventually."

"Figure out what?" Tricia asked innocently.

"Who killed Eli Meier."

"And who's that?"

Nadine's eyes blazed. "Me, you idiot!"

"You've made a big mistake," Becca practically growled.

"Shut up," Angelica hissed.

"I just want to know why you killed Eli," Tricia said, not only to stall for time but because if Nadine hadn't outed herself, would she have been considered a suspect at all?

"I told you, he'd been scamming Dan for years. The diner's about to go under—then where will we—I—be?"

It seemed a pretty flimsy motive for murder.

"The idiot picked a fight with me," Nadine went on, "and I lost it. Meier kept laughing at me—telling me what a sucker I'd married. He was right about that. He kept going on and on and I got more and more angry so I pulled my gun out of my purse and shot the bastard on the spot."

Just like that?

Tricia's gaze was riveted on the gun's barrel. "And now you're going to shoot us."

Nadine's smile was positively wicked.

THIRTY-SIX

The harsh light from the storage facility's security lights had bleached all the color from everything and everyone, making the situation even more surreal.

Tricia's mouth went dry. "And to think I actually felt sorry for you."

"Well, now I feel sorry for *you*. And I'll make this easier on all of you," Nadine said. "Just turn around, get down on your knees, and it'll be over before you know it."

"No," Tricia said coldly. "If you're going to kill us, you have to look us in the eye."

Nadine shrugged. "If that's the way you want it." She gave a snort of laughter.

Running footsteps distracted the women and movement to her right caused Tricia's gaze to stray from the barrel of the gun. It was Edward hurtling toward the group.

"Stop!" he hollered.

Nadine turned and fired, hitting Edward, who jerked back, but somehow remained on his feet. Nadine pumped another two shots into his body and he staggered before falling backward to the ground.

Without conscious thought, Tricia let out the same kind of guttural yell Pixie had made when she'd attacked Dan, and lashed out with her foot as she'd seen her assistant manager do—connecting with Nadine's right hand, sending the gun flying.

Becca was a blur as she rushed at Nadine, knocking her to the asphalt.

Angelica already had her phone at the ready, punching in the numbers 911.

Nadine rolled over onto her stomach, palms to the ground to push herself up when Becca shoved her back to the ground and sat on her backside. "Oh, no, you don't," she cried as Nadine's arms flailed, trying to knock her off. "Find something to tie her up!"

Tricia rushed to the back of the rental truck, where she found a number of thick, black bungee cords, grabbing two of them. Between her and Becca, they managed to restrain Nadine, who was screaming abuse. The struggle took the better part of a minute, during which Angelica told the dispatcher about their predicament.

"Oh, put a sock in it," Becca said, and stuffed one of her work gloves into Nadine's mouth.

Now that Nadine was subdued, Tricia raced to Edward's side. She crouched down to assess his injuries. The front of his jacket was sodden with blood. With nothing to make a bandage from, Tricia stripped off her jacket and stuffed it inside Edward's, hoping it might help to staunch the flow.

Edward's eyes blinked open and he groaned. "Getting shot . . . really hurts."

"Why did you try to stop her?" Tricia asked, feeling an amalgam of fear, awe, and helplessness.

"Fred told me you . . . were Pixie's best friend."

The sound of a siren broke the relative quiet. Becca had abandoned her prisoner. "How's he look?" she muttered.

Tricia shook her head, declining to answer.

Becca held up the key card that opened the storage facility's gate. "I'll go let the cops and EMTs in," she said, and took off as fast as her bum leg would let her.

Edward groped for Tricia's hand, trying to raise his

head. "You tell Pixie . . . I'm not a monster. You tell her . . . I'm not like my birth father."

"You're not," Tricia assured him.

He laid his head back down, his breathing labored.

Tricia held on to his cold hand and swallowed, tears filling her eyes.

"Hold on, Edward," she told him. "Please hold on."

THIRTY-SEVEN

 Tricia hadn't waited for the ambulance to leave the storage facility before she called Pixie.

"What am I supposed to do about it?" an anguished Pixie cried.

"I don't know. I just thought you ought to know."

A long silence followed.

"Where are they taking him?" Pixie asked.

"Southern New Hampshire Medical Center."

Tricia heard Pixie sigh. "All right."

"Are you going there?"

"I don't know. I just don't know. I'll talk to you later."

The call ended.

Tricia watched as the ambulance took off. At least Edward was still alive. With him losing so much blood, she hadn't expected him to survive this long.

Antonio had swung by and dropped Sofia off, and Angelica had used Tricia's car to take the girl back to her apartment to wait for the blessed event. She'd give her story to the cops the next day.

Tricia saw Ian speaking with Becca and walked over to join them, feeling suddenly exhausted.

"We meet again under unfortunate circumstances," Ian said in greeting, his voice subdued.

"Unfortunate indeed."

Nadine had been hauled off and sat in the back of one of the police SUVs, glowering at them.

Ian's expression was bland. "So, you found another one."

"Another what?"

"Killer."

"Oh, that!" Becca said in dismissal. "It's Tricia's life's work."

Tricia scowled at her frenemy.

"I'll want you both to come to the station to make a formal statement."

"We've told you all we know. Does it have to be tonight?" Tricia asked.

Ian seemed to consider the request. "I guess not."

"I need to open my store at noon tomorrow. Can I come in before that?"

"Anytime after eight," Ian replied.

Tricia nodded.

"Chief!" called one of the officers.

"Excuse me," Ian said.

Becca inspected Tricia's face. "How well did you know that young man?"

"Barely at all."

"He's going to die, isn't he?" Her tone was so innocuous.

Tricia sigh. "It doesn't look good. Can you give me a ride back to the municipal parking lot? I want to pick up my car and head to the hospital. I think someone should be there for Edward."

"The poor schmuck. But, hey, that was some kung fu move you made to disarm Nadine."

"It was something Edward's mother taught me."

Minutes later, Becca steered the van through the streets of Stoneham and pulled up in front of the parking lot. "Text me later and let me know how the kid makes out, will ya?"

"Sure. And thanks for the ride."

"Thank *you* for the tapes," Becca said, and bent to pat the plastic carrier that sat on the floor beside her.

Tricia walked through the parking lot to retrieve her car.

It was a quiet ride to the hospital some twenty minutes away. She didn't bother with the radio, but she found it hard to concentrate on anything other than her feelings of guilt and worry.

Upon her arrival, she was informed that due to the Health Insurance Portability and Accountability Act, the hospital could not give out any information on Edward's condition. She'd figured as much, but they did say he'd been admitted. Tricia wasn't sure what to do, so she sat down in the ER's lobby and waited. It wasn't long before she heard her name called.

"Tricia!"

It was Pixie.

Tricia rose to her feet and intercepted her friend.

"What's going on?" Pixie asked, sounding distraught.

"They won't tell me anything. HIPPA rules."

Pixie shook her head and frowned. "Let's see if pulling the mother card will help." She marched up to the receptionist on duty and asked for information on Edward and was told he was in surgery and she could wait in the surgical waiting area.

"Where's Fred?" Tricia asked.

"He didn't want to come in. He's squeamish that way. He'd prefer to sit in the car and freeze."

Tricia nodded. If Pixie wasn't going to hold it against him, Tricia decided she wouldn't, either.

"Will you come and wait with me?" Pixie asked.

"Of course." No way would she leave her friend alone at a time like this.

Several other people sat waiting when they signed in and asked for news about Edward, getting the same information they were given in the ER. Tricia and Pixie sat in the upholstered, but not very comfortable, chairs to wait. The others were soon greeted with good news about their loved one and left the area.

"Would you like some coffee? I could go find some," Tricia offered.

Pixie shook her head. "Thank you for being here. I almost didn't come. But then . . . I didn't want him to die with no one here."

"Who said he's going to die?"

Pixie turned a hard gaze on her employer. "From what you told me on the phone, I'm surprised he even made it to the hospital, let alone surgery."

"That's a good sign, wouldn't you say?" Tricia offered, trying to remain optimistic, although she certainly didn't feel that way.

Pixie said nothing but turned her gaze to the carpeted floor.

They sat there, not speaking, not looking at each other, for nearly half an hour before a scrubs-clad man approached. "Family of Edward Dowding?"

Pixie stood up. "I'm his mother."

How hard had it been for her to say that? Tricia got up to stand beside her friend.

"I'm very sorry, Mrs. Dowding—"

"Poe. Ms. Poe," Pixie corrected him.

"But your son didn't survive the surgery."

Pixie staggered a little and Tricia reached out a hand to steady her.

Dry-eyed, Pixie swallowed and nodded. "I'd . . . I'd like to be with him for a while. Would that be possible?"

"Certainly. If you'll give us a few moments, we'll call you when—"

"I understand," Pixie said, interrupting the physician.

"I'm sorry," he said again. "But his injuries were just too—"

"Thank you," Pixie said, and swallowed.

The doctor headed back for the surgical suites.

"Oh, Pixie. I don't know what to say," Tricia said, and hugged her friend.

"That's okay," Pixie said, her voice muffled against Tricia's shoulder. "I don't know what to say, either."

Tricia pulled back. "Would you like me to go in with you?"

Pixie shook her head. "I need to do this by myself."

They sat back down, but it was only a few minutes before Pixie was called away.

Tricia remained in her seat, feeling desolate. She hadn't liked Edward Dowding, but she hadn't thought his relationship with Pixie would end this way.

And then it occurred to her that Ginny was somewhere in the same hospital. Tricia pulled out her phone and texted Antonio.

It won't be long now, came his reply.

How ironic. Pixie had just lost her son, and Ginny was giving birth to hers.

With nothing better to do, Tricia texted her sister, bringing her up to date on what had happened.

Please tell Pixie how sorry I am, was her reply. Since you're at the hospital, maybe you could take some pictures of the baby for Sofia and me?

Tricia said she would. And then she waited some more.

After what seemed like hours, but was more like half an hour, Pixie reappeared, still dry-eyed. She practically fell into the chair next to Tricia.

"How are you?"

"I'm . . . better. I told him everything. I explained everything. I only wish I could have done it when he was alive. But I couldn't look at him. Even in death, he was the spittin' image of Al. For some reason, I couldn't forgive him for that—even now. I feel like such a shit."

"Oh, Pixie!" Tricia chided her. "You know, he asked me to tell you that he wasn't a monster. He wanted you to know that he wasn't like Al."

Pixie shook her head and frowned.

"And one more thing," Tricia said, feeling her throat begin to close. "When I asked him why he ran to confront Nadine Reed, he said he did it because he didn't want me to get hurt. He knew I was your friend and he wanted to protect me . . . for you."

Pixie's eyes filled with tears and finally, she cried.

* * *

It was a long walk back to the emergency room exit where Fred was waiting with the car. "I want you to take some time off from work," Tricia said.

Pixie shook her head. "No. I don't want to sit around and mope. It'll be easier if I try to get back to my usual routine. So I'll see you bright and early Monday morning."

"Only if you're up to it," Tricia reiterated.

"I'll be there. Please tell Mr. E what happened. It'll be bad enough going over it with Fred on the way home. I don't want to have to do it again."

"Okay," Tricia promised. She hugged her friend and watched her get into the car and drive off.

Just then Tricia's phone pinged. She quickly glanced at Antonio's message. Come and meet your nephew.

And so she did.

THIRTY-EIGHT

 It was a lovely summer day in late June when Ginny and Antonio held their belated open house/meet-the-new-member-of-the-family celebration. Tricia closed Haven't Got a Clue several hours early so that she and her staff could all attend the celebration with other friends and business associates who worked at or owned businesses along Stoneham's main drag who had been invited, along with Ginny's parents, who'd traveled from Florida.

Of course, the star attraction of the party was two-month-old William Alessandro Barbero, affectionately known as Will, who had been happily passed around to be tickled and kissed by the closest of family and friends.

Ginny had explained that her father's middle name was William but confided to Tricia that the baby had actually been named after Mr. Everett, who seemed proud enough to bust each time he got to hold the little bambino. Will's middle name came from Antonio's birth father, which had pleased Angelica as well.

The food catered by the Brookview Inn was superb, and the drinks—both hard and soft—flowed freely. Everyone seemed to be having a good time. Well, except perhaps for one guest.

Pixie and Fred stood near one of the food stations,

where a waitress from the Brookview Inn served hors
d'oeuvres. Pixie held a tall plastic cup with a lime wedge
garnish clinging to the rim, while Fred held a nearly empty
bottle of Rick Lavoy's craft beer. Since Edward's death,
Pixie had dressed in either black or other subdued colors,
but on that day, she'd chosen the cheerful Snow White dress
that was among Tricia's favorites. Pixie hadn't bounced
back as quickly as Tricia would have hoped. She'd suggested Pixie might want to seek the help of a psychologist,
but Pixie was adamant that she wanted to work things out
for herself.

"My, don't you look nice today," Tricia said in greeting.

"Yeah," Pixie agreed, "we clean up nicely."

"I'm so glad you decided to come after all," Tricia said.
Pixie had been on the fence earlier that day.

"I'm sure glad," Fred said, smiling. "This is a great
party."

It was, too. Good food, good drinks, good people.

Fred drained the last of his beer. He proffered his empty
bottle. "I think I'll go get another. That is, if you don't
mind, honey."

"Go for it," Pixie encouraged him.

Fred raised his bottle as though in a toast and went in
search of a replacement.

Pixie watched him go, looking sad. These days, that was
her usual expression. It broke Tricia's heart. She reached
out and touched Pixie's shoulder.

"I went to his grave again this morning," Pixie said. "I
don't think I've ever really expressed how much I appreciate you, Angelica, and Ms. Dickson-Chandler for paying
for Edward to have a decent burial, something I could never
have given him."

"He saved our lives. We owed him that much."

"But it wasn't expected, and most people wouldn't have
done it."

Tricia liked to think that she wouldn't be grouped in the
"most people" category.

"The thing is . . . some part of me loved Edward . . . and

yet I knew I could never *really* love him because of the way he was conceived," Pixie said. "And if I'd known how miserable his short life would be, and that he would be murdered like his father, I would have made a different decision about carrying him to term. I thought I was doing the right thing. But to know he never had a happy life is a burden I have to live with for the rest of *my* life."

Tricia wasn't sure how to react to that statement, so she said nothing.

Pixie seemed to shake herself. "Well, that's not a very cheerful subject. I'm done mourning—at least in front of other people, Fred included. *I'm* still alive. *You're* still alive, and it's summer, my favorite time of year."

"I thought the fall was your favorite?"

"In the *fall* it is. Now it's summer and *now* it's my favorite."

Tricia often had trouble following Pixie's logic, but if it made her happy to think along those lines, Tricia was more than willing to go along with her.

"Now, I'm going to get me a refill and let Antonio cook me one of those hot dogs and I'm going to stuff my face full of potato chips and worry about the calories tomorrow."

"Sounds like a plan," Tricia agreed.

Pixie gave her a smile that actually seemed genuine and for a moment Tricia missed the gold canine tooth that used to grace that grin.

Ginny strode toward them.

"I'll catch up with you in a bit," Tricia promised her assistant manager.

"Great. Wonderful party, Ginny," Pixie said.

"I'm so glad you and Fred could come. Eat, drink, and be merry!"

Pixie proffered her nearly empty cup. "On my way to do just that."

They watched her leave, heading for the makeshift bar.

"How's she doing?" Ginny asked, sounding worried.

"Better. It's a hard thing to lose someone you didn't know you loved."

"I can imagine. Any word on Nadine Reed? I haven't heard much since her arrest."

"I heard through the grapevine that she's going to plead insanity thanks to the mental cruelty she's suffered during her marriage."

"That's a stretch, isn't it?"

"I'd say so."

Ginny's gaze traveled across the yard to where Angelica was holding little Will—hogging him, really, so that others couldn't get their hands on the baby. She absolutely loved being a *nonna*.

But then Ginny's expression underwent a change from motherly love to one of frustration. "Oh, no! What's *she* doing here?"

Tricia turned to see Becca Dickson-Chandler walking across the grass toward the tent with a wrapped gift in hand. "Ginny darling," she called as she approached.

Ginny plastered on a fake smile. "Why, Becca, we weren't expecting you," she said with a grace Tricia knew to be artificial.

"I've had this gift sitting in my car for ages and just happened to be driving by." Sure, and she always wore pearls and a knockout summer dress when she tooled around the village. She handed the package to Ginny. "It's just a little something for the new baby. My, you look fabulous. Looks like you've already lost that baby weight and are in tip-top shape." Her gaze drifted toward the new tennis court beyond the tent.

"Thank you," Ginny said tightly.

"And I wanted to let you know that my offer to come work for me is still open. I just know you'd make a fantastic manager of the first in my chain of tennis clubs."

"Yes, well, I'll be back at my job at Nigela Ricita Associates on Monday."

"You've still got time to change your mind," Becca said. "I pay very well. And I'm a real sweetheart to work for."

Tricia and Ginny exchanged skeptical looks.

Becca looked over their shoulders. "Is that a bar over

there? I'm just a little bit thirsty. We'll talk later," she said, and started off toward those who were standing and chatting near the booze.

"I'll bet she tries to poach at least half the people attending the party," Ginny grumbled.

"Let her try. Her reputation precedes her," Tricia remarked.

But then Ginny's expression changed once again—this time to one of joy. Still holding her grandson, Angelica strode toward them. Ginny held out her arms to take Will from her, but Angelica wasn't giving him up that easily. Instead, she held him closer and kissed the top of his dark hair.

"You are spoiling that boy," Ginny scolded her.

"That's what grandmothers are supposed to do."

Ginny's gaze strayed and Tricia looked to see that Ginny's mother was watching them with a look of longing.

"I think Ginny's mother would like a shot at her grandson, too," Tricia said. "You get to see him anytime you please—"

"I do not! I've gone at least thirty-six hours without seeing him and on more than one occasion."

"Ginny's mother will only be here until tomorrow. Don't be so greedy."

"Well, if you put it that way," Angelica groused, and handed the baby over to his mother. "I've got dibs on him next," she called as Ginny walked away.

The sisters took in the attendees.

"Isn't it nice to be surrounded by so many of our friends and associates?" Angelica said.

"Watch out for Becca—or some of them may no longer *be* your associates," Tricia warned. "She crashed the party."

Angelica's jaw dropped. "How crass!"

"And she pitched that manager's job to Ginny again."

Angelica scowled. "Well, this means war."

"What do you mean?"

"I'm going to see if *she's* got any employees who might be better suited for Nigela Ricita Associates."

"Oh, please. Don't stoop to her level."

"All is fair in love and business."

"I believe the quote is 'war.'"

"This *is* war!" Angelica declared, and stalked off in Becca's direction.

Tricia watched her sister, knowing that Becca was about to be bombarded with the Angelica charm-and-sweetness treatment and she didn't even feel sorry for her. And as she gazed at her friends and family, she was filled with a warm feeling of affection.

That is until she saw Ian McDonald walking across the lawn with a deeply serious—and possibly annoyed—look on his face, and that could mean only one thing: someone in Stoneham had been found dead.

Now, who?

TRICIA'S AND ANGELICA'S HAPPY HOUR REPASTS

GRANDMA MILES'S CHEESE PUFFS

INGREDIENTS
1 cup water
2 tablespoons butter
½ teaspoon salt
⅛ teaspoon cayenne pepper
1 cup all-purpose flour
4 eggs
1¼ cups shredded Gruyère or Swiss cheese
1 tablespoon Dijon mustard
¼ cup grated Parmesan cheese

Preheat the oven to 425°F (220°C, Gas Mark 7). In a large saucepan, bring the water, butter, salt, and cayenne pepper to a boil. Add the flour all at once and stir until a smooth ball forms. Remove from the heat and let stand for 5 minutes. Add the eggs one at a time, beating well after each addition. Continue beating until the mixture is smooth and shiny. Stir in the Gruyère or Swiss cheese and mustard. Drop by rounded teaspoonfuls 2 inches apart onto greased baking sheets. Sprinkle with the Parmesan cheese. Bake for 15 to 20 minutes or until golden brown. Serve warm or cold.

Yield: 4 dozen

HOT CLAM DIP

INGREDIENTS
2 (6½-ounce) cans minced clams
¼ pound (1 stick/8 tablespoons) butter
1½ cups cracker crumbs
1 medium onion, minced
½ teaspoon lemon juice
Crackers or chips

Preheat the oven to 350°F (180°C, Gas Mark 4). Drain the juice from one can of the clams. (Discard juice or save for another use.) Melt the butter in a microwave-safe bowl and add the drained clams, the other can of clams with the juice, the crumbs, onion, and lemon juice. Pour into a shallow baking dish and bake for 30 minutes. Serve hot with crackers or chips.

Yield: 2½ cups

SLOW COOKER GRAPE JELLY MEATBALLS

INGREDIENTS
2½ cups grape jelly
1 (18-ounce) bottle of sweet barbecue sauce
Hot sauce (optional)
2 pounds frozen prepared meatballs

Place the grape jelly and barbecue sauce in a slow cooker
and stir to blend well. If desired, add hot sauce for a bit of
fire. Stir in the meatballs to coat. Cover and cook on high
for 3 to 3½ hours, stirring halfway during the cook time,
until the meatballs are thoroughly heated and the sauce is
simmering.

Yield: 15 to 20 servings

SWEDISH MEATBALLS

INGREDIENTS
¾ cup seasoned bread crumbs
1 medium onion, chopped
2 large eggs, lightly beaten
⅓ cup minced fresh parsley (or 4 tablespoons dried
    parsley)
1 teaspoon coarsely ground pepper
¾ teaspoon salt
2 pounds ground beef

GRAVY
½ cup all-purpose flour
2¾ cups milk

2 cans (10½ ounces each) condensed beef stock,
   undiluted
1 tablespoon Worcestershire sauce
1 teaspoon coarsely ground pepper
¾ teaspoon salt

In a large bowl, combine the first 6 ingredients. Add the beef and mix thoroughly. Shape into 1-inch meatballs (about 50). In a large skillet over medium heat, brown the meatballs in batches. Using a slotted spoon, remove them to paper towels to drain, reserving drippings in the pan.

For the gravy, stir the flour into the drippings and cook over medium-high heat until light brown. Gradually whisk in the milk until smooth. Stir in the stock, Worcestershire sauce, pepper, and salt. Bring to a boil over medium-high heat. Cook and stir until thickened, about 2 minutes. Reduce the heat to medium low and return the meatballs to the pan. Cook, uncovered, until the meatballs are cooked through, 15 to 20 minutes longer, stirring occasionally. Serve hot with toothpicks.

Yield: 8 to 12 servings

CHEESE STRAWS

INGREDIENTS
¼ pound (1 stick/8 tablespoons) butter
2 cups all-purpose flour
¼ teaspoon cayenne pepper
1 pound sharp cheddar cheese, grated
Salt to taste

Preheat the oven to 400°F (200°C, Gas Mark 6). In a medium bowl, cream the butter until light in color. Add the flour, cayenne pepper, cheese, and salt. Roll out the dough on a floured surface. Cut the dough into strips 5 inches long and ⅜ inch wide. Place on a greased baking sheet and bake for 6 minutes or until golden brown. Cool on the baking sheet. Store in an airtight container for up to 1 week.

Yield: 36 straws

ACKNOWLEDGMENTS

Thanks to members of the Lorraine Train for their support: Amy Connolley, Debbie Lyon, Rita Pierrottie, and Pam Priest.

Keep reading for an excerpt of
Lorna Barrett's next Booktown Mystery

A QUESTIONABLE CHARACTER

from Berkley Prime Crime

The sun had been up for a little over an hour when Tricia Miles arrived on her sister's doorstep on that early Monday in June. It was to be a busy day, what with welcoming the Chamber of Commerce's summer intern, getting him settled, and attending to her vintage mystery bookstore, Haven't Got a Clue.

Tricia and her sister were co-presidents of the Stoneham, New Hampshire, Chamber—a job they'd held for nearly six months. It had been a rocky experience trying to revive the operation their predecessor had so diligently tried to destroy. Thanks to Angelica's previous tenure at the organization's helm, and Tricia's involvement as her woman Friday, they'd slowly been rebuilding the trust of their members. But welcoming the new intern was only one part of the day's plan.

Angelica Miles was a woman of many talents—and two personas. She was a successful businesswoman in her own right, owning the Cookery book and kitchen gadget store; Booked for Lunch, a small retro café dedicated to the midday meal; the village's day spa, Booked for Beauty; and a half share of the village's most expensive bed-and-breakfast, the Sheer Comfort Inn. But it was her alter ego, the secretive Nigela Ricita, who commanded the utmost respect, and sometimes animosity, for transforming the

somewhat sleepy village of used bookstores known as
Booktown into a wildly successful tourist attraction. NR
Associates owned the Brookview Inn, the local pub (the
Dog-Eared Page), the Happy Domestic home/gift shop, a
food truck, a real estate office, the other half interest in the
Sheer Comfort Inn, and the most recent addition to the NR
portfolio, the *Stoneham Weekly News*.

When Tricia thought about her sister's business acumen,
she sometimes suffered from an inferiority complex—but
not for long. Angelica actually spent little hands-on time
with her companies since she'd built a team of top-notch,
experienced individuals. She acted as the CEO of her em-
pires, letting her son, Antonio Barbero, take on the day-to-
day supervision. His wife, Ginny Wilson-Barbero, was the
company's marketing director and mother to Angelica's
grandbabies, little Sofia and baby Will.

On that morning, Tricia had agreed to accompany her
sister to NR Associates' new world headquarters, a historic
granite-clad building located off the village's main drag. The
former mansion had been owned by Asa Morrison, another
of the village's founders, who'd made his money producing
whiskey and whose stately house had been built some hundred and fifty or so years before. During its life, it had been
a home, a hospital, a school, and, most recently, office space.
It was to be upgraded in the latter configuration with a new
roof, HVAC, and plumbing before Angelica would personally choose the furniture and decor.

The workmen usually came to get started around seven,
which was why Tricia and Angelica had decided to set out
to check on the progress of the renovations an hour before
the construction crew arrived for the day.

Tricia texted her sister. I'm here.

Be right down.

Tricia would have been pleased to use the occasion to
get in part of her morning three-mile constitutional, but she
knew her sister would insist on taking her car. The five-
block walk was probably too far for her to ever walk, even
though she'd given up her stilettos earlier that year.

Sure enough, when Angelica appeared she clutched her car keys in her right hand. She looked smart dressed in a peach cotton sleeveless blouse, black slacks, and sandals, sporting a black fanny pack that she'd never be caught wearing in a business setting, so she obviously didn't expect to be seen at that time of the day and especially at the construction site. Tricia's attire wasn't much different. She'd chosen a pink tee and jeans but would change into her usual sweater set and black slacks once the workday commenced. The weatherman had predicted an unseasonably warm day. It was already in the seventies. She'd be glad of the sweater once she cranked up the AC in her shop upon her return.

"Let's go," Angelica said brightly. "I want to make a list of things I want to be completed by the end of the week."

"Isn't that up to Jim Stark?" Tricia asked. Stark was the contractor Angelica had hired to complete the mansion's renovations. Tricia had worked with him, too, but these days the firm was booked solid months in advance. So much so that lately Stark's clients had been dealing with his right-hand man, Sanjay Arya, a personable man in his thirties with a ready smile and a reassuring presence.

"I hardly ever talk to Jim anymore," Angelica lamented as she started up the road toward the village's municipal parking lot where the street residents kept their vehicles. Angelica might not exercise as much as Tricia, but if she cared to, she could have excelled in competitive walking.

"When I do get to speak to the boss man, I always feel like him consulting his phone is more important than anything I have to say."

"He's a busy man."

Angelica glanced at her sister with disdain. "And I'm a busy woman."

She was indeed.

They arrived at the lot and headed for Angelica's car. Neither of them spoke until Angelica pulled the car onto Main Street and headed for the mansion.

"We should have done this yesterday," Tricia said. "Especially if you don't want to run into the workmen."

"Are you kidding? Sunday is my busiest day of the week."

That was when Angelica hosted their weekly family dinner, although since baby Will had made his appearance two months ago, they'd been gathering with the Barberos in their newly built home. Dragging the kiddies out took a lot of effort, but Angelica had adapted. She'd either have the meal catered or would bring the ingredients for a delicious meal to the fabulous kitchen she'd designed for the family. In addition to Tricia and the Barberos, their "family" also consisted of Tricia's friend and employee Mr. Everett and his wife, Grace. They'd been accepted as the children's honorary great-grandparents.

Angelica pulled up in front of the mansion, which at this point bore a rather ramshackle appearance. Landscaping was one of the last items on the list of things to be completed.

The sisters exited the car and stood before the building. Tricia studied Angelica's face. She could tell her sister was looking at the mansion with an eye to its future appearance.

"I love this place," Angelica muttered. "If only it was feasible to return it to its original use." She shook her head, looking wistful.

"You've got big bucks," Tricia commented.

"I do, but what would I do, one person living in so large a home? Besides, the older I get, the less I want or need."

Tricia was beginning to think that way herself. She looked at her watch: 6:10. If they wanted to be out before the workers showed up, they'd better start their inspection. She said so.

Angelica approached the lockbox hanging from the dull brass handle on the big oak door, punched in the code, and removed the key to the former palace, unlocking the door and letting them in. Antonio must have given her the combination to the electronic lock. Tricia hadn't visited the building since Angelica's initial walk-through almost a year ago. Everything took so long. Permits, zoning, architectural plans. She'd been told that the future NR offices had actually been put on an accelerated schedule. Even so, the timeline for finishing the job was still almost a month away.

Dust caked every surface. Where it had come from was anyone's guess. Random lumber and metal framing materials were piled in what had once been the home's grand foyer. It would be a shame if the beautiful marble floors were covered instead of being restored.

"I thought we should start on the second floor and work our way down," Angelica said, and headed for the grand staircase.

"They're not going to replace these magnificent stairs, are they?" Tricia asked, appalled at the idea.

"No. I was adamant about that," Angelica said as they made their way to the second floor. "But they'll be placing laminate on these floors," she said, indicating the scuffed wide pine flooring beneath their feet.

"Why? It looks like it's in good shape."

"And I want to keep it that way."

Tricia studied her sister's expression. "What are you planning to do with this place in the future?" she asked with suspicion.

"Nothing. Nothing at all," Angelica said innocently.

Tricia didn't believe her. Perhaps Angelica *did* hope to restore the old building to its former glory after all—just not at this time.

They wandered through the upper rooms, admiring the cove moldings, the ceiling medallions, and other features before taking the back—or servants'—stairs to the main floor.

"What's your favorite part of the renovation?" Tricia asked.

"It'll be the communal kitchen. I had the most fun choosing the appliances and furniture."

"Is it located in the original kitchen?"

"Yes, but unfortunately, it'll be reworked on a smaller scale. Still, we're keeping some of the original features. Want to see the work in progress?"

"Why not?"

Angelica might not have visited the site much in person, but she seemed to have memorized the layout, for she led Tricia through corridors until they came to a door that was ajar. Angelica pushed through it.

The room was large and two of the walls had been stripped back to the brick. Like the foyer, boxes of building supplies littered its floor. Vintage subway tile covered two of the walls near where an old porcelain sink marred by rust stains sat and another where an old range must have stood.

Tricia nodded toward a large dark door to the left. "Butler's pantry?" she guessed.

"Yes, and it's magnificent. We were going to use it as a supply cabinet, but that was before we decided to lease some of the space to other businesses." She sighed, once again wistful. "I can just imagine all the crystal, silver serving dishes, and cutlery that were once stored in it." She strode across the room, threw open the heavy door, and gasped. "Good grief!"

"What's wrong?" Tricia asked, coming up behind her sister. She came to an abrupt halt as her gaze raked across the cracked tile floor. Huddled in the corner was the body of a man with a head of dark hair matted with blood that had pooled around it.

Tricia groaned. "Why does this always happen to us?"

About the Author

LORNA BARRETT is the *New York Times* bestselling author of the Booktown Mysteries, including *Clause of Death*, *A Deadly Deletion*, and *Handbook for Homicide*. She lives in Rochester, New York.

CONNECT ONLINE

LornaBarrett.com
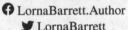 LornaBarrett.Author
LornaBarrett

Ready to find
your next great read?

Let us help.

Visit prh.com/nextread

Penguin
Random
House